To Don

I hope you enjoy the read

Unholy Fire

Very best wishes

Don

March 2013

By

Don Stratton

To Pauline, whose encouragement and
support never falters

Acknowledgements

Writing is ultimately a solitary business. One sits down and writes—alone. But it's only possible because of the considerable help of many people. I'd especially like to thank Rick Morrow for starting us both on the writing road, and I'm happy to say we're both still at it. We meet regularly and continue to review each other's work. I'm especially indebted to Carol Gaskin, of *Editorial Alchemy* who edited this novel not once, but twice. She was a bottomless well of knowledge on the nuts and bolts of the mystery-writing genre. Her invaluable critiques improved the work immensely and I'm forever grateful. I'd also like to thank the many successful writers I had the privilege to interact with at Mystery Florida in Sarasota. Their encouragement was greatly appreciated and their suggestions have born fruit throughout this work. A special thanks to those who read earlier versions and offered their input including, Audrey Deanhardt, Fred and Claire Norton, Jim Stratton, Rick Morrow and of course, my chief supporter and daily editor, my wife, Pauline Stratton.

Copyright © 2012 by Don Stratton

Unholy Fire

Published by Tuscany Press 2012

ISBN   978-0-9859459-0-9

All rights reserved. No part of this publication may be reproduced, stored in a retrieval system or transmitted, by any means, electronic, mechanical, photocopying, recording or otherwise, without the prior permission of the copyright owner

. . .

This book is a work of fiction. All of the names, characters, places, and incidents are products of the author's imagination or are used fictitiously. Any resemblance to actual events, locales, or persons, living or dead, is entirely coincidental.

To kill a man is not to defend a doctrine but to kill a man.

Michael Servetus

Prologue

The condemned man was bound hand and foot. He stared at nothing as he rode in a prison wagon pulled by a mule from his jail cell in Geneva to a hill south of the city called Champel. Binding to a stake and a horrible death by fire awaited him at his destination.

He'd been condemned for heresy against the Church. William Farel, a leading figure in his condemnation, rode in the wagon with him, harassing him relentlessly. The wagon trundled along the rocky path canopied by overarching branches of old oaks that reached out to him like the long, withered arms of the dead.

"At least save your soul by recanting your heresies," pleaded Farel, a close associate of John Calvin, the Protestant reformer. "Ask God's forgiveness. He might spare you the eternal flames of hell."

The condemned man, one Michael Servetus, ignored him and did not respond. He was terrified. Too terrified to speak. He was so scared he'd been unable to eat the meager food they'd brought him earlier. He'd vomited just looking at it.

Oh my God, don't let the pain cause me to recant. Oh my God! Is this really happening?

Most of the townsfolk assembled were aware that a heretic had been condemned to burn at the stake, but knew little beyond that. They cared even less. Watching a burning was entertainment, an occasion to get drunk, and that's what most of them planned to do.

Soon the sad procession arrived. Servetus broke into a cold sweat and faltered as his guards tightened their grip, half marching, half dragging him up a set of wooden steps, where they chained his body to the stake. One chain was looped around his neck, binding him tightly against the rough-sawn pole.

Servetus gazed at the rose-gray sky, savoring his last moments on this earth, and experienced an unexpected sense of calm. He reflected on the events that had brought him to this place. Only three months earlier, he had been confidently reassuring his friend Pierre LeGrand, a printer in Vienne, in southwest France.

"Pierre, it will be fine. There will be no publisher's name. Not even the location of publication will appear in the book. Like you, I've no desire to incur the wrath and punishment of the Inquisition. But we have spoken of this, you and I. This work needs to be made available to the people."

"Please, Dr. Villanueve, I beg you to reconsider," whispered Pierre, pacing and wringing his hands. "This could put us in terrible danger. I mean danger for our lives."

Villanueve continued as if he hadn't heard the man's plea. "We will print a thousand copies of my *Christianismi Restitutio*—The Restoration of Christianity—here in this abandoned barn. Then we'll secretly send the volumes in bales to Lyon. When Lyon celebrates the Easter fairs, they'll be put on sale. From there, copies will make their way to Frankfurt and the great book markets of northern Europe."

Pierre nodded dubiously.

"Don't worry, Pierre, you're doing a good thing. Have courage. Be assured that God is on your side."

But Pierre did worry, and Villanueve knew he had reason to. If the authorities discovered that Pierre had published this work, his life would be over. Pierre also knew that Villanueve's real name was Michael Servetus and that he had taken the name Michael Villanueve from his birth town in Spain to hide from the Spanish and French Inquisitions and the Protestant Inquisition as well. He had offended the leaders of all of these movements with the theological arguments he'd been publishing since 1531. To avoid their grasp, he'd changed his name, attended medical school in Paris, and had been practicing medicine in Vienne ever since.

Servetus heard LeGrand whine, his growing fear obvious. "But sir, is it really necessary to include your correspondence with John Calvin? This alone could produce your greatest danger. For all practical purposes Calvin is now the ruler of Geneva. He's become even more important to the Reformation than the great Martin Luther himself."

Servetus used the iron voice he adopted whenever he spoke of his theological convictions. "The letters stay. They clearly show how Calvin and his *Institutions of Christian Religion* are in error, and that the path back to true Christianity lies in the spirit of my *Christianismi Restitutio* that we're printing here today."

He and Calvin had been corresponding for many years. They both saw themselves as Protestant reformers but disagreed on how the Reformation should proceed. Villanueve felt that Calvin and Luther had not gone far enough—that their idea of reform still maintained too much Catholic dogma.

"Did you know, Pierre, that I sent Calvin a copy of the *Christianismi Restitutio* earlier, and what did he do? He didn't even comment on it. Instead he sent me a copy of his own error-filled *Institutio*, as if reading that alone would clearly refute my writing."

"But sir, was it wise to send his book back with all those insulting comments? I've heard he was so furious that he said if his authority was of any avail he would not suffer you to get out alive if you ever come to Geneva."

Servetus sighed, shook his head, and continued. "Pierre, the Christian church has taken a seriously wrong turn. This concept of the trinity makes no sense. Jesus was not another being of the Godhead, separate from the father. No!" he almost shouted. "Jesus was God himself come to earth."

Pierre nodded fretfully. He had heard all of this before, or course. He was even persuaded to believe some of it. Nevertheless, he continued to pace.

Servetus spoke more gently. "Pierre, the Bible makes no mention of a three-part God, but speaks only of one God. How can Christians support monotheism, then worship a God who is split into three parts? At best, the trinity manifests the forms that God can bring into play. We know that Christ did not always exist, but was created when God chose to come to earth."

Pierre shrugged. "Bien sur, mon ami. But—"

"And this concept of original sin, I'll have no part of it!" Servetus's voice rose again. "Calvin's theology proposes that all people are totally depraved and that God's grace is restricted only to those few that he calls 'God's Elect.' Surely God's grace abounds, and humans need only the intelligence and free will that all of us possess to grasp it!"

Servetus folded his arms across his chest and Pierre, seeing his friend was not to be dissuaded, gave in.

"Bon. Then shall we get on with it? We have much to do if we are going to print a thousand copies, and the sooner we are out of here the better."

In the end, Pierre only printed five hundred copies, and a month later when Calvin was shown the newly published *Christianismi Restitutio* containing the copies of his correspondence with Servetus, he knew immediately who the anonymous author was. Not only was he furious that such a heretical piece of work would be presented to the public, but he was enraged by the personal embarrassment the published letters could cause him. He wrote at once to the local Catholic inquisitor in Vienne and told him that he had a heretic in his midst, one Michael Servetus, operating under the name Michael Villanueve.

The local inquisitor arrested and interrogated Servetus, but with the help of a sympathetic guard, Michael had managed to escape. Knowing he was no longer safe in France, he decided to go to the Kingdom of Naples, where he planned to practice medicine. Many of his Spanish countrymen had previously fled to Naples, which was controlled by a Hispanic ruler. They'd been trying to escape the horrors of the Spanish Inquisition and to enjoy greater religious liberty. There he felt he would be safe and his writings accepted.

But he made a fatal mistake. After wandering like a hunted animal for months, he decided it was too dangerous to travel to Naples through Spain by going over the Pyrenees. So he took a route through Switzerland and into northern Italy instead.

In Geneva, Servetus spent the night at an inn, and the next day being Sunday, dutifully attended church. The rules of conduct for living in Calvin's Geneva required that everyone attend church on Sunday. Unfortunately for Servetus, someone recognized him and alerted Calvin, who quickly had him arrested, no doubt fearful that Servetus was there to spread his heretical views and upset the Reformation that he'd set in motion in Geneva.

The charges against Servetus, drawn up by Calvin, were based mainly on the *Christianismi Restitutio*, a book Calvin described as full of blasphemies. The writings of Servetus over the past twenty-four years were also introduced as evidence. He was charged with various heresies, such as challenging the tenants of the trinity, infant baptism, and the immortality of the soul, and destroying the very foundations of Christianity itself. Further, he was charged with attacking the reputation of Calvin by claiming he was guilty of all kinds of blasphemies. And finally, of course, he was an escaped prisoner.

No time was wasted; the trial began the next day. The venue was the Little Council of Geneva. The prosecuting attorney read the charges against Servetus, who had been sworn in. In response to the accusations of heresy and blasphemy raised by Calvin, Servetus calmly stated that he would use scripture itself to refute all of the charges.

But he had greatly overestimated the persuasive power of his own theological arguments, and more so, the control that Calvin held over the court. The court quickly found Servetus guilty as charged and voted that he be taken to the suburb of Champel and burned at the stake the next day, along with his heretical books. In a pious effort to show his Christian compassion, Calvin tried to get the judgment changed to the supposedly more humane sentence of beheading, but was overruled by the court.

Stunned by the judgment and the rapidity of his undoing, Servetus nevertheless had little time to contemplate his fate. He was aware of the custom that a copy of the writings done by heretics would be placed below their feet at the stake. That night, the night before the execution, Servetus asked that he be allowed to write in the copy of his book that was to be burned under his feet the next day. He was told that all of the five hundred unbound copies of the *Christianismi Restitutio* that the inquisitors were able to assemble would also be burned with him. His last request was granted. He supposed that the authorities didn't care what he wrote, as it would go up in flames and that would be the end of it.

Taking the time he had left, he wrote a message on the unprinted borders of the last pages of the book the guard had brought him. Servetus knew that what he was writing expressed arguments he had never made before; arguments he'd deliberately refrained from making in his own defense at the trial. He explained in this message why he had not included them at the time. He also included a 'code' to the location of a secret ancient scroll that he claimed supported his arguments.

Servetus was allowed one visitor that night. He asked a man who was quietly sympathetic to his views to please try to surreptitiously bring him the copy of the *Christianismi Restitutio* that Servetus knew the man had. When he did, Michael exchanged the copy he'd written his message in with the one his friend had brought. Michael asked the man to preserve the copy with its message. At great risk to himself, the man did as Servetus asked.

Now, as Servetus stood chained to the stake, he saw his visitor from the night before moving through the crowd. Even though his neck was fixed in an upright position by a chain, his eyes followed the visitor until the man turned toward Servetus and quietly nodded his head. Servetus nodded his head in response, as if to say "thank you."

On his head, the executioners placed a straw crown filled with sulfur, indicating that he was soon going to Hell. When the executioner began his work, Servetus whispered with trembling voice, "Oh God, oh God!" William Farel, frustrated by his inability to get Servetus to recant, snapped at him: "Have you nothing else to say?"

This time Servetus replied to him. "What else might I do, but speak of God?"

The execution lasted more than two hours. The executioners, to prolong the agony, had deliberately used green firewood. Throughout the ordeal, Farel and other reformers of Geneva danced around him and taunted him, trying to get him to renounce his blasphemy. Nevertheless, Servetus refused to recant.

As this unholy fire on the altar of death consumed him, he cried out in a loud voice, "Oh Jesus, son of the eternal God, have pity on me."

To be saved from the stake Servetus only had to state, "Jesus Christ the eternal Son of God."

Instead, resolute to the end, his last words were: "Jesus Christ, Son of the eternal God."

Chapter 1

MENDEZ CASTLE, MADRID, SPAIN
PRESENT TIME

Basilio grew increasingly convinced the man was deranged. Had he always been like this? How had he missed it before? The man hadn't physically hurt him, at least not yet, but he wouldn't leave, so Basilio tried once more.

"Look. I don't know what you're talking about. It's not in my collection. It never was. I don't know anything about it. Where did you get this idea, anyway?"

The man paced and glowered. He was as tall as Basilio's six feet but considerably younger and stronger than the ninety-two-year-old man.

"Look, Mendez, I know you've got it. I know what you're planning to do with it. Just tell me where it is— *now*!"

How could he possibly know? From the time he'd taken possession of it in 1942 Basilio had only told three people about it. Two were his closest friends, and the third had every reason *not* to tell anyone. The real irony was, he didn't actually have it. He didn't even know precisely where it was. He couldn't tell even if he wanted to. And what did the man mean, he had a right to it?

The intruder, his face now just inches from Basilio's, grabbed him by the shoulders and shook him. "You won't get away with this." With that he slammed Basilio into the chair.

Hyperventilating, the old man found himself staring at the ceiling of his library. Then looking down, he watched as the man stomped to the single oak door that was the only access to the room. There he paused and fixed a withering stare at Basilio.

"This isn't over, Mendez. The *Restitutio* is mine. I'll get it. One way or another." With that he left, slamming the door behind him.

Basilio Mendez exhaled loudly. A proud man with patrician white hair, he was the current heir to the ancestral Mendez family title and fortune. He clutched his chest, willing his pounding heart to be quiet. The very existence of the book had been a carefully guarded secret for so many years. But now he knew he had to call the police. No question about it. He'd just been threatened, and the man *had* gotten physical. Damn.

He went to the door and opened it to make sure the intruder was really gone. He poured himself a large brandy and tried to calm down. For the first time, since he'd taken possession of the book, nearly seventy years earlier, he was afraid. Not for his physical wellbeing. He assumed at his age he wouldn't live much longer. Basilio's fear was that the man could interfere with the plans he had recently set in motion.

He finished his brandy and poured another one. Unable to readily shake his growing anxiety, he paced the perimeter of the library.

He wondered how the man could know about the *Christianismi Restitutio*. The bastard had even implied he knew what Basilio had planned. It just wasn't possible. Dr. Lazodelavega would never have told him or anyone else. Hugo Alvarez would never tell either. The only other people who even knew about it were his close wartime friend, George Blackwell, who'd been dead for fifty years, and Señora Honoria Calderon, who'd given it to him in the first place, and she'd been dead even longer. Where was the leak?

His breathing gradually returned to normal and the brandy finally began to take its longed-for effect. Basilio returned to his desk in front of the library's immense stone fireplace. He leaned back in his chair and sipped his drink, beginning to convince himself that his plan would still work.

Twenty-five feet on a side, and completely lined with bookshelves from its Spanish tile floor to its oak-beamed ceiling sixteen feet above, the library had always been his favorite retreat when he wanted to be alone. Comfortable leather chairs, in groups of two, provided snug reading zones. The leatherbound books on history, art, science, geography, and philosophy collected largely by his ancestors, lent the room a pleasant musty aroma. Basilio's own additions to the shelves gave him a satisfying sense of continuity with his ancient and noble family.

Freed from the need to earn a living in the conventional sense, the old man had devoted his life to philanthropy and scholarship. A passionate bibliophile, his collection of books, manuscripts, documents, and implements of torture related to the Spanish Inquisition of the sixteenth century was extensive, having been started by his ancestor, Count Allisandro Mendez, in the seventeenth century.

Basilio himself wasn't interested in collecting the actual torture devices that had been used against heretics and Jews. Others of his ancestors did that. Instead, he collected historical papers and books related to the trials. These included such documents as writs of arrest and orders for appearance before the inquisitors. The collection even held entire or partial trial transcripts. The poor souls condemned by these tribunals were ordered to undergo torture or death by formal documents signed occasionally by public officials, but most often by the holy inquisitors of the Church.

Basilio had gone to considerable expense to have the entire collection properly catalogued four months back, hiring Professor Isandro de la Peña of the University of Madrid's history faculty to undertake the task. The professor was a world-renowned scholar on the Inquisition and had done an excellent job.

Just then Basilio heard a loud crashing noise from the great hall outside his library. Fearing the man had returned, he set down his drink, picked up the telephone, and pushed number one on the speed dial. His son Alfonso's voice mail came on. *Damn, where was he?*

"Alfonso, I think there is an intruder in the castle. I'm in the library now. Take care of it."

Knowing his son wouldn't tolerate an intruder, Basilio hoped he'd just stepped out of his office momentarily and would get the message quickly. Still, puzzled by the noise, he cracked open the library door and looked around the lofty hallway of the castle. Something large must have fallen over, but everything he could see was intact. Carefully, scanning for his earlier intruder, he moved along the hall to the single door of the large room behind the library where the torture implements of the collection were housed. He quietly opened it and stepped in looking around. He was relieved to see and hear no one. Thin strips of natural light shone through the narrow vertical slits in the walls, originally designed for archers, bathing the collection in eerie, wan sunlight.

He crept down the side of the room that housed the large torture devices, past the Judas Cradle and continued quietly past the rack and the knee splitter. Suddenly he heard a noise from the other side of the room, where the smaller implements were kept. He couldn't see across the center of the room, which was filled with large replicas of horrific torture machines built by his ancestors to specifications found in old documents. But he knew he wasn't alone. The bastard must be over there looking for the book. He'd probably knocked something over and made the large noise heard earlier.

Basilio slowly turned around and retraced his steps to the entrance. Maybe the man hadn't heard him come in. He'd leave and get back to the library until Alfonso got help.

Once back in the library, he locked the door from the inside and felt safe. While he waited for help to arrive, he thought of his meeting many years before with Señora Honoria Calderon at her ancestral estate in Toledo, the meeting where she'd entrusted him with the priceless book. It happened during World War II.

Both her husband and two adult sons were sympathetic to the Axis powers and she was afraid they might ultimately let the book fall into the hands of Herman Goering's art looters. Personally, she abhorred everything they stood for, and she knew that Basilio, like herself, was sympathetic to the Allies. Now, close to seventy years later, he was justifiably concerned about the uproar the book's unveiling would likely present. Nevertheless, he felt an old and personal obligation to Señora Calderon to make it available to scholars and the world at large. He remembered his surprise when she'd told him about it.

"Señor Mendez, I want to give you, for safekeeping, a most remarkable copy of the *Christianismi Restitutio*. By Michael Servetus."

Basilio took in a sharp breath. The *Christianismi Restitutio?* As an Inquisition historian, Basilio knew, of course, that Michael Servetus had been burned at the stake. The publication of his book, the *Christianismi Restitutio* was ample evidence of his heresy in the eyes of the Protestant Reformation and the Catholic Church. He also knew that all copies of his books had supposedly been burned with him. *How had this one survive the fire?*

Expecting his surprise, she smiled sagely, "Señor Mendez, you should know that the night before his execution, Michael Servetus wrote a final message in the margins of the last pages of this book. This message provided arguments he was afraid to use in his defense at the trial, arguments that he claimed would have only added to his list of 'heresies' in the eyes of the court. He claimed these arguments were based on knowledge he'd gained from reading an unknown ancient scroll dating from the time of Christ. He also included in this message obscure language that referred to the location of this scroll. To my knowledge, none of the very few people who had ever seen this message over the centuries, had been able to decipher it and locate the scroll, including me."

Taking a deep breath and letting it out slowly, Señora Calderon nodded, then said, "This incredible message is included in the copy of the *Christianismi Restitutio* that I'm entrusting to your care."

As Basilio recalled his stunned disbelief at the memory of that meeting so many years before, he sipped more brandy and smiled to himself. Thinking about it reminded him that he'd wanted to validate a historical point concerning the Calvinists who supported the Protestant Inquisition. His library contained history books on every imaginable era and people. Basilio, like many of his ancestors, had long appreciated the lessons history taught.

He crossed over to the rolling ladder that he used to reach the tomes that sat on shelves high on the wall. He pushed the ladder to the reformation history collection and then locked it in place. Still spry for his age, he climbed the ladder almost to the top and found the history text he was looking for. As he stretched to shift the weighty volume from its spot, he heard a noise at the door. He twisted and looked down to see the iron latch move and the door open. His prior visitor had returned and had somehow unlocked the door. Basilio made no sound while the man began rifling through the drawers of his desk.

Outraged at this intrusion, and regaining his courage, he shouted, "Hey, what are you doing?"

The visitor jumped, equally startled to see Basilio teetering on the ladder to the right of the door. The intruder paused and then ran to the ladder, released the brake, and started shaking it.

Basilio, terrified, shouted. "What the hell are you doing?"

The ladder jerked side-to-side and trembled, so he had to grip the side rails to prevent being shaken off.

"Stop, you idiot, I'll fall."

The shaking became more violent, and Basilio's ancient fingers lost their hold. He flailed the air as he went over backward, falling toward the hard Spanish tile floor.

"H—help me . . ." he whispered as he caught sight of the visitor, leaving the library—empty-handed. Then there was only blackness.

Chapter 2

THE BLACKWELL RANCH
CHARLOTTESVILLE, VIRGINIA

Professor Hunter McCoy had been in San Diego at the Experimental Biology meetings. He and his two postdocs were presenting four papers on pulmonary physiology that were the culmination of several research projects they'd conducted in Hunter's lab when he'd gotten the call from Shay Blackwell.

Four days later, at the end of the conference, he'd returned to Virginia and was now sitting in the comfortable chair Shay had offered him in the library of his estate in rural Charlottesville.

Hunter was a big man, just over six-foot-two, and his strong arms, back, and chest were only slightly masked by the loose-fitting silk Hawaiian shirt he wore with his tan slacks. His short hair, flecked with premature gray, topped a handsome face with blue-green eyes that could sparkle with warmth or stare with a frightening ferocity. They were sparkling now as he greeted his old friend.

"Glad I got you before you left town," Shay told him. "You probably already have plans for the summer, but I could sure use you again."

Hunter remained quiet and waited.

Shay paused dramatically, then asked, "Ever heard of Michael Servetus?"

Hunter was momentarily confused and then brightened as he leaned forward, smiling. "As I recall he was a sixteenth century physician, burned at the stake for heresy." Stroking his chin and looking up at the ceiling, he tried to recall even more. "I believe he met his fiery fate near Geneva at the hands of—let me see now—oh yes, John Calvin and the Protestant Inquisition."

Hunter leaned back in his chair, feeling smug, and waited for Blackwell's reaction. His brief wait was rewarded.

Tossing his hands up in mock surrender, Shay said, "Now why am I not surprised you know that?"

Hunter chuckled at Blackwell's surprise. "Come on, Shay, you know my field at the med school is physiology, right?"

"What's physiology got to do with heresy?"

Hunter clasped his hands behind his head and stared at the ceiling. "Interestingly, one of poor old Dr. Servetus's supposed crimes was committing physiological heresy."

Blackwell knit his brows. "Physiological heresy?"

Hunter, enjoying Shay's puzzlement, lowered his gaze from the ceiling and looked at him. "Yup. He had the audacity to be correct when he explained how and why blood circulated through the lungs."

"If he was correct, what was the problem?" Blackwell asked. "And anyway, what does circulating blood or the lungs have to do with heresy?"

Really taking pleasure in this conversation now, Hunter stretched and enlightened him. "You've asked the right question, Shay. It would, and should, have been a good thing except for one prickly little fact. The Church didn't like it. You have to understand that for the previous thousand years, medical people pretty much accepted the second-century physician Claudius Galen's version of everything medical, including his explanation of blood flow through the lungs, even though it was completely wrong.

Of course, to be fair, no one knew it was wrong at the time. But Galen, always a practical man, was careful to lace his pronouncements on physiology with the tag line, 'One can see the wonder of God in this system.' You see, bringing God into it, made it 'correct' in the eyes of the Church. And of course once it got that imprimatur, any alternate views were heresy."

"Of course," said Shay with a grin. "Then the task I'd like you to do for me should appeal to you on several levels."

As Blackwell launched into a story about an unopened letter to his father from a Spanish nobleman named Basilio Mendez, Hunter sat back and let Shay tell it in his own words.

Blackwell ran his hand through his thinning, sandy gray hair. He was beginning to get a pattern baldness that his father had not lived long enough to develop. He hadn't inherited his father's height, but at a slim and fit fifty-nine, his friendly, handsome face had the same engaging smile as his late father.

"I'd been going through my late father's papers, something I do occasionally just to get a feel for the man who had died along with my mother years earlier in a boating accident.

"I've been through these things many times," gesturing to file cabinets along a wall.

Then Blackwell picked up an envelope off his desk and handed it to Hunter. "But I never noticed that envelope before. I don't know how I could have overlooked it, maybe because it was sandwiched between two boxes of unused embassy letterhead stationary. Anyway, for some reason I went through his stuff today and there it was. As you can see, it's addressed to my father and postmarked Madrid, Spain, March 2nd, 1947. It had never been opened."

Hunter knew that Shay's father, George Blackwell, had been with the American Embassy in Madrid during the war. Following the cessation of hostilities in 1945, he had returned to the United States and completed a graduate degree in business and marketing at the University of Virginia. He married and produced one child, Shay. Shay's Aunt Margaret, his father's sister, had told him what she knew of her brother's exploits with the embassy during World War II. But her knowledge of his real activities was limited to what a sister and housewife could find out in those eventful days.

Margaret and her husband Frank had taken Shay in and raised him as their own after his parent's deaths and he'd come to love them as if they were his biological parents. They'd worked hard to help fund his education at the University of Virginia, and Shay had eventually named his daughter, Margaret after his aunt. Later, when he'd developed a successful business empire of his own, Shay's resources far outstripped theirs and he was able to learn more about his late father's activities. He'd discovered that during the war his father's real assignment as Undersecretary of Foreign Affairs at the U.S. Embassy in Madrid had been to gather intelligence.

Spain, then under the Franco Regime was officially non-belligerent but made no attempt to hide its Axis leanings. George Blackwell's special assignment was to learn all he could about underground groups in Spain that would be likely to support the Allies. He was also tasked to gather intelligence on groups that offered assistance to the Axis powers of Germany and Italy in order to neutralize them.

"Hunter, that letter was from a good friend of my father's who'd helped him during those years in Madrid, one Count Basilio Diego Mendez."

Hunter examined the letter again noting that it was standard business letter size, and held the personal crest of the Mendez Family embossed directly into the paper. The return address read Mendez Castle, Castillo de Aldovea, Spain and was addressed in a man's bold script to Mr. George Blackwell at 4216 Park Place, Charlottesville, Virginia.

"That was my father's address when he first returned from Spain after the war," remarked Shay, when he saw Hunter examining it

"Any idea why he didn't open it?"

"I don't know, Shay mused. I mean—nowhere in his papers have I found any other unopened envelopes."

Hunter shrugged. "Maybe it got lost in the stationary box, and since he didn't need the paper once he was out of the system, he never bothered to look in there again, just like you didn't until today."

"I suppose. Still, it's strange. Let me read it to you." Shay took the envelope back from Hunter, removed the letter and read it aloud to him.

My dear Friend,

I hope this letter finds you well and happily reunited with family and friends. Since the end of the war in Europe the diplomatic intrigue in Madrid has been reduced to determining the leanings of the Franco Government regarding public or private ownership of the new city sewer system, not exactly the heady stuff of the old days, my friend. Still, one can't argue with the happy cessation of hostilities even though the road back to normalcy will be long and costly for many countries, including Germany, so destroyed by the war.

It is so ironic that Spain, spared the brunt of the destructive power of the war, should still be in the grip of a dictatorial government, while the rest of the continent, presumably even Germany and Italy, will be developing democracies. Nevertheless, my family has been here for centuries and has survived many regimes, and I expect that this too shall pass.

"There are several references to Basilio Mendez in my father's papers," Shay said, interrupting his reading.

"Come on, Shay, keep going. What else does the letter say?"

Shay continued:

On another front: regarding our common interest in the Inquisition, I have acquired a most remarkable item. It is unquestionably the most important artifact in the collection.

Shay read on in silence, leaving Hunter staring at him in frustration. Finally he nudged Shay's arm. "I'm still here. What does it say?"

Shay continued to read in silence, then stopped. "He's telling my father about a book written by Michael Servetus, who was burned at the stake just as you said, Hunter. He says there are only three known copies in existence today, all in national libraries in Europe.

"Your father was interested in the Inquisition?" asked Hunter, in a surprised disbelief.

"Apparently so. I didn't know that," said Shay. "I'm sure there's a lot about him I don't know." He continued reading aloud:

My dear George, quite remarkably I have acquired a hitherto unknown fourth copy of the Christianismi Restitutio. It is authentic, complete, and supposedly better preserved than any of the other three and is signed by Servetus. The author also wrote a message in the margins of the last pages, not included in the other known copies. This message refers to a lost source of first-century evidence that has the potential to change the way we view Christianity itself. I can't tell you any more unless we meet in person. This is surely the most incredible, rare, and potentially dangerous book in existence today.

Now, to the point of my letter to you: I have acquired this book quite legitimately under circumstances that require considerable delicacy and care if its safety and access to future historians is to be maintained.

I would like you to return to Spain, briefly, to meet with me concerning its future. I'm afraid I can't be more forthcoming at this time, but be assured that I need you now, my friend, as you have needed me many times during your time in Madrid.

I will, of course, cover all of your expenses in this endeavor. Please let me know of your decision as soon as you can.

With affection,
Basilio Diego Mendez

They both sat quietly for a moment. Finally, Hunter said, "This looks pretty important, Shay. It's a shame he didn't open it. I wonder if they ever had any other correspondence?"

Shay shook his head. "No. And I've been over his things pretty thoroughly."

"You never found any reference to this book in any of your father's papers?"

"Nope, not a hint. The only references to Basilio Mendez relate to their friendship, and that he'd cooperated with my dad during the war, by supplying him with valuable intelligence."

Shay, who had been pacing back and forth, moved behind his desk, sat down and leaned back. "Let me explain what I'd like to do, Hunter. I've been planning for some time to make a large donation to the University of Virginia. Since you're on the faculty there, perhaps you know that I'm a member of the University Board of Trustees. I've even served as its chairman more than once."

Hunter *did* know this even though Blackwell had never brought it up. Hunter learned it on his own when he'd investigated Blackwell after he'd hired him for a short-term job a year ago.

"Anyway," continued Shay, "The University is currently in the midst of a fundraising campaign and several brick-and-mortar projects are being seriously looked at. The one I've been considering funding is an addition to the library to house the rare book collection. I think it would be super to offer to fund the new addition and to present the library with the fourth copy of the Servetus book as the centerpiece of what would instantly become one of the most important collections in the country, maybe even the world.

"Of course all of that would depend on whether the book actually exists, whether it is still in the Mendez family collection, and whether they would be willing to sell it to me. Usually rare works like this, when they do become available, are typically auctioned in order to get maximum revenue for any sale. I'll try to avoid that by making a generous but fair offer up front.

"I tried to contact Basilio Mendez," he continued, "but it seems he recently died by falling off a ladder in his library. I spoke with his son Alfonso, a very unpleasant man, who said there was no such book in his father's collection and not to bother him again.

"Nevertheless, Hunter, would you be willing to fly to Spain, meet the Mendez family, find out if they do or don't have the book, and if they do, whether they would be willing to sell it to me?"

Hunter slowly stroked his chin but didn't reply. He knew why Blackwell didn't fly to Madrid himself. Shay had previously told him about the boating accident that had killed both his parents in 1954. His father had been thirty-eight years old and Shay was three at the time. Although he was on board with them, he had little remembrance of the accident. He learned later that they'd just stopped to refuel his father's motor launch at a marina near Cape Charles on Chesapeake Bay. The best guess of the authorities that investigated the accident was that a spark had set off fumes in the engine compartment when they were preparing to dock. The subsequent explosion had destroyed the boat, part of the dock, both of his parents, and part of Shay's inner ear mechanism. The damage to his equilibrium system had left him so susceptible to motion sickness that travel by plane or boat was impossible.

After graduating from the University of Virginia, Shay, who had inherited his father's intelligence and business prowess, had become a successful venture capitalist and eventually a philanthropist. He'd accumulated a substantial fortune by buying small but potentially lucrative companies that were in financial trouble, improving them significantly, and then selling them for a profit. He was a fair man who took care of his employees and those of the companies he traded. In return, he became a multi-millionaire.

Early in his career, when financing for his ventures was difficult to attract, it seemed that funding would often mysteriously appear at the last possible moment. Rationally he couldn't fathom that it was just luck, but

Shay was never able to find any reason to believe otherwise.

"Of course I'll cover all your expenses" Shay added, "including whatever you need to authenticate the book, if you find it. And rest assured, your remuneration would be generous in keeping with our past contract. I've taken the liberty of assembling a list of people capable of authenticating the book, if you find it."

He picked up a stack of folders on his desk and handed them to Hunter. "Here are their dossiers. If you would rather use someone else, that would be okay too. Who you choose is entirely up to you.

"Scarlet will be your contact person until you have something to report to me directly. Think of her as your travel agent, banker, and general expediter. I know you got along well with her on the last assignment you did for me, and I'm sure you'll find her to be just as efficient as ever."

Hunter took a moment before answering. He was conflicted by competing priorities. He knew that his dad was expecting him to spend the summer helping build a sunroom on their cabin on Lake Superior. Ever since Hunter's younger brother Gary's death, his dad had somehow seemed older and less full of life. Hunter added this observation to his own already considerable guilt for not protecting his brother during the pursuit and capture of the terrorist, Mahmud e Raq in the mountainous region of Pakistan bordering Afghanistan. Hunter had led that black-ops operation. If he took this job he might be away for a good part of the summer, leaving his dad alone. On the other hand, this assignment was exactly the kind of "find-and-correct" work he enjoyed doing when he wasn't focusing on his academic career at the medical school. In the end, the intriguing nature of the assignment won out. "I'll do it."

Chapter 3

CHARLOTTESVILLE

It was late afternoon on Sunday when Hunter left the Blackwell Ranch. The sunlight streamed through the trees casting long shadows over the pastures used by the horses when they weren't housed in the stables nearby. Blackwell's driver, who had taken him directly to the ranch, now drove him home to his loft on the top floor of an old converted warehouse not far from his office at the University. There he showered, dressed in chinos and a yellow silk shirt, and headed out to dinner at Angelo's, an Italian restaurant in his neighborhood where the owners and staff knew him well.

It was a beautiful early summer evening so he decided to walk. He strolled down tree-lined streets with quaint shops and unique storefronts. There wasn't a chain operation in sight. Of course, it also took him past Annie's Antique Shoppe. When Annie had sold the store and left for New York, the new owner wisely kept the name. Annie had been very successful, and the store had gained both a local and regional reputation for great finds and fair prices.

Hunter missed her a lot. They'd met during his first year teaching at the medical school. He'd been trying to furnish the loft and needed help. On a whim, without even having any decorating scheme in mind, he'd stopped in her store. He'd found himself looking at a pair of matched table lamps when he heard her magical voice for the first time.

"May I be of any help, sir?"

Hunter turned and saw a petite young woman with shoulder-length blonde hair and an enigmatic smile, looking up at him. He'd often thought later that he fell in love with her right there, first the voice and then the smile. He'd gazed at her for a moment, seemingly spellbound, before regaining his composure and answering her.

At Angelo's he took a table by the front window, where he could see her shop. He and Annie often sat there, at that very table, talking and drinking wine after one of Angelo's wonderful cannelloni dinners.

"Hi, Hunter, good to see you again. It's been a while."

Hunter acknowledged Kenny De Luca, Angelo De Luca's oldest son. He ordered the cannelloni.

Their first year together had been everything he could ask for. They were together as much as both of their jobs would permit, and she'd introduced Hunter to the world of antique furniture. Surprising himself, he'd become somewhat of an amateur connoisseur. Since he'd had no furniture of his own to speak of, his first purchase was a wonderful highly carved French desk from the late eighteen hundreds that stretched his budget to the limit. It had come from a castle in Belgium and was seven feet wide with drawers and slots in the upper back and twelve drawers in the base unit. It had become the hub of his home office, and his first antique purchase. Over the next year Annie helped him pick out even more pieces. Whenever they could they traveled together, focusing on purchases for the store and, where Hunter's salary would allow, furniture for him. Hunter had never been happier. And then it all ended.

She'd suddenly announced she was moving to New York to open a shop there. An opportunity had come up that she couldn't ignore was the way she put it. It was all very mysterious, and though he could have insisted on an explanation, something inexplicable told him not to. At first he'd thought they could still work it out, the long-distance romance thing. In the end it was Annie who said it wouldn't work and they needed to go their separate ways.

In the sixteen months since she'd left, Hunter had dated others, and even became somewhat serious about an epidemiologist from the campus, but nothing lasting seemed to come from any of it.

Enough of this; he shook off his melancholy. He knew he had to get back to the issue at hand—the project he'd agreed to do for Shay—finding the *Christianismi Restitutio.*

After dinner he returned home, fixed a perfect Manhattan on the rocks with a twist and read the dossiers of the recommended authenticators that Blackwell had assembled for him.

Whoever did the background checks on these people was very thorough, he decided when he'd finished. Not only did the dossiers include their professional credentials, which showed that they all were more than fully qualified to carry out the authentication, but they also provided a psychological assessment of each person's personality, ability to make informed decisions, and their likelihood of cooperation with a guy like Hunter in charge. Also included was an assessment of their likelihood to take on such a task and whether their passport was current.

Hunter decided that the candidate who best fit all the qualifying criteria was a woman named Genevieve Swift, who was currently an assistant curator in the documents section of the Bibliotheque Nationale in Paris. She was twenty-nine years old and spoke fluent Spanish as well as German, English, Greek, and French. Further, she could read Latin and Hebrew. She held dual British and French citizenship.

She was born in England to a French mother and English father who were both professors at Cambridge. The father's field was medieval history and the mother's was astrophysics, an unusual combination that produced a daughter with an appreciation for science but a passion for history.   Her own Ph.D. from the Sorbonne was in Renaissance History, and she had published several important papers on the Reformation and the Inquisitions of the sixteenth century. If the book existed and Hunter could find it, she would be the authenticator he'd use.

The next day, Hunter called Shay and told him that he needed a week before he could start on the project. He had to get back to Upper Michigan and tie up a few loose ends before he could begin the search for the book.

Taking that week turned out to be a serious mistake.

Chapter 4

BIG BAY, IN MICHIGAN'S UPPER PENINSULA

The Laughing Whitefish restaurant and bar in Big Bay was a fixture in the small fishing village situated on the shore of Lake Independence. The warm midday breeze blowing off the vast immensity of Lake Superior, just to the north and east, gently ruffled the curtains in the open screened windows and convincingly signaled the end of another long winter in Michigan's Upper Peninsula. The McCormick Wilderness Tract and the Huron Mountains lay immediately to the west.

Hunter was on his second refill and wondered, not for the first time, how Chilly Johnson consistently brewed the best coffee in the U.P. Nothing smelled this good in the morning. Hunter had even bought a pound of the stuff from him and tried to brew it at home. The result? Ordinary coffee. He finally concluded Chilly just had a gift. As he sipped his third cup of coffee, he was enjoying the story Henry Lahti was telling him and his dad, Ed McCoy, as the three of them sat at their usual table.

"I'm telling you, Ed, she had to be eighty at least. I was right behind her in line at the Wal-Mart checkout. The clerk was this young, smart-alecky kid who looked at the baseball bat she'd plunked down on his checkout counter and asked if it was for her grandson. She fixed him with a level withering stare and said in an icy tone, 'No—it's for me.'"

Hunter sipped his coffee and waited as Henry paused gleefully, then continued his story. "The kid took a second look at her as he was running the charge through. He says, 'No way. What are you going to do, keep it under the bed and if some creep breaks into your house bop him on the head?' She glared at him and said, 'Listen, sonny, I play center field on my softball team and dented my old bat from hitting so many homers."

"Ha! That's an old bat for you," Ed remarked. The three men laughed at the pun, but Henry wasn't done yet.

"So after taking her money and putting the bat in a bag, the kid thanked her for shopping at Wal-Mart, backed up a step, and told her to have a nice day. I think he was a little worried she might bop *him* on the head. I wanted to ask her if she was just putting the kid on about the softball team, but she was long gone by the time I checked out. What do *you* think, Hunter? Could some woman in her eighties really play on a softball team?"

Hunter, grinning, slapped his hands on the table. "Too bad you two old geezers didn't have a chance to ask her, she might have let you join her team." Laughing, he added, "Heck, I'd even come to watch that." Hunter pushed his chair back and rose. "Now if you two guys will excuse me, I've had too much coffee and need to go sharpen my skates." He headed toward the men's room.

"Sharpen his skates?" He heard Henry ask Ed.

"Why not?" Hunter's dad said. "Last time he got up to pee he'd said he was going to band practice. Both men grinned, their mutual affection for Hunter obvious.

Just as Hunter was returning, three men wearing camouflage-hunting clothes entered the restaurant. They were big and noisy, all over six feet. Seeing no empty tables they walked over to the one shared by Ed and Henry.

"You're done here. Get up and get out," said the biggest one. "We're taking this table."

As he began to pull Ed out of his chair, Hunter strolled up, and in a voice all the more menacing by its soft flat tone, said to the man, "Take your hands off him—now."

The three men looked confused when Hunter, still staring at the big man, called to Chilly Johnson, the bartender and owner of the Laughing Whitefish, who was watching things unfold from his place behind the bar. "Chilly, open the front door. I don't want to break anything when I throw them out."

"Yeah, I'll do that, Hunter. The last time it cost me a new window."

Hunter, who hadn't taken his eyes off the big man, added, "You know, Chilly, on second thought, this dumb looking guy here's big enough I think you'd better open both doors."

Chilly hurried to the doors to do as he was told. Then the biggest of the three strangers recovered his composure, dropped Ed back in his chair, pumped himself up and said,

"Screw you, we're taking this table," and he moved forward and swung a huge fist at Hunter's head.

To Hunter, it all unfolded in slow motion, as such situations always did for him. He'd first became aware of his capacity to slow things down when he was just a school boy. One day during school recess the class bully had decided that Hunter was to be his new target. As the bully charged Hunter with the intent of knocking him down, Hunter saw all of his movements in slow motion as if they were occurring under water. So he had plenty of time to step aside and shove the bully to the ground with both of his hands on the attacker's back as he flew by. When the bully got up swinging, again in slow motion to Hunter's eye, he simply ducked and the swing missed badly. The gathering crowd of schoolmates started to laugh at the bully, who was being so easily outclassed by Hunter. Then the teacher showed up and the incident was quickly over. This unique phenomenon only seemed to occur in situations in which Hunter's safety, or someone close to him, was threatened. It had protected him many times over the years, but never more so than in his former work as an agent for the Defense Intelligence Agency, the DIA.

This time, as before, when the big guy threw his punch, Hunter had plenty of time to assess it and duck below. As he straightened up, he drove his left fist into the man's chest, just below the sternum, with all the force of the trained fighter he was. When the blast doubled the big man forward, Hunter smacked his right fist into the man's jaw and the lights went out. The big guy tottered back on his heels and fell with a thud to the floor.

As his buddies stood by with their mouths gaping in amazement at the ease with which their leader was put out of commission, Hunter picked him up by his belt and shirt collar and carried him to the open double front doors. As Chilly stepped back, Hunter tossed the man out into the parking lot. Then, following him out and searching the unconscious man for identification took his wallet and found a Michigan Driver's license stating he was Thomas B. Hayes from Detroit.

As Hunter walked back into the room the other two put their hands up.

"Hey, easy now, we're leaving. We were just kidding man."

After they had gone, Chilly, still with a smile on his face said "Thanks, Hunter. Every time something gets broken in here my insurance premiums head further north."

"Always glad to help, Chilly."

Once seated again, the three friends ordered lunch, and Hunter relaxed as Ed and Henry Lahti made plans for another fishing trip, the following Tuesday, on the Yellow Dog River. The brookies were biting, and the friends were overdue for some more pan-fried trout. Hunter rubbed his knuckles. The big guy's jaw had been like hitting a cement block.

After they ate and said goodbye to Henry and Chilly, Hunter and his dad headed south on the Big Bay road to their place on a bluff overlooking Lake Superior, about halfway between Big Bay and Marquette. Because of the many black bears they saw in the area, they'd decided to call their place Anue, which meant black bear in the Wyandot Indian language. The French name for the Wyandot tribe was *Huron*, meaning "wild boar." The French thought that the Mohawk haircuts of the Wyandot warriors looked like the bristles on a wild boar's neck. Hunter grinned at the thought; he liked knowing his local history.

After a few minutes Ed said, "Thanks for your help back there, son. I don't think I could have taken that guy by myself." Then he puffed his chest out a little. "Maybe I could have, but probably not."

With a knowing smile on his face, Hunter said, "Hey, everything I know I learned from you, Dad."

"Not how to dispose of a guy that big, you didn't."

Hunter laughed. "Well then, we'll thank the Marines and my good genes for that." Back at the cabin, Hunter immediately began splitting logs with an axe. Henry Lahti had dropped off the pickup load of logs the day before, claiming that the big white birch tree he'd cut down two years earlier, the one that threatened his garage, was finally ready for logging. Still worked up over his encounter at the Laughing Whitefish, Hunter needed the physical release.

Hunter was aware that he'd had to fight down the fury that surged to the surface when the man grabbed his dad. He often worried that he wouldn't be able to keep the surging power of it under control. Luckily, he'd dispatched the man so easily there wasn't time for it to take over. He'd watched the rage develop over the years and knew it was getting worse, not better. Violence, or even the threat of it to those in his care, was usually the trigger that brought it on. And then there were the nightmares. Hunter tried to fool himself into thinking he had it under control, but deep down he knew otherwise. He also knew it was somehow linked to the border incident in Pakistan.

What kind of assholes would pull that crap on two old guys having lunch? Hunter knew the answer as soon as he thought about it. He had encountered men like them before. Too many times, he thought, men whose self-esteem came only at the expense of others. Fortunately that part of his life was past. At least Hunter hoped it was.

Feeling the early afternoon sun on his back as he replenished the woodpile, the muscles in his strong young back, shoulders, and arms rhythmically contracted and relaxed under a sheen of sweat as he split the larger logs. The ache in his knuckles was gone. By the time he'd been at it for two hours, the afternoon sun was beginning to set over the Huron Mountains to the west, and Hunter felt rejuvenated.

After a fine dinner of brook trout that Ed had caught earlier that day in the Yellow Dog, Hunter and his dad sat on the deck in their old Adirondack chairs, enjoying the blue-black night sky that majestically framed their view of Lake Superior. The clear sky was alight with stars, and the breeze off the lake was welcome and made Hunter glad he was home, even if only for a week. This, coupled with the smell of pine and the lingering aroma of the trout dinner cooked on the grill, did its job, and Hunter began to relax. Both men were comfortable with their silent companionship. Often they sat together for hours with little conversation to interfere with their reverence for the big lake and the land they both called home.

That wouldn't be the case tonight.

An hour later, the silence was disrupted by a snap. It sounded like a small twig breaking. Hunter heard it first. Both men heard a second snap a moment later.

Hunter, immediately alert, said, "Dad, get in the house now, stay low, and kill the lights."

Hunter followed him inside a moment later, retrieved his Beretta 9 mm. from its hiding place under the kitchen table, inserted the clip, and slid a second one into his pocket. Ed had turned off all the lights by now, and they met in the dark kitchen toward the rear of the cabin, where Hunter retrieved his Winchester from its place near the back door.

Hunter indicated that Ed should stay down. "It might just be an animal, but it could be another one of those armed break-ins we've been reading about recently."

A sudden burst of automatic fire shattered the living room window and worked its way across the front of the cabin, loudly punctuating a vivid denial of the animal theory.

Hunter's senses and instincts quickly accelerated to maximum readiness. He gave his dad the rifle. "Stay in the kitchen and keep low. I'm going to slip out onto the back deck where I'll be able to hear any outside movement."

He waited for his eyes to adjust to the dark. The black wash of trees slowly became individual trunks and branches. He stood still, scanning for signs of movement. Years of training and experience taught him that patience and vigilance were his best offensive weapons when stalking. Few men were better at it than Hunter McCoy.

Soon he heard footsteps on the pine needles off to his left. The man presumably was moving around to come at the cabin from the rear. The assailant was clearly not a skilled woodsman, based on the level of noise he was making. Hunter stayed low, but was now able to see the silhouette of a man moving from the cover of one big pine to another. He could hear no others. The man appeared to be alone.

Hunter moved quietly off the deck and around to the back of their sauna, a structure separate from the main house. From there he stealthily crept through the woods to a position he estimated to be roughly thirty-five feet behind the intruder. Using tracking skills he'd honed over the years, he silently approached to within five feet of the man. He had yet to make a sound of any kind. He took an isosceles shooting stance and leveled his gun at the man's back.

"Drop it! Now!"

The man stiffened. Hunter could sense his hesitation. "Don't even think about it."

"Okay. Okay. Take it easy," the man said.

Hunter kept his aim on the man's back "Slowly put your weapon on the ground in front of you."

"All right, take it easy."

Surprised, he identified the voice immediately. Then, Hunter's voice took on a steel-hard edge. "Put your weapon on the ground in front of you. I won't ask again. Do it now. Then turn around slowly."

With that, the man quickly fell into a roll, brought the automatic rifle around, and fired a burst, but only managed to wound a few trees before Hunter, who saw it all happening in slow motion, fired six rapid shots that caught the man squarely in the chest.

Hunter bent over him and studied his face. He confirmed it was the same man he'd thrown out of the Laughing Whitefish earlier in the day. Now he was dead, with six closely placed 9 mm. rounds in his heart. Hunter's pulse was racing. *Damn it. The man shot first. I had to kill him. But six shots? One would have been enough. Jeez!*

He tried to slow his breathing and push the dark surging animal fury back below the surface. He used a stick to pick up Hayes's weapon. Hunter could see it was a MAC 10 machine pistol.

Not hearing any other sounds to indicate the man's buddies might be with him, Hunter carefully crept back into the cabin to tell his dad that he was all right and the shooter was dead.

Not finding him immediately in the kitchen, he called quietly, "Dad, where are you?" "Dad, it's okay. I'm all right. Where are you?

Just then Hunter almost stumbled over him. He looked down and saw his dad lying motionless in a pool of blood slowly spreading away from his head.

Chapter 5

Hunter was pacing his dad's room in Marquette General Hospital when Ed McCoy fluttered open his eyes and woozily stared up into the ample bosom of a very pretty young nurse wearing a nametag that declared she was Bev. Nurse Bev, who had just finished taking his vital signs, signaled to Hunter and the sheriff that it was okay for them to come forward.

Hunter watched as his dad reached for his aching head and discovered it was covered in the back by bandages. "What happened?" he croaked, dry-mouthed.

"That's exactly what I want to know," said a stern and unsmiling Sheriff John Destramp, who had just arrived. His deputy, Mike Fragale, had responded to the shooting the previous night at Anue and had taken a statement from Hunter. Nevertheless, Fragale told Hunter that he would have to tell it to the sheriff again in the morning.

Hunter described the assault on their house, and how a stray round from Hayes's machine pistol had creased his dad's head and concussed him.

Ed McCoy groaned, no doubt with a headache registering ten on a ten-point scale. "I was shot?"

"Yeah, Dad, you were. How about that, not a scratch from Viet Nam, but you manage to get shot right in your own back yard."

Ed closed his eyes and took several deep breaths.

Sheriff Destramp mused out loud to no one in particular, "What the hell was Hayes doing with an automatic weapon shooting up your cabin? Getting in a bar fight is one thing, but shooting up a house isn't something we see every day around here." Shaking his head, he admonished Hunter and Ed not to leave town until he completed his investigation.

"Don't worry, sheriff, we're not going anywhere," Hunter assured him.

Hunter stayed in Ed's hospital room that night, sleeping in a chair. The next morning, satisfied that he was all right, the doctor cleared Ed for release.

Still grumpy, his dad flopped down in the passenger seat of the Ford pickup. "You know, Hunter, I don't know if I'm more pissed at that monkey who shot up the cabin and almost killed me, or at this damned headache."

When they got to the cabin they discovered it was now a crime scene, roped off by yellow police tape. Ed called Henry Lahti, who said they could stay at his place as long as they needed. Henry's house was on the Yellow Dog River, about five miles south of where it emptied into Lake Independence at Big Bay, and about eight miles from Anue.

Like Hunter and Ed, Henry was a 'Yooper,' born and raised in the U.P. He was a game warden who worked for the DNR in Marquette County. Hunter had met him just three years before, when he'd bought Anue, then called the "Niemi place," off county road 550, halfway between Marquette and Big Bay.

After three days of staying with Henry Lahti who'd been a gracious host, Hunter and Ed were anxious to get back to their own place. When they finally got the call that they were to report to Sheriff Destramp so he could return their house to them, they greeted the news with relief.

Hunter drove the pickup on the way into Marquette. "What do you think, Dad, we okay with the sheriff?"

"Oh yeah. I've known John Destramp for many years. He's a good cop. He knows the truth when he sees it."

Hunter eyed him with concern. "How's the head?"

Rubbing the spot where the swelling had gone down, Ed replied, "Well, apparently it's as hard as yours, because I seem to be all right."

Hunter laughed. His dad was going to be okay.

At the sheriff's office, they were ushered in to see him immediately.

"Hunter, Ed. Have a chair. Here's what I was able to find out. The State Police picked up the two buddies of your midnight stalker shortly after they crossed the Mackinac Bridge, south of Mackinaw City. They confirmed that Hayes said he was going after you. That you'd sucker punched him and he wouldn't take that from any man. They told him that he was nuts and that you'd beat him fair and square and that they were going back to Detroit. He was on his own if he was going to go after you. They claim they had no idea he was going to use deadly force. Turns out that Hayes has a long rap sheet of assaults going back years. He had a nasty temper.

"Ed, can you think of any reason why Hayes might have been after you?"

"You've got to be kidding, sheriff, said Ed. "I'm an old man. I spend my time fishing. Who'd want to bother me? I didn't even know the guy."

Slowly shifting his gaze, Destramp said, "What about you, Hunter?"

"None that I can think of."

Sheriff Destramp studied Hunter for a few moments before he shrugged and got up from his chair. "All right then, you're free to return to your cabin. My people are done there. As far as my office is concerned, the shooting was justified and the matter is closed."

Hunter paused at the door as they were leaving. "Sheriff?"

"Yeah?" Destramp paused, removed his glasses, and wiped them with his handkerchief.

"If you find out anything more about this episode, you know, like if Hayes actually had a motive other than just being an asshole, you will let me know, won't you?"

Destramp replaced his glasses and continued to eye Hunter for a moment longer. "You're not holding anything back on me, are you, Hunter?"

"No, sheriff, I'm not."

The Sheriff, unlike most locals in the area, knew most of Hunter's background and was comfortable sharing information with him. "All right. You'll know anything we find out."

Destramp knew that after graduating from Northern Michigan University, Hunter had enlisted in the Marines as his father had done years earlier, during the Viet Nam War. When his tour was up he'd received an honorable discharge and planned to return to graduate school. He'd put his plans on hold, however, when a man from the U.S. Defense Intelligence Agency (DIA), a division of the Department of Defense, approached him as he was mustering out.

"Capt. McCoy, my name is Jim Maddox. I have a proposition to make to you."

Ultimately, Hunter became a civilian agent of the DIA's Directorate for Human Intelligence. For the next four years he pursued international criminals and terrorists whose paths linked them to the United States. Because of the international criminal aspects of much of his work, Hunter frequently worked with Interpol, the international police organization. The United States National Central Bureau—the USNCB—was the American group that linked all United States police organizations to Interpol's General Secretariat in Lyon, France. Hunter frequently tapped Interpol's intelligence databases whenever his DIA work had an international criminal component. And, to the delight of Interpol, he frequently supplied them with intelligence in turn. His relationship with them was so good they offered him a job at Interpol headquarters Lyon if he ever left the DIA.

Relieved the episode at the cabin was over, Hunter and Ed returned to Anue. Surveying the damage done by the automatic rounds, they estimated it would take a week or so to repair the carnage.

Later, after Hunter had showered and changed into jeans and a light sweatshirt, they had dinner and, as had become their custom, they retired to the two Adirondack chairs on the front deck to watch the twilight colors change on Lake Superior as a prelude to the night to come. Hunter mixed himself his customary perfect Manhattan on the rocks, and Ed had his usual Jack Daniels on ice. They sat quietly for a while, enjoying the outdoors with its spectacular view of the vast, cold lake. The rhythm of the waves washing over the ancient rocks fifty feet below the edge of their lawn, synched with Hunter's own breathing and gave him a sense of oneness with the big lake.

He thought about the man he'd just killed. It wasn't the first time he'd killed a man, but it was probably the first time he didn't know why. And why had he shot him six times? He remembered the first shot, but not the last five. Who wouldn't remember shooting a man five times? The coroner had told him all six shots were through the heart. What had he become? Was he really that deadly, that efficient?

Hunter's reverie was interrupted when Ed set his drink down on the table between them. "So, do you think you can stay for a while this summer?" he asked lightly.

Hunter tried to shake off his confused thoughts as he dreaded the answer he had to give.

His dad continued, "The reason I ask is that I'd thought it would be nice to get started on the sunroom."

Both Ed and Hunter had decided that they needed to enlarge the cabin's deck and convert it to a glassed-in sunroom. The sunroom would not only provide relief from insects, but also from the harsh winds that frequently blew in from Superior. They'd have a great panoramic view of the lake, as well as the tall stands of pine and white birch on either side of the grassy front lawn, which extended to the edge of the cliff that overlooked the rocky shoreline that was constantly battered by Superior's waves.

Hunter still hadn't answered, so his dad continued. "Your classes don't start until mid-August, so if you get back to Charlottesville by the first of August you should have plenty of time to get ready for those first-year medical students."

Four years earlier, after completing his Ph.D. in physiology, Hunter had accepted a position as assistant professor in the Physiology Department at the University of Virginia Medical School in Charlottesville. He'd discovered, much to his relief, that he liked teaching and was actually quite good at it. Professor Thornberry, the man who'd encouraged him to pursue the Ph.D. after he left the DIA, had been right. Of course it didn't hurt any that his classes were composed of bright, young medical students eager to learn all they could.

It was shortly after settling in at the medical school in Charlottesville that he'd decided to buy Anue. It had worked out well. His dad lived there year round and took care of the place. Hunter would come up in the summers to fish and spend time with him. His mother had died when Hunter was ten, and Ed McCoy had raised him and his brother Gary after that. Since Gary's death, his dad was the only family Hunter had and vice versa.

As darkness settled over the lake, the sky came alive with stars and Lake Superior became a vast inky blue canvas dotted by the lights of two inbound iron-ore carriers headed to the ore docks near Presque Isle. Hunter thought

that the Indian word for superior, Gitche Man'ito, the Great
Spirit, was right on the money.

"Hunter?" said Ed.

"Yeah?"

"This other job you seem to have now, you know what
I mean. Not the academic one with the university, and not
the government work you did after your stint with the
Marines, but the freelance stuff you do. I've never asked
you about it, and you haven't volunteered anything. Maybe
you could at least tell me if I should be worried when
you're away on one of those projects."

Hunter met his father's eyes. It wasn't as if he had
anything to hide or was ashamed of. But he knew that,
alone up here in the cabin while Hunter was away on these
jobs, his dad would already be feeling lonely and probably
worried about him. Hunter didn't want to add to that.

"It's certainly different from what I do at the med
school."

Ed McCoy leaned forward and turned to face him.
"Can you tell me about it or shouldn't I ask?"

"Sure. You can ask." Hunter took a sip of his drink
and thought for a moment before continuing.

"It's not any formal kind of job. I don't work for the
government anymore. The Pakistan business took care of
that. I'm not a spy or anything like that. I just help people
find things. I try to keep any risk to a minimum."

His dad, settling back into his chair, nodded. "Glad to
hear it. But what exactly do you do?"

Hunter had often asked himself the same thing. *What
exactly is it I do?* It wasn't work with a tidy job
description, like professor, golf pro, or commercial
fisherman. Well, maybe it was a little like a fisherman, he
thought.

"I guess it started when an old colleague from the
Corps called and asked me for a favor on behalf of his
sister," he said. "She'd been a final candidate for an

assistant professorship of archeology at the University of Michigan, but didn't get the job. It went instead to a guy who'd stolen her work and presented it as his own. They'd been on the same dig in Ethiopia, collecting fossils of early man. Since they were colleagues, they kept their research notes together in a single notebook. As a more seasoned investigator, the guy convinced her at the time that that was the most efficient way to do it. Then he took the notebook.

"The brother asked me if I could try to recover the notebook, if it still existed. According to his sister, the notes would clearly show that she, not he, made the discovery and actually wrote the paper that described it. My friend thought that since I was now in 'the academic business' as he put it, but still a Marine buddy, maybe I could help set things straight."

Ed sipped his Jack Daniels and grinned. "Bet you did it, right?"

"It wasn't too difficult. To put it briefly, I found the notebook in the basement of the guy's house. When I confronted him with the evidence and why I was looking for it, and what I intended to do with it, the man promptly resigned his position at the university in disgrace, and the assistant professorship went to the sister instead."

"Wow, what a low life."

"Yeah, he was." Hunter recalled the fear in the man's eyes when he'd been found out. He took another swallow of his drink and continued. "This led to another case, if you want to call it that, of what I call 'find and correct' jobs. The sister of my buddy recommended this one. It involved a missing bid on a construction job in the northwest corner of Seattle. A new electrical contracting company composed of ex-cons who were trying to get their lives together by building this legitimate business asked for my help. They were constantly having their bids disappear from the general contractor's office. The client wanted to know if I would find out how this was happening, and do something about it.

"So I investigated, and it turned out that the foreman for the general contractor had a brother with a competing electrical subcontracting firm, and he was removing the bids. After I got him alone and 'explained' how things were going to change from now on, their bids stayed in the pool and they were in business. This took a little physical persuasion, as he thought he was a tough guy. Later, when he was recovering from this delusion, he contacted his brother and told him the fix was off."

Hunter downed the last of his drink. "I don't go looking for this work, Dad, but I seem to be good at it. I only require that clients tell me how they found me. Who recommended me? Also, and this is important, no one in Virginia, nor any of my clients, know about this place, about Anue. This life we have here, you and I, this is ours, and I want to keep it that way. So to answer your question, should you be worried? I don't think so."

Ed nodded thoughtfully. "And that's it? Just those two jobs?"

"After the ones I've described for you, I've had three others since. I have no set fee for my services. The clients, of course, pay all expenses. Beyond expenses, my fee is what they think my service has been worth to them when the job is done. So far, no one has been difficult about the amount or method of payment."

Hunter didn't tell his dad that these jobs also satisfied some dark need within him for putting himself in danger. A need he didn't really understand. It wasn't rational at all. Maybe it was his way of beating the rage. Maybe he needed the danger to dredge it up, if only so he could confront it and beat it back down again. He tried not to ponder it too much or delve too deeply into it. He suspected it was probably linked to his failure to protect his brother on that secret mission across the border into

Pakistan to capture Mahmud e Raq—a failure he couldn't allow to happen again for anyone else in his care. Maybe he just had to prove to himself over and over again that he could be depended on. He didn't know, but it somehow made him whole, filled a gap, satisfied a need. But it also scared him.

Deciding he couldn't put it off any longer, Hunter clasped his hands. "Dad?"

"Yeah, Hunter?"

"A week ago, right after classes got out, a former client that I'd previously done 'find-and-correct' work for asked me to help him again. He said he had another job I might be interested in. I met with him and I agreed to take it.

"So when do you start this new job for him?"

Hunter's face formed the answer.

Ed sighed dejectedly, knowing what was coming. "I understand, Hunter. The only bad thing is that now I'll have to wait a little longer to get that darned sunroom built."

Hunter was pleased his dad understood, but still felt a little guilty. He hadn't been completely honest with him. A few months earlier, he'd received a visit from his old DIA handler, Major Deacon Wogen. In the seven years since they'd last talked, Deacon had been promoted to full Colonel and was now Assistant Director of the DIA. He'd personally come to Virginia with a proposition for Hunter. He wanted him to consider rejoining the agency on an ad hoc basis. Deacon promised that he would respect that Hunter's first obligation was to his academic career and that the agency would not interfere in that. In fact, it was the very reason he visited Hunter. Deacon explained that from time to time the DIA's investigations ventured into higher academic areas. Deacon asked if Hunter would be willing to 'advise' them in these investigations. They reasoned that Hunter's academic position would afford him credibility that the agency simply didn't have.

Hunter initially turned him down. But then a strange thing happened. It was almost as if Deacon knew him better than he knew himself. Over the next two weeks, Hunter slowly began to reconsider the offer. That dark need in him for action and danger that he didn't want to reflect on too closely was ever-present. His tranquil academic life was already being nicely offset by the excitement of his occasional "find-and-correct" jobs. But this offer from Deacon suggested the potential to fan the flames of his need for adventure even more. Hunter had always respected Deacon, and just as he was beginning to think he'd call him back and tell him he'd reconsidered the offer, Deacon called him first and offered the job again.

This time Hunter didn't hesitate in saying yes.

Chapter 6

PUERTO DE SOLLER, MAJORCA

The afternoon sun was playing in diagonally through the large windows of her studio looking north over the Bay of Soller. The villa was nestled into the mountainside on the northwest coast of Majorca, off the coast of Spain in the western Mediterranean. It looked down on the picturesque old town of Puerto de Soller and its harbor filled with multicolored small pleasure boats. It was everything Alicia Mendez needed: her personal retreat and the place she felt most at home. She'd been working on a large oil of a local beach scene when the afternoon post arrived.

Recognizing that it was from Hugo Alvarez, her grandfather's longtime attorney, she opened the letter immediately. He was calling the family to his office in the city center of Madrid for the reading of her grandfather's will. She knew that while Alvarez was younger than her grandfather, he'd handled his affairs for many years, and the two men had also become good friends.

Her semester completed at the University of Madrid, she'd moved back to her villa in Majorca and was devastated when she'd learned of her grandfather's death. She'd flown back to Madrid for the funeral of course, but afterward, with nothing to keep her in Spain for the summer, she returned to Soller. Her classes at the University of Madrid didn't start until September. Now she had to make the trip back again. Still, she knew her grandfather would have wanted her there.

Her flight of a little over an hour arrived on time and she took a cab to Hugo Alvarez's office. Her father, Alfonso Mendez, age sixty-two, a widower, and Basilio's only heir, was already present and seated. Alicia was Alfonso's only daughter. A slender, attractive young woman of twenty-five, she had shoulder-length dark brown hair and shared her father's fine features with high aristocratic cheekbones. Absent was Alicia's twenty-year-old brother Rafael.

Alicia had greeted the attorney warmly, and then sat, looking at everything in the office except her father.

"Where is that damned son of mine?" growled Alfonso. "His grandfather dead, the family money at stake, and where is he? No doubt somewhere with his head in the stars again. What a useless and stupid hobby for a male member of the Mendez family."

Alicia fumed inside. She had spoken with her brother and knew why he wasn't there, but held her tongue and remained silent.

Alfonso was a tall man like his father had been, with refined handsome features and graying hair. He was wearing an expensive tailored business suit, with dark tie and Ferragamo black leather shoes. Alicia had chosen a tasteful black dress with a matching jacket and low-heeled shoes that, while attractive, were not of the same quality as her father's ensemble.

"Thank you for coming, Señor Mendez, and you also, Señorita Mendez," Alvarez began. "As you know, I have been Basilio's attorney for many years. Over those years he has amended his will several times. Of importance to you, however, are the directives in this, his final will," tapping the papers on his desk. "It is available to you to read in its entirety, but I would like to inform you now of its principal provisions.

"To you, Señor Mendez, your father leaves Mendez Castle, its furnishings and art, the lands that make up the Mendez holdings in Spain, and the majority of the family fortune."

Alphonso grunted in acknowledgement.

"To you, Señorita Mendez, your grandfather leaves the villa in Majorca, the collection of Inquisition artifacts, and an endowment that will pay seventy-five thousand euros per year, a figure that, at the discretion of your father, will be increased to one hundred twenty-five thousand euros at such a time as you are awarded a university degree."

A small smirk appeared on Alfonso's face at this announcement. Alicia stared straight ahead, stiffening a little.

"To Rafael Mendez, an endowment that will pay seventy-five thousand euros annually with an increase, again at the discretion of your father, to one hundred twenty-five thousand when he reaches age thirty.

"There are other small bequests to Basilio's housekeeper, his gardener, and his chauffeur. Do either of you have any questions?"

Alicia was not surprised when her father spoke up.

"Thank you, Señor Alvarez," said Alfonso. "You have been a good friend of my father's over the years, but as you know I have my own attorneys, and when this business is settled they will be handling the family business affairs from now on."

"Of course, sir, as you wish," replied Hugo Alvarez with a slight bow.

"Señor Alvarez," said Alicia, "as you probably know, I am currently residing in the villa in Majorca. Does the bequest of the villa include its furnishings and art as well?"

"Yes, Señorita, rest assured it does."

"Also," she continued, "does the provision for granting me the collection include all the furnishings— the historical implements and documents and their display cases and cabinetry as well?"

"Yes, it does. The granting of the castle and all its furnishings and artwork to your father specifically *excludes* everything associated with the collection. And I'm instructed to tell you that if you wish, the collection may remain there and you are to have complete access at all times."

"Thank you," she said. Then she waited until her father rose, glowering, and departed. Not once did father and daughter look at or speak to one another.

Alicia drove her rental car to the small apartment she'd taken near the University of Madrid, subsequent to her recent decision to continue her education. It was inexpensive and certainly didn't reflect the grandeur others might have expected of Basilio Mendez's granddaughter. But it was all she could afford on her relatively small allowance, an allowance controlled by her father. It had been considerably more substantial when she had been living with him in the large house adjacent to Mendez Castle.

As she drove, she reflected on how that situation had become untenable and finally compelled her to leave, resulting in her current state of relative financial strain.

After high school she'd enrolled at the University of Madrid, majoring in art. Her grandfather Basilio had approved, but her father said she should not waste her time with such a frivolous pursuit. She should instead study something important, like business. Of course he had never gone to college himself, and over the years had managed to make money with his portion of the family funds only by using the same money managers his father had. Nevertheless, he insisted that it was his business savvy alone that was responsible for their livelihood and lifestyle.

For a time she ignored him. Alfonso placated his aging father, largely by leaving him to his library and collection. This left him plenty of time to harass Alicia as she tried to study and paint. The more she tried to ignore him, the more verbally abusive he became. The last straw was when he used a hunting knife to slash a large oil painting she had just completed as a class project for one of her favorite professors.

She swore at him and vowed she was through with him forever. She'd always had access to the villa in Majorca. Fortunately her father had never shown any interest in it. But it was perfect for her. She moved there and continued painting on her own, with no further formal education until her recent reenrollment at the University. As a result of hiring an attorney she could barely afford, her father was forced to continue providing her a small allowance.

She'd had mixed feelings about the settlement announced this afternoon by her grandfather's attorney. Having legal title to the villa would remove much of the uncertainty she experienced in living there. Further, the seventy-five-thousand-euro annual endowment payment would be considerably more than her father had been giving her.

Also, when she completed her degree, the income would increase to a quite comfortable one hundred twenty-five thousand euros. But one part didn't sit well: the last provision that stipulated if she completed the degree, her income would increase, but only at her father's discretion.

What did that mean? She'd have to ask Attorney Alvarez. Surely her grandfather, who had approved of her choice to study art, would not have given his son, who he knew did not approve, the option of denying the increase. Yes, she would have to ask Señor Alvarez what that meant.

Chapter 7

Dr. Arnaud Laurendeau stood as tall as his five foot five inches would allow while he addressed the Grand Council of the Large Hadron Collider in its boardroom at the CERN headquarters building near the collider outside Geneva, Switzerland.

CERN was an acronym for The European Organization for Nuclear Research. Its signature project was the Large Hadron Collider, so called because it was designed to crash large hadrons—protons, and lead nuclei—into each other in order to study the smaller subatomic particles and energy these collisions produced. Most of the time it was just referred to locally as the collider.

Laurendeau was appropriately proportioned for his short stature, but his head of thick long black hair with its wild curls would have looked better on a taller man. Although he was forty-two, he had a surprisingly boyish face. As a member of the Grand Council and the former head of the Physics Department at the Institute for Nuclear Physics in Lyon, he expected to command the respect and attention of his colleagues. He had been speaking now for ten minutes.

"I'm telling you, gentlemen, we need to consider the possibilities. What if they're correct? And I have to tell you I believe they've made a plausible case. We can't just ignore it out of hand. Our search for the Higgs boson here at the collider could itself *be* the cause of the continual string of accidents and disasters that have impeded our operations up to now."

The Chairman of the Grand Council, world-renowned particle physicist Giuseppe Ambrosi, who was presiding over the meeting, visibly clenched his jaw and rolled his eyes skyward, but remained silent for now.

Laurendeau continued. "Consider the record. In 1993, the Americans abruptly cancelled their Superconducting Supercollider program just when they were on the verge of discovering the Higgs boson. In 2000, the LEP, another or our CERN accelerators, was on the verge of discovering the Higgs when *its* funding dried up. And our own LHC has been continually beset with problems just when *it* was ready to start up. Coincidence? Maybe—maybe not. Then, a little over a year ago, a chunk of bread *somehow* got into an electrical substation, causing the super-cooled magnets in sector 81 to overheat dangerously. All of these events are consistent with the paper's predictions— predictions that suggest that the discovery of the Higgs boson could lead to events so catastrophic to the future, that the future is somehow sabotaging the present to prevent its discovery."

Unable to contain his annoyance any longer, Chairman Ambrosi shouted, "For God's sake, Laurendeau, are you completely out of your mind? You're supposed to be a scientist. Christ, man, act like one. You're standing here asking us to take seriously the idea that little green men from the future are time traveling back to Geneva to sabotage the collider? Are you nuts?"

Pausing to take several deep breaths to calm down, Laurendeau, mortified, glowered at Ambrosi. "Do me the courtesy to listen to what I have to say, before you dismiss it out of hand."

"We know what you're going to say already," snapped the chairman. "God knows, we've heard it enough. We've all heard you and we've all read that nonsense. How in the world that crap got peer-reviewed and published is beyond me. What nonsense."

Laurendeau, now fully humiliated and enraged, narrowed his eyes. "You pompous, irresponsible ass," he hissed. "Those respected scientists did not publish 'crap,' as you call it.   And other respected physicists have published their concerns about the potential of the collisions creating thousands of black holes that could jeopardize our very existence.   Their concerns can't be ignored."

"Laurendeau.   You're through.   I'm having you removed from the Council immediately.   I've had enough of your crackpot theories on sabotage and black holes swallowing up the universe. They make good copy for the world press, but they're bad science. Your time is up. We're moving on to new business."   With that the chairman slammed down his gavel.

Six months after this disastrous meeting, Dr. Arnaud Laurendeau still stung from the public rebuke at the council meeting, believed his motives in protecting the safety of mankind were noble and true. When he'd originally been employed by CERN and appointed to the ruling Grand Council, he'd continually cautioned them to take seriously the concerns of those scientists who were fearful of the consequences of the high-speed collisions that were being planned.

He wasn't opposed to the collider.   Like all particle physicists, he was driven to uncover the secrets of the universe. Indeed, he was a highly successful and respected contributor to the field, with many publications in internationally peer-reviewed journals. This was why he'd been elected to the collider Grand Council in the first place.

He was respectful of the potential power of the collider interactions and the incredible discoveries that might be possible. He certainly wanted them to go forward, but he also believed that they should be conducted as safely as humanly possible.

Right from the start, he'd been continually thwarted by the chairman, who regularly challenged his science and even his basic intelligence in a demeaning way before his colleagues on the council. When he was finally fired at the insistence of the chairman, he went back to his former position in the physics department at the Institute for Nuclear Physics in Lyon. He was crushed to find that his former colleagues in the department, as well as his colleagues in the larger particle physics community, treated him with disdain. His peer-reviewed funding dried up and he quit in disgrace. He'd never married and found himself more alone than he'd ever been in his entire life.

He was sitting alone now at a sidewalk café in Lyon, trying to quiet the conflicting thoughts whirling around in his head. *Why can't those morons see that the consequences of going ahead, without considering the potential catastrophic harm, are just too great? The human race—indeed, potentially all life on Earth—could be in serious jeopardy. I've done everything I could. I tried reason. I even pleaded with them. Nothing. Their minds were closed, and they wanted no part of slowing down. No threats were real in their eyes.*

Laurendeau got up and paced, catching the eye of his waiter, who approached him,

"May I help you, sir?"

"No. Yes. Bring me a Stella."

"Certainly, sir."

With that Laurendeau sat down again.

I've got to stop them. Surely the greater good is what's important here, isn't it? Surely God would be on my side in this. He'd have to be.

For some time now, Laurendeau had been contemplating a plan that would force the Council to reconsider his recommendations. Since he'd been fired, he couldn't appeal to them directly, but he'd thought of a plan that would allow him to do it indirectly. He was convinced it would work, but he'd been constantly agonizing over the morality of it. To get an answer, he'd even gone to confession and asked a priest. He recalled the circumstances.

He'd been tormenting himself all day over what to do about the potential dangers of the collider when he found himself walking outside the majestic Basilica of Notre-Dame de Fourvière. Ostensibly a Catholic, he hadn't been to mass or confession in many years. Suddenly, he was overcome with the need for guidance from the church and he found himself walking into the cathedral. It was huge and mostly empty. He could see a few penitents kneeling near a side confessional where, presumably, a priest sat inside, hearing confessions. When his turn came, he again surprised himself by entering the stall and kneeling in the dark.

When the slide opened, he found himself saying, "Father, my soul is troubled."

"What is it, my son?" asked the priest.

"I find myself in a position to do an enormous amount of good for many, many, people."

"That doesn't sound like it should trouble your soul," replied the priest.

"No, it's not that, Father. I'm happy to do this for them. What bothers me is that in order to do it, a few people would be hurt."

"I see. You're facing the eternal dilemma of, "Does the end justify the means?"

"Exactly. That's exactly it." Laurendeau was amazed. The man had gone right to the heart of it.

"I see. Let me ask you. Are you one of those people who would be hurt?"

"No, Father."

"Then you have a difficult choice. I can't make it for you. Indeed, no one can. All we can do in a situation like this is to ask for God's help. Pray for guidance. You might even ask yourself what you think Jesus would do under the circumstances. What I'm telling you, my son, is that you need to make the choice. And be assured, if you ask for God's help, you won't be making the choice alone."

Laurendeau did just that. He prayed for guidance. He prayed for clarity. He prayed that God would not allow him to make the wrong choice. Finally, after two weeks of this, he believed he had his answer.

Chapter 8

The seat belt sign had just clicked off on the panel above Hunter's first class seat on an Air Lingus flight to Paris via Dublin.   It was early evening, three days after telling his dad about the job he'd be doing for Shay Blackwell. He'd told him truthfully that he didn't know how long it would take, but that when he got back they'd build the new sunroom together.

The perky young flight attendant, who Hunter had already learned was from Oklahoma City, brought him a cocktail and assured him, accompanied by a knowing smile, that shortly she would personally bring him dinner.

The overnight flight was scheduled to arrive at Charles De Gaulle Airport in Paris just before ten AM. That would give him time to freshen up before his appointment.

Once he'd decided on Genevieve Swift, Hunter had phoned her office. He'd made sure to do this early enough in the morning to catch her about mid-afternoon Paris time. He'd wanted to reach her at work. She answered her phone in French, but when Hunter introduced himself, she instantly shifted to English with a delightful French accent that was every bit as attractive as the picture in her dossier. He decided to stick with the truth as much as possible in his initial request for her help.

"Ms. Swift, my name is Hunter McCoy. I've been hired by an American businessman, Shay Blackwell, to locate an important book from the mid sixteenth century relating to the Inquisition and I would like your—"

"What book is that?"

"—Expertise in authenticating it," he finished after being interrupted. "Actually, I would prefer to meet you in person before—"

"You tell me?"

"—I tell you."

They'd agreed to meet at her office in the National Library the day of his arrival at two PM.

Hunter had flown from Marquette to Charlottesville first because he needed to meet with Scarlet to set things up and to get his loft ready for a period of absence. At the Blackwell building, just off the historic downtown mall, Scarlet immediately jumped up and greeted Hunter with a hug.

"Hunter, I've missed you. Mr. Blackwell told me about your project and that you'd be stopping by to report in."

"Hi, Scarlet, good to see you too. Pretty as ever, I see."

Scarlet blushed. "Oh go on, you."

Scarlet was of an age somewhere north of sixty, but dressed with a style and attitude that helped her look much younger. She'd gotten her name from her mother because of her red hair. But later, when she married Homer O'Hara and became Scarlet O'Hara, she really came into her own. Shay Blackwell had hired her many years before, when he was just getting started. She showed up one day and said she could do all his organizing and he would be free to conduct his business. She was true to her word, and after a one-month trial period he'd found her to be so valuable that he took her on full time and gave her a raise that he could barely afford at the time.

Hunter knew that she could be a formidable barrier to anyone she decided should not be bothering Blackwell. On the other hand, she could be a master at expediting last-minute travel, finances, and problem solving of almost any kind. She was fearless, tenacious, and totally loyal to Shay.

Hunter was happy to have access to her talents during the upcoming project. She'd been so efficient during his last work for Blackwell that when he submitted his final report on the outcome, he brought flowers and chocolates to Scarlet as well. From that point on he was on her "A" list.

"If you were only a little older, or we lived in cougar town . . ."

"Scarlet, if it weren't for Homer . . ."

"Sure, sure. I know," she said with a mocking smile. "Anyway, what do you need?"

Hunter told her and she said she'd have everything ready for him to pick up the next day.

He'd decided that rather than head straight for Spain to meet with Alfonso Mendez, he'd first find out what he could about the Servetus book. He could do this and interview Genevieve Swift at the same time. So he had Scarlet arrange a flight to Paris. In addition, she made hotel arrangements, provided access to a rental car if needed, an international smart phone, and a company Visa card in his name. She also handed him five thousand euros. The digital cell phone was even equipped with a GPS application with access to all areas in Europe, with his hotel, the National Library, and Mendez Castle in Spain all pre-bookmarked for him.

Hunter was startled to hear a pleasant feminine voice say, "Excuse me, sir, I've brought your dinner."

"Thanks."

"Would you like me to freshen your drink?" the flight attendant asked, in a voice more suited for an evening's date than for a working flight.

Smiling, with his blue-green eyes amped to the max, he matched her evening voice.

"Only if you'll have one with me."

When she demurred, Hunter smiled and sighed. "I guess I'll have to settle for coffee alone then."

After his dinner Hunter reread Genevieve Swift's dossier and wondered what she would think of his quest. He tilted back his comfortable first-class seat and promptly fell asleep. He didn't wake until the cabin lights came on and the pilot announced that they would be landing in Paris in about one hour. He had coffee and juice and steamed his face with a hot towel.

After collecting his bag and clearing customs, he took a taxi to his hotel and prepared to start his day. Jet lag had never been a problem for Hunter. It was as if his body clock started fresh with each sunup regardless of the time zone difference.

He snacked on fruit that had been provided in his room. Since he'd decided that a rental car would be a nuisance in the busy city of Paris, he took a cab to the National Library to meet with Ms. Swift. He admired the mixture of old and very modern structures that made up the immense complex located on the left bank of the Seine River, between the Simone-de-Beauvoir footbridge and the Bercy Bridge. He'd read that the National Library of France traced its origin to the royal library founded at the Louvre by Charles V in 1368. By 1896 it had become the largest repository of books in the world, but had since been surpassed by other libraries. Still, impressively, the library housed over twenty million volumes.

The cabby dropped him off at the Francois Mitterrand site, where he entered one of the four multistory modern buildings. Even though the cabby knew the way, Hunter also tracked their route using his smart phone GPS system and was amazed that it directed him practically to the front door. He was also impressed that the cabby hadn't taken him there via a longer and more expensive route. At the immense front desk, the receptionist told him to take the elevator down two flights to the archive's offices, where he should find Mademoiselle Swift.

The archive's offices were much like those of many office buildings, composed of one-person movable cubicles with a desk, a bookcase, and a computer. He had been given her cubicle number and found it with no trouble. When he got there she looked up from her desk and said, "Je vous demande pardon?"

"Excuse me, I'm here for an appointment with Genevieve Swift."

"Oh, you must be Dr. McCoy." She shifted to flawless English with the accent Hunter found irresistible from their earlier phone conversation. "I'm Genevieve Swift."

She rose and he shook hands with her, struck by her beauty. She was tall, at least five-foot-eight with a slim but definite female form. She looked fit, like a runner. Her fashionably cut dark hair framed an exquisitely pretty face with equally dark eyes. She wore what appeared to be an expensive dark business suit over a pink blouse open to reveal a necklace and matching earrings of rainbow sapphires. When she smiled, as she was doing now, her eyes lit up with even more amperage.

"Let me get you a chair, monsieur, so we can sit and talk," she said.

Before she could get the chair in question Hunter said, "Ms. Swift, I still need to get settled in my hotel. I know we've just met, but if it's all right with you, could I simply take you to dinner this evening and—"

"We could discuss things then?"

"Yes, we could discuss things then," said Hunter with a sigh. "I'm staying at the Hotel Arioso. We could perhaps eat there. They're supposed to have an excellent restaurant."

If she was bothered by the sudden shift in the situation from a routine business meeting in her office to a potential dinner date, she didn't show it.

"Oui, I know the hotel well. In fact my flat is not far from there. Of course, you've just arrived and must be exhausted. Why don't I meet you at the restaurant at, say, nine this evening."

"That'd be great," Hunter replied, musing that "early bird specials" certainly didn't originate in Paris.

Later that evening, the maître d' directed Hunter to a table. Previously he'd asked the man for the best table in the room and had tipped him generously for the privilege. Shortly after nine PM Genevieve entered and checked her coat, which revealed that she was wearing a simple black dress, with minimal jewelry and makeup. Again, Hunter couldn't help but notice how pretty she was. More than pretty, she was gorgeous. Her pale porcelain-like skin and her dark eyes fringed with long lashes helped to make her striking. If she lived up to her dossier, this could be most pleasurable. She spotted him, smiled a greeting, and walked to his table. They shook hands briefly and sat down.

They enjoyed a delicious dinner of braised veal with an excellent dry red wine, during which they talked about their relative academic backgrounds. They soon dispensed with the formalities and began addressing each other as Hunter and Genevieve. Eventually Hunter decided to come to the point.

"Genevieve, what I am about to tell you is potentially a major event in the rare book field. I must presume that you can listen to what I have to say, and treat it with—"

"The utmost discretion," she said, nodding soberly.

"Yes, exactly," said Hunter. "Excuse me. Do you always finish—"?

"Other people's sentences? Oui, pardon—I do. I'm sorry. I always finish sentences for people. I've been doing it for as long as I can remember, and I really am trying to stop. I know it's annoying, but my brain just thinks ahead and my mouth goes along for the ride. Please go on," she urged him.

After ordering more wine he proceeded to tell her about George Blackwell, Basilio Mendez, Shay Blackwell, the long lost unopened letter, the phone call to Alfonso Mendez, and what Blackwell had hired Hunter to do. When he finished, she shook her head.

"Hunter, I've never heard the slightest hint of there being a fourth copy of the *Restitutio*. Believe me, in the rare book business, rumors fly hot and heavy that there are additional copies of rare books. You say that Señor Mendez was a reputable man and unlikely to make up such a story, but I have to tell you, such rumors almost always turn out to be untrue."

"Well, this too may turn out to be untrue. The son says he knows nothing about such a book. But my employer is basing his belief on the deep friendship between his father and Basilio Mendez. He believes it would be completely out of character for such a good friend to—"

"Deceive his father that way," she said.

Hunter hung his head as if in surrender and said, "Yes."

"Pardon, I mean, sorry, I'm afraid you'll just have to get used to me. If such a book actually exists, it would be incredibly valuable, not only monetarily but also for the historical value of the message that Mendez said Servetus wrote in the last pages before he was burned at the stake. So how do you intend to proceed? I can't authenticate something that doesn't exist. And for that matter, and please don't take offense, I don't understand why your Mr. Blackwell hired you, an academic scientist, to track this book down. Why you?"

Hunter smiled. "I often get hired to find things. I'm good at it, and I've done similar work for Blackwell before. It rarely requires my science background, but often makes use of other skills I have."

She raised an eyebrow but let his comment pass.

"It appears that our starting point should be Madrid," Hunter went on. "I'll meet with Alfonso Mendez and try talking to him again about the book. He also has a daughter who might be of help if Alfonso won't talk with us."

"Us?"

"Yes. I'm hoping that you will accompany me to Madrid to authenticate the work if we find it, or to let me know if I'm going down blind alleys, historically, so to speak."

"Accompany you to Madrid? You want me to go with you to Spain?" She paused and narrowed her eyes. "Dr. McCoy," not Hunter anymore, "I've just met you today. I know nothing about you. I have a job that requires me to be here, in Paris, at the National Library, at my desk. You can't be serious."

"I know this must seem pretty unconventional to you. I assure you it's strictly—"

"Business?" she finished. "Oops! There I go again," she said, and put her hand to her mouth.

"Yes. Business," he smiled. Finishing his sentences could be annoying. But as the evening progressed, Hunter was surprisingly beginning to find it somewhat endearing. And the French accent in her soft voice made her that much more attractive. And while they were now speaking English, and she was exchanging 'yes' for 'oui' and 'sorry' for 'pardon.' the accent stayed and only added to her charm.

"Also," he continued, "you will be generously paid for your time and expertise. In fact, to put you at ease, I'd like you to talk through a video Skype connection to Shay Blackwell himself, and also to his amazingly efficient secretary Scarlet, who, by the way, will do everything in her considerable powers to make our travels smooth. If the two of them can't convince you that it will be safe and worth your while professionally and financially, I'll travel on my own and ask for your help only when I have something for you to authenticate."

"Even if I were to agree to travel with you, I have a job here. I can't just up and leave."

"Blackwell has authorized me to tell you that he will make a generous contribution to your department to offset the time you would be away. If you agree, he will make this offer himself to your director through very formal and proper channels."

"You seem to have thought of everything."

"Well, not everything. We haven't ordered dessert yet."

Chapter 9

Hans De Groot hated having to get up so early to go to work even though he loved his job as a theoretical physicist assigned to the ALICE team at the Large Hadron Collider. A slim young man of twenty-nine with a Ph.D. from MIT, his specialty was particle physics. This morning he was driving the Route de Meyrin past the south end of the runways at Geneva International Airport on his way to the collider site, west of the main urban area of Geneva. He sipped his morning coffee while listening to Geneva's Radio Cité belt out Swiss pop hits. In spite of the morning rush hour traffic, he was happily thinking about his upcoming meeting with Dr. Lautrec, the head of the ALICE project.

Hans had become fascinated right from the start when the European Organization for Nuclear Research (CERN) planned to build the collider with the cooperation of thousands of scientist from over one hundred countries. He was in high school at the time, but already knew that his future was in particle physics. When CERN commenced digging the oval-shaped tunnel, some seventeen miles in circumference almost three hundred feet below the surface near the French border with Switzerland, even Hans's high school physics teacher felt the boy would work there someday.

By the time Hans had completed his Ph.D., the tunnel, which crossed the border between France and Switzerland four times, was finished. The tunnel housed beam pipes designed to carry subatomic particles that physicists planned to accelerate to near the speed of light. At various points in the circular racetrack, the particles traveling in opposite directions could be made to smash into each other. At these intersection points, a variety of very sophisticated detectors would be looking to examine the even-smaller particles these collisions would produce.

Finally, Hans was hired by the LHC and joined other physicists who hoped that analysis of these collisions would lead to answers to some of nature's best-kept secrets Over the past twenty to thirty years, scientists had been able to describe with ever increasing clarity the fundamental particles that make up the universe. These relationships, the stuff of quantum physics, were incorporated in what was known as the *Standard Model.* Still, physicists acknowledged gaps and unanswered questions that they hoped the collider could answer. Hans contemplated these questions every day.

For example: What is mass? Why do tiny particles weigh what they do? Why do some particles have no mass at all? The Higgs Theory, proposed in 1964, offered answers and was central to the Standard Model. However, the core of the Higgs theory, the Higgs boson, was a particle that remained undetected. One of the LHC detectors, the ATLAS, was designed to look for this elusive particle.

Initially, Hans had hoped to be assigned to the ATLAS project. But, as his young American colleagues would say, the ALICE project was way, way cooler. He'd get chills just thinking about it. The ALICE project asked, what was matter like in the first second of the Universe's life? Virtually all physicists accepted that the ordinary matter of the universe is made up of familiar particles called atoms.

These, in turn are composed of protons and neutrons, which are in turn made up of quarks held together with gluons. These gluon bonds are very strong and hold the atoms together. But in the early stages of the universe after the Big Bang, conditions would have been too hot for the gluons to hold the atoms together as they now do. The current thinking was that in the first seconds after the Big Bang, the quarks and gluons would have been a very hot mixture called quark-gluon plasma. And thus the goal of ALICE: Showing that this quark-gluon plasma was more than a hypothesis.

Hans was especially proud to be asked to lead his small team. They were all first-class particle physicists. Even though some of them hadn't actually met before joining the team, they knew each other through their published theoretical works on gluons, quarks, and the possibility of the quark-gluon plasma. Hans suspected that his selection as team leader was based on his last paper, which had received critical acclaim in *Physical Reviews*.

He and his team at ALICE had come up with some workable experimental designs they were convinced would yield critical information on quark-gluon plasma. His job this morning would be to convince Lautrec that their experiments were important enough to warrant dedicating more collider time to them.

Of course, all of the heads of the other teams set to use the ALICE detector felt the same urgency for their projects.

No matter, thought Hans. *When he hears our plans he'll acquiesce. After all, he's a fair man. He'll know good science when he sees it.*

Within the next few microseconds several things happened in rapid succession. First the starburst pattern appeared in the driver's side window of Han's car. Next, a small opening, approximately 9 mm. in diameter, occurred in Han's left temple. Then a bullet traveled through the thin temporal bone into the soft midbrain and exploded into fragments that turned his brilliant mind to mush.

The car careened off the road, miraculously missing other traffic, and slammed into an embankment.

For Hans, his ten AM appointment was eternally cancelled.

Chapter 10

Alicia Mendez and her friend, Isabella Gomez, met for lunch in the student union after their eleven AM class in European Art History. It was early in the semester and both young women liked the way the new class was going. Today's lecture dealt with historical authentication, and both had found it fascinating.

They were the same age, twenty-five, but while Isabella had continued her schooling without interruption and was now a graduate student, Alicia had just recently started back after taking a "sabbatical," as she called it, for several years.

Isabella's Norwegian mother and Spanish father had left her with light skin and blond hair that she wore short and straight, setting off her blue gray eyes. Her plumpness was of her own doing. She was the exact physical opposite to slim, dark, pretty Alicia. As friendly as Alicia, she had an earnestness about her that allowed her to tackle and complete projects like the graduate degree she was working on now. They'd been talking about their current art history instructor.

"He's sure better looking than *my* major professor," said Isabella with a laugh. Then she added, "of course, I'm not working with Isandro de la Peña because of his looks."

"What's a major professor?" inquired Alicia. "I don't know that term."

"It's a graduate student term. It refers to the guy who directs your thesis."

Putting on a mock haughty tone for her friend, Alicia said, "Oh, that's right, I keep forgetting that you're working on a Ph.D." She laughed, then grew serious, "God, that seems so incredibly difficult. I'll have all I can do just to complete my undergraduate degree."

Alicia took a bite of her salad and washed it down with a little iced tea and thought about a conversation she'd had with Isabella several months ago.

Isabella had told her that Professor de la Peña was one of the world's leading scholars on the Inquisitions of the sixteenth century. She'd told Alicia that most people don't realize how extensive the Inquisitions were. "They tend to think only of our own homegrown Spanish Inquisition. But it wasn't just in Spain and didn't just involve the Catholics. There was a Protestant Inquisition as well. Even the civil governments were involved." Alicia had learned that de la Peña only took on students who were interested in doing research on some aspect of the Inquisitions.

When Alicia asked her what she was going to work on, Isabella said,

"I'm not sure yet, but I'm leaning toward a comparison of John Calvin's and Martin Luther's responses to the Inquisitions going on in their spheres of influence."

"What a coincidence," Alicia had said. "My grandfather has a pretty extensive collection of Inquisition artifacts. I wonder if Professor de la Peña would be interested in seeing it?"

"I wouldn't be surprised if he already knows about it," Isabella had told her. "He knows most of the collections in Spain. In fact, he's been asked to evaluate and catalog many of them."

"Do you suppose he'd mind if I asked him about my grandfather's collection?" Alicia had asked her.

"No, I'm sure he'd be happy about it."

Alicia recalled thinking about her grandfather. She knew that he'd never advertised or made much of a deal about his collection. She'd decided that she would check with him first.

"Let me think about it," the old man had said when she reached him on the phone later. "You know the collection is not a great secret, but I enjoy not having it open to the public at this point. Still, it probably would be a good idea to have it properly evaluated and catalogued. Stop in this evening, and we'll talk about it."

Two days later, Alicia had sat in Professor de la Peña's office, a large room on the second floor of the remodeled old house that housed the offices for several history professors and their graduate students. It was a typical professor's office: bookshelves everywhere, overflowing with manuscripts, books, papers, and paraphernalia, seemingly gathered from around the world. The professor himself was seated at his desk behind a clutter of documents and reference books. He appeared to be in his mid-to late forties, with a full head of dark hair and a somewhat homely face wearing a frown.

Without getting up, and barely looking at Alicia, he'd said, "What do you want? I see that you're not a student in any of my classes. I'm busy here today and don't have much time. If you're from the student newspaper, I don't give interviews."

Taken aback by his curt condescending attitude, Alicia, recalled standing taller and saying in her best upper class voice, "Professor de la Peña, you're partly correct. I am indeed, *not* one of your students. I am also *not* from the student paper or any other newspaper. I want to talk with you about an Inquisition Collection— that is, if you have the time," she added casually.

The professor, picking up on the stiffened backbone he detected in her frosty voice, now looked up fully as if to see her for the first time, he lowered his reading glasses slightly, and peered over them.

Seeing that he now appeared to be interested, Alicia pointed to the chair he hadn't asked her to take. "May I?"

De la Peña pushed his chair back and waved to the other chair in the room, "Please do. What collection are you referring to?"

Alicia, feeling she was now in charge of the conversation, continued, "Are you familiar with my grandfather, Count Basilio Diego Mendez?"

"Familiar? No, I don't believe so," said de la Peña. "Should I be?"

"He is a Spanish nobleman whose family has been collecting Inquisition artifacts since the seventeenth century. His collection of implements and documents is extensive."

Professor de la Peña raised his eyebrows. "Strange that I don't know of this collection; I'm familiar with most of them in Spain. Where is it located?"

"It's housed in Mendez Castle, just on the outskirts of Madrid in Castillo de Aldovea.   I'm here at my grandfather's request to ask you to consider evaluating and cataloging his collection. Your graduate student, Isabella Gomez, and I have become friends here at the university, and through a conversation with her I was informed of your expertise in this area." Alicia was amused to find she had taken on a rather imperious air as she said this.

Considerably more friendly now, de la Peña smiled showing large yellow teeth. "I would be most happy to. I've cataloged many collections in Spain, but very few that began shortly after the Inquisitions themselves. Tell Señor

Mendez that I will call on him and would be happy to accept a commission to do the work."

With that, Alicia rose and told the professor she would convey this information to her grandfather.

As he stood for the first time and came around his desk, she saw that he was much taller then she had thought. He took her outstretched hand and bowed slightly. "Good day, Señorita Mendez. Until we meet again."

Alicia recalled that she'd left, hoping she'd been doing her grandfather a favor.

Now he was dead.

"Alicia, are you okay?" Isabella asked, startling Alicia from her reverie. "What are you thinking about?"

"Oh, yeah. Just thinking about my grandfather. He was so happy to finally have his collection authenticated and organized, and now he won't be able to enjoy it. I know he was happy with Professor de la Peña's work, Isabella, thanks for putting me on to him,"

Isabella took a bite of her sandwich and paused before speaking. "You know, about that, it's strange."

Alicia looked at her, "What's strange?"

"I don't know if there is any connection," said Isabella, "But lately de la Peña hasn't been himself. He's gotten less friendly and it's getting harder to get in to see him. It's not just me. His other grad students have noticed it too. But what's strange is it started right after he completed the work on your grandfather's collection."

Chapter 11

Hunter was having coffee and a freshly baked croissant with dollops of orange marmalade at the bakery he'd found around the corner from the hotel Arioso. The sun was shining and he was ready to get to Madrid and start looking for the book. But first he had to convince Genevieve to get on board.

On the short cab ride from his hotel, Hunter called Scarlet on his international smart phone. He explained that it would be useful if both she and Shay could assure Genevieve that she'd be safe traveling with him to Madrid. He suggested that a Skype video call on Genevieve's computer might be best.

After the setup approvals were arranged, Genevieve called Blackwell's number while Hunter was again, drawn to her striking beauty. Her computer had a large monitor, and Shay Blackwell's image immediately filled the screen. It was apparent to Hunter that he was in his office and at his desk.

"Ms. Swift. How nice to meet with you. I want you to know that we're pleased you're considering helping us with the authentication of the *Christianismi Restitutio,* if Hunter can locate it. I'm sure he's explained why locating and possibly purchasing this book is of importance to me personally. I am well aware of your expertise in this area and I am prepared to immediately authorize a check to your account in the amount of ten thousand euros for agreeing to authenticate the book if it can be found. Please understand that if the book is not found, the ten thousand euros are still yours.

"In addition, if you agree to accompany Hunter on this project, I will cover all of your expenses and pay you an additional ten thousand euros when the search is over, again whether it is successful or not. Further, if I am able to acquire the text, you, as a Renaissance scholar, will of course be given the first opportunity to examine it and prepare any scholarly reports you think are appropriate.

"I understand your reluctance to travel with a man, a stranger really, having only just met him. For what it is worth, you can trust him, and if for any reason I needed someone with me in a dangerous situation, Hunter would be the man. Having said that, there is no reason to believe that this trip will be dangerous in any way. Now, do you have any questions of me?"

Genevieve seemed impressed by the man's sincerity and forthrightness although confused by the reference to danger. She sat back in her chair and thought for a moment. "I still don't understand why I'd need to go with Hunter now. Why not wait until he locates the book and then ask me to authenticate it?"

"Hunter and I have discussed this and believe that, while there is a good chance that the book exists, authenticating the manuscript's provenance is as important as authenticating the work itself. If it is indeed missing, your background in the history of tracking such books might prove invaluable in locating it."

Genevieve raised her eyebrows. "I see you understand my area of expertise, monsieur. But, if I were to consider accompanying Hunter on this trip, I still have the problem of my job here. I can't just take an unannounced leave."

"Of course. Perhaps if I were to gift your department with that new Spenser digital acquisition system that your department head has been coveting but can't afford, Dr. Allard might be able to spare you for a short time. I would, of course, do this through formal channels as a gift from my company to your department through the National Library."

Genevieve frowned. "You have been very thorough in your research, sir."

Shay laughed. "There's no need to be suspicious, mademoiselle. I just wanted to remove any obstacles. I like to work with the best."

Genevieve hesitated, and then grinned. "Well, perhaps that would convince Dr. Allard."

Shay brightened. "Wonderful, wonderful. And now I would like you to meet the lady who will supply you and Hunter with expert help in all things related to travel and finances during your trip. Please meet Scarlet O'Hara. Yes, I know—but that's her real name. She has three grown children and three grandchildren, and I couldn't operate without her."

The picture shifted to the outer office where a cheery Scarlet sat at her desk.

"Why thank you, Mr. Blackwell," she said.

"Genevieve, honey, trust this man," said Scarlet. "Both of these men. They are what they say they are, and you can believe what they say. Well, wait a minute. On second thought, Hunter once said he was going to bring me a Christmas present for a job he did for us in Texas last year, and then promptly forgot."

"Wait a minute, Scarlet," interrupted Hunter, with a hint of indignation in his voice. " I didn't forget. Don't you remember the video games Santa brought for your grandkids and installed on your TV in the guest room?"

"Was that you? I wondered who did that. They loved it." Scarlet exhaled with an exaggerated sigh, "Well, okay, Genevieve, then you can trust him completely."

When they signed off Hunter and Genevieve sat for a moment in companionable silence.   Genevieve was thinking and Hunter was letting her do it, quietly and by herself. Finally, she said, "Okay. I'll do it. Here's what we need to do first."

She explained to Hunter that they should start by having a look at the copy of the *Christianismi Restitutio* in the National Library's rare book room. She had seen it before but now would be a good time to examine it again. She explained that she could obtain a digital copy of the entire manuscript and download it to her laptop, which she'd take with them. The digital copy wouldn't convey the nuances of paper, color, texture, and age that the original would, though, so she said that Hunter should see an original copy. She would set up an appointment with the director of the rare book collection.

Hunter and Genevieve entered the office of the director at four that afternoon. In order to view the document they had to undergo the tedious task of filling out reader registration forms for the research library and apply for a research pass for Hunter. Genevieve already had a pass. On the application they described that they were doing academic research on Servetus's incorporation of information about pulmonary circulation to his theological arguments in the *Christianismi Restitutio*. She was the historian and Hunter was the scientist. They agreed that there was no reason to mention the existence of a possible fourth copy of the book to the director.

Once they were cleared, the director took them into the viewing room, where they could examine the text that was encased in a locked glass case. The title page of the book was in view. It was, of course, in Latin, but Genevieve assured Hunter that she could obtain from the library's general collection an excellent English translation by Christopher A. Hoffman and Marian Hiller of all 734 pages. She also could read Latin with little difficulty if they found the original fourth copy.

The director unlocked the case for them. They donned surgical gloves and were allowed to touch it and turn a few pages to get a sense of its physical makeup. They'd been required to surrender all cameras and cell phones at the door. Further, the room was dimly lit and two library guards were stationed nearby. Special security cameras began recording them as they entered and continued until they left twenty minutes later.

After thanking the director, they returned to her office where they compared notes. They decided that what they'd seen of the book was not different from their digitized PDF version.

Hunter called Scarlet again. She told him that Allard had decided it would be prudent for Mademoiselle Swift to take some time off to help Mr. Blackwell. Hunter grinned. "Okay, then. We'll need two tickets for a morning flight to Madrid day after tomorrow and two rooms at a hotel with an open-ended departure date. I'll also need home and office phone numbers for Alfonso Mendez."

Leaving Genevieve to take care of her business, Hunter decided to spend the day sightseeing around Paris, since he hadn't been to the City of Lights in several years. In the morning he dressed in running clothes and shoes and set off on what turned out to be an eight-mile run through the city. After he returned to his hotel and showered, he set off on a walking tour of the neighborhoods surrounding the national library. Something nagged the back of his brain while he did this. In fact, he'd had that feeling even during his earlier run, as if he were being followed. Using his highly tuned tradecraft, he walked for two more miles and wasn't able to detect anyone. Finally, convinced he was only imagining it, he stopped at a sidewalk café along the Seine and had an afternoon coffee. After an hour he slowly walked back to his hotel, determined to double check that he had all the papers and materials needed for their flight tomorrow to Madrid.

Chapter 12

Between the early summer flowers lining the walkways and the coeds wearing bright colors to replace the darker attire of winter, the campus of Kyushu University in Fukuoka, Japan was a bustling kaleidoscope of changing light.

Professor Akahiko Kagawa had just finished his lecture to his graduate level particle physics class and was walking back to his office, accompanied by a student who wanted to ask him for help on some of the more difficult points in his lecture. Aki loved these moments. Right after a lecture the students always had very focused questions that made the interaction much more enjoyable than when they were just trying to grasp the rudiments of the material.

"Professor, I still don't understand how a particle can exist but not have mass. If it's there, taking up space it's clearly made up of something, isn't it?" asked Shiro, the student.

"Look at it this way," the professor explained. "A sumo wrestler is clearly bulkier than you are and obviously weighs more. Even in a zero gravity situation, the sumo wrestler would have more mass than you. It would take more effort to push him and set him in motion than to get you moving. So why does he have more mass? Because he is composed of many more atoms than you are.

"So the real question we need to ask," he continued, "is what accounts for the mass of the individual atoms? What about the mass of the particles that make up the atoms? What accounts for their mass? The current theory is that a field called the Higgs field permeates all of reality, and we think that a particle's mass arises from its interaction with the Higgs field. The theory also demands that the field has an associated particle called the Higgs boson."

"And the Higgs boson is what you will be looking for in Geneva?" asked Shiro.

"That's right. It is the only hypothesized particle remaining to be found to complete our understanding of the Standard Model of particle physics. I've been asked to work with the ATLAS detector at the Large Hadron Collider and to design experiments to show that the Higgs boson either exists or it doesn't."

"I still don't understand how a particle like the Higgs boson can give mass to another particle," said Shiro.

Aki thought for a moment. "Well, think of it like this. You're at a big party, milling around with other guests who are evenly distributed throughout the room, when the newest, most beautiful Japanese movie star comes through one of the doors. As she walks across the room, fawning people begin to gather around her and move with her. As the group gets larger she gains mass and is harder to slow down. Once stopped, she and her crowd of admirers are harder to get started again. This clustering effect is the Higgs mechanism postulated by the British physicist Peter Higgs in the 1960s. It imagines a lattice-like network called the Higgs field that permeates the universe and affects the particles that move through it."

They reached Professor Kagawa's building, and Shiro thanked him for his help and headed off in another direction.

Aki climbed the stairs to the elevated first floor of the physics office building walked cheerfully to his office. His mail had been placed in the slot outside his door, and he collected it before he unlocked his office and sat at his desk.

Today was Monday, and by Saturday he needed to be packed and ready for his flight to Geneva. He was eager to get started with his work and to meet the members of his team who had already gathered in Switzerland at the Large Hadron Collider site.

As he sat back in his chair and thought of the work to come, he sensed rather than saw a presence behind him. Puzzled, he began to turn his head just as a wire cut into his neck and was pulled tight by invisible hands. In less than a minute Kagawa was dead.

Chapter 13

The house had been selected for its location. It was on a busy street, in a busy neighborhood in the city center of Geneva. There was so much traffic that no one paid attention to whether a car belonged in the neighborhood or not, so it was perfect. Arnaud Laurendeau had made the decision to buy it and convinced the others. Not surprisingly they were quite impressed by his cleverness.

He'd had the small dining room and equally small living room converted into a larger single room that was dominated by a rectangular oak table with five chairs placed around it: two chairs on each side and Laurendeau's chair at the head. The other end of the rectangle had no chair. This space was reserved for the occasional sixth person who met with them. This person stood, gave his report and received his orders.

While he waited, Laurendeau recalled the meeting at his Geneva apartment where Kurt Walker told him of the Servetus message purportedly relating to the collider.

"You're not going to believe this, Arnaud, but what if I could show you that over four hundred years ago— four hundred years— a scientist predicted that it would be necessary to sabotage the collider here in Geneva in order to protect mankind from its potential consequences."

"What? Laurendeau leaned forward in his chair and set his drink down. "Four hundred years ago? What are you talking about?"

"I know, I know," said Walker, "What if someone— this scientist I'm talking about—predicted the unacceptable risks of the collider—over four hundred years ago, mind you. If you can show those clowns on the council this prediction, they'll have to listen to you."

Laurendeau, now fully alert, asked, "What are you talking about? Nobody knew about colliders four hundred years ago. What prediction are you talking about? Who made it? Where is it?"

"Okay, let me tell you," said Walker, raising his palms as if to hold off a charging Laurendeau. "If you search the Internet for information on predictions, you get about three hundred million hits. I'm not exaggerating. I've being searching this way for years, looking for information for my books, and I've barely made a dent. Well, about a week ago I came across a website that referred to a book written by some guy named Servetus, a heretic of some kind, who was burned at the stake in the sixteenth century right here in Geneva."

"A heretic? Burned at the stake? What the hell is this, Kurt? Come on, I thought you had something."

"Wait, it's coming," said Walker, clearly enjoying his moment of suspense. "It seems he was a doctor who also liked to write about God and stuff. Anyway, he wrote this book that got him in trouble with the Church. All the copies got burned up with him except for two or three that survived and are in a few big libraries in Europe. But that's not important for us. What's important for us, is that there is another copy out there— somewhere; nobody seems to know where— that includes a special message that Servetus wrote the night before his execution."

"Kurt, for God's sake. Get on with it, man!"

Kurt continued, dragging out his story, to Laurendeau's frustration. "The website didn't say, and there's no word-for-word description of the message. But apparently a scholar in eighteenth century Spain is said to have seen it and claimed that it referred to a source of information that could dramatically threaten the accepted version of Christianity that exists today."

"Christianity? We're talking about physics here, not the Church."

"But," continued Walker, as if he hadn't been interrupted, "for our purposes, he also referred to a future worldwide catastrophic event that would be prevented by a time traveler from the future right here in Geneva. It referred specifically to an accelerator and a collider. Don't you see, Arnaud? This reference goes back to the fifteen hundreds, long before we ever dreamed about the LHC. Hell, long before we even had people studying particle physics. Long before anyone even heard of particle physics." Kurt grinned smugly, waiting for Laurendeau's reaction.

Laurendeau sat stunned, thinking of the possibilities. After several minutes, still not having said anything, he strolled to the bar and slowly poured himself another scotch. He walked to the window and stared down at the Rhône, sipping his drink. Finally, as if waking up from his reverie, he said, "What's the name of this book?"

Kurt smiled. "It's called the *Christianismi Restitutio. The Restoration of Christianity*."

"All right, we need to find out everything we can about it. You're our computer search expert. Drop everything else you're doing and get on it. "And Kurt?"

"Yes?"

"Don't fail me on this. That book could be just what we need."

Laurendeau always waited until the others were seated around the table before he entered the room. He had scheduled today's meeting so they could receive a report from Kestrel and give the man a new assignment. The others had now all arrived and taken their seats. It was time. He strode into the room and greeted them.

"Thank you for being on time, gentlemen. I know that your schedules are full and you have other commitments aside from our group. However, none of those commitments are more important. On this we all agree."

Heads nodded around the table.

"Kestrel is back from Japan and will give a report momentarily. When he is finished, I'm going to give him another assignment. A young, and I mean young, twenty-year-old particle physicist from Spain, Rafael Mendez, will shortly join the LHC team. He will be put in charge of designing experiments to study supersymetric particles in dark matter. This is the subject of his doctoral dissertation and will, no doubt, be the basis for his experimental plans. Presumably, that's why they brought him on board.

"His work will be particularly abhorrent to you, Thorbjorn," He addressed the dour Norwegian to his right. Thorbjorn Asplund was a physicist from Oslo who believed the real threat from the planned experiments investigating dark matter and energy was the possible creation of many tiny black holes, which he felt could feed on each other and grow to truly cataclysmic proportions, potentially threatening the entire earth. Most reputable scientists had addressed this fear and had long downplayed the possibility, but not to the satisfaction of Thorbjorn Asplund. He would do anything to stop this catastrophe from happening, even if the rest of the scientific community treated him as an oddball.

"I know his work," said Asplund with obvious disgust. "Those fools on the Council will undoubtedly approve anything he designs. You're correct to single him out. He's got to be stopped."

Laurendeau inwardly smiled. He knew all about Asplund's very public encounters with young Mendez at the International Particle Physics Congress last year in Paris. Mendez took apart Asplund's doomsday arguments handily and made the Norwegian look like a crackpot in the open discussion session that followed.

Nodding in agreement was the Dutch physicist Maarten Hoffman, a serious man with a full beard, small black eyes set in a round head, and an equally round body. He sat in the chair to the leader's left. Hoffman believed that the search for the hypothetical subatomic particle called the Higgs boson was being impeded through sabotage by some action from the future, possibly time travelers who were behind the continual series of events that had caused the LHC to malfunction month after month since its completion. He believed these actions were essential because the answers to the questions sought by the collider research teams would prove so cataclysmic to the future.

He never failed to point out that he wasn't alone in this idea, as two respected physicists had recently published a theory suggesting that the future can change the past if the past becomes dangerous enough to jeopardize that very future. Hoffman hated the very existence of the collider, which this year was going to try to find the boson through several planned experiments.

Next to him was Otto Fleischer. Otto wasn't a scientist and he wasn't a writer. He was a man with a deep suspicion of any attempt to alter atomic structure, especially anything that attempted to split subatomic particles. A deeply religious Christian, Fleischer was convinced that God would not approve. He didn't really understand much about it, but completely absorbed the fears of the others who sat around him. His oft spoken religiosity often rankled his fellow more secular members of the group but was overlooked in consideration for his real value to them—his checkbook. Fleischer was heir to a Swiss family fortune valued at over 100 million euros. The empty chair was for Kurt Walker.

This was the group the leader had assembled to stop the work of the Large Hadron Collider until all their safety concerns were properly addressed. They strongly believed that all steps to impede the work of the collider were justified by the greater good. Each, like Laurendeau, preferred to think that his own motives were purely to protect the safety of humankind. Most denied that their wounded egos and public humiliation were factors in their collective actions.

Laurendeau continued. "As you have no doubt noticed, Kurt Walker isn't with us today. I've sent him on a special mission to track down leads on the fourth copy of the *Christianismi Restitutio*. This is the book I told you about at our last meeting. If it exists and is all we think it is, it will be a tremendous help to our cause."

Maarten Hoffman nodded in agreement while Thorbjorn Asplund looked bored. Otto Fleischer licked his lips and nervously checked his watch.

"It's time to bring in Kestrel," said Laurendeau as he pushed a button below the table. A moment later the door at the end of the room opened and in walked a man whom they were all slightly afraid of, even though they tried not to show it.

Kestrel stood at the end of the table. He was a slim man of medium height with dark hair, eyes, and complexion. He carried himself with a catlike grace. His real name was Alain Moreau, and he was a Frenchman from Marseilles. His business was killing, and he had been at it since he was a youth of seventeen. He was now thirty-four and commanded a high price from his employers. He killed equally as efficiently with his hands as he did with a variety of weapons.

He waited with a look of superiority on his face that he made little effort to hide.

"And how did your trip to the Orient go?" asked the Leader.

In a soft voice, which only made him seem more menacing, he said, "Your Professor Kagawa has been taken care of. He won't be designing any more experiments."

"Did you have any trouble?"

Kestrel glowered at him and then at each of the members of the group in turn. "If you expected trouble, you employed the wrong man. I told you, there would be no problem."

"Yes, yes, you said that," commented Laurendeau. "We appreciate the, how shall we say it, the *quality* of your work. Now we have another job for you."

He explained about the next target, young Rafael Mendez.

Chapter 14

Rafael Mendez was packing his few belongings at his apartment in Zaragoza, not far from the University, when the phone rang.

"Rafe, it's Alicia," his sister said. "I need to talk to you about some things. It's probably better if we do it in person. I was thinking of driving there today, if you're free for a while."

"Sure. I'm just packing for my move to Geneva next week, but I always have time for you. I'll make reservations for lunch. It will take you about that long to get here from Madrid."

"Geneva? Why are you going there?"

"I'll tell you when you get here."

Rafael loved his big sister. She'd shielded him from his classmates who saw his scholarly habits and brilliant mind as grounds for abuse during his early days in school. Nerd and geek weren't complimentary terms. His father wasn't much better. While he wasn't as hard on him as he was on Alicia, he wasn't supportive of him either. Alfonso Mendez would have preferred a son who was athletic and would grow up to be an accomplished businessman, an aggressive type who'd take over the family fortune and run the business.

Instead, Rafael Mendez, at just twenty years of age, was a prodigy even by math and physics standards. It's often been said that mathematicians and physicists do their best work before the age of thirty. Rafael wouldn't receive his Ph.D. in experimental particle physics from the University of Zaragoza until next year. Not because he wasn't qualified right now. He was. No. It was because tradition and University policies dictated that the degree couldn't be awarded to anyone younger than twenty-one. Indeed, Rafael's published dissertation, on "Supersymmetric Particles and the Search for Dark Matter," had earned him a spot on the Large Hadron Collider team that would try to answer questions on the make-up of dark matter and dark energy.

Rafael had once tried to explain to his father that everything seen in the universe is made up of ordinary particles called matter. This included everything from goldfish to supernovas. But all this matter makes up only 4% of the universe. All the rest was composed of dark matter and dark energy. But dark matter and energy were incredibly difficult to detect and could only be studied by the gravitational forces they exerted. His father couldn't have cared less, saying it was all just a bunch of dark crap as far as he was concerned.

Rafael would be the only non-Ph.D. working on the CMS detector program at the collider facility. But that would only be a technicality, as the other members of the team knew him well through his many published research papers.

Experimental particle physics in Spain was a young field. It really began when Spain rejoined CERN in 1983. Major centers for the study of experimental particle physics in the country were at the University of Madrid and the University of Zaragoza in the Aragon region.

Rafael hadn't been to Madrid since his grandfather's funeral, almost six weeks earlier. His grandfather's death and the funeral had been quite troubling. Sure, he was an old man, but to die like that, falling off a ladder. It wasn't right. It should have been peacefully, in his sleep. He knew Grandfather had probably left a will, and he was probably in it, but he hadn't checked on it. He was more interested in his own career than he was in the family fortune.

Alicia arrived just after noon. She burst in and gave her brother a huge hug. Rafael was a slim young man of medium height with a mop of unruly black curly hair, an impish grin, and bright dark eyes that hinted at the alert mind within. He was wearing jeans and a dark blue tee shirt with a picture of Darth Vader and the words "Dark Matter Matters" printed on the front.

"Okay, tell me why you're moving to Geneva," she said with mock accusation.

"Let's go and eat first. I'm starved. I haven't had anything since last night. I've been tying up loose ends and starting to pack."

They drove to a quiet neighborhood restaurant that Rafael frequented and got a nice table outside in the shade of a large umbrella. After they'd ordered tapas, he explained.

"Last week I received a call from Dr. Gersbach, the Director of the ATLAS and CMS experiments at the Large Hadron Collider outside of Geneva."

"I've read about that place," said Alicia. "They're going to split atoms or something."

"Well, sort of." Rafael chuckled. "The director asked me if I would be interested in designing experiments to answer questions about dark matter and energy. I jumped at the chance, and given that I'm essentially done with all of my work at the University, I could begin almost immediately.

"You have to understand, Alicia, this is the chance of a lifetime for an experimental particle guy like myself. That collider will be the best experimental workshop in the world. Just to work there will be a thrill, but to design and carry out my own experiments, that's icing on the cake."

Finally, after another half hour of describing what he would be doing at the LHC, Rafael said, "But wait, you drove here to talk about something else and I've been babbling on like an idiot."

She laughed. "Babbling on, maybe. But certainly not like an idiot. I'm proud of you and your accomplishments, and Father should be too."

She immediately knew that was a mistake. Her comment definitely put a damper on the mood.

They looked at each other as if to say, *do we really want to talk about him?*

They silently agreed that they didn't.

"So what's on your mind, Alicia?"

"Rafael, I'm very proud of your appointment in Geneva, and I'm extremely happy for you too. I know you didn't want to come to the reading of Grandfather's will, so I'll tell you what it said. Father gets the bulk of the fortune, the property, and the businesses. He left you and me essentially the same thing. I'll get an endowment that will pay 75,000 euros per year that will be increased to 125,000, with father's approval, if I complete a college degree."

"Oh, for God's sake," said Rafael in disgust. "What does he have to do with it?"

"It's okay, I talked with Señor Alvarez, Grandfather's attorney, and he explained it to me. The clause is there just to make sure there's money to pay for it. As long as Father doesn't lose it all somehow, which would affect him too, he's required to approve the increased endowment. So the stipulation is not as bad as it sounds.

"In your case, you'll start receiving 75,000 euros annually immediately with a similar increase to 125,000 when you reach thirty."

Rafael took all this in and then looked questioningly at Alicia. "So, is that why you came up, just to fill me in on the provisions of the will?"

"More or less."   Then swallowing somewhat nervously, avoiding his eyes, she continued.   "But in addition, I've been given the villa in Majorca and the collection. I hope that's okay with you?"

"Of course, of course. You're the only one who ever used the villa anyway. It's always been yours and it should be. And you know the collection never meant anything to me. I've been in my own world of math and science for as long as I can remember. In fact Grandfather would often say to me, 'Rafael, you are a man of the future and not of the past. Pursue your physics as far as you can. Your sister, the artist, even though she doesn't know it yet, is the proper keeper of things historical. Her temperament and love of the humanities dictates that she will eventually look after the collection and make the proper decisions for it.'"

Alicia tipped back in her chair, both relieved by Rafael's acceptance and astounded and moved by this news. Their grandfather had never spoken of this to her directly. But as she thought about it, she knew he'd been right.

Chapter 15

MADRID

Hunter and Genevieve flew out of Paris's CDG airport at 8:20 AM and arrived at Madrid-Barajas International a little over two hours later. They picked up their car, a silver Mercedes S class, and drove to the Bausa Hotel. Scarlet had described it as small, but extremely elegant and fashionable. It was. They were assigned two adjoining rooms on the first floor. When they checked in, the concierge gave them a message from Scarlet indicating that she had contacted Alicia Mendez and they were to meet her for dinner at ten that evening at the Bausa restaurant. Hunter called Scarlet on the cell phone and asked why they were seeing the daughter and not the father.

"It seems that Daddy," Scarlet replied mockingly, "was unavailable. His secretary said he calls people—people don't call him."

"Nice," said Hunter.

"Oh, it gets even better," she said, shifting to an even more snooty voice. 'If you would give me your name and address,' she told me, 'my office will email you an application form that you can fill out and submit on line. If I approve it, I'll ask Señor Mendez if he would accept a call from your Mr. Blackwell. Oh, and by the way, there is a rather long waiting list.'"

"Obvious Sonny is overly impressed with his own importance," said Hunter.

"You think?"

"And his gatekeeper is even more impressed with hers. So how did we get to the daughter?"

"It seems that she and Daddy have different ideas of their importance. I got her cell phone number. Don't ask how, just say 'Scarlet, you're amazing.' I explained that two scholars, one from America and one from France, would like to interview her about her grandfather's Inquisition Collection, if she would be so kind as to meet with them."

"And she agreed to meet us at the restaurant rather than at the castle?" asked Hunter.

"She doesn't live at the castle. Apparently she and Daddy don't see eye-to-eye, so to speak."

"Thanks, Scarlet, good work. Oh, I forgot . . . Scarlet, you're amazing."

"I know. And by the way, I hear the paella is great. Bye-bye," she said, and rung off.

"Wow. How does she do that from across the ocean?" asked Genevieve.

"I've learned not to ask Scarlet how she does anything. Her greatest joy is doing the impossible sooner than you ask for it, then saying quite modestly, 'Sorry it took so long.' She's a gem."

Hunter would have preferred to meet with Alfonso Mendez himself, but he considered the possible advantage of meeting instead with his daughter—Basilio's granddaughter. Since Alfonso had already declared to Shay his unwillingness to cooperate, maybe his daughter's estrangement from daddy could work to their advantage. Who knows, she might even cooperate with them out of spite.

They had quite a bit of time before dinner, so they decided to park the Mercedes and take a half-day minivan tour.   Neither had been to Madrid before.   They settled back and enjoyed the warm sunny day as they were driven through the city's famous avenues, followed by a visit to the huge Prado Museum with its Goya collection.

Hunter and Genevieve were already at the table in the Bausa Hotel's restaurant when the maître d escorted Alicia Mendez to their table.   Hunter rose and was surprised to greet such an attractive Spanish beauty.   He hadn't known what to expect, but this slim, dark, attractive young woman wasn't it.

After introductions he said, "I'm afraid my Spanish is not as good as Genevieve's, but I'll do the best I can."

"Oh, my goodness, don't worry about that. I've been speaking English since my school days," Alicia answered.

Hunter kept the conversation to generalities during dinner. Alicia Mendez seemed to be a most pleasant young woman.   She was apparently single, a student at the University of Madrid, and spent her spare time at her villa in Majorca. Her interests included art and architecture, and she had traveled to the United States, Britain, and all of continental Europe. Hunter could see Genevieve's delight that Alicia had visited the Bibliotheque National in Paris and believed the Dominique Perrault-designed new towers that contained the major collections to be among the most beautiful buildings in the world. The two women got along nicely.

Hunter saw to it that he and Genevieve only admitted to being scholars.   Genevieve referred to herself as a Renaissance historian and Hunter as a scientist.   He explained that they were interested in her grandfather's collection.

Following the dinner they retired to the hotel's well-appointed library, where they settled into comfortable chairs and, over aperitifs, Hunter began to discuss what he and Genevieve were really after.

"Señorita Mendez," he began, "I've been hired by Shay Blackwell, the son of an American named George Blackwell, who was a good friend of your grandfather's in Madrid during the Second World War. Your grandfather wrote George Blackwell a letter in 1947 that remained unopened until recently, when Shay Blackwell found it among his father's things." He went on to explained how her grandfather and George Blackwell had met and became good friends. "If you'd be so kind, I'd like you to read a copy of this letter now," said Hunter.

While she read it, Hunter tried to interpret her changing facial expression. It seemed to go from curiosity to concentration and then to confusion. Setting the letter in her lap, she brushed her hair back behind her ear and stared for a moment before saying, "I don't recall there being such a book in my grandfather's collection, and I'm reasonably sure of this, because just before his death, he'd had the collection evaluated by an authority, a professor at the University of Madrid. I'm sure my grandfather would have mentioned it to me if it were there."

"Have you spoken with this professor about the cataloging?" asked Genevieve.

"Yes. As a matter of fact, I'm the one who brought him to my grandfather's attention. However, I have to say, I've never felt comfortable around parts of the collection. I find it macabre, with its torture tools and documents of conviction and execution. I often wonder why my family ever bothered collecting those things over the years."

Hunter asked her, "Do you remember the professor's name?"

"Of course, Professor Isandro Rodriquez de la Peña."

"Alicia, can I give you our cell phone numbers in case you do manage to come across any information on the book?"

"Yes, that would be okay, although I can't imagine what."

Hunter wrote their numbers on a notepad that he found on the end table near their chairs and handed it to Alicia, who put it in her purse.

Obviously uncomfortable with the topic of the collection, she politely rose and said that she had enjoyed meeting them but now she had to be going.

"I'm sorry that I can't help you."

Hunter stood and said, "Well if you do learn anything, we'd surely appreciate if you'd call us."

Hunter and Genevieve remained in the library and tried to decide what to do next. They wondered why Alicia appeared to be troubled by talking about the collection. It might be, as she said, that it was just scary stuff, but they couldn't help thinking there was more to it than that. Was it the discussion of the book? Why would the book bother her? Maybe it was the Professor.

"Let's consider the possibilities," Hunter said. "Basilio Mendez could have lied to George Blackwell in his letter about having such a book. But why would he do that if they were such good friends? Did he just want to see him again and figured such a 'find' might lure him back over the Atlantic for a visit?"

They both agreed that didn't make much sense.

Hunter continued. "Maybe the book was, in fact, in the collection as Basilio stated in the letter, but he later sold it off, or his son Alfonso did. Perhaps one or the other needed the money its sale might bring, or maybe they were keeping it but were trying to avoid paying the huge inheritance tax that would probably accompany passing it on to Alfonso."

Hunter made a mental note to check on line to see if there were any public records available in Spain on such sales and taxes.

"Or maybe the book is still in the collection and for whatever reason Alfonso and Alicia are lying to us," Genevieve countered. "Remember, Alfonso told

Blackwell there was no such book in the collection. Maybe we should try to find out who actually owns this collection. Is it Alfonso, Alicia, or both of them?"

Hunter was becoming increasingly impressed with his traveling companion. Initially he'd been afraid she might slow down his investigation. Instead, much to his delight, she was turning out to be an asset.

He smiled approvingly. "That's a very good idea."

Genevieve blushed a little, and looked away, but quickly returned to their discussion. "You know, there is another possibility. Maybe the professor who did the cataloguing came across the book in the collection and thought, 'I'll just keep this little gem for myself and not report it.' Later, after the old man died, he was relying on the possibility that the son and granddaughter didn't know it existed."

Hunter nodded thoughtfully. "Maybe it's time we pay a visit to the professor."

Chapter 16

Using Genevieve's laptop Hunter Skyped Shay and told him what they'd learned so far. He excused himself when Shay asked to speak to Genevieve, and when he returned a few minutes later the connection had been broken and Genevieve just looked curiously at him for a moment.

"What?" he said finally.

"Apparently there's more to you than meets the eye. Your Mr. Blackwell seems to think there's *nothing* you can't do. He told me again I should have complete faith in you. She cocked her head, raised an eyebrow and appraised him. We'll see," she said smiling.

Hunter had no idea what Shay had told her, but he sighed. *If you only knew! No. It's going to be okay. I won't let anything happen to you. The nightmares seem to be going away. Maybe it's going to be all right. Maybe I'm finally getting back to normal, whatever that is.*

Since Gary's death, Hunter had become less confident about having people depend on him. Always present was that nagging doubt in the back of his mind. Would he be there when they needed him if push came to shove? Or would he let them down in some way at a critical moment?

Hunter ended this negative reverie. "I think we need to view the collection ourselves, if for no other reason than just to get a feel for what we are getting involved with."

Genevieve agreed and they decided to call Alicia
Mendez to see if she'd show it to them, even if the book
weren't there, just because they'd come so far and were
interested. Then he realized they didn't even know how to
contact her since Scarlet had made the call earlier to set up
the meeting at the Bausa Hotel's restaurant.

So Hunter set up a Skype connection with Scarlet to
find out. She came into view on the computer screen and
said "What can I do for you today?"

Hunter replied, "We need to see Alicia again and I
forgot to ask for her phone number last night."

Scarlet immediately turned to her desk. "Give me a
minute."

They could see her typing and manipulating the mouse
pads for three different computers. In ninety seconds she
returned her attention to Hunter and Genevieve. "Sorry it
took so long. Alicia's cell phone is shut off right now but
she is currently playing golf at the Real Club de la Puerta
de Hierro, which is about five kilometers northwest of
Madrid. Her tee time was at eight AM and she's planning
to have lunch in the club restaurant when her round is over.
If you plug the address into your phone's GPS system, you
should be able to get there in time to have lunch with her.
Bye-bye, dearies" and she shut down the connection.

Genevieve stood there with her mouth open. "How
does she do that?"

"Like I said, I—"

"Don't ask."

They drove to the club, where they just caught Alicia
coming in after her round. She was surprised to see them,
and when they inquired if it would be all right to ask her a
few more questions she said, "Find a table in the restaurant,
and I'll join you in a few minutes after I freshen up."

Over lunch they explained that they'd regretted having
to bother her, but that her father was impossible to get in
touch with.

"Couldn't get past Miss Nasty, could you?" said Alicia. "You know, she once asked me to fill out a request form to see my own father. That's when I knew I'd had enough. I moved out of the house next to the castle shortly after that and have been living on my own since."

"So is the collection in the castle?" asked Genevieve.

"Oh yes. And I do have access. My father wants me to take more interest in the place, but except for the collection that I inherited from my grandfather, I want nothing to do with it or him. My brother Rafael has his own life, and he's not interested. I haven't decided yet what to do with the collection, although we did improve the display room's lighting, furniture, and climate control system. So for the time being, it will stay where it is in the castle."

"We?" queried Hunter.

"Yes. Surprisingly, my father paid for the update. It seems he thought the room was a mess also."

"What does your brother do, if you don't mind my asking, Señorita Mendez?"

"My brother is five years younger than I am. He's a particle physicist and a sort of a genius, really. Though he is only twenty, he lives in Zaragoza and has just completed the work for his Ph.D. at the University there, and will be leaving soon to take up a position with the Large Hadron Collider in Geneva. I'm very proud of him."

"Do you suppose it would be all right if we called on him and asked him about the book?"

"Oh, he wouldn't know anything about it, even if it did exist. As I said, he's in his own world of physics and has never been interested in the collection. Still, I'll give you his address and phone number and you can ask him yourself."

"Thank you," said Hunter. "Alicia, I wonder if we might ask another favor of you. Since we've come this far, and we're both professionally interested in this historical period, we wondered if you might allow us to view your Inquisition collection?"

"I don't see why not. Personally I find it all quite horrible, but I can understand how the historical significance would be of interest to scholars. Why don't you come to the castle about four this afternoon? I'll open it up for you."

Thanks to Scarlet having preprogrammed the GPS application on Hunter's cell phone they arrived at Mendez Castle on time. Traffic was heavy on the Autopista M-50 until they pulled off onto the M-206 heading south where the surrounding countryside became less urban and more rural. As they approached the castle, they could see that adjacent to it was a large, twentieth-century European-style house. As they got closer still, they could see that it was attached to the castle itself. It appeared to have been built in the early 1900s, with whitewashed stucco walls and a tiled red roof. The windows all had wooden open shutters that were held back by decorative iron fasteners. Two large oak doors, stained to match the shutters, greeted visitors who climbed up the ten steps to a wide entry porch that ran the length of the house. On this porch beautiful potted plants and flowers framed the setting.

Alicia had instructed them to pull into the large circular driveway in the courtyard and come to the front door. When they pressed the doorbell button, she answered the door herself. She took them into a comfortable sitting room and offered them a chilled glass of sangria, which they each took.

"As you will see when we enter the castle proper, it is not a place one would want to live, hence the construction of this house by my great grandfather at the turn of the last century. My father lives here by himself now, but maintains an office downtown, where he conducts his business."

"Forgive me, Alicia, but your father doesn't appear to want us here. Are you taking a risk of offending him by allowing us in?" asked Genevieve.

"Yes, probably. But you must understand. My father is a private and often difficult man, and as you have discovered through your interaction with his office staff, he won't meet with people his secretary hasn't pre-approved."

Then, with a defiant toss of her head, she continued. "But I'm my own person, the collection is now mine, and I choose to give you access."

Hunter and Genevieve followed her as she led them from the house to the castle and the collection. They were enchanted by the progressive transformation of the relatively modern home into the castle as they walked from one to the other. The temperature dropped slightly to add to the sense that they were now in a structure completely different from the one they had just left.

"It's a creepy feeling, isn't it?" asked Alicia. "I never fail to sense the falling away of centuries when I take this walk."

In Hunter's mind, the cave-like passageway gave him the feeling of a time machine of sorts, and he found himself letting go of the present as his mind drifted backward over the years.

"All right men, get ready. You hear that distant thunder? Our F-18s are pounding the enemy on the Afghan side of the border. Our job's here, in Pakistan, at that cave you see ahead of us, right now. We're going to get this bastard out of there alive and complete this mission. The black-faced special ops team stayed low, waiting their orders from Hunter.

Intelligence tells us that Mahmud e Raq, is inside. This entrance is the only way in or out. A lone sentry armed with a Kalashnikov was sitting wrapped in his robe to keep out the cold. *"Stay down, I'll take him out."* Hunter did, silently and efficiently. Two of his men dragged the body into the bushes nearby. Hunter issued commands. *"McKenzie and McCoy, you take up positions on either side of the opening. No sound. The rest of you follow me into the cave."*

On entering the cave, one of his men set off a booby-trapped alarm. *"Shit. Go! Go!"* They rushed the cave and there he was, Mahmud e Raq, sitting on a carpet with three other men. They grabbed for their weapons, but the Marines opened fire and cut down the guards. They were all over Mahmud e Raq before he could get to his weapon. He was knocked unconscious and carried from the cave.

"McKenzie and McCoy, watch our tail. Stay alert. We're taking this bastard down the mountain now." Just then the firefight began and—

"Hunter. Are you paying attention?" asked Genevieve with a look of concern on her face. "Alicia is giving us a history tour of the castle."

Hunter snapped back to the present. As he refocused his mind he realized he was sweating and hyperventilating. His heart was racing. Refocusing, he managed a self-deprecating smile. "Sorry, I— I'm sorry. My mind was wandering."

Genevieve eyed him curiously and gently touched his arm.

Alicia showed them the great hall, the kitchens, and the library that her grandfather loved so well. She pointed out the large desk with side library table that she said her grandfather used when he worked in the room.

They left the library and walked down the hall to a room just behind it that she indicated held the collection. As they approached the door she told them again that she was never comfortable going into this room and never went in alone. They entered a large rectangular open space. She turned on the overhead lighting and the room was suddenly bathed in brightness. This made up for the rather dismal light that had filtered through the small slit openings in the wall, now fitted with glass windows.

The front two-thirds of the room was separated from the back section by a wall of glass with a single glass door connecting the two.

The larger room held numerous devices of horrific design. The smaller physical artifacts were under glass in specially designed display cases, as in a typical museum. The large devices, on close examination, had unimaginably horrible purposes as described in the display plaques that accompanied each. Some of the devices were original and others were replicas built from medieval illustrations.

There was the Judas Cradle, also called the Spanish Donkey, in which the victim was seated on a tall triangular seat where he or she was slowly impaled as weights were added incrementally to each leg. Then they saw the rack, on which the victim was bound by the ankles and wrists and slowly pulled in opposite directions designed to dislocate every joint in the body. Next to this was the Knee Splitter, a popular torture device used during the Inquisition.

"My God," said Genevieve, "how could anyone commit these atrocities on another human being? It's unimaginable."

Next was the Inquisitional chair. Hundreds of sharp and rusty spikes stuck out from every surface of the chair— back, seat, back of legs, and arm rests. The accompanying plaque said the victim was strapped tightly into the chair and the torturer would then press him down onto the spikes, increasing the pain. Sometimes the chair was even heated so the spikes could slow roast the victim as well.

On separate pedestals were the thumbscrew and the head crusher. The latter did what its name implied. It was an iron screw device in which the victim's chin was placed on a lower iron bar, while a metal cap was slowly screwed down on the top of the skull, eventually crushing it during the questioning.

The display cases held equally disturbing pieces of equipment. These included the heretic's fork, an iron device with a spear at both ends that was wedged under the chin and to the sternum and held in place with a strap. When the victim was exhausted, he impaled himself. There was the lead sprinkler, which looked much like a holy water sprinkler except it was filled with molten lead and sprinkled over the victim.

For women victims there was the breast ripper, whose metal claws gripped the breasts and when pulled would literally tear them apart. Equally awful was the pear that was inserted into the mouth, rectum, or vagina. Then a screw mechanism would make its pointed "leaves" expand inside of any of these orifices, resulting in severe internal mutilation.

Genevieve groaned. "I think I've had more than enough."

Hunter agreed.

As they looked for Alicia they realized that she hadn't accompanied them on this walking tour but was sitting on a bench by the glass wall partition that separated the room into its two sections. As they walked toward her and Alicia spotted Genevieve's blanched complexion, she said, "Now you see why I don't like coming here?"

Next she led them into the glass-enclosed portion of the room, which was carefully climate-controlled to preserve the paper documents. Wooden cabinets with wide, shallow pullout drawers held the Inquisition documents. When the items were to be viewed, they were carefully placed on a table designed for scholars to examine them, even though Basilio was the only one who'd actually done so until recently.

Alicia showed them the cataloguing report by Professor de la Peña. Hunter studied the table of contents and saw that it covered the papers, documents, and other written works kept in the cases. Included were documents about the church's restrictions on the movement of Jews and instructions on how to prosecute Protestants, including by hanging. Sixteenth-century maps outlined the ghettos, depicting where Jews could live and where they were allowed to keep businesses. Handwritten regulations described when Jewish women could be out of the gated areas and what they could wear. The catalogue also cited sketches of prisons and extensive lists of banned books. Hunter could see documents of execution, orders for arrest and interrogation, and instructions on how inquisitors were to behave both on and off the job. There appeared to be no mention of the *Christianismi Restitutio* by Michael Servetus.

As if sensing Hunter's frustration, Alicia said, "As you can see, we have no record of the book you're looking for."

"Can you think of any reason your grandfather would have told George Blackwell that he had such a book?" he asked. "Did you know your grandfather well enough to speculate?"

"I have no idea, and I did know my grandfather well. He was more of a father to me than my own father was."

"Do you have a sample of your grandfather's handwriting so we could compare it to the signature on the 1947 letter? Maybe the letter's a fake, and your grandfather never wrote it," said Hunter.

"I'm sure we can find a sample of his signature somewhere in the library."

Alicia led them out of the collection room and back into the library with its walls of books. She opened his desk drawer, went through a few files, and soon found a document with Basilio Diego Mendez's signature on it. It appeared that the same hand had written both signatures.

A deep booming voice startled them all. "What the hell is the meaning of this, Alicia? Who are these people and what are they doing here?"

In the doorway to the library stood a tall man with his hands in fists on his hips. He was dressed in a business suit, had a head of white hair, a piercing glare, and an angry expression on his face.

"These are guests of mine, Father, and I was showing them the collection and giving them a tour of the castle. Let me present—"

"I don't care who they are, they have not been approved to be here," roared Alfonso.

Alicia, in a tone that surprised Hunter by the stiffened backbone it implied, said, "They don't need any approval; they are my guests, and I'll take them anywhere I like."

"Who are they?" growled the man.

"I'm trying to tell you. This is Dr. Hunter McCoy of the University of Virginia in the United States, and this is Dr. Genevieve Swift of the Bibliotheque National in Paris. May I present my father, Alfonso Mendez."

Hunter put his hand out to shake hands, but was ignored by Alfonso, who just grunted.

"Why are you here? What do you want with us?"

Hunter smiled pleasantly. As tall as Alfonso was, Hunter had him by an inch, and he could see that it really irritated Alfonso not to be able to look down on him. He tried, but the effect was lost when he couldn't make eye contact and look down at the same time.

"Your daughter has been kind enough to allow us to view the collection," Hunter answered. "We're scholars interested in this time period in Spanish history. We had thought that your collection might possibly contain a fourth copy of a book published by Michael Servetus, the *Christianismi Restitutio*."

"That damned book again." The man snapped. "We don't have it. Why would you think we did?"

"If you will permit me, I would like to show you a letter written by your father to George Blackwell in 1947, in which he invited Blackwell, a good friend of his from the war years, to come to Madrid and view it. Apparently it was part of his collection."

"Let me see that." Alfonso demanded.

Hunter took the copy of the letter out of his jacket pocket and handed it, in the envelope, to Alfonso, who examined the envelope, then withdrew and unfolded the letter. He read it. Then he read it again, frowning all the while.

"I don't understand this. It looks like my father's handwriting and signature, and it even looks like his style of phrasing, but I know nothing about this book. My father never mentioned it to me, and I'm certain we don't have it in the collection. In fact, he'd recently had the collection evaluated, just before his unfortunate accident killed him. I've read the evaluation and cataloging report, and I remember no such book."

"Were you completely familiar with all contents of the collection?" asked Genevieve.

Ignoring her, he said, "I understood that the evaluator and cataloger, Professor de la Peña, was a very reputable person and I have no reason to disbelieve his report. Now, if there is nothing else, I would like you to leave."

"Just one more thing, if you don't mind," said Hunter. "You said your father's death was an unfortunate accident. How'd he die?"

Alfonso glowered at him for several seconds before answering. "If you must know, he died in this very room. He was up on that ladder over there, presumably looking for a book, when he fell off and hit his head on the tile floor. He was ninety-two years old and shouldn't have been up there in the first place, but he was."

"I see," said Hunter. "Was the collection always in the same room and was it there that the professor did his work?"

Alicia answered. "Yes, it's always been in that room. But the torture items were scattered all over, covered in dust in no particular order. The documents, which were my grandfather's primary interest, were cared for in a much more organized way. He kept them in the cabinets you saw in the room behind the glass wall. He had that room modified to preserve them, but never did the same for torture devices. They never meant that much to my grandfather."

Alfonso added, although no one had asked, "When the professor was finished and gave his report to my father, he left. The man had done his job. There was no book."

Alicia showed them out and they thanked her for her help.

Hunter and Genevieve left and on the drive back to town talked about the visit and what to do next. They both agreed that Alfonso would interfere with their search if he could. He might even be hiding something, but they couldn't be sure what.

"Did you have a chance to examine the library?" Hunter asked Genevieve. "What if there was a safe or climate-controlled storage space there too? Might he have kept the Servetus book in the library? None of the other documents were books."

"It's possible," said Genevieve. "But I don't suppose we'll be allowed back in to look."

Hunter heard a ringtone and glanced over when he saw Genevieve open her purse and take out her cell phone. She pressed a few buttons on the screen. "Mon dieu!" she gasped.

"What is it?" Asked Hunter, alarmed.

The color drained from her face and Genevieve began to shake. Then she dropped the phone in her lap.

"Genevieve, what is it?"

Her voice cracked. "I—I don't know."

She turned and looked at Hunter, He could see she was terribly agitated and trembling.

"Genevieve, for God's sake, what is it?"

She slowly picked up the phone and with a shaking hand, gave it to Hunter.

He saw a text message on the screen.

Genevieve Swift
Fear torture and death by the Inquisition
Stay away from McCoy
Cease looking for the book
This will be your only warning

Chapter 17

Badly shaken by the message she'd gotten on her cell phone, Genevieve demanded that Hunter tell if there was something going on he hadn't told her about`. Hunter immediately found a café, convinced they needed to talk about it.

Hunter leaned forward across the small table, took both of her hands in his and tried to reassure her. "I've kept nothing from you, Genevieve. I have no idea what that text is about. Now let's think about who knows we're even looking for the book. Aside from Shay and Scarlet, we've only talked to Alicia and Alfonso. The only other one is my dad and he doesn't know about you. We can safely rule out Shay, Scarlet and my dad. That leaves only Alicia and Alfonso."

Genevieve was recovering her composure and nodded in response. "Alfonso is sure not a fan of our snooping around, and he all but ignored me when we were there," she added, still unable to completely mask her anxiety about the message.

"My money's on him too," agreed Hunter. "There's no reason for him to have been that upset by our presence unless he's got something to hide."

Genevieve twirled her hair in her fingers and thought for a few minutes in silence. "It's certainly not my superior at the Bibliotheque. He doesn't even know precisely what he was releasing me for. He was just happy enough to give me the time in exchange for that digital data acquisition system."

Hunter agreed. "And the Director of your Rare Book Room only knew that we'd wanted to view the *Christianismi Restitutio* for a research project we were planning, not that we're searching for an unknown fourth copy."

They sat quietly for a while each thinking of additional clues.

"What I can't figure out," Hunter finally said, "is why someone would warn *you* off the search instead of *me*," "You'd think if someone doesn't want the book found, I'd be a bigger threat in that regard than you would," said Hunter, vocalizing his thoughts. "What could you bring to the search that would be so threatening?"

Genevieve pondered this, having had the same thoughts. "Maybe, for some reason, they don't want an ancient book scholar to see it, and since you're not that, you're not a threat."

"But that doesn't make any sense," Hunter mused. "Once the book is found, scholars will see it anyway since Shay intends to donate it the University of Virginia.

"Genevieve, I've been thinking. Maybe you should go back to your job and leave this to me. Once I've got the book we can use you for authentication. That's what you'd originally suggested anyway."

Genevieve, thought about this and didn't say anything for several minutes. Finally she looked at Hunter, her doubt replaced by conviction. "No. I'm going to stick with it. You'll just have to look out for me."

Hunter slowly smiled and appraised her anew, beauty, brains, and the soul of a fighter too. "Are you sure?"

Squaring her shoulders and thrusting out her chin, she took her hands back from Hunter and made fists. "I'm sure."

As they drove to the campus, Genevieve tried to put the threat behind her and read aloud information about the University of Madrid that she'd found on her laptop. "It's the largest university in Spain, with an annual enrollment of close to one hundred thousand students, and it dates back to the Middle Ages. It offers seventy-six distinct degrees arranged with respect to four areas of knowledge: Humanities, Mathematics and Natural Sciences, Health Sciences, and Social Sciences. There are over twenty-five hundred tenured professors."

"Wow! I'd hate to have to sit on that tenure committee," quipped Hunter, happy to see that Genevieve's mood had brightened, although he was very much concerned about the threat to her.

They drove through the campus, following the GPS directions on the cell phone. The drive was interrupted many times by large numbers of students crossing the streets from building to building as they went from class to class. In that respect it was like any large university anywhere in the world. Young people lugging books and bags, laughing in groups, walking alone silently, cutting across lawns and generally looking busy.

The cell phone GPS signaled that they'd reached their destination and almost miraculously, a car pulled out of a parking space next to the building just as they arrived. Hunter knew that most buildings in Europe were considered new if they were less than two hundred years old. By that standard, this was a modern building, less than one hundred years old. It was a medium sized, three-story structure of stone with the tiled roofs common to Spain.

Hunter and Genevieve entered through the glass doors that were considerably newer than the rest of the building and found Professor de la Peña's office. They entered and were politely greeted, in Spanish, by the professor's secretary, a middle-aged woman.

Looking embarrassed she said that the professor was sorry, but that he couldn't meet with them now or at any time.

"I'm sorry, I don't understand," said Hunter. "If something has come up, can we schedule another appointment?"

"I'm afraid the professor will not be able to meet with you at all," she said.

Hunter, no longer smiling, said, "Would you explain that please?"

Shifting uncomfortably in her chair, the secretary said, "I'm afraid I don't know any more than what I've told you. Professor de la Peña has gone for the day and told me to tell you that he would not meet with you."

Hunter could see they were getting nowhere. He took Genevieve's arm and steered her out of the office and down the hall. "There is no reason he shouldn't see us, unless somebody warned him off," he said. There is no way he could have even known about us before yesterday or today. It had to be somebody in the Mendez family."

They noticed a young woman, presumably a graduate student, in one of the small offices along the hallway. The door was open and the nameplate read Isabella Gomez. Hunter gave Genevieve a nudge. Picking up on Hunter's hint, Genevieve knocked lightly.

"Excuse me, I'm Dr. Swift and this is Dr. McCoy. Do you work with Professor de la Peña?"

"Yes," the young woman answered, "I'm working on a doctorate with him."

"We just had an appointment with him and he was apparently too busy to see us today. Do you know where he might be?"

The girl shrugged. "You shouldn't be surprised. He is too important or busy these days to see anybody, including me."

Hunter and Genevieve looked at each other, picking up on the sarcasm.

Hunter asked, "If he acts this way, why do you work with him?"

"He wasn't always this way. It started last year, just before Christmas."

They asked what happened and she said she didn't know. "I guess he just got too distracted. It was right after he was hired to assess a private collection."

"Would that be the Mendez collection?" asked Hunter casually.

"Why yes," the girl said, lifting an eyebrow, surprised that they knew about it. She briefly described how he'd changed, and then she returned to her work.

As they were exiting her cubicle, they spotted a familiar face entering de la Peña's office: Alfonso Mendez.

On the way back to the hotel in the car they drove in silence for a while.

"What do you suppose that was all about?" asked Genevieve finally. "Why would Mendez be seeing the professor? Especially if he was supposedly gone for the day."

"Maybe we convinced Alfonso that there really was such a book in his father's collection, and he's confronting de la Peña as to why it wasn't included in the report," said Hunter. "Maybe he thinks the professor stole it during—"

"His assessment of the collection," inserted Genevieve.

"His assessment of the collection," sighed Hunter.

"Or," said Genevieve, perking up, "maybe Alfonso has the book and is trying to sell it, and figures the professor would know its value and possibly even—"

"Some potential buyers," said Hunter, going on the offensive in this round of the sentence-finishing duel.

"Exactly," said Genevieve, smiling enigmatically at his getting into the game.

"Perhaps the professor did find the book in the collection and Alfonso paid him to keep quiet about it, and with us snooping around he stopped in to—"

"Remind him of the need for discretion," said Genevieve.

"Yup."

"That would even explain why the professor doesn't want to see us."

"Could be. And Spanish inheritance taxes are pretty stiff too," said Hunter. "I looked them up on your laptop while you were calling the professor to set up the appointment. It seems that Spanish citizens who are beneficiaries pay a death duty or inheritance tax of up to 50 % of the value of the gift to each beneficiary, except in the case of a gifted house, where a tax discount of 95% is available. The duty is based upon the value of the property at the date of death. So if the book actually exists and is of considerable value, simply owning it as a result of inheritance would be very costly. Unless, of course, you owned it but no one knew about it. Or if you inherited it, kept it quiet, and sold it to a private collector and did not report the income for taxation."

Genevieve countered with, "But the book, if it exists, would be part of the collection, and Alicia, not her father, inherited the collection. Maybe we could find out if she reported it on her taxes."

"There's a problem with that," said Hunter, "Property taxes are public but income taxes aren't. So there's no way to find out through the public records."

Hunter decided they did have another lead to follow. During their talk with the graduate student she had let on that the professor had recently visited something called The Michael Servetus Institute, but she hadn't known why. While she knew that Servetus was an historical figure during the Inquisition, she didn't believe that the professor had ever mentioned him or for that matter had ever been to the Institute before. When they asked if he went by himself, she said she didn't know but assumed he went alone.

They looked at each other and both nodded in agreement to the unspoken suggestion.

"The Institute?" queried Genevieve.

"Let's go," agreed Hunter.

Chapter 18

DRIVING FROM MADRID TO THE MICHAEL SERVETUS
INSTITUTE

The GPS unit indicated a four-hour drive from Madrid on the N-II northeast to the foothills of the Pyrenees.

As they drove through the ever-changing Spanish countryside, they speculated on why the professor might have traveled to this isolated institute, located in the relatively remote little village of Villanueva de Sijena, the birthplace of Michael Servetus.

"Maybe Alfonso has the book and asked the professor to travel to the Institute to see if they were interested in buying it," offered Genevieve while adjusting the air conditioning.

"Perhaps," said Hunter. "Or maybe he was going to the Institute to see if they already had acquired it. After all, Grandfather Mendez was purported to be quite altruistic and may have given it to them as a gift. Genevieve, I've got an idea. Since Zaragoza is on the way to the Institute, why don't we call Rafael Mendez and see if we can meet him for lunch and ask him—"

"If he knows anything about the book?" finished Genevieve.

Hunter paused for a moment and then looked at her. "Genevieve?"

"Yes?"

"I just wondered, are you still trying to work on that finishing sentences thing?"

"I know. I know. But it's hard. I've been doing it so long. I promise, I'll try harder," she said. "Anyway, stopping to see the brother sounds like a good idea. I'll call while you drive."

She put her cell on speakerphone and a young man answered on the second ring.

"My name is Genevieve Swift. I'm a curator with the National Library in Paris, and I just met with your sister, Alicia yesterday. I have some questions about research I'm doing that has a bearing on your late grandfather's collection. I'm currently driving from Madrid to Villanueva de Sijena. I'm stopping for lunch in Zaragoza, and wondered if I might meet with you and ask you some questions concerning the collection?"

"What sort of questions?" asked Rafael. "I don't know very much about it. I'm sure my sister told you—"

"Yes, she did," interrupted Genevieve, "but you know how it is. "Sometimes we know things we aren't aware we know, until asked. I promise you we won't take up much of your time and we'll buy you lunch as well."

"We?"

"Oh yes, sorry. I'm traveling with a fellow researcher, Hunter McCoy. He's a physiologist from the United States. Our research involves medieval history, theology and, oddly enough, physiology. If you'll see us, we'd greatly appreciate it."

"Well, I don't know what I can contribute, but I do have to eat. How about El Cachirulo?" He gave her the address and she plugged it into the GPS system.

As they approached Zaragoza, Genevieve had looked up the city on her computer.

"Zaragoza is the fifth largest city in Spain," she informed Hunter. "The city of three quarters of a million represents a crossroads between Madrid, Barcelona,

Valencia, Bilboa, and Toulouse, France, all of which are within about two hundred miles of the city."

A short time later they pulled into the driveway of an old but stately Aragonese home that had been converted into a restaurant. As they exited the car, Hunter swept the parking lot with his eyes.

"What are you looking for?" asked Genevieve.

"I'm not sure. Probably nothing," Hunter replied.

Ever since the threatening message for Genevieve to stop looking for the book, he had been on heightened alert.

Seeing nothing suspicious, he finally said, "Let's go meet Mendez and have lunch."

They walked up a wide flight of steps into what must have been the entry to the house. The inside was furnished with several dining tables and chairs. The tables were covered with white tablecloths, each with a small vase of fresh summer flowers. The room had walls of stone with oak beams and many paintings of bright Spanish scenes, adding a warm, inviting charm to the old house.

A young man spotted them immediately and got up from his table.

"You must be the two who just called me. I'm Rafael Mendez," he said, extending his hand first to Genevieve and then to Hunter.

Even though Alicia had told him Rafael's age, Hunter was surprised at how young he looked. "Thanks for seeing us on such short notice."

"Well, like I said, I can't imagine I'll be able to tell you anything my sister couldn't, but I do need lunch," he grinned as they made their way to his table.

They ordered and each had a mango-iced tea that was the specialty of the house.

While waiting for the food to arrive, they explained to Rafael everything they'd told his sister about Shay Blackwell, the wartime friendship between George Blackwell and his grandfather, the letter, and the missing book. They explained about their unsuccessful visit to the professor and why they were on their way to the Servetus Institute.

As they'd been warned, Rafael had nothing new to offer. He'd never heard of such a book and knew practically nothing about the collection.

Hunter noticed a single man enter the room and sit at a table with his back to the wall. As they ate he noticed that the man seemed to be staring at their table more often than not. Hunter's internal alarm system began to ping. But the man didn't appear to be looking at him or Genevieve. Instead, he seemed to take particular interest in Rafael. He was good. He didn't stare at Rafael continually, but his gaze kept sliding back to him. The man neither ordered food nor did he seem to be interested in anyone else. Hunter noticed that he simply sipped coffee and, when his gaze did find their table, he appeared to be looking exclusively at the youngest Mendez heir.

Hunter had an idea. "Rafael, I don't want to alarm you, and I don't want you to look right now, but there is a man sitting by himself with his back to the wall behind you. He's wearing a black nylon jacket over light tan pants, and he seems to be taking an interest in you. If you can do it casually, let me know if you've ever seen him before."

Rafael blinked in surprise, but played along. He strolled to the front desk and asked the girl at the register for a pack of gum. After paying, he unwrapped a stick and walked back to the table, casually scanning the room. When he got back to his chair he said, "Never saw him before. What's going on?"

"Probably nothing, it just looked unusual, that's all." Hunter couldn't explain it, but something wasn't right here. He recognized the flight or fight response of his autonomic nervous system kicking in. He could feel his body loosening up and preparing for action. What could be triggering this reflex now? Was the rage coming, could that be it, but why? Maybe it triggered his early warning system. He hadn't noticed that relationship before. He maintained his focus on the situation and tried to remain calm.

When lunch was over, Rafael said he was sorry that he couldn't have been more help, but that he was leaving the next day for Geneva, where he was going to join the Hadron collider team, and he had to get back home and finish packing.

They all got up, shook hands and wished each other well. Then Rafael left as Hunter and Genevieve stayed behind. While Hunter awaited the check, he noticed the man in the black jacket rise and follow Rafael out. Rafael got in his car and drove away, and the man quickly followed him in a brown van.

"Something's wrong here," said Hunter. "I don't like it."

Deciding to see if the man in the van really was following Rafael, Hunter left cash and a tip on the table and led Genevieve quickly to the car. The young man didn't live far from the restaurant, and within minutes Rafael pulled his car into the parking lot of slate gray apartment building and went inside. The van eased into position around the corner, partially hidden by a copse of trees.

Hunter drove past the van, pulled over to the side of the road, and told Genevieve to stay in the car, lock the doors, and not let anyone in but him. He'd be back shortly. He walked back, but took a direction that would bring him into a position in the trees where he could see the van between himself and Rafael's building. He paused about fifteen yards from the van, which was idling perhaps thirty yards from the building.

Hunter was fully armed. Genevieve hadn't noticed it yet, and that was his intent. He was licensed to carry in the States, and often did, but of course he wasn't licensed in Europe. Nevertheless, he had contacts in Europe who could supply him with anything he needed for a fee. He had used them in the past for his government work with the DIA and Interpol. His contact in Paris had come through, as he had on several previous cases. He also knew that if he was caught with a weapon he was on his own.

The man in the van was looking through binoculars at a window on the second floor near the corner of the building. It was obvious to Hunter that he had been here before and knew exactly which window was Rafael's. Next Hunter saw him set down the binoculars and set up a sniper rifle.

"*Son of a bitch*," Hunter muttered under his breath.

He quickly redialed Rafael's number on the cell phone.

"Rafael. This is Hunter McCoy."

"Hello again. What's up?"

"Don't go anywhere near your main front window. That man I asked you about, is outside in a van with a sniper rifle aimed at it. He followed you from the restaurant, and I followed him."

"What? My God. What the hell does he want?"

"That's the question. Stay away from the window. I'll deal with him."

As if he had heard the conversation, the man lowered the rifle, turned, and faced Hunter. Hunter knew there was no way he could have seen him, but the sniper was looking directly at Hunter as if he could. He pulled out a pistol, aimed it squarely at Hunter, and fired. Hunter moved just before the silenced round was discharged. He already had his own weapon out and fired back with six consecutive rounds. He saw the man jerk and grab his shoulder. He'd hit him. The man ducked down and sped off, with Hunter emptying his clip into the back of the rapidly receding van.

Hunter called Genevieve and told her to come to the apartment. Next, he called Rafael and told him he was coming up. As Hunter reached the main entrance to the building, Genevieve drove up. They quickly climbed the stairs together to Rafael's flat.

Hunter knocked and said, "Rafael. It's Hunter and Genevieve. Let us in."

"What's going on here?" Rafael blurted. "I have lunch with you people and the next thing I know you tell me I'm being stalked by a killer and my parking lot sounds like a war zone!"

"Now take it easy," said Hunter. "Let's try to think this through. Can you think of anyone who'd want to harm you?"

"Harm me?" cried Rafael. "Are you kidding? I'm a scientist, not a damn gangster."

Hunter knew he had to calm him down, quickly. "Rafael, trust me, we are not your problem. But you do have a problem. That man outside in the van meant business. After I called you he put down his rifle and turned directly toward me in the woods behind him and fired a round from a silenced gun. He missed, and I unloaded a clip on him. I'm sure I winged him, but he got away in the van."

Genevieve jerked around, staring at Hunter. "What? You unloaded a clip on him?   What do you mean you unloaded a clip on him?"

"I'll explain in a minute, but first I have to make a call."

Hunter asked if there was a public phone in the building. Rafael said, "Use mine," and Hunter replied, "No, it might be tapped."

"Oh, this just gets better and better," remarked Rafael. Then he said, "There's a public phone in the lobby."

Hunter went down the stairs to the lobby, where he found the phone booth. Genevieve and Rafael trailed after him. He used his international calling card and punched in a number known only to a few people on the planet.

A woman's voice in perfect English said, "McMurtle Manufacturing, how may I help you?"

"I'd like to place an order for seventeen front-end loaders by noon tomorrow," Hunter replied.

After a pause, a man's voice came on the line. "Is it really you, Hunter?"

"It's me, Deacon. In the flesh."

"To what do I owe the honor of talking with the dishonorable Hunter McCoy?" he said with a touch of warm humor.

"Listen, Deacon, it may be nothing, but I want to give you a heads up anyway. I'm in Spain on business of my own, which caused me to meet a young physicist who's been recruited as a scientist with the Large Hadron Collider in Geneva. He's supposed to be traveling there soon to begin work. Today he was the target of what look liked an assassin who would have succeeded, except for my scaring him off."

"The Large Hadron Collider? Wait a minute. I have something here. Hold on."

After a few minutes, Deacon was back. "Is your boy by any chance a particle physicist?"

"Yes, he is."

"Hunter. This could be important. Stay with him. I'll get back to you at this phone within the hour." And he hung up.

Genevieve stood with her hands on her hips. "Hunter, I demand to know what's going on."

"Me too," said Rafael.

Hunter knew he couldn't continue to keep them in the dark. Rafael had a right to know he was a target, and Genevieve certainly deserved to know just whom she was traveling with.

"Look, maybe it's time you both learned some things about me. Rafael, I don't want to scare you, but your place may be bugged. Let's go sit over there." He pointed to a cluster of chairs in the corner of the lobby. "That way I can hear this phone ring."

Hunter told them of his former connection to the Defense Intelligence Agency and the kind of work he did in general without going into any detail. He explained that he was skilled in international investigation and apprehension of terrorists and violent criminals. In his work he often utilized the services of Interpol. Now that he was a professor, that life was mostly behind him. He explained that he still used his investigative skills occasionally, but now it was to help individuals rather than governments find things. His work for Shay Blackwell was one of those assignments.

"But who did you call?" asked Genevieve with furrowed brows, just now beginning to understand those 'other skills' Hunter had referred to earlier.

"My old station chief in Europe. He sounded as if there might be some link between the attempt on your life, Rafael, and the collider. We'll have to wait for—"

The phone rang. Hunter raced over to it and picked it up. "Is my order ready?"

"Hunter, my boy, you are on to something big. Your man's lucky to be alive. Someone is killing particle physicists newly assigned to the collider program. The first was a Dr. Hans De Groot, killed in Geneva six weeks ago. The second was Dr. Akahiko Kagawa in Fukuoka, Japan, three weeks ago. They were both definitely murders. Apparently your man was next on the list.

"Now listen to this carefully. It looks like Interpol is already on this case and they're sharing information with Swiss law enforcement and the Japanese. With this attempt on your boy, they'll know for sure a plot is underway to kill collider scientists. I'll contact Interpol and tell them what you've discovered. I'll also contact Director Jones at the Department of Justice and see about updating your liaison with the USNCB and Interpol. And, as of right now, you're reactivated with DIA. I'm also authorizing you to carry that Beretta you picked up in Paris. You do know you're currently not authorized to carry over there?"

Hunter paused for a moment before answering. "I should have known that Henri would be required to tell you about my weapon request," Hunter said glumly.

"Yes, you should have. Not losing your touch, are you, my boy?"

"Probably, but not by much."

"I'll assign someone at DIA that you can contact. He'll do what he can to get you information. Just leave the major investigation to Interpol and the local authorities."

"Thanks, Deacon." Hunter hung up.

Hunter explained what he could to Rafael and Genevieve.

"My God," exclaimed Rafael, when Hunter told them about the two murdered physicists. "I knew De Groot and Kagawa. They're two of the best particle men in the world. Why is this happening? Who'd want to do this?"

"Can you think of any reason someone would want to prevent you and the other scientists from working at the collider?" inquired Hunter. "I seem to recall that there were public fears of creating black holes that might swallow up the earth as a result of the collisions planned there."

"That's nonsense," said Rafael, shifting into the pragmatic scientist mode that Hunter himself had used from time to time when dealing with the widespread science illiteracy of the public. "Even at full power, the energy created by the collisions we have in mind is less than that of two mosquitoes colliding. Even if black holes are produced, they'd be smaller than what nature produces all the time by naturally occurring cosmic particle collisions."

"Still, there might be crazies out there who don't want to take the chance and think killing scientists is the way to stop it," said Genevieve.

"The problem," said Hunter, "is that whoever is doing this must have access to some highly classified information. For instance, the two dead physicists and Rafael here hadn't even reported to duty yet. How did the killer even know about them and their recent appointments to the collider team?"

"It certainly wasn't common public knowledge," said Rafael. "I didn't even know the other two had been appointed to the project."

"So obviously someone with that kind of inside information is involved," said Hunter. "Rafael, the safest place for you is in Geneva at the collider. My contact told me that their security has been beefed up due to the increased threat. We need to get you there as soon as possible. When can you be ready to go?"

"I still need to finish packing but I'm almost done. I can be ready in an hour or two, but my airline ticket is for the day after tomorrow."

"That's too long. Let me arrange for later today. I'll travel with you to Geneva and get you safely settled in. Genevieve, you can take the car back to Madrid and stay at the hotel. I'll catch a flight from Geneva and meet you there early tomorrow."

He hated the idea of leaving her alone, but didn't feel he had much choice.

Genevieve gazed at Hunter and frowned. "Please don't be late."

Chapter 19

"The bastard," Kestrel said out loud. It had to be a lucky shot. No one had ever stopped him on a job before, much less shot him. His shoulder stung like hell. It was only a flesh wound but deep enough and had to be dealt with. Still, he knew it hurt, as much from the humiliation as from the wound itself.

It was lucky he'd seen the glint of light off the man's gun in the side mirror of the van, since he couldn't see the man himself, hidden as he was in the leaves. He couldn't believe he had been so careless that he'd let him get that close without picking up on it.

He'd ditched the stolen van in a mall parking lot and stolen a small, three-year-old Volkswagen Jetta from the employees' parking lot behind the mall's large anchor store to replace it. He drove to a chemist's and bought antiseptic, bandages, and some peroxide to clean and dress his wound.

He'd never failed at an assassination before. He'd never even come close to failing. The more he thought about it, the angrier he got. Those idiots in Geneva, stupid as they were with their crazy ideas about black holes and time travelers, deserved his best for the price they were paying him and he hadn't given it to them. He knew he had to take out the man who shot him before he could get on with the hit on the Spanish physicist. But first he had to find him.

He took a chance and went to the airport at Zaragoza, guessing the target would try to get out of the city as soon as possible and head for the supposed safety of the LHC with its high security. He figured Mendez would take a Geneva flight. Like Hunter, he'd learned long ago that patience in a hunt is one of an assassin's best allies. He waited at the main entrance and was rewarded three hours later when he saw Rafael Mendez and the tall muscular man enter the main lobby and head to the Swissair desk. It appeared that the big man was in charge, as he did all the talking. Only the young man checked in luggage. That was good. If the big man stayed behind he could take him out here, and then get a flight back to Geneva to finish his contract. He shadowed them to the entrance of the security check, where they shook hands, and he could see that only the young man went through security. Good, the big guy was staying.

He studied him closely. He saw that his prey moved with a graceful coordination that bespoke agility and power at the same time. This wasn't a man to take lightly. He took his eyes off him briefly as a siren went off in the opposite direction near the entrance. When he looked back the man was gone. Nothing else had changed; there was still a line going through security, but the man was gone. Irritated and agitated, he got up from his seat and looked everywhere but couldn't spot him. Well, at least he knew he hadn't gotten on the plane, since he didn't go through security. Kestrel decided to keep looking, and when he found him, he'd kill him.

But first, he needed to call Laurendeau. He dialed the number and waited for an answer. "There has been a complication with the assignment in Zaragoza. A man interfered with my work. He appears to be a professional and may have been sent to stop me."

Laurendeau, panicky, shouted into the phone. "My God, man, how did you let this happen?"

Kestrel took several deep breaths, intentionally audible to Laurendeau, followed by a long period of silence that finally got through to the physicist.

"Sorry. I didn't mean that. I don't know what to say."

Finally Kestrel said, "I'll take care of him."

Forty minutes later in the skies over the Pyrenees, Rafael asked, "Do you think he was at the airport?"

"I don't know, but if he was, he's sure I didn't get on the plane. Thanks to my former boss pulling a few strings with his Spanish counterpart, I was able bypass the main airport security check that's visible to everyone."

Even more surprising, Hunter thought, was that Deacon had managed to get him a DIA identification badge and a USNCB ID as well. A courier, carrying the new documents, had caught up with him at the airport and delivered them. He was now properly credentialed. How Deacon had arranged all of this in a matter of hours, Hunter had no idea.

"I'm sure the shooter will stay in Spain, looking to take me out before he does anything else. He can't afford to keep me around. He can't take the chance I'll mess up his work again."

The plane landed at eight-forty PM and Hunter got a rental car and drove them to CERN headquarters at the LHC site, where he was impressed with the security he saw everywhere. Deacon had told him they were going to ratchet it up in response to the killings. He was right. Hunter saw to it that Rafael got registered and was assigned an apartment in the secure zone for visiting scientists who were on temporary loan to the facility. Once he was sure Rafael was safe, he bid him farewell, accompanied by a promise that he would check on him later and keep him informed.

He checked into the Holiday Inn Express at Geneva International Airport. The next flight to Madrid wasn't until 9:30 the next morning.

Chapter 20

MADRID

Genevieve drove straight back to Madrid after leaving Hunter and Rafael. She hated to be alone, but knew that Hunter had to get Rafael safely to the scientist's housing complex at the collider. As she drove she thought about the warning text message and what she had gotten herself into.

Who would care If we find an old book or not? No, that's not the right question. Who would care if I were part of the search? Hunter hasn't gotten any warnings, just me.

As she approached the outer regions of Madrid, Genevieve thought the large black car behind her was driving a little too closely. She was nervous and still frightened about the text message. She knew it would be easy from now on to see anything that was even a little unusual as a threat. It was probably nothing. Still, she sensed she should be on her guard. She had been threatened after all. The black car seemed to fall back a bit and wasn't quite so close now. It was probably nothing.

The black car was still there as she moved over to the far right lane in anticipation of her exit to the right in a few miles. The black car stayed in its lane. Maybe it's just my imagination she thought. She found herself having to slow down in the right lane. Apparently most of the traffic was going to exit with her. She reached the exit and began to turn off. She saw the black car continue on down the highway. Good, she'd only been imagining it after all.

Relieved, Genevieve took a sip of the coffee she'd bought prior to starting her drive back to Madrid and her hotel. Her plan was to stay in the room until Hunter returned in the morning. She'd order room service. Thinking about that brought her around again to who might be threatening her. After ten minutes of fruitless speculation she had to admit she had no idea. It just didn't make any sense. She couldn't imagine herself as a threat to anyone. She tuned the car radio to a music station, settled back, and continued driving.

She was now on a road running parallel to the highway and another exit was coming up. She'd stayed in the right hand lane because the off ramp from the highway appeared to merge into her left lane. Traffic off the highway looked light with only a few cars taking this exit. The area was mostly rural with the city still up ahead. Then she saw it. The black car she had seen earlier exited and was now about five hundred yards ahead of her traveling in the same direction.

Her anxiety returned even as she told herself it was nothing but a coincidence. Besides, he was ahead of her and driving at a higher rate of speed and would soon be gone. She was proven right, when after a few miles he disappeared. Once again relieved, she told herself she was being silly and no one was after her. Ten minutes later she was approaching her next turn. This one would take her into the city and the safety of her hotel room. She planned to call Hunter as soon as she got in to tell him she was safe.

Just then her head snapped to the left at the same instant she heard a crash and her car slammed right toward the edge of the road. She fought for control and found herself on the shoulder with the right wheels riding on the grass while she went to her brakes and brought the car to a stop to the right of the pavement partially down a culvert. She sat stunned, gasping one large breath after another.

Frightened, she had no idea what had just happened. She look quickly back out onto the road to see if other cars were nearby when she saw a Volkswagen van pull off the road and park behind her. An elderly couple got out of the van and knocked on her window, shouting. Genevieve rolled down the window and heard the woman, clearly agitated, shout, "My God, are you all right? We saw it all. That car deliberately hit you. Are you all right dear? Should we call an ambulance?"

Genevieve tried to bring her hyperventilation under control. She could feel herself already beginning to get light headed.

"Put your head down, dear, you'll be all right," the concerned woman said.

Genevieve did, and in a minute she was feeling better. She unbuckled her seat belt, moved her arms and legs to make sure they worked, and tried to open the door. It was jammed. She lifted her legs over the center console, opened the passenger door, and stepped outside.

The man and woman put their arms around her while she walked back and forth for a moment.

"I'm all right. Nothing seems to be injured. What happened? Did you see it?" Genevieve asked, her breathing finally coming under control. "Did a car hit me?"

"Yes it did. And it was no accident either," her husband said. "He went to pass you and when he was along side, probably a little back in your blind spot, he jerked to the right and slammed into you and took off at high speed. I tried to get the license number but it all happened too fast."

Genevieve stopped walking. "What color was the car? Did you see?"

"Yes," the woman said. "It was black. And big."

Genevieve called Hunter as soon as she was back in the hotel room. The couple had driven her there and she'd called the car rental company to pick up the car. She told him what had happened and what the couple had seen.

"It was no accident, Hunter. I'm sure it was related to the text warning."

"All right, Genevieve, listen carefully. Stay in your room. Don't go out anywhere. Call room service for food and anything else you need. Don't let anyone in. I'll come straight there in the morning when I get in. Okay?"

"That was exactly my plan, Hunter. Get here as fast as you can."

A relieved Genevieve threw her arms around him the next morning when he came through the door. "Hunter, it was awful. I'm so glad you're here."

"Me too," agreed Hunter. They went out for lunch, much to Genevieve's relief after being 'locked up' in the room for so long. Again, they speculated on the likelihood that the road incident and the text were related and who might be responsible. They came to the same conclusions they'd reached earlier. They had no idea.

Hunter filled her in on the events since he'd left her yesterday.

Back at their hotel, Hunter decided that it was time to bring Shay up-to-date on recent developments. Waiting until two PM in order to assure he was in his office, Hunter set up a Skype call to Charlottesville and reported on the meeting with Alicia, the events at Zaragoza, his temporary link to DIA and Interpol, the warning to Genevieve, her road episode, and their commitment to the task at hand, namely finding and acquiring the book.

He told Shay they were going to leave the next day to travel to the Michael Servetus Institute at Villanueva de Sijena to interview its director.

That night the nightmare was back. *The explosion from the land mine flung Gary into the air, lifeless. No. Not Gary. Pieces of Gary flew upward. There's no blood. Why is there no blood? No blood, just pieces of body, an arm, a leg, a hand, Gary's head.*

"Hunter? Hunter! Are you all right?" A woman's voice and pounding on the door between their adjoining rooms. The handle turned and the door opened. Wearing a robe over her nightie, she peered in and saw him sitting up in bed, shaking, with his hands over his face. "Hunter. What's wrong?" He looked up still shaking and sweating heavily.

She sat on the bed and asked him again, "What's happening? Did you have a nightmare?"

Running his hands over his wet face and back through his hair, he stared at her with a ferocity she'd never seen. She backed up, afraid.

"Hunter, wake up." She took another step back and shouted again, "Hunter. Wake up, now!"

He shook his head, and saw her for the first time. Genevieve.

"Hunter, are you okay? Are you awake?"

He wiped his dripping face with the sheet. "Yes—yes, I'm okay. I'm awake. Give me a minute." He rolled the sheet back, and wearing his boxer shorts, got up, went to the bathroom, and splashed water in his face. He returned to the bed, where he sat on the edge.

She took his hand and asked again. "Did you have a nightmare?"

How could he answer her question? Yes, he'd had a nightmare. It certainly was that. But it was more too. It was the anger within him. It took over his body, as it always did. It urged him on and got him ready to fight.

What set off the land mine that killed Gary?   I don't know. It's become a blur, a fading memory.   I just don't know. Maybe I've got it wrong.   Maybe the anger isn't something that's gotten into me, maybe it's just who I am.

Finally, exhausted, he looked at her. "Yeah. It was a nightmare. I get them sometimes. I'm sorry I disturbed you. It's okay, really. I'll be all right."

Genevieve went back to her bed and lay awake for some time, thinking.

That was no ordinary nightmare.

When the time was right, she'd ask him about it.

Chapter 21

The next morning, the only reference either made to the nightmare was a casual comment from Hunter: "Sorry I woke you up last night. I'm normally not so noisy." Then he refocused on the events with Rafael and the assassin. "We have to tell Alicia about this. I called her and she's expecting us."

They arrived at Alicia's second floor walkup near the university twenty minutes later. Hunter told her about the assassination attempt, and the high security that surrounded Rafael now. Like Genevieve, she was most startled by the gunplay.

"I don't understand. Why did you have a gun? You're a scientist."

"Alicia, we've told you the truth. I'm, a scientist and Genevieve works at the Paris National Library. We've been hired to determine if the Servetus book exists, to authenticate it, and to make an honest offer to purchase it. I also occasionally work for the U.S. Defense Intelligence Agency and with Interpol. I've tried to help protect your brother, and I assure you I'll do whatever I can to find out who was responsible for the attempt on his life. For now, I don't think you or your father is in any danger. But if you notice anything suspicious, anything at all, please call me immediately or call the police."

"Please don't let anything happen to my brother. He's all I have," Alicia pleaded. "What are you going to do now?"

He told her they were going to the Institute to meet the director.

After leaving Alicia, he and Genevieve set out from Madrid. As they approached Zaragoza for the second time in two days, Hunter said, "A black Volvo sedan's been trailing us since we left Madrid. Let's stop for lunch when we get to Zaragoza and see if it shows up." Hunter couldn't help wondering if it had anything to do with the warning to Genevieve and the attack of the black car. Of course, it could also be Rafael's potential assassin. He sure as hell wanted to find out.

They pulled over for petrol and lunch at a restaurant/fuel station just off the highway near Zaragoza. It was a huge pull-off frequented by tour buses that used it as a lunch stop for their passengers. After a lunch of ham and cheese sandwiches, they continued on the A-131 toward Sarinena. The road became progressively worse, with potholes and cracks, so Hunter had to drive with an extreme measure of caution. It seemed to him that he was suddenly cautious about everything he did. They passed a beautiful lake and soon reached the town of Fraga. The GPS said they were now only 17 km from Villanueva de Sijena, birthplace of Michael Servetus and home of the Institute. The Volvo was nowhere to be seen.

They pulled into the village of Villanueva de Sijena about two-thirty PM. The village was in a verdant valley in the shadows of the Black Mountains and the snowcapped Pyrenees to the north. The GPS was surprisingly accurate, even providing the names of the streets in this small village. Hunter and Genevieve followed the guide through the town to the Institute, a cluster of buildings centered by the restored birth house of Servetus.

A receptionist greeted them and appeared a moment later with the director, who looked to be in his sixties. He seemed genuinely pleased to see them.

"Welcome, welcome, please come into my office so we can chat. I'm Cristobal Lazodelavega, director of the institute. Dulcinea, would you be so kind as to bring us some tea?"

The director's office was neat and tidy, like the man appeared to be. He immediately reminded Hunter of Edmund Gwenn who'd played Santa Claus in that old movie, Miracle on 34th Street. He had a cherubic smile, a full white beard, and twinkling eyes. He was also appropriately rotund. They liked him instantly.

Genevieve explained that their research centered on a paper they were coauthoring concerning why Servetus included his findings on pulmonary circulation in the *Christianismi Restitutio.*

"Wonderful," the director responded, beaming with delight. "Scholars have been pondering that one for a long time."

"Exactly," said Hunter. "We believe that Servetus knew what he was doing. We think his intent was to further emphasize the Church's views on the trinity, original sin, infant baptism, and other teachings were wrong. We know the Church backed Galen's incorrect interpretation of circulation because he'd proclaimed it had to be the work of a wonderful God. We believe that Servetus was saying to the Church, 'You were wrong about the circulation, and you're wrong about these theological points as well.'"

"Excellent," said the director, clapping his hands. "How can we at the Institute help you?"

"Well, could we have a tour of the institute for starters?" asked Genevieve.

"Yes, of course, my dear," said the director. "I'll show you myself. Here, take my arm."

They walked up the stairway from the ground floor to the first floor above. The walls contained several panels with explanations of Servetus's life and works.

"This floor contains the library, one of the most important rooms in the house for scholars such as yourselves," said the director. "We have one of the most comprehensive collections of documents, books, and photographs related to Michael Servetus and the Royal Monastery of Sijena. We also have computer facilities, including a printer and scanner."

Since the house was an old wine-producing facility, it was not surprising to find preserved wine and oil cisterns placed about. The house was also a museum, depicting life in the sixteenth century. Hunter and Genevieve saw a completely reproduced sixteenth century chemical laboratory and a pharmacy.

As they were walking to the nearby barn, which had been restored and was now used for exhibitions, Hunter asked the director if he had ever heard rumors of a fourth copy of the *Christianismi Restitutio*, besides the three known copies.

The director paused in his commentary, stopped walking, and gazed at Hunter for an uncomfortably long time before speaking. His angelic smile wavered. "No, I have never heard of such a book."

Hunter realized the director was clearly disturbed by the question. "It's just that we have heard rumors to that effect and we simply wondered if you had too," he said.

Dr. Lazodelavega repeated that he knew nothing of such a book. He looked thoughtful for a moment and then added, "But recently two others asked me the same question."

Genevieve smiled warmly. "May we ask who they were?"

"The first was a very unpleasant fellow from Madrid, a professor at the university. I believe his name was de la Peña. I told him what I told you; I know nothing about it."

"And the second?" asked Hunter.

"He was a science fiction writer, Kurt Walker— an American, currently living in Geneva, I think he said. He told me he was interested in ancient predictions and had some crazy idea that this fourth copy had a message from Servetus that dealt with future predictions or something equally crazy."

"Interesting," said Hunter. "Dr. Lazodelavega, could you suggest a hotel in town where we could stay for a while, since we'd like to avail ourselves of your wonderful library to do some of our research?"

Apparently pleased to be off the topic of the book, the director brightened up again and said that he would recommend they stay at Casa Helvetica. It was located downtown and had rooms and three modern apartments, which he understood were delightfully furnished and had excellent views of the mountains to the north.

After checking in at the hotel, they found a quaint restaurant in the main square called La Bodega. It was an old livery that had been restored by the owners into a fine restaurant. The original main dining room was decorated in stone and wood and had a massive fireplace.

"Your question about the book certainly got a rise out of the director," said Genevieve. "He was clearly being cautious about something." She put on a small pair of reading glasses he'd seen her use before to study the menu. To Hunter, this only added to her charm.

"I know," he agreed, "and I have a feeling that there was more to it than just his being reminded again—"

"Of the—oops." Genevieve clamped her hand over her mouth. "Sorry. I was going to say the unpleasant professor," Genevieve added anyway. "I just can't seem to stop myself. I am trying though, Hunter. I really am."

Hunter patted her hand. "It's okay. I'm getting used to it." Then he continued. "And if he did have the book—let's say Basilio gave it to him for the Institute—why isn't it displayed? Surely it'd be the crown jewel of the place. They'd probably even build a special room to display it. There'd be no reason for him to deny having it," said Hunter.

"How about tomorrow morning we go back to the Institute and check out the library holdings?" said Genevieve. "Maybe we could ask the director if he knows why the professor was interested or if he thought he was representing someone else."

Just then, Hunter saw a small red circle move to the center of his forehead in the reflection in Genevieve's reading glasses. He dove for the floor dragging her with him just as the glass-covered framed print behind him exploded. He could feel her heart pounding as he covered her with his body. He slid off her and said, "Over there, quick," pointing to a three-foot-high partition that separated the tables in front from the wait staff route to the kitchen. Hunter got Genevieve behind it and told her to stay down. He ran to the front wall, drawing his gun, and glanced out the window in the direction the shot must have come from, just in time to see the black Volvo pulling away, its tires squealing.

He ran back into the restaurant and Genevieve flew into his arms. She held him tightly while he smoothed back her hair. They stayed that way for a moment trying to calm each other. Hunter whispered in her ear, "Are you okay?"

Genevieve was still hyperventilating so Hunter continued to hold her. Finally, she broke their embrace. "Mon Dieu, what was that? What just happened?"

He pointed to the shattered print behind the table they'd been sitting at. "That was a sniper round meant for me. Remember that black Volvo I thought was following us to Zaragoza? The shooter was driving that car."

11

By now the other two couples in La Bodega's dining room, and the kitchen staff and manager had gathered around them, demanding to know what was going on. Hunter took over. He pointed to the owner. "Call the police." He asked if anyone was hurt. No one was. He told everyone they had to wait for the police, who would want to interview everyone concerning what had just occurred.

While they waited for the police to arrive, Hunter and Genevieve took a table. Genevieve was still shaking a little but said, "I'm going to be okay. Hunter, what's going on? Do you think it was the man who was after Rafael or, was it the guy who threatened me?"

"I don't know. It could be either of them. Maybe it's just one man, the same man responsible for both. I just don't know. I wanted Rafael's shooter to think I was still in Spain, so he would leave him alone. He might be the one trying to stop me, you, or both of us." Hunter made an instant decision.

"Genevieve, you've got to quit this now. Go back to Paris. It's too dangerous."

"I'm not leaving. I told you."

"I know you did, but things have changed. It's gotten worse. We might have two separate threats out there. I can take care of myself. Believe me, they're not as good as I am even if they think they are. But you have no defenses against them."

"Yes, I do."

"What?"

"You."

They were silent for a while. Hunter had no doubt he could deal with both of these threats if left on his own. He might even be able to do it with Genevieve still here. But could he take the risk with her life? He had no right to ask this of her. In fact, he wasn't asking her to. He'd just told her to go home, for the second time. Still, he had to admit she'd proven herself to be a real asset so far. But could he take the risk?

Genevieve interrupted his thoughts as if she'd been reading them. "Hunter, I won't get in your way. I know this is what you do, and believe me I'll let you do it. I can still be a big help to you in the search for the book. We both know that. And besides, I don't take well to threats."

Hunter looked at her, still thinking she should leave, but again admiring her toughness.

"Okay, for now, but we'll take it a day at a time and reevaluate the situation again later."

They returned to speculating on who might be behind the threat to Genevieve. As they had earlier, they drew a blank. It just didn't make any sense. On the other hand there were several possibilities to the threat to Hunter. First, and probably most likely, would be Rafael's would-be assassin, the one Hunter had apparently wounded. If he was the LHC killer, Hunter knew the man would try to get him so he could get on with his contracts. Presumably, Rafael wouldn't be the last physicist to be targeted.

Hunter continued. "We know Alfonso isn't happy with us. He probably knows we went to see the professor. If they have something going on, he may be having us followed to see what we're up to."

Genevieve rubbed her hands together. "Yes, but following is one thing; turning a killer loose is quite another."

"You're right. Somehow I just can't see Alfonso doing that. Maybe it's the professor, although I can't think of why. Although, if he is guilty of something—say, fudging his report, or worse, stealing the book if it was in the collection—he'd be very apprehensive of two characters like us snooping around."

"Characters like us? You may be a character, Dr. McCoy," Genevieve said with a returning sense of indignation, straightening her posture and assuming an imperious demeanor, "but I certainly am not."

Hunter smiled. "No, you're not a character." Taking both of her hands in his, he kissed her gently on the lips and said, "But you and your reflective glasses are a lifesaver." They continued to hold hands for a moment, gazing in each other's eyes, both sensing the beginning of something more.

It took two hours before the local police detective was satisfied that he had all the information he was going to get from Hunter and Genevieve. They'd been honest with the detective and told him that a black Volvo had been following them and the shooter was driving it. They also told the detective that they didn't know who the shooter was or why he did it.

Back at the hotel, they stopped at the doors to their adjoining rooms. As Genevieve turned to enter her room, he took her in his arms and held her close. She tilted her head upward and kissed him. Their embrace tightened, the threats and dangers of recent days beginning to fade. Slowly and reluctantly, she stepped back and they separated as Hunter opened her door. He walked her inside but left the lights off. In a voice soft as the moonlight filtering in through the window of the darkened room, Hunter said, "If you'd like I'll leave the door between our rooms unlocked, just as a precaution."

"No. Stay with me. Don't leave me." He took her in his arms and kissed her again and a slow heat grew between them rising to match the unleashed passion of the second kiss. His hands found the buttons on her blouse and began to undo them one by one. She undid the snap of her slacks and stepped out of them, turning her attention to removing Hunter's shirt. Soon they were naked and lying on the bed with only the moonlight playing over the curves of their bodies. In the end, the terror of the day slipped away along with any inhibitions that may have remained between them.

Chapter 22

THE MICHAEL SERVETUS INSTITUTE,
VILLANUEVA DE SIJENA

Over breakfast at the hotel, Hunter and Genevieve discussed the need for strict vigilance. From now on she would stay as close to him as possible. Although it was unspoken, they both knew that security wasn't the only reason they'd share one room and one bed from now on. After breakfast, they drove back to the Institute and spent an hour investigating the holdings of the library. As the director had said, the collection was extensive. If Hunter and Genevieve were actually interested in writing the paper they had described to Dr. Lazodelavega, this would be the place to start.

While they were examining the holdings, the director came in and beamed.

"Good morning. I hope you found the hotel to be acceptable."

"Oh it was, thank you for the recommendation," said Genevieve, "and La Bodega restaurant was—exciting."

A puzzled look came over the director. "Exciting?"

"You had to be there," added Hunter.

"I see," said the director, not really seeing at all. "Will you be staying for a while to use the library facilities? I can have an archivist assigned who can help you find what you need."

"No, thank you, Director, I'm afraid we need to get back to Madrid today for some other business," Hunter told him. "But we'll no doubt be coming back soon, and then we'd certainly appreciate the help." He paused. "By the way, you'd mentioned that unpleasant professor who asked you about that fourth copy of the *Christianismi Restitutio*. Was he by himself?"

"I only saw him. If someone else was with him, I didn't see him—or her." Again, the Director looked wary. "If you don't mind my asking, why are you so interested in this?"

"We just find it strange that while we're here doing research on the science and theology relationship in the *Christianismi Restitutio*, we hear a rumor about the existence of a fourth copy, and then you're visited by a professor and a science fiction writer asking about a fourth copy. It's just unusual, that's all."

"Yes—I suppose it is," mused director.

Their drive back to Madrid was uneventful. They didn't see the black Volvo again. Hunter felt sure they weren't being followed. They spent the time discussing what they knew. Hunter suggested that they should make another attempt to see the professor, whether he wanted to see them or not. They decided to drive straight to the University and show up at his office unannounced.

Genevieve was silent for a while as they drove and then said, "Hunter? I've been thinking. The attempt on Rafael's life seems clearly linked to the collider murders. The collider is in Geneva. Is it just a coincidence that the other man who asked the director about the book, the American science fiction writer, lives in Geneva?"

"I've been thinking about that too. A science fiction writer who is looking for the fourth copy because it has a message from Servetus referring to predictions? It doesn't sound right. The Geneva connection could just be a coincidence, but most cops aren't comfortable with coincidences, and neither am I."

When they pulled up, they were surprised to see yellow crime scene tape surrounding the campus building, and police cars and officers on the scene. A small crowd of mostly students had gathered around, talking animatedly to each other.

They walked up to a uniformed officer behind a roped-off area and asked what happened.

"I'm sorry folks, you'll have to step back. This is a homicide investigation."

"Homicide? Who was killed?" asked Hunter.

"A professor, apparently. You'll have to step back please"

"But we had an appointment with Professor de la Peña"

"Well I'm afraid it's been cancelled, just like the professor."

"He was the one killed?"

"Yes."

They stepped back and joined the crowd of students.

"Hunter, this is starting to get scary," Genevieve whispered. "We're supposedly only trying to find and authenticate a book. In the meantime, we're being followed, shot at, threatened by a hit man or someone else, and now the professor who cataloged the collection is dead?"

"Something's going on, all right. Let's talk to the investigating officer."

Hunter approached the policeman at the tape again. "I'd like to talk to the man in charge. I might have some relevant information."

"What kind of information?" asked the officer, now beginning to show more interest in Hunter.

"Information that the investigator-in-charge will find useful," said Hunter. He wanted the man's cooperation, but didn't want to go into details with him here.

The officer pondered this for a moment, then went into the building and returned with the "man" in charge, who turned out to be an attractive, tall dark-haired woman. She wore black slacks, a white blouse, and a tan blazer. The shield on a cord around her neck identified her as an inspector with the National Police.

"I'm Inspector Lupita Delgado of the Policia Nacional. I'm in charge of this investigation. Who are you?"

"Inspector, my name is Hunter McCoy, and this is Genevieve Swift. We came here to see Professor de la Peña. We just got into town."

The inspector eyed them both and had her assistant write their names down in a notebook.

Unsmiling, she asked, "And what do you know about this?"

"We had an appointment with the professor two days ago. He originally agreed to see us. But when we arrived, his secretary said he'd changed his mind and wouldn't meet with us after all. One of his graduate students suggested that he'd recently visited the Michael Servetus Institute in Villanueva de Sijena, and since we're doing some research on Servetus, we drove up there to see the Institute. The director remembered meeting the professor.

"Also, someone driving a black Volvo sedan followed us to the Institute and tried to kill us last night. We returned today to try again to see the professor, and found this situation."

Inspector Delgado's assistant had furiously tried to write it all down.

The inspector was immediately alert. "Someone tried to kill you last night?"

"That's right. We gave a complete statement to the local police. It should be on file by now," Hunter told her.

The inspector contemplated this for a moment. "Getting back to my case," Delgado said, "Why would you come back if you were already told that he wouldn't see you?"

"We thought if we caught him by surprise, he'd at least give us a few minutes," said Hunter.

"May I see some identification, please?"

Hunter and Genevieve produced passports. Delgado examined them and asked where they were staying. They told her and she said, "Wait here."

Taking their passports, Delgado went to a police van that was parked near the scene and disappeared inside. Fifteen minutes later she emerged and waved them over. The inspector said that she had done a background check on both of them and that they were indeed who and what they said they were.

"I'm relieved to know I'm who I think I am," said Genevieve, somewhat peevishly.

"Ms. Swift," Inspector Delgado said, unsmiling, "in my business, the police can make mistakes and criminals can go free by taking people at their word. A little checking is prudent and wise. No offense was intended. Your credentials are impeccable and your background is clean."

She turned to Hunter. "You're a professor at the medical school in Virginia. You've also worked for the United States Department of Defense as an intelligence agent, and you've worked with Interpol. I wasn't able to access any information about what you did for them. It seems it was classified."

"You did do a thorough check in a short time, Inspector," said Hunter.

"Yes, I did. But now what I'd like to know is, are you on official business in my country?"

Hunter had a feeling that Delgado was a good cop and that he should trust her as long as nothing she did impeded his activities. She might actually be of benefit to them in their search for the book and maybe even in the collider business. He followed his instincts and decided to take her into their confidence. He told her about their business for Shay Blackwell, the letter, their visits to the Mendez family, and the link to the professor and the collection. He also told her about the attempt on Rafael's life and how it was probably linked to the collider murders. He informed her that he was now seconded to DIA and Interpol and showed her his credentials.

Delgado considered the information and thanked him for telling her and asked him to keep her informed if he learned anything related to her murder case.

They returned to the Bausa Hotel, where Scarlet, following Hunter's instructions, had booked one room for them. Hunter chuckled as he imagined her eyebrows raising after he told her that they would be sharing one room from now on in the interest of safety. After lunch they used their laptops and the room's Wi-Fi network to search for background material on the professor, Alfonso, Alicia, Rafael, and Dr. Lazodelavega. Sometimes these fishing expeditions yielded crucial information. Later, as they were ready to head downstairs to dinner at the restaurant, Hunter's cell phone rang. It was Alicia Mendez.

"Hunter, I talked with Rafael, and he told me how you helped him. Thank you so much for watching out for him. He appreciated the way you handled the situation. He's doing fine and loves his work. It's really all he ever cared about—that, and me. He says the level of security is extremely high and that he feels safe in the compound with the other scientists.

"I found something that might be of interest to you. I hadn't thought about this earlier, but my grandfather kept a diary. It was in the castle library along with his other papers. I'd skimmed through it before, right after his death, and I didn't recall there being anything about a book in it. But since your visit the other day, I've reread it in detail, and while there are still no references to this book, there are some references to George Blackwell. If you would like to see the diary, you can."

Hunter looked up at Genevieve and raised his eyebrows. "Thank you, Alicia, we certainly would like to see your grandfather's diary."

Genevieve had a look of puzzlement and anticipation on her face.

"Would tomorrow morning be all right? We could be there by ten."

"Yes, that would be fine. I'll meet you at the house."

After dinner they walked for a while through a nearby park. Couples were walking hand in hand, and music came from somewhere above the storefronts where most Madridians lived in the city. As they walked Genevieve took his hand and said, "Tell me about yourself, Hunter. I don't even know if you have any family. After all, it's only fair. You have a complete dossier on me, with who knows how many secrets about my life in it, and I don't know anything about you, other than that you're a professor, you're some kind of agent, and you have talents that make an important man like Shay Blackwell trust you unconditionally. Come on now, let's sit over there on that bench and you can give me the scoop."

They sat, and Hunter said, "There's not a lot to tell." He explained about growing up in upper Michigan near Lake Superior. He described how his dad had raised him after his mother died and how he and his dad worked to get him through college with a degree in biology. He referred briefly to his stint in the Marine Corps followed by four years with the Defense Intelligence Agency. He didn't supply any details but simply said that the lure of science brought him to graduate school and to his present career as a medical school professor.

"How did you happen to get this job with Mr. Blackwell?"

Hunter wondered how much to tell her but finally decided she had a right to know this. "Shay was planning to buy a company in Texas that makes components for satellites. The company was privately held and totally owned by a guy named Tommy Traggert. Blackwell's auditors were still working on the books when his investigators uncovered some shady dealings between Traggert's firm and a small health insurance broker he was using to provide coverage for his employees, some two hundred and fifty people. Shay asked me to look into it, find out the extent of any illegal practices that were going on, and come up with a way to correct it."

"So how did that go?"

Hunter chuckled as he remembered it. "After considerable digging, I was able to find out that the owner of the brokerage—with Traggert's full knowledge and cooperation—was contracting with a major insurance company for coverage, but claiming to the employees that the premiums were higher than they actually were. The employees were led to believe that the company was paying the major portion of the premium, and that their portion, while still significant, was considerably smaller than it would be otherwise, and they should be thankful for that. In reality they were paying for almost the entire premium, thereby saving Traggert's company considerable money while still claiming to provide first-rate health insurance for his employees. The broker was paid handsomely for his part in this deception."

"Then what?"

"Shay wasn't happy about this owner trying to sell him a business while keeping illegal activities from him.

So he asked me to correct the situation in a most interesting way."

"What did you do?"

"I'll admit that I technically did break the law. I posed as a government agent. I drove the owner of the brokerage to Traggert's home. I confronted them with all of the evidence that the 'Agency' had collected that showed their duplicity in the fraudulent scheme to extort money from the employees.

"Blackwell's auditors had calculated just how much additional money each employee had actually paid over the years for their coverage. I gave the two men a choice. They could quietly write out a check to each employee for the additional amount plus interest and refer to it as a rebate for their good claims history, or the FBI would be more than happy to prosecute them to the full extent of the law for extortion, embezzlement, and fraud."

"Wow. Obviously they chose to pay up?" said Genevieve.

"Oh yeah." Hunter grinned. "This was actually a pretty good outcome for Blackwell, because now he could buy the company for a fair price and turn it around without the burden of the negative publicity of the potential scandal."

Genevieve was quiet for a moment. Then she asked about his dad, and he told her that he still lived in Michigan and that he visited him whenever he could. He didn't tell her about the cabin on the big lake. He didn't normally talk to anyone about his personal life and didn't talk about the cabin at all. It just seemed to be the safest thing he could do for his father. Besides, his dad had a right to his privacy, and Hunter wouldn't compromise that. Even though it appeared that she really wanted to know and wasn't just being polite, he continued to keep that part of his life secret. Her question made him think about the plans for the sunroom, and how his dad was going to have to wait a little longer before they could start on it, although he was certain his dad was drawing up plans even now.

Genevieve twirled her hair with her fingers. "No women in your life, Hunter?   Surely there must be someone."

He paused before answering.   "There was, but it—it didn't work out."

Genevieve nodded, accepting that was all he was prepared to say.

As they walked back to the hotel, they were quiet until they got to their room where Hunter was forced to admit that Scarlet had made her only mistake up to now. They didn't need two beds.

The next morning they arrived at the castle house, as they now called it, promptly at ten. Alicia let them in and took them to the castle library, where she opened a drawer in Basilio's large desk and produced a black leatherbound diary with a zipper. The name Basilio Diego Mendez was embossed in gold leaf on the front.

"As I said on the phone, I've been through it before and there is no reference to the book you're talking about. But he did mention George Blackwell."

"I'm not surprised," said Hunter. "They knew each other in Madrid during the war, when George was an undersecretary in the United States Embassy until he returned to the States in 1945."

"Here, I'll show you the reference." She opened the diary to the pertinent page and they found that George Blackwell apparently returned to Madrid on March 2, 1947 for a short time.

Genevieve said, "Look at that date! It's exactly the same date—"

"As the postmark on the unopened letter to George Blackwell from Basilio Mendez," they both said in unison.

"Of course. That's why the letter was unopened," said Genevieve. "They crossed in transit."

"Sure," said Hunter, "that explains it. When George Blackwell eventually got back to America, he'd already met with Basilio and presumably had already been told, during their visit, all that was in the letter. He probably just never saw any need to—"

"Open it," finished Genevieve.

Hunter asked Alicia if she could think of anywhere that her grandfather might have kept the book, if it indeed existed. Did he visit other collectors, or have friends who were collectors?

"I have no idea."

"What the hell are you doing back here?" roared Alfonso Mendez as he stormed into the room, his face an angry, ruddy hue. "This has got to stop. This is my home, and I won't have it. We have nothing for you. That damned book doesn't exist. I want you out of here now, and if you come back again, I'll have the law and the dogs on you. Now get out!"

Genevieve and Alicia rolled their eyes at each other as they watched the irate Alfonso leave the room.

They thanked Alicia at the front door and left.

On the drive into the city, Genevieve said to Hunter, "Try this on for size. Maybe de la Peña somehow learned of the existence of the book during his assessment. Maybe Basilio kept records along with the artifacts, records that we never got to examine, records that described the book. Maybe de la Peña saw the records but never actually found the book itself. Let's say Basilio kept it somewhere else. Maybe the professor told Alfonso about it and offered to use his talents to find it in return for a hefty cut of the profits from any sale it might generate."

"Could be," said Hunter. "Or maybe Alfonso had the book all along and used the professor to determine its value. Since it wouldn't show up in the inheritance list after Basilio's death—"

"It couldn't be taxed," said Genevieve. "But why would any of this lead Alfonso to kill the professor, if that's where we're going with this speculation?"

Hunter agreed. "That's the right question."

"Maybe the professor threatened to go to the police or the taxing authorities and tell them about it unless he was paid off. Alfonso doesn't strike me as someone who would submit to extortion very well."

Hunter called Delgado and filled her in on their activities and offered their speculations on Alfonso and the late Professor de la Peña. She wouldn't comment on their speculation but did offer some new information on Basilio's death.

"We got something from searching the professor's office safe, McCoy, an appointment calendar, older than the one on his desk. It showed the professor was scheduled to see Basilio Mendez, at the castle, on the day he died. We've since gathered corroborating evidence from Basilio's housekeeper that he actually showed up shortly before the old man fell off that ladder. The professor had opportunity and motive, it's possible he shook Basilio Mendez off that ladder and his death wasn't an accident after all. If he weren't already dead, the professor would certainly be, what you Americans call a 'person of interest' in Basilio's death."

Chapter 23

Hunter and Genevieve made no progress in trying to figure out why the page in Basilio's diary for the date he'd met with Lazodelavega had been removed. Beyond their earlier speculations, they came up with nothing,

"It's almost noon, Hunter, how about we go down to lunch in the hotel restaurant?"

Hunter grabbed his jacket. "Sounds good to me. Let's go."

They were on the fifth floor and the elevator door opened immediately on the first button-push. Surprisingly, they had the car to themselves as they started their descent. Suddenly the car stopped between the third and fourth floor.

"What the hell?" Hunter pushed the Lobby button again and waited. The car wouldn't move. Just then they heard a hissing noise.

Hunter, immediately on alert scanned the walls, floor and ceiling and all corners of the elevator car. Nothing.

"Hunter, what's going on?" Panic in her voice now. "Why aren't we moving?"

Hunter tried the emergency phone. Nothing. It either wasn't connected or had been cut. He looked up. The elevator car was very modern and had a grid-like ceiling fixture designed to provide indirect lighting. He saw no opening.

The hissing continued.

"Hunter, I'm scared." More panic in her voice.

"Stay calm. We'll get out of here."

The hissing continued. Was some kind of gas being released? He had to find it soon or get them out of here fast.

He grabbed the grid-like lighting fixture above and tried to pull it free reasoning there had to be an access to the car through the roof. It wouldn't budge. He looked around for something, anything to pry it loose. Handrails circled the car. He tried to pull one free. Again, it was firmly fixed.

"Genevieve, listen to me. Call the hotel desk on my cell phone. It's in the directory. Tell them where we are. I have an idea."

She fumbled with the phone trying to comply.

Hunter grabbed the ceiling grid with both hands and lifted his feet of the floor and pushed off the wall with all his might. The grid loosened a little. He did it again, loosening it more. He kept trying as he heard Genevieve finally get through to the desk.

"We need help. Were stuck in the elevator. You have to get us out now. Please hurry."

Finally, the grid came lose and pulled free from the ceiling and Hunter crashed to the floor. He looked up and saw what he'd hoped was there, an access door.

Oh no, he thought. *No handle.*

It appeared to be held in place by four roughened twist bolts in each corner. Reaching overhead as high as he could, he attempted to twist one. It didn't move. He tried another. This one loosened a little and he kept at it. It was unscrewing. He got it out and started on another. That one also loosened and he removed it. After he removed the third bolt he returned to the first one. It still wouldn't move. Then he saw the problem. Unlike the other three, it was smooth and he couldn't get any purchase on it. He needed some traction.

"Genevieve, have you got a nail file, or emery board?" Moving sluggishly as if she were succumbing to the unknown ether, she nodded her head and fumbled in her purse and came up with an emery board. Hunter took it and wrapped it around the bolt with the abrasive side in. He pressed as tightly as he could with his thumb and forefinger and twisted. Nothing. He tried again. This time he felt it move. He tried again. Yes. It was definitely turning. He removed the emery board and was able to unscrew the last bolt with his fingers alone. When it was out he slammed the access panel with his fist and the door opened to the rush of fresh air into the car. The effect on both of them was instantaneous. They took huge gulps of fresh air, realizing for the first time that they'd been deliberately breathing as shallowly as they could to avoid inhaling whatever was coming into the car.

Hunter immediately grabbed the opening above and heaved himself upward. Then he saw it. Duct- taped to the top of the car was an aerosol can of harmless compressed air rigged to slowly release its contents into the car along with its hissing sound. But what he saw next to it was anything but harmless.

A half-pound of plastic explosive was pressed onto the surface. A blasting cap was pressed into it. The cap was connected to a wired cell phone that would, no doubt, detonate the instant it received a call from an outside phone somewhere. Hunter immediately pulled the blasting cap from the plastic explosive and dropped it along with the wired cell phone over the side of the car and let it drop to the bottom of the shaft to get it as far away from the explosive as possible. Ten seconds later he heard the muffled explosion of the blasting cap several floors below them. The explosive didn't respond.

Hunter dropped back and gathered Genevieve in his arms just as the car started to move upward. It stopped at the fourth floor and the door opened and they quickly emerged to find the hotel staff waiting for them.

"I ask you again, McCoy. Is the search for this book worth it?"

Inspector Delgado, Hunter and Genevieve were sitting in the hotel lobby. Delgado had arrived faster than Hunter had thought possible after he'd called. It turned out she was already in the area on other police business.

"The elevator is now a crime-scene. We'll check the air canister for prints and the plastic explosive as well. Leave this to us. Don't try to investigate this on your own." Then looking directly at Hunter, she said, "Do you hear me, McCoy? This is my jurisdiction."

Hunter hesitated briefly before answering. "Yes, Inspector, I understand."

"Either someone seriously doesn't want you looking for this book, or the collider killer sees you as a threat and wants you out of his way. Either way, I don't see him stopping as long as you're around. Maybe the best thing for you is to quit this and return to the United States." Then she turned to Genevieve. "And you, Ms. Swift, would be much safer back in Paris at your job at the National Library. My advice is that you both should go and leave it to us and Interpol to catch this guy."

Hunter agreed, at least as far as Genevieve was concerned. He had absolutely no intention of quitting himself. "Genevieve, the inspector is right. This has become way too dangerous for you. After today's threat, you must go back to Paris. When I find the book, I'll bring it to you for authentication. It's the only reasonable thing to do."

Hunter could see she was thinking it over seriously for the first time.

"Tell you what," she said. "We'll talk about it later."

Kestrel was confused. He'd dialed the remote phone and waited for the explosion. He absolutely should have heard it. He was just across the street He didn't know how it could have failed. He was an expert at all forms of death including remote explosions using plastic explosives. The man should be dead by now. He'd seen him and the girl step into the elevator on the fifth floor from his recessed redoubt three doors down from the man's room at the hotel. Once the elevator door closed and they were between floors he pressed the remote he'd rigged up to the elevator circuit breaker in the basement. It worked beautifully. The elevator stopped between the third and fourth floors. This gave him plenty of time to exit the building and take up his position across the street. He admitted to himself that he'd waited a little longer than he should have before dialing the detonator cell phone, but then he'd wanted the man to panic before he killed him thinking he was being gassed. He couldn't just kill him without taking a little revenge for wounding him. But how could it not have exploded? Later, when he saw the police arrive, he knew it was best to retreat.

He called Laurendeau but refrained from telling him about his failed attempt to kill the man in the elevator.

"I know exactly where he is and he'll be eliminated today," Kestrel told Laurendeau.

Laurendeau wasn't satisfied. "How can you be sure? If he's a professional, won't he be harder to stop?"

"He would be except he's preoccupied with the search for some old book anyway."

"An old book?" What are you talking about?"

"When I was tailing Mendez, I remotely activated his cell phone microphone with some specialized equipment I have and eavesdropped on a conversation between Mendez, the man and a woman he was with. I did this at a restaurant in Zaragoza the day the man interfered with the Mendez hit. It's a sophisticated system that lets me pick up and record any nearby conversation. Their phones don't even have to be on."

Laurendeau was momentarily confused, and then, his voice rising, said, "The book, man, what was the name of the book he's looking for?"

Kestrel took out his pocket recorder and played back the recording and got the information he needed. "The man's name is Hunter McCoy. He claims he's an American scientist and he's traveling with a woman, Genevieve Swift, from the National Library in Paris. They're looking for a book called the *Christianismi Restitutio* by Michael Servetus. He claims it's a rare unknown fourth copy. Don't worry. I'll take care of the man and the woman too."

Laurendeau was momentarily paralyzed.

"No! No! Don't kill them," shouted Laurendeau. "I can't believe it. This is too good to be true. You can't hurt them. Do you understand? Don't hurt them. Follow them. I have to have that book. Do you hear me? I have to have that book. Once they lead you to it, get it from them and bring it immediately to me. After that, you can do what you want with them. If you get me that book your commission will be doubled."

Chapter 24

Apparently it really does rain in Spain, and heavily. With the sky completely overcast it looked like it was going to continue all day. The gray day was a perfect reflection of their moods. Being a murder target definitely sours your outlook. After all they'd been through they were still no closer to finding the book.

They decided to return to the Institute and re-interview Dr. Lazodelavega. On the trip back they were on the lookout for the black Volvo or anything else out of the ordinary, but as far as Hunter could detect, no one was following them. Either whoever it was had changed cars, gotten better at avoiding detection, or didn't like to drive in the rain.

They reached the Institute later that morning and found a police car out in front with its roof lights cycling. The rain had let up a little. They parked the Mercedes and went inside, where it was apparent that whatever had happened, must have happened in the director's office. Lazodelavega was outside his office door, gesturing to a policeman who was busy taking notes. Through the open door Hunter and Genevieve could see that his office had been ransacked.

"Director, what's happened?" asked Genevieve.

A dejected Lazodelavega turned glumly to look at them. "Oh, hello. It's unbelievable. Someone broke into my office and made a mess of things. It must have happened overnight. This is the way I found it when I came in this morning."

The man looked distressed and depressed, in contrast to his usual cheery self.

The policeman said, "Director, we have what we need for now. Don't touch anything. We'll dust for fingerprints before we go and contact you later this afternoon or tomorrow." Closing his notebook and pocketing it, he nodded to Hunter and Genevieve on his way out.

"What a mess," said the director, shaking his head. "Off hand, I can't see that anything has been taken. It seems it was just vandalism. Why would anyone do such a thing?"

"Director, could we find a place to sit? We have something to tell you that may or may not have something to do with this break-in," said Hunter.

They retired to a small back room that served as the mailroom and the coffee room. There was a table in the middle with chairs around it.

They sat down and Hunter told the director that they hadn't been entirely forthcoming with him when they'd met two days before. He told him about George and Shay Blackwell, about the Blackwell and Basilio Mendez connection, the apparently missing fourth copy of the *Christianismi Restitutio*, and about the black Volvo and the murder of Professor de la Peña. Then he told him about the attempt on Rafael's life and the shooting in La Bodega restaurant. As he spoke Lazodelavega wrung his hands and looked increasingly alarmed.

"We don't know," Hunter concluded, "but perhaps whoever was following us, for whatever reason, may also be looking for this book. Maybe he thinks it's here. If that's the case, he may be back to search the rest of the place. Hopefully the police will provide some surveillance for the Institute for a while."

The director rubbed his hand across his face as he assimilated this information. When he finally did speak, he said that he needed to think about what they'd just told him. He would like to join them for dinner that evening, if possible. "Then it will be my turn. I may have something to share with you."

Later that afternoon the police from the local Guardia National come back and Hunter watched them do a remarkably good job of investigating the break-in. If anything, they were even more thorough than they had been investigating the shooting in the restaurant. He suspected that the Institute was an important part of the little town's identity and that the police took a dim view of this "desecration." They thoroughly canvassed the neighborhood, asking if anyone had seen anything unusual during the night or early in the morning at the Institute. They interviewed all of the staff to see if they'd noticed that anything had been disturbed or missing. They had the director's secretary examine his office to see if she could identify anything missing.

Hunter and Genevieve didn't see the director again until that evening, when they met for dinner at Casa Helvetica. Their table was in the corner, at the director's request, and they kept their voices low. He told them a remarkable story.

"Six months ago I received an invitation from Señor Basilio Diego Mendez in which he asked me to visit him at his ancestral home in Madrid. He said he had some very important business to discuss with me. When I arrived, Señor Mendez told me that age had caused him to begin thinking about the possibility of declining health. He expressed that he was reasonably healthy then, but that he wasn't getting any younger and he had decided that it was time to make arrangements for the eventual disposition of a rare and historic artifact.

"He explained that he had an undocumented fourth copy of the *Christianismi Restitutio* by Michael Servetus. Further, he told me that next year he would donate it to the Institute. I was not told where the book was currently located. Further, he instructed me to say nothing of the existence of the book or of these arrangements, or he would find another final resting place for the manuscript. As far as I knew, the only living persons who knew of the existence of the book were Basilio Mendez and myself. I have never repeated this to anyone, until now. I figured that it was all right to tell you since you have a legitimate reason to know, and besides, this year the book will somehow be transferred to the Institute in accordance with his wishes. I can only assume that arrangements have been made, probably in Basilio's will."

After talking about it for a while, the three of them concluded that the inquiries Hunter and Genevieve had been making about the book had probably stirred the pot, so others had heard about the book and were trying to get it. They made a list of all those who would have heard of the book by now: Shay Blackwell, Scarlet, Hunter and Genevieve, Inspector Delgado, the director, Alfonso, Alicia and Rafael Mendez, the late Professor de la Peña, Kurt Walker, and possibly other people unknown to them. The list was growing.

The three of them agreed to meet in the morning in the coffee room before Hunter and Genevieve returned to Madrid.

Hunter and Genevieve drove to their hotel, and Hunter phoned Shay to bring him up to date on their latest findings while Genevieve showered.

When she came out of the bathroom, her hair was toweled dry and clung to her neck in loose curls. Her face had a rosy glow from the hot water. The black nightgown with a sheer robe thrown over it did little to hide her curvaceous figure.

Hunter looked up and did a double take. "Wow, you sure know how to make a guy forget about searching for a silly book. Where's the long nightshirt you wore last night?"

"Oh that. I checked out the boutique in the hotel. It had some great clothes. So I bought this. I thought after all we've been through, it might be, I don't know, uplifting."

"It's certainly lifting something up," Hunter said with a knowing smile as he slowly removed her robe and gown. Before long the search for the book and the unknown threat to their lives were distant memories.

In the morning, they drove over to the Institute for their early meeting with the director. Hunter felt fulfilled, almost complete, again. Not since Annie had he felt this way about a woman. He wasn't sure where this was going, but he knew that it felt right.

When they arrived, the secretary told them that the director hadn't come in yet. This was unusual, as he was always the first one to arrive at the Institute every day. He usually put on the first pot of coffee. Hunter's radar began pinging and he suggested she call his house and see what was holding him up. She did, but got no answer.

"I don't like this," he muttered to Genevieve.

The secretary gave them the address of the director's house. When they got there no one answered the doorbell or responded to his rapping on the door.

Hunter walked around the modest house looking in windows, most of which had the blinds drawn, and could see nothing unusual. Returning to the front door, he knocked again then pounded as loud as he could. Still nothing. Figuring he had nothing to lose, he used a large rock from the flowerbed beside the front step to smash the window beside the front door. He reached in and opened it. The house had been ransacked.

Un-holstering his berretta, he said, "Genevieve, call the police and stay back." He began a search of the house for the director. He found nothing, but could see that whoever had torn up the place had been thorough: drawers spilled, books pulled off shelves, furniture overturned, kitchen cabinets opened. Someone had clearly been looking for something.

Still, there was no sign of the director. Looking out a kitchen window at the rear of the house, Hunter could see a detached two-car garage. With Genevieve close at his heels now, they approached the small garage door and Hunter slowly opened it with his weapon ready. They weren't ready for what they saw.

Tied to a chair, quite dead with a single bullet through his forehead, was Director Lazodelavega, his face twisted in agony.

"Oh my God," breathed Genevieve as she looked away. "Oh my God— is he—"

"Yes. He's dead," whispered Hunter. "Stay back." He searched the garage. The place was empty. Whoever had done this was gone.

Genevieve, almost unable to speak, stammered, "H— hunter, look at his hands."

Hunter did and saw that his fingers all appeared to have been crushed by something. Then he noticed a towel on the dead man's lap with something obviously under it. He used the barrel of his gun to lift the towel and there, placed almost reverently on Lazodelavega's thigh, was the medieval thumbscrew they had seen earlier in Mendez Castle.

Four hours later, after dealing with the police and Lazodelavega's distraught secretary, Hunter and Genevieve were back at their hotel room. Neither felt like eating, Hunter realized he was unusually quiet and he could see that Genevieve was beginning to notice too. She suggested, although they weren't hungry, having dinner might take their minds of the horrific scene they'd witnessed earlier in the garage.

La Bodega, where Hunter had almost been killed, didn't seem like a good idea to her so she told him she'd find another restaurant. He gave here an "okay," without much enthusiasm.   They drove around and found the restaurant, La Cerdera.   It served a traditional Catalan menu, was quite attractive inside, and the food was very good.

He knew Genevieve was concerned by his silence but he couldn't help it. He tried opening up a little over dinner but was still unusually quiet. Finally, she put her knife and fork down and her palms on the table, and looked directly at him. "Are you all right?"

He sighed and looked up, nodding his head. "I'll be okay. I just keep thinking what a nice man he was and what a horrible way to die. No one should have to go through that."

Genevieve took his hand and was surprised to find that she was comforting him instead of the other way around. "I know, I can't get it out of my mind either. I hope I can sleep tonight."

Hunter withdrew his hand, made two fists, and then slowly opened them and put his hands palms down on the table.

"What is it," asked Genevieve, startled by his sudden move.

Hunter signaled the waiter and ordered a second glass of wine for each of them. Sensing he was going to open up, Genevieve remained silent and waited until the wine arrived.

Hunter puffed out his cheeks and slowly exhaled. He told her about the operation in Pakistan. How it was a DIA operation and he was in charge of the black ops squad. How his brother had died in the land mine explosion. He told her the nightmares began shortly after that and occurred intermittently. He told her he couldn't help feeling like he'd let Gary down. He wasn't there when his brother had needed him. Had he let the director down too?

He knew it was irrational on one level but still, there it was. He couldn't get past it. He recognized that the guilt over not protecting Gary, and now maybe Lazodelavega, was one thing, but the anger—the *dark thing*—that boiled to the surface when someone he cared for was threatened, that was a new phenomenon.

That night they were both glad they were sharing one room.

Chapter 25

The Rhône River flowing past Arnaud Laurendeau's Geneva apartment gave most of the building's tenants the kind of comfort and pleasure that water views typically elicit in those who could afford them. The steady flow of the water almost forced one to reflect on the direction and flow of one's own life. But today Arnaud Laurendeau had no need for such contemplation as he stared down at the river.

He was both pleased and displeased with the information Kestrel had extracted from the director before killing him. Kurt Walker had been correct. Lazodelavega had been lying when he'd said earlier that he knew nothing of a fourth copy of the *Christianismi Restitutio*. Not only did the man know about the book, but also a Spanish count, Basilio Diego Mendez, was scheduled to donate the manuscript to his Institute sometime this year. Lazodelavega had also confirmed what they'd already learned from Kestrel, that Hunter McCoy and the woman, Genevieve Swift, were searching for the book as well. A man named Shay Blackwell had hired them.

When Kestrel offered to explain how he got the man to talk, Laurendeau declined. He knew Kestrel was a psychopath who thoroughly enjoyed his work. Still, he preferred to be kept in the dark on his more deviant

activities.   Not that Laurendeau was squeamish himself.
He wasn't troubled in the least by the murders he and his
group had ordered Kestrel to perform.   They were
necessary.   Anyone could see that.   But, he didn't enjoy it
the same way Kestrel did.   For Laurendeau the murders of
the young physicists would protect the world from the
unchecked consequences of the collider discoveries.   In
fact, Laurendeau had come to believe it was his Godly
mission to sabotage the LHC.

If he could only get his hands on the Servetus book and
its supposed message predicting the dangers of the
experiments, he could prove it as well.   He'd show those
supercilious bastards at the collider and his former
colleagues who now treated him with derision, that he'd
been right all along.   He was becoming thoroughly
comfortable with his divine mission.   After all, he believed
the Bible was full of justified killings and murders.

He'd ended the phone conversation with Kestrel by
telling him that, for now at least, his primary function was
to find the book.   If he could do it on his own, okay.
However, he was not to interfere with McCoy's search for
the book.   He suggested that Kestrel stay close to McCoy
and the girl, so if they found it, he could move in and take
it.

Laurendeau poured himself a cognac and gazed out
over the river below.   In spite of ordering Kestrel to try to
get the book, he had begun to have doubts whether the
Servetus message was going to be all he'd hoped.   Even if
it were found, would it deliver the punch he needed?   Was
it really even possible that Servetus wrote about the collider
way back in the sixteenth century?

Laurendeau called Walker and told him that the
website he'd told him about earlier—the one with the
reference to the Servetus message— was no longer
available.

"Really?   Let me try."

Laurendeau waited while Walker presumably went online to find the site.

After a few minutes, Walker came back on the line. "You're right. That's strange. I wonder why it was pulled down?"

"You're sure it was really there?" Laurendeau asked with suspicion.

"It was there. I gave you the printout with the URL printed on it," said Walker, somewhat indignantly. "I sure didn't make it up."

Laurendeau tried to suppress his anger. "What about the guy who reported having read the message? What was his name? Renaldo something. You said he read it sometime in the eighteen century. Can we check on him? The Internet must have something on him."

"His name was Renaldo Quintero. The website didn't say anything about him. Just that he was a scholar."

"Kurt, you're better at this stuff than I am. Get on your computer and scour it for information on this guy. Maybe he wrote something about the Servetus message that's buried in an archive somewhere, something that never made it to the Internet. We need corroboration in case Kestrel fails to find it. I'm going to look too, but I'm counting on you, Kurt. Get it done."

Chapter 26

MADRID

The morning after finding the director tortured and killed in his own garage, Hunter and Genevieve returned to Madrid and resumed the search.

"We need to get back into that library at the castle," Hunter told Genevieve. "There may be more in that diary than the one page we've seen that mentioned George Blackwell's return trip to Madrid after the war. Maybe there are some references that could give clues as to the whereabouts of the book."

"Why don't we just ask Alicia if we can look at the diary again, or even let us photocopy it?" asked Genevieve.

"I don't know, exactly, it's just a feeling I have. You know, we've only given our cell phone numbers to Alicia. Whoever texted you that threatening message, had to have your cell phone number. Now I don't think Alicia's behind the threat. There are ways to get someone's cell phone number if you really need to. Scarlet does it all the time. I just think we've worn out our welcome through the front door, such as it was."

"How are we going to get around that?"

"I'm going to use those other talents that Shay told you I have. I want you to stay here at the hotel. Lock the door and use the deadbolt. Put your phone on 'vibrate' and keep it next to your body. Don't let anyone in but me. I'll do the same, and we can stay in touch by texting without making excess noise."

Genevieve shook her head and looked worried. "I don't like this. What are you going to do?"

"I'm going to slip into the castle tonight and have a look. Don't worry. I'm quite good at this sort of thing. I've done it many times before. On our two trips there I made notes of the alarm system and I'll be able to deactivate it easily."

She rolled her eyes. "Why am I not surprised?"

Later that night Hunter drove to a wooded area about a quarter mile from the castle. He parked the car far enough off the road that it couldn't be seen. He hiked the rest of the way to the castle, staying off the road to remain undetected. On his previous visits he'd noticed that there was no way to break into the castle itself from the outside. But he'd seen that the final hallway they passed through from the house to the castle had a small, low window just big enough for him to slip through. Fortunately there was no moon to illuminate the wall, and he safely crept along the back of the house and castle. He quickly deactivated the alarms, opened the window, and was inside within a few seconds. He followed the hall they'd taken twice before to the library. Inside it was pitch black, with no windows and no lights.

Using a flashlight app on his cell phone, he made his way to Basilio's large desk, where he'd kept the diary. It was still there. With no indication that he'd triggered any alarms or had alerted anyone, he opened the diary and began to read.

Hunter found no reference to Lazodelavega, but he did find confirmation that Basilio had hired Professor de la Peña to catalogue and evaluate the collection. Just as Alicia had told them, it wasn't Basilio who extended the offer to de la Peña. It was the other way around. The professor had offered his services to Basilio upon learning that he had an Inquisition artifact collection, from Alicia. Further, it turned out that de la Peña had called Basilio and offered his services about the same time Dr. Lazodelavega alleged that he was contacted by Basilio and told of the book. What did that mean? Were they linked somehow?"

Hunter put the diary away and looked through the other drawers of the big desk. In a lower drawer, he found a ledger. On examination he found that it was a record of events related to the collection. It included separate listings going back to 1942. It included records of purchases and sales, and visits to research centers.

The ledger also included the names of a few people who visited the collection and the dates they were there. The first recorded visitor to the collection, on November 15, 1942, was none other than George Blackwell of the U.S. Consulate. After this, Hunter noted entries for four other individuals with Spanish surnames over the next five years. He made a note to himself that they'd need to check out these people to see if they knew anything about the book, perhaps one of them had it. He wrote their names in his notebook.

Most of the ledger entries involved the purchase and sale of Inquisition documents of various types. His purchases were for documents relating to the Church, the Inquisitors, and the civil authorities. Nowhere was there any reference to the *Christianismi Restitutio.*

Aside from seeing George Blackwell's name in the ledger, the other odd finding was that in 1947, after the war, Basilio had visited the Osterreichische National-Bibliothek in Vienna, the Bibliotheque Nationale in Paris, and the Library of the University of Edinburgh in Scotland. Bingo. Those visits weren't coincidental, thought Hunter. These institutions held the other three known copies of the *Christianismi Restitutio.*

Hunter made another note to himself. They needed to check with the libraries to verify that Basilio actually did make these trips to see the original copies in 1947. Hunter wondered what this meant. Maybe he *did* have a fourth copy and needed to see the other three in order to authenticate his holding. And another thing, either Basilio didn't yet have the book when George Blackwell visited the collection in 1942, or if he did have it, for some reason he didn't show it to him at that time. He found nothing to suggest that they should abandon their search.

He heard a noise outside the library. He quickly killed his light and ducked under the desk. The door opened and the overhead lights came on. A voice that sounded like Alfonso's called, "Is anyone in here?" After a moment the light went out and the door closed. He could hear the footfalls walking in the direction of the main house. Hunter must have made some sound that brought Alfonso in here. He'd have to be more careful.

Using the camera on his cell phone, he carefully photographed every page of the diary and the ledger. He then put everything back exactly where it belonged, then slipped out of the library, made his way back to the window, and exited as he had entered. He reactivated the alarms and headed for the cover of the woods.

Back at the hotel, Genevieve's relief was more than professional concern. She threw her arms around him and held on tightly for a long time.

Chapter 27

MADRID AND SALAMANCA

Their room became a kind of command center. Hunter downloaded the complete set of digital photos he had taken of the diary and ledger onto both of their computers. Genevieve, because of her connection to the international library system, would try to find out if Basilio actually did visit and view the copies of the *Christianismi Restitutio* at the French, Austrian, and Scottish libraries in 1947. She set up her computer on one end of the desk in their room. Hunter, working with his own laptop on the other end of the desk, was responsible for locating the four individuals who, in addition to George Blackwell, were said to have viewed the collection between 1942 and 1947:

> Tomas Garrido
> Alejandro Santiago
> Guillermo Bustos
> Tiago Rodriquez

There were no addresses. An initial perusal of the Madrid phone book showed that there were four Tomas Garridos, nine Alejandro Santiagos, three Guillermo Bustos and one Tiago Rodriquez. He started with Tiago Rodriquez. Tiago was a twenty-three-year old high school teacher who had no relatives that he knew of named Tiago. He was readily ruled out as a candidate when he said that he had just moved to Spain from Canada only that year.

The Bustos and Garridos listed proved to be dead ends as well, and Hunter was working his way through the Santiagos, when he remembered something he had read in the ledger the previous night in the library. It hadn't meant anything at the time, but now it did. He checked the appropriate ledger page from the digital photos on his computer. There it was: "Alejandro came all the way from Salamanca."

Maybe he was checking in the wrong city. He got the Salamanca phone directory on line and typed in Alejandro Santiago. He instantly got a hit.

> *Santiago, Alejandro   352 Calle de Pinto*
> *Tel. +34 9232218344*

Hunter called the number and spoke with a woman who said that Alejandro Santiago was her father. She stated that she lived with him and was his caregiver. Hunter introduced himself and asked if he and a companion might come to Salamanca to interview her father. He explained that he was an American scholar who was traveling in Spain. He'd been asked to say hello by the son of a man who worked in Madrid during the war and may have known her father.

She said that he was an old man and they could come, but that the visit would have to be short as her father tired easily. Hunter assured her they would be considerate and hung up.

He looked over the top of his computer screen at Genevieve. "I've got one of them. He's in Salamanca. How would you like another nice drive through the Spanish countryside?"

An hour and a half later they were driving northwest out of Madrid on the way to Salamanca, the highway gradually elevating through the central mountain system in Spain. As the scenery rolled by, Genevieve commented, "I was able to verify that Basilio did visit each of the sites that have copies of the *Christianismi Restitutio*. While two also had records that showed he actually viewed the manuscripts, I'm sorry to say that my own institution, the Bibliotheque, didn't. I can trace him to the Paris holdings at that time, but can't link him to the rare book room. It was in a different building back then and the records are incomplete during the German occupation."

"That's probably not important. He clearly was trying to view all three, and we can assume he did," said Hunter, focusing on the road.

They came out of the mountains onto a high rocky plain and continued driving on the AP-51 highway to Avila, where they got on the A-50 for the final leg to Salamanca. Their GPS estimated the total driving time at two hours 39 minutes.

Genevieve's computer offered up the information that Salamanca was considered one of the great Renaissance cities in Europe. The Plaza Mayor, the central square in the city was known as the 'living room" of the Salmantinos.

"Does that computer of yours also suggest where in the city our boy is?" asked Hunter.

"He's in the central city, east of the University and a few blocks east of the Plaza."

The GPS faithfully took them to Santiago's home. The bigger problem was finding a place to park the Mercedes. Parking was always at a premium in these old medieval cities; people left their cars wherever they could find space. With the exception of the middle of the streets, everything else was fair game. Following apparent local customs, they parked straddling the curbing, half on the street and half on the walkway, a block and a half away from the Santiagos.

They knocked on the door of the small brick house, barely distinguishable from the others in the area and seemingly connected by a common wall. A somber woman in her late sixties wearing a black dress and black sensible shoes opened it. When they identified themselves, she led them to a small but tidy living room in which an old man sat hunched over in a wheelchair, a blanket wrapped over his lap and legs.

She began to introduce them to her father when he interrupted her and said, with a remarkably strong and clear voice that didn't match the figure in the chair, "You must be the American and you're his charming companion."

They finished the introduction themselves.

Señor Santiago shook hands with both of them. Then, looking at his daughter he said, "Marcelina, why don't we go outside in the back under the tree?"

"Yes, Father, I've already set it up for you."

Pushing her father's wheelchair, she indicated that Hunter and Genevieve were to follow. They emerged into a small courtyard where a large, gnarly olive tree shaded most of the space.

The frail but surprisingly alert man brushed wisps of white hair from his forehead and directed them to two chairs. Marcelina briefly disappeared, then returned with tea and cakes on a tray, which she set on a table between the old man and his guests. Hunter found the tea remarkably tasty with a hint of apples and spices. The cakes were wonderful too. He complimented Marcelina on both and she beamed, shattering her image as a stern gatekeeper.

"My daughter is a wonderful woman and I'm happy to have her, although some poor soul of a man is alone tonight because he didn't marry this lady."

Marcelina flushed. "Oh, Father, we've been through this before," she said in what Hunter assumed was an old and never fruitful avenue of discussion.

"Now then, what do you want to know about the old days? It seems those times are *all* I can remember clearly anymore."

In answer to their questions, Señor Santiago said that he remembered viewing Basilio's collection but didn't recall seeing or hearing about a book such as they described. I'm not saying it wasn't there, but if it was, I don't remember seeing it. Then he delivered a jolting remark. "This is the second time someone has come to ask about the existence of this book. A man from Madrid was here about six months ago inquiring about it."

They showed him a picture of Alfonso Mendez and ask him if this was the man.

After adjusting his glasses and peering closely at the photo, he shook his head. "No, I've never seen that man before."

"Did the man give you his name, Señor Santiago?" asked Hunter.

"Yes, he was a professor in Madrid. Professor de la Peña."

"What did the professor want exactly?" asked Genevieve.

"Like you, he knew that I had viewed the collection in 1944 and wanted to know if I had seen the book that you're talking about. I told him I didn't remember. Then he got quite upset and said I was lying. Can you believe that? He said that he knew I was there and that I'd kept the book for myself. I told him that he was talking complete nonsense and should get the hell out of my house. That's when Marcelina stepped in and told him to leave immediately or she would call the police.

"Then he suddenly became friendly again. I think he said that Señor Basilio Mendez had recently died, and that he'd been instructed by the Mendez family heir to offer me a considerable amount of cash in return for the book. I insisted again that I knew nothing of such a book, and my daughter escorted him out the door."

"Señor Santiago, is there any way you would know the exact date of this visit?" asked Hunter.

Marcelina went to the kitchen and returned with a calendar. On it was noted the date of the strange visit, April 23rd.

Hunter and Genevieve thanked the Santiagos for their help and hospitality and left. As they walked down the street and reached their car, Hunter noticed movement on the roof of a two-story house across the street to his left. He whirled around freeing his Berretta in the same fluid movement only to hear a muffled gunshot and see a man on the roof jerk, clutch his chest and drop.

"Get in the car and keep low," he yelled to Genevieve as he scanned the scene trying to determine what happened. Seeing no one, he stayed low behind his parked car as he watched Genevieve get inside.

Seeing no one else, and with his gun ready, he crossed the street. The building had an iron fire escape ladder bolted to the side of the building. Continually scanning the area and seeing no one, he quickly climbed to the roof where he found a man on his back with a single bullet wound to the chest bleeding into his gray shirt. His sniper rifle was propped on an air conditioning vent. In a second Hunter could see that it was pointed at their car below. He bent down and determined the man was dead.

He looked at all the adjacent rooftops and up and down the street. He saw no one. He saw no open windows. The shot that killed him had clearly been silenced. No homeowners heard it and came forward to investigate. He checked him for ID and found none. Still cautious, knowing there had to be a second man—the one who shot this guy—Hunter used his cell phone camera to photograph the sniper rifle, the dead man's face and, under high magnification, his fingerprints. Then he unbuttoned his shirt and checked him for any recent wounds other than the obvious bullet through his heart. Confused, he found none on his torso, arms, or hands.

The local authorities responded to his call and quickly secured the crime scene. Hunter explained to the Inspector and chief detective what had happened. It took an hour at the crime scene and another three hours at police headquarters before he and Genevieve were allowed to leave. Hunter had finally convinced the detective that this might be the same man who shot at them at La Bodega. They should compare the ballistics on the slug taken from the wall at La Bodega with rounds fired by this weapon. They should also compare it to the slug taken from the scientist shot on his way to the collider in Geneva. The dead man might be the collider killer. As Hunter expected, this is when they began to take him seriously. The collider killings were becoming big news throughout the European press and TV. Trying to stay out of it, he hadn't informed them of his DIA and Interpol connections.

Ten minutes away from the house and before starting the drive back to Madrid, Hunter pulled over and called Ken Slocum at the number Deacon had given him. Slocum was the resource Deacon had assigned to cooperate with Hunter and fill any requests that were within reason. He told Slocum about the sniper attempt at La Bodega and what had just happened here in Salamanca. Hunter e-mailed the facial photo and fingerprints to Slocum and asked him to find out what he could about the dead man.

Slapping his hand on the steering wheel in frustration as they drove back to Madrid, Hunter tried to guess what was going on. "Who the hell shot this guy? Apparently there is someone out there with a reason to keep us alive. Whoever shot him saved our lives today. But who would do that? And why would he be trying to protect us?"

Hunter's cell phone rang: Slocum. Hunter put it on speakerphone so Genevieve could listen.

"McCoy, I got some answers off Interpol's database. Your dead guy is one Julian Baltz. He was a bad apple with a long record. He started out with petty crime and worked his way up. After doing time for a botched bank job, in Bern, he seems to have shifted gears and graduated to doing murder for hire. He's been good at it and he's managed to stay out of trouble by giving the police nothing to go on, even when they've suspected he'd been responsible for a hit.

Hunter thanked him. "Good work, Slocum. Any information on who might have hired him?"

"None."

"McCoy?"

"Yeah?"

"You do know, the DIA officially has no interest in these killings, right? They're not related to American defense in any way.

"I know that"

Breaking the connection and continuing to drive, Hunter turned to Genevieve. "Let's summarize. Julian Baltz was presumably hired by someone to stop us from searching for the book. He's probably the one who took a shot at us in La Bodega and missed, and tried again today, and was killed. He might also be the source of the threatening note to you to quit the search for the book and the guy who tried to run you off the road. Whoever shot him today was apparently trying to protect us. We don't know who that is, or why he'd do it. And then, we still have the question of who tried to kill Rafael.

Genevieve twisted around in her seat pulling her legs up under her. "How can you be sure Baltz isn't the one who tried to kill Rafael."

"The man I shot outside Rafael's was wounded in the upper body somewhere. I know I hit him. I saw him grab his shoulder. Except for the shot to the chest that killed him, Baltz didn't appear to be wounded and I checked him out thoroughly."

They drove in silence, each trying to come up with a plausible explanation, for who and why. Finally, Hunter said to Genevieve, "Here's something off the subject that also doesn't make sense. Santiago told us that on April 23rd the professor *might* have said that Basilio recently died. If I remember correctly, he didn't actually fall off the ladder until May 6th, two weeks later."

Chapter 28

Back in Madrid, Hunter called Inspector Delgado and told her of their visit to Alejandro Santiago. She immediately wanted to know how Hunter obtained his name. He couldn't very well divulge that he got the name by breaking into the Mendez home and castle in the middle of the night and going through Basilio's personal papers.

"Alicia Mendez told us that Basilio had a diary in which there was a reference to George Blackwell, and she invited us to read it. His name was mentioned as having visited the collection in 1944." It was just a minor twist on the facts.

Hunter told her about the attempt on their lives by Julian Baltz, killed by a person unknown, who'd probably saved their lives. He gave her the digital photos he took of Baltz, his sniper rifle and his prints. Of course he also told her about how he had Interpol ID the man.

Delgado paused for a moment, cocked her head and sat back in her chair, clasping her hands under her chin. "Are you sure looking for this book is worth it, McCoy?"

"Frankly, Inspector, I'm beginning to wonder that myself."

"You say that the professor told Santiago that Basilio Mendez was dead two weeks before it actually happened." It was said as a fact and not a question. Then she volunteered a bit of information on the professor's death that he didn't know.

"The knife in the chest is definitely what killed the professor, but his death was peculiar in another way."

"What do you mean?" said Hunter.

"The autopsy showed a high level of a drug called metoprolol in the professor's blood."

"That's a beta blocker often given for hypertension," said Hunter. "What's so strange about that?"

"What's strange is, that while de la Peña *did* have high blood pressure, and his doctor prescribed this medication for him, he'd been taking one 80 mg tablet per day for several years. He knew how to take the stuff. The level in his blood stream was more consistent with taking eight-to-ten pills at once. He said, further, that the level found in the professor's blood would probably drop his heart rate and blood pressure low enough to produce a state of unconsciousness."

"Apparently the professor's knife wielding attacker wasn't going to take any chances that he'd fight back," Hunter remarked.

"Exactly our conclusion," said Inspector Delgado.

Genevieve had been working her computer during the phone call to Delgado and motioned Hunter over.

"What have you got?" asked Hunter.

Genevieve grinned. "Guess what I found when I went over Basilio's diary?"

"Tell me."

"A page appears to have been very carefully removed. The date for this page would have been January 25."

"And?" said Hunter.

"Don't you see? That's the date that Dr. Lazodelavega said he visited Basilio in the castle and was told about the book and the future donation of it to the Michael Servetus Institute."

"Interesting. Show me."

Looking carefully at the image on the screen, he could see that whoever had removed the page must have done it with a razor blade in order to do such a precise job of it.

Genevieve said, "I wouldn't even have noticed it but I was keeping track of the time line and I spotted the break in days."

They speculated as to what might have been on the page and who would have cut it out.

Was it Basilio himself, who, after recording the evening's talk with Lazodelavega, decided this was not the kind of information he wanted in his diary? Or did someone in the household take it, and if they did, why?

Genevieve ventured yet another possibility. "Maybe it was the professor. The Inspector told you there was circumstantial evidence that he'd killed Basilio. Maybe he also killed the director and was trying to keep secret the existence of the book and/or Basilio's intention to donate it to the Institute."

"And if that's true, the professor's killer must be someone with access to the house, and specifically, with access to the library," said Hunter. "The most likely candidates are Alfonso and Alicia, and my bet is on Alfonso. He's been opposed to our inquiries from the beginning."

"However," Genevieve added, "Alicia's helpfulness would be a nice cover if she were guilty. But, if she is the one, why would she take the risk of showing us the diary at all?" Then, answering her own question, Genevieve said, "Of course she did only show us the reference to George Blackwell meeting with Basilio in 1947 which was pretty innocuous. The rest of it we got by ourselves, thanks to your breaking-and-entering skills."

"Hunter?"

"What?"

"Do you think it possible that Alicia could be behind the threat to get me off the search?"

He paused before answering. "It's hard to believe, but at this point, I think it's best to suspect everyone." Then he asked her, "Did you find anything else in the diary during your examination?"

"Only this entry in Latin on July 15, 1950. I can translate it, but I'm not sure how it fits in with anything."

Hunter looked at the page and saw:

In inhalation quod respiratio illic est an navitas quod a vivax divinus phasmatis, utpote Is, per suus phasmatis suscipio spiritus of vita relinquo virtus ut populus quisnam es in orbis terrarum quod phasmatis illis quisnam ingredior in is.

"I think I see inhalation and respiration in there. What does it say? Can you read this for me?"

"Sure. It roughly translates:

In the inhalation and exhalation there is energy and a lively divine spirit, since He, through his spirit, supports the breath of life, giving courage to the people who are in the earth and spirit to those who walk on it.

Not knowing what to make of this, Hunter relayed Inspector Delgado's findings about the autopsy report and the metoprolol. He asked Genevieve to continue examining the diary and ledger. He was going to pay a visit to Alfonso Mendez at the castle.

Without telling Delgado what he had in mind, he drove to the castle and was ushered into the sitting room by the housekeeper. Alfonso Mendez appeared a few minutes later.

"What are you doing here, McCoy?"

"I wanted to see a reference to my employer, Shay Blackwell," Hunter lied. "Your daughter showed me your father's diary on an earlier visit. In fact it was the visit when you told me to get out and not come back again."

"And yet here you are."

"Since I didn't get to see the reference at that time, I've returned, hoping you'd let me see it."

"All right, smart ass, I'm calling the police to have you arrested for trespassing." Alfonse picked up the telephone and prepared to call.

"I'd think twice about calling them if I were you. The evidence already strongly points to you for the murders of Professor de la Peña and Dr. Lazodelavega."

He put the phone down. "What are you talking about? What evidence? I haven't murdered anyone."

"Your car was seen leaving the professor's office around the estimated time of his death." Hunter knew this was a stretch, but he was fishing.

"That's impossible. I've only been there once and he was fine when I left. I already told this to the Inspector when she questioned me earlier. As far as I know, the only business he had with this household was with my father, and he sure as hell didn't kill the professor."

"That's right, he didn't. Your father was already dead at the time."

"Who is this other guy, this Lazo— something?" demanded Mendez.

"His name was Dr. Cristobal Lazodelavega, the founder and director of the Michael Servetus Institute."

"I've never heard of him, and what the hell is the Michael Servetus goddamn Institute?"

Hunter explained that Alfonso's father was planning to donate the missing book to this institute and had said as much to Dr. Lazodelavega in June of last year.

"So what? My father could do anything he wanted to with the collection. It was always his personal property anyway. I still know nothing of this book you talk about."

Hunter decided to take a risk. "It may interest you to know that the medical examiner has determined that Professor de la Peña was doped with a large quantity of metoprolol, which you take for high blood pressure."

"Are you nuts? I don't take anything for high blood pressure because I don't have high blood pressure. And my father didn't have high blood pressure either, and never took a goddamn pill in his entire life."

Hunter was beginning to think that maybe Alfonso might actually be telling the truth. Then he made a decision. "You know, you're right. I've been barking up the wrong tree. I'll leave you alone and I won't be back again, trust me. However, Señor Mendez, I have just two last questions, if you would. Question number one. Have you seen the professor since he did the work for your father?"

"I went to his office recently to pick up a second copy of his assessment. My daughter wanted a copy. I asked him to prepare one for her."

"Question two. Would you be able to tell if anything was missing from the Inquisition collection?"

"Missing? Why would anything be missing?"

"Could you tell?"

"I think so. Why."

"I'll tell you after we look."

Alfonso sighed. "Then will you leave us alone?"

"I promise."

Alfonso's skepticism showed as he snorted.

After they reached the collection and Alfonso looked around a bit, he said, "Over here. It looks like the thumbscrew is missing. It should be right here, on this stand, next to its label."

Hunter asked him, "Do you have any idea how long it's been gone?"

Alfonso, regaining a little of his typical belligerence, said, "Dammit, McCoy, what's going on? What's this all about?"

"Dr. Cristobal Lazodelavega, the director of the Michael Servetus Institute in Villanueva de Sijena, was murdered at his home recently, after being tortured, apparently with your missing thumbscrew."

Chapter 29

Delgado blew up when Hunter called and told her he'd interviewed Alfonso Mendez and that he'd seemed genuinely surprised that the thumbscrew was missing.

"Look McCoy, let's get something straight. You're a visitor in this country and your Interpol connection has no bearing on this case. This is a police matter, and it's my investigation. I've already interviewed him once regarding de la Peña's murder and was going to see him this afternoon regarding the thumbscrew. If I find you interfering again, just once, I'll haul your ass to jail. Do I make myself clear?"

"Perfectly, Inspector. You're right. Sorry, it won't happen again. Then he added, "If I do talk to Alfonso again, it will only be about the book and I'll leave the investigation of the Professor's murder to you."

Inspector Delgado decided it was time to interview Alicia Mendez. She and Detective Jorge Reyes met Alicia in her apartment. Alicia, wearing jeans and a white blouse, answered the knock on the door, curious by the two serious looking strangers.

"Señorita Mendez, I'm Inspector Lupita Delgado and this is Detective Jorge Reyes of the police." They showed their credentials. "We're investigating the murder of

Professor de la Peña and we thought you might be able to help us."

"Me? I don't know anything about it."

Delgado tried to put her at ease. "You know how it goes. Sometimes we know things we don't even know we know, until someone asks. In any case, we're just starting this investigation."

"Okay. Come in."

Her apartment was small but nicely set up. It looked like the furniture came with the place but she had arranged it effectively, and took a minimalist approach to decorating. The walls were covered with fine art prints and a few oil paintings that looked to Delgado as if they were expensive and genuine. She wasn't surprised given what she'd learned about Alicia's major in art and her relatively wealthy background.

"Have you ever met Professor Isandro Rodriquez de la Peña, the man who evaluated your grandfather's collection; excuse me, your collection?"

"Yes."

"Have you ever been to his office?"

"Yes. I asked him to consider looking at my grandfather's collection."

"Have you ever been to his house?"

"No, of course not."

"Did you kill Professor de la Peña?"

"What? What's going on here?

Delgado smiled reassuringly. "I'm only asking routine questions as part of a murder investigation. We have to ask these questions of everyone"

"Do I need an attorney?"

"Like I said, we're only asking routine questions, but if you'd like an attorney, you're certainly free to call one."

An hour later, after a few phone calls, Alicia had her attorney present and the questioning continued, this time in a questioning room at police headquarters.

"Señorita Mendez, did you kill professor de la Peña?" asked Inspector Delgado.

"I already told you I didn't. Aren't you listening? Why would I? Plus, I couldn't overpower a large man like the professor. Look at me. I couldn't do that. I'm not strong enough."

"Do you know what metoprolol is?"

"Why?"

"Answer the question please"

"Yes. It's a medication for hypertension."

"Do you have high blood pressure and do you take this medication yourself?"

"You must know I do or you wouldn't ask."

"Answer the question please."

"Yes. I take metoprolol."

"Does your father have hypertension?"

"My Father? I don't think so, no."

"Did your grandfather have high blood pressure?"

Her attorney interrupted. "Is there a point to these questions, Inspector?"

"Yes, counselor, there is." She turned back to Alicia.

"Did your grandfather have hypertension?"

"No. Not that I'm aware of," Alicia said. "He didn't believe in taking pills."

"So you are the only family member with hypertension. Is that correct?"

"I suppose so."

"You suppose so? Can you explain why a coffee cup with traces of metoprolol would be on the professor's desk on the day of his murder?"

Alicia swallowed and bit her lower lip, confusion and fear showing on her face.

"Inspector, unless you're charging my client with something, we're leaving now. This interview is over."

"In a minute, counselor. I'm only asking questions at this point."

"All right, but my client can leave at any time, Inspector."

"Of course. Ms. Mendez, do you know a graduate student at the university named Isabella Gomez?"

"Yes, I do."

"Did she tell you that Professor de la Peña, her major professor, might be willing to evaluate and catalog your grandfather's collection?" asked Delgado.

"She did mention that, yes," said Alicia warily.

"Did she also tell you that she'd found a note in the professor's things that led her to believe he might be planning to steal a rare and extremely valuable book that he thought was in your grandfather's collection: the Servetus book. Let me see now— the *Christianismi Restitutio*?"

Alicia had been slouching in her chair, but suddenly sat up straight and raised her voice. "No, absolutely not. She never told me such a thing. I never even heard of such a book before Hunter McCoy and Genevieve Swift told me they were looking for it. Why won't anyone believe that?" she cried.

As Alicia rose to leave, Inspector Delgado put up her hand and said, "Just a few more questions, if you would, Señorita Mendez."

As Alicia sat back down, Delgado asked, "Ms. Mendez, do you know Dr. Cristobal Lazodelavega?"

"No, I've never met him," said Alicia.

"But you know of him?" queried the inspector.

Alicia, looking confused, answered, "I know that Hunter and Genevieve were going to an Institute somewhere in Aragon where they said he was the director, I think."

"Have you ever been there yourself?" asked Delgado.

"Good heavens, no. I don't even know where it is. What is this all about, Inspector?"

"Do you own a thumbscrew?"

"A what?" cried Alicia.

"You know, a thumbscrew. One of those medieval torture devices, like the stuff you have in your collection." Inspector Delgado gazed evenly at her eyes.

Her attorney asked, "What is this, Inspector? What are you getting at?"

"It might interest you to know, Ms. Mendez, that a few nights ago, Director Lazodelavega, was tortured with the thumbscrew from *your* collection. He was found dead in his garage with a bullet in the brain and your thumbscrew on his lap."

"What?" cried Alicia, her face twisted in confusion and horror, "Oh my God, how awful, but you must be wrong. I'm sure the thumbscrew is where it belongs in the collection."

"Well, you'd be wrong. It's not there. It was on the man's lap, as I said." She paused.

"Ms. Mendez, where were you two nights ago between six PM and midnight?"

"What? Why are you asking me that?"

"Where were you?"

"I don't know, let me think." She looked upward as if checking an imaginary calendar. "I remember, I was at the University library from about five-thirty until they closed at midnight. I was working on a paper in the art history section."

Delgado asked, "Can anyone verify that? Were you with anyone?"

"Sure, I checked out several books, and the library scans all students in and out electronically."

"Thank you," said Delgado. "We'll check that out."

"What a horrible thing to happen to that man. How did someone get the thumbscrew, if it is mine?" asked Alicia appearing relieved now that the questions appeared to be over.

"That's what we plan to find out," Delgado said.

Chapter 30

Detective Jorge Reyes knocked on Inspector Delgado's office door and walked in.

"What is it, Jorge? What've you got?"

"Inspector, you're going to be interested in this. A search of the professor's home turned up a near-empty prescription bottle for metoprolol in his name. It seems the professor, like Alicia Mendez, had hypertension and took the medication daily. The bottle was a three-month supply filled almost three months ago. There are two pills left which is about right. He'd normally be getting a new bottle soon. He got them filled at a local pharmacy. I checked and the pharmacy claims a new bottle of ninety was recently picked up. We can't find it anywhere in his house.

"That's not all, Inspector," said Jorge. "A check of the professor's phone records shows that Alicia Mendez called the professor *at his home*, just before he started to evaluate the collection. She left a message on his answering machine saying she'd be happy to bring him a list of some of the major items in the collection to help him decide if he wanted to evaluate it."

"So," said Delgado, "she could have gone to his house, brought the list, excused herself to use the bathroom and noticed he took the same medication she did."

Delgado pushed back her chair and tapped her fingers on the surface of her desk, thinking. "Something else, Jorge. I did a background check on Ms. Mendez and found out that she may have been a suspect in a vicious attack on a classmate when she was in school in Switzerland. It seems that Alicia and this girl were up for the same award, and the girl was attacked with a knife and disfigured. Alicia was never charged, but she, and several other girls, *were* suspects at the time."

Hunter called Delgado to see if there had been any progress in identifying the elevator bomber. She assured him that they were analyzing the aerosol can and the plastic explosive and would know soon if they produced any leads. Then she suggested again that he and Genevieve go home and leave it to the authorities. Undaunted, Hunter then asked her if she had any leads on who killed Director Lazodelavega. She reminded him that his murder wasn't her case, and pointedly, it wasn't his either. She was looking for the professor's killer. When he asked how that was going, she hesitated.

"Look, McCoy, I know you have a vested interest in this, but let's be clear. This is a murder investigation. I have no obligation to share information with you."

"I understand, Inspector."

Nevertheless, she sighed and said, "We have no credible suspects yet, but we're definitely looking at Alphonso Mendez, Alicia Mendez, and the graduate student, Isabella Gomez."

"I don't think it's Alicia and I don't think Alfonso did it either. Good luck, Inspector," Hunter hung up before she could respond.

He'd tried and failed again to get Genevieve to go home. As she had before, she told him that she felt safer with him than she would by herself. Hunter, in spite of his better judgment, again acquiesced.

Even though Delgado had warned him to leave the case to her, Hunter said to Genevieve, "Let's have another chat with that graduate student."

Hunter rationalized that, because of her connection to the professor, he had a right to question her about the book. If she volunteered information about the professor that might help find his killer, he'd give it to Delgado.

When they arrived at the university they found that Isabella was no longer in her original office. The secretary told them that she was now working with a different professor in an adjacent building. His name was Professor Echevarria.

The two went next door to a building almost identical to the one they were leaving and found Professor Echevarria's office.

The professor didn't have a secretary and answered his door himself when Hunter knocked.   Hunter introduced himself and Genevieve as scholars collaborating on a project regarding the Inquisition. He explained that they'd had an appointment to see Professor da la Peña before he was killed. Since they obviously couldn't see him, they'd like to talk with his former graduate student, Isabella Gomez, instead.

"I see. I'm sure she'll talk with you. Her office is just down the hall."

As they got up to leave, Hunter asked, "By the way, how is she working out for you?"

"Very well. She's a hard worker. I'm glad to have her in my program. In fact, she's even changed her dissertation topic since coming to me. It seems that she has recently developed an interest in the writings of Michael Servetus."

Hunter and Genevieve looked at each other, and said in unison, "Michael Servetus?"

"Yes. She's presented an interesting dissertation proposal focusing on his heretical writings, especially a book called the *Christianismi Restitutio*."

They found Isabella's office with no difficulty. This office was as small and already as cluttered as her other one had been.

Her door was open, so Hunter poked his head in and said, "Excuse me, Ms. Gomez, do you have a few minutes?"

Isabella looked up, startled. "Oh, it's you. Sure, come in." Then seeing that Genevieve was with him, she said, "Let me get another chair."

The plump graduate student pushed an open box of chocolates aside and pulled in a chair from the hallway and they all sat down.

"Ms. Gomez," Hunter began, "we're sorry to hear of the death of Professor de la Peña. I know you were working closely with him and his death must have caused you to interrupt your studies."

"Yes, it did. But Professor Echevarria has agreed to take me on through the completion of my degree. He's been very helpful."

"I'm sure he has," murmured Hunter, "We were just wondering if you've had any thoughts on who might have killed your previous mentor?"

She shrugged. Her blues eyes registering confusion under her raised eyebrows. "No, I don't."

"Earlier, when we talked with you, you'd said that he started acting strangely after he cataloged the Mendez collection."

"That's right. He started to get mean after that. I guess I never should have told Alicia about him."

Hunter snapped to attention. "You know Alicia Mendez?"

"Yes. We were taking a class together, European Art History. We had lunch together several times and had become friends. In fact, I was the one who told her about Professor de la Peña's interest in the Inquisition. When she told me her grandfather had an extensive Inquisition collection, I told her the professor would probably be interested as he'd cataloged several important private historical collections throughout Spain."

Hunter asked Isabella if Alicia had ever met the professor.

"I'm sure she did, because I know he cataloged the collection."

Hunter asked, "Did you and the professor continue to get along all right after he—changed?"

"We got along great, and then he just changed. Like I said, he got rather testy and mean. Why are you asking me this?"

She began twisting back and forth in her swivel chair, nervously fingering the silver band on her index finger. It was a small thing, but Hunter picked up on it. This conversation definitely bothered her.

"Sorry, I didn't mean to offend you. I'm sometimes accused of being too nosy."

She pushed back her chair and stood up. "You know, I've told all of this to university security and to Police Inspector Delgado. I don't want to talk about it anymore. You'll have to excuse me. I have work I need to do."

They thanked Isabella and left. They were walking back to the first floor when Genevieve said, "What do you make of that?"

"I don't know."

Hunter phoned Delgado and asked if Isabella had alibis for the times of the murders, not only the professor, but Lazodelavega and maybe even Basilio himself. Hunter had to admit it was a stretch, but he thought she might want to check on all of them.

"Damn it, McCoy, you're getting close to seeing the inside of my jail. What are you after here?"

"My gut says to check out Isabella. That's all"

Delgado hung up on him.

Chapter 31

MENDEZ CASTLE

Now that he had to keep McCoy alive until he found the book, Kestrel wondered how he could speed up the process. He listened again to the taped conversation between Rafael Mendez, McCoy and the girl. He learned that McCoy thought young Mendez's father, Alphonso, knew something about the book but was denying it. He'd heard Rafael Mendez say he didn't know if his father knew anything about it but it wasn't impossible. He told McCoy that if he did know he certainly wouldn't tell them about it. He didn't like dealing with outsiders.

"So he doesn't like dealing with outsiders," sneered Kestrel, out loud to himself. "Maybe it's time he met an outsider he *really* won't want to deal with."

He went to the castle house and was admitted to the library after telling the housekeeper that he had valuable information that would be most welcome to Señor Mendez concerning the American who had been bothering him, Hunter McCoy. After a ten-minute wait, Alphonso arrived in the room demanding to know who he was and why the hell he was here. Kestrel removed his hand from his jacket pocket and stuck his silenced pistol in Alfonso's belly.

"What—what the hell are you doing?" shouted Alphonso stepping back and knocking over a small table behind him.

Kestrel pressed the gun harder into Alfonso's shirt backing him up even more while staring with cold, dispassionate eyes directly into the man's increasingly fearful and confused face.

Sensing the man was all bluster and had no real backbone, Kestrel decided to threaten him right here. "You have something I want, and you're going to give it to me now."

Looking at the gun, but regaining some of his indignant natural attitude, Alfonso stood tall and defiant. "Just who the hell do you think you are, pointing a gun at me, and why should I give you anything of mine?"

"You, Senor Mendez, have a copy of the *Christianismi Restitutio* that my employer wants. You'll give it to me now and I might let you live. If not, you will surely die, here, now."

"That damned book again. I told McCoy and I'll tell you. I don't have the damned thing. Nor, do I know where it is, if it even exists."

Kestrel studied the man for a moment. Then nodding his head as if he'd made up his mind on something said, "Take me to your Inquisition collection."

When Alfonso hesitated, Kestrel silently and with lightning speed produced a blade in his other hand and laid it up against Alfonso's neck and said in a dead voice filled with menace as much from its tone as from the words, said, "Oh you'll take me Senor, or you will die right here in a pool of your own blood."

Holding the gun steady and level on Alfonso, Kestrel marched him around the room housing the large torture instruments. Kestrel amused himself by reading the descriptions of how each device was used. Some, he was familiar with but one really caught his attention. Its simplicity appealed to him. "Señor Mendez, I believe I've found just the thing to encourage you to be more forthcoming."

The horror on Alfonso's face gave Kestrel a deep sense of satisfaction.

Eldora Munoz, Alfonso Mendez's housekeeper, was beginning her work in the old castle. It was her day to clean the library and the collection rooms.   Señor Basilio Mendez had always treated her well and often told her to take a chocolate or two from the bowl he always kept full on his large desk in the library, where she was working now.   She loved cleaning the library.   Unfortunately, the chocolates were gone, along with the old man.   Still, Alfonso was okay to work for. He wasn't as friendly, and he didn't have bowls of chocolate about, but he treated her well.   She didn't like having to clean the room that housed all of those horrible machines.   Prior to Senor Basilio dying, she'd never had to clean the room behind the library that housed them. She'd heard about them, of course, but she'd never actually seen them. Señor Basilio had never required her to clean the room, and for that she was thankful. But then when Alfonso and Alicia had the room expanded and improved after Señor Basilio died, they wanted the room regularly cleaned.

Eldora had just finished the library and was on her way to the collection room. She pushed her mop bucket ahead of her, opened the door and switched on the light. Then— she gasped. She tried to scream but couldn't. Her breath caught in her throat.   Horrified, she stumbled from the room, knocking the mop bucket over.

When Inspector Delgado arrived, the crime scene people had already secured the area, and the coroner was on the way. Inspector Delgado showed her credentials to the policeman at the entrance to the castle home and was met by her deputy detective, Jorge Reyes, who had responded to the initial call from Eldora, the cleaning lady.

"What have we got, Jorge?" asked Delgado as they walked down the passageway from the house to the castle.

"It's ugly, Inspector," Jorge replied, looking pale and sweating. "After ten years in homicide, I thought I was ready for anything. But nobody's ready for this. You'd better prepare yourself."

Armed with this caution, Delgado, suddenly and uncharacteristically nervous, found herself outside the door to the collection room. She took a deep breath and walked in.

Jorge, sensing what to expect, quickly gave her a barf bag. She'd never been sick at a crime scene, but no crime scene she'd ever seen was like this. Her stomach told her to use the bag but she managed to hold it together.

Alfonso Mendes, naked, eyes bulging wide open in agonized horror, hands tied behind his back and dead beyond a doubt, sat astride a tall sharp V-shape wedge of wood. Delgado immediately recognized it as the "Spanish Donkey" she had seen earlier when she'd visited the collection with Alfonso. It was one of the most horrifying torture devices ever used by the Inquisition. Weights had apparently been added in increments to Alfonso's feet until eventually, enough weight had been added to cause the wedge to slice through him, splitting him in half up to the chest.

Delgado again battled the feeling that she was going to be sick. "What kind of animal would do this, Jorge? What kind of a sick shit? Christ. Look at that. This wasn't a quick death. Someone wanted information and slowly did this to get it. The poor bastard had to have spilled anything he knew. How could he not?"

Jorge, not looking too good himself, repeated what he'd said earlier. "I thought I'd seen everything."

The coroner arrived and had the same reaction as Delgado and Jorge. When he'd recovered he told Delgado the obvious.

"Cause of death looks like impalement, but I'll have more detail when we get the body to the lab."

Delgado thanked him and spoke for a while with the crime scene techs, then interviewed the housekeeper, who was being taken care of in the library. She had nothing to offer beyond what she had told Jorge. She'd walked in and found him there.

After the crime scene people were through and the coroner had removed the body, Delgado returned to headquarters. She had just sat down when her phone rang. It was Hunter. She told him what they'd found at the castle.

The phone couldn't hide Hunter's revulsion. "What a scene that must have been."

"It was, and believe me, you didn't want to see it," she said. "Even though you told me she didn't get along with her father and might have a motive, I can't believe Alicia Mendez would be capable of this. I haven't met anyone in my years on the job that I think could have done this crime, and I've met some real scum."

"Have you told Alicia yet, inspector?"

Hunter could hear Delgado take a deep sigh. "Not yet, but I will."

"Inspector?" said Hunter.

"What?"

"I don't think she killed the professor either."

She hung up on him again, in what he was beginning to think was becoming a habit.

Chapter 32

Delgado just couldn't bring herself to imagine the Mendez girl capable of killing her father in such a horrible way. However, she continued to believe her to be a credible suspect in the murder of the professor. McCoy's annoying insistence on her innocence, didn't make sense. Still, she knew he was a professional and she knew how important gut instincts were in this business. Reluctantly, she decided to re-interview Isabella Gomes and to conduct this interview in the young woman's office at the university.

She and Reyes took the two chairs that Isabella offered, and she began with a pro forma apology. "Señorita Gomez, I'm sorry to bother you again, but you know how these things are. They never seem to be quite done."

Isabella nodded her head, while clearly not understanding what the inspector meant by that. Delgado adjusted herself on the hard straight office chair, trying to get more comfortable. When that failed, she explained, "We'd like to go over your friendship with Alicia Mendez again, if you don't mind."

"I don't understand. I've already told you everything I know."

"I'm sure that's true, but sometimes other facts inadvertently come out in the retelling of a story."

"Okay, what do you want to know?"

"Alicia Mendez agreed with your statement that you told her about the professor and his interest in the Inquisition. She also agreed that she told you about her grandfather's collection and even asked you about the possibility of the professor looking at the collection."

Isabella nodded. "That's right. That's all true."

Delgado continued as if there'd been no interruption. "Further, she agreed with your statement indicating that she might even ask him about it." Looking directly at Isabella, Delgado said, "Now here's where we have some confusion." She jabbed a finger at Isabella. "You say you found a note from the professor slipped into the back pages of his report that referred to the fact that he'd just learned about a book called the *Christianismi Restitutio,* that should have been, but wasn't, in the collection when he evaluated it. And what else did it say? *He'd have to ask Mendez about it.* Was that it? Further, you said you told this to Alicia Mendez because you thought the professor might have plans to get it for himself, that he'd even estimated the value of such a book at one million euros."

"Yes. That's exactly what happened," exclaimed Isabella, lifting her chin with defiant conviction. "I told her about it because I wanted her to know that the professor knew about the book."

"And what did she say to that?"

"She told me she didn't know anything about such a book. And then she thanked me for telling her."

Inspector Delgado leaned forward in her chair and stared directly at Isabella. "Alicia Mendez denies that you ever said that. She said you never mentioned such a note and you certainly didn't warn her about the professor."

"That's a lie," shouted Isabella, standing up and pacing to the window. "I did find the note and I did tell her about it. I don't know if she ever confronted him about it or not, but I did tell her about the note." She sat back down glowering. "She's lying. I don't know why, but she's lying."

Trying once again to get comfortable in the hard chair, Delgado asked, "Señorita Gomez?"

"What?" snapped Isabella.

"This note. The one you say the professor had among his things. Where is it?"

"I told you when you asked before. It was in the back of his report on the Mendez collection. It was just a loose piece of paper. It was there when I saw it last. If it's gone now, I don't know what happened to it."

Delgado got up to leave. "Thank you, Señorita Gomez, I know this is difficult. We're just trying to get the whole picture of what happened. I hope we won't have to bother you again."

When they were back in the car, Jorge asked, "What do you think, boss? I think she's holding something back."

Inspector Delgado paused before answering. "I do too. I don't know what's missing, but she's not telling us the whole story."

Hunter still had something he had to work out with respect to Alicia. It'd been nagging him for some time, but he had been too busy to deal with it. Did Alicia have anything to do with the attack on the girl in the Swiss school when she was a student there? Delgado had told him about it, but he just couldn't put any faith in the idea. He thought there must be some way he could find out.

He called Slocum and told him he needed information on a possible criminal assault on a young woman in a gymnasium at St. Gallen in or around 2000. She had been slashed and attacked, presumably by a classmate, and he wanted to know if there had ever been a resolution.

Hunter could hear Slocum drawing in a deep breath and exhaling slowly. "You do know McCoy that I work for the Defense Intelligence Agency and not the police, right?"

"I know, Ken, just do what you can."

Two hours later, Slocum called back. "Okay, here's what I could find out. The case was quite adequately handled by the Swiss Canon's own local law enforcement people. The perpetrator was identified and confessed to the assault. But of course she was underage and was dealt with in juvenile court, and the issue generated no local publicity at all. Her records were obviously sealed, so I can't identify her to you or even tell you what nationality she was. She was apparently punished rather severely, but seems to have straightened her life out and is now married and has two children. I was told that she heavily bears the pain of her misdeed and will for the rest of her life. Does that help you at all, McCoy?"

"It does. Great work, Ken, thanks." Hunter hung up and leaned back in his chair. *I knew it. Alicia had nothing to do with it.*

Chapter 33

MADRID

Inspector Delgado clasped her hands behind her head and stared at the ceiling of her office at police headquarters. She was thinking about the two women, Isabella Gomez and Alicia Mendez. They both had motive to kill the professor. The professor was threatening Isabella's future career by jeopardizing her degree, and that can be a powerful motive. If the book was as valuable as McCoy said it was, Alicia, as heir to the collection, stood to lose a fortune if the professor got his hands on it. Neither woman had a solid alibi for the estimated time of the murder. Alicia, at least, had a solid alibi for Lazodelavega's murder but not for the professor's. Her phone rang, waking her out of her reverie.

"Homicide, Delgado."

"Inspector, this is Hunter McCoy. Just for your information, Alicia Mendez wasn't involved in that student attack at the Swiss school several years ago. The local police caught the student, a minor at the time, and she confessed to slashing the girl. After serving her probation, she married and had two children. I know it's not really germane to your case, but I thought you should know anyway."

Delgado replied in an icy tone. "Thanks, McCoy. You're right; it's not germane," and she hung up.

She thought about asking McCoy how he could have possibly gotten that information, but then figured she really didn't want to know. So she sat back and thought more about the two women. Is the Mendez woman actually innocent? Both she and the grad student, Isabella Gomez, seem to be hiding something. Neither of them has been completely truthful. Maybe they did the murders together. No, I don't believe that. Still, maybe I should take a closer look at the Gomez woman. She sat in silence for a few more minutes. Then having made up her mind, she opened her door and called to Detective Reyes. "Jorge, get in here."

After getting a search warrant for Isabella Gomez's apartment and office at the university. She and Detective Reyes knocked on the door of the apartment first. It was on the second floor over a dry-cleaning establishment on Calle de Guzman and a short walk from the university. When Isabella answered the knock on her door, Delgado handed her the warrant and told her they were authorized to search her apartment.

Startled, Isabella said, "What are you talking about? I don't understand."

"A search, Señorita Gomez. Detective Reyes and I are going to search your apartment. You may stay and watch. We're authorized to look everywhere and anywhere."

"But what are you looking for?" she protested.

"We'll know when we find it," replied Delgado. With that they began a meticulous search. The warrant actually authorized them to look for the murder weapon that had been used on the professor. They knew it was a long shot. Surely, if she had stabbed the professor, she would have gotten rid of the weapon in such a way they'd never find it. Still, killers did stupid things like keeping evidence all the time, evidence that could convict them. You never could tell what a thorough search might turn up. Two hours later they'd found nothing. Then, Reyes stepped out of the kitchen and signaled for Delgado to come in.

"What have you got, Jorge?"

Cracking a large smile, Jorge said, "Look what we have here, Inspector. It was in a bag on her kitchen counter."

Delgado saw that Jorge was holding a plastic bag with the name and logo of de la Peña's chemist on it. Inside were two prescription bottles with the name Isandro de la Peña on the labels. One was for Metoprolol and the other was for Lipitor. She examined the Metoprolol label and saw that it was a ninety-day supply and had been filled just two weeks earlier. She unscrewed the cap and could see that the seal had been broken. Replacing the cap, she carefully put the bottle in an evidence bag.

Delgado and Reyes continued their search and found nothing else of interest. No murder weapon. Inspector Delgado concluded that they were done with Isabella's apartment and the search would continue with her office at the university.

Returning to the living room where Isabella sat glumly on the sofa, Delgado asked, but it was really an order, "Señorita Gomez, I'd like you to accompany us downtown to headquarters. We'll have some additional questions for you later."

A half hour later, after dropping Isabella off at the police station, they showed their warrant to the department chairman, and began their search of Isabella Gomez's office. They spent ninety minutes going through everything in the office, her files, her desk, and the books on her small bookcase. They found nothing. They went though her wastebasket and they examined the bottoms of her desk drawers and her single small file cabinet. Nothing.

Frustrated, Delgado went back to the chairman's office and asked him if she used any other space regularly besides her office.

"Not that I know of, Inspector, but you should ask Professor Echevarria, he'd be more likely to know. After all, he was responsible for getting her the new office."

"New office? What do you mean, new office?

"When she worked with Professor de la Peña she was in the building next door in another office. After she began working with Echevarria, he had her move closer to his group of graduate students. That's when she moved to the office you just looked at."

"So is someone in her old office?"

"No, Inspector, we don't need it right now since the death of Professor de la Peña. The few graduate students he had have all been reassigned. I believe that office is still empty."

Delgado and Reyes quickly found her old office and began a second search. This time it was easier since the bookshelves were empty as was the desk and file cabinet. Just when they thought this was going to be another dry run, they hit pay dirt. Underneath the plastic liner in the otherwise empty basket of a paper shredder, was a steel letter opener. Delgado cautiously picked it up so as not to contaminate it. She could see that it was long and sharp, and had what could be dried blood on it.

As she was placing it in an evidence bag, Jorge said, "Inspector, that letter opener looks like a match to the set on her desk in the other office."

On returning to Isabella's current office they saw a wooden holder on her desk that held a scissors, a ruler, and an empty slot, presumably for the letter opener. The design on the ruler and scissors matched perfectly with that on the letter opener they'd found.

The police lab quickly determined that there was dried blood on the letter opener, but it would take a few days before they could determine if it was the professor's. That was enough for Delgado to hold Isabella.

Delgado walked into the questioning room and sat at the table opposite Isabella and her court-appointed attorney. She gently placed a report between them and stared at Isabella.

"So why did you do it, Isabella? Was it so you could get the Servetus book for yourself? Or did you just hate the professor so much that you decided to kill him? Which was it?"

Isabella gasped, stunned. "I don't know what you're talking about. I didn't kill him. Why are you doing this?"

It's no use, Isabella, we've got it all right here," the Inspector said, patting the folder on the table. "We have the murder weapon."

"I don't understand," cried Isabella. "What murder weapon? I didn't kill anyone, ever."

"Where's your letter opener?"

"What letter opener?"

"The one that's missing from your desk set in your office at the university," declared Delgado, staring her right in the eyes. "The one we found in the shredder basket in your old office, the one with your fingerprints on it, along with traces of the professor's blood. The one that is a perfect match to the set on your desk with an empty slot where the letter opener normally goes. That letter opener, Isabella."

Isabella sat back in her chair, looking lost and confused, but most of all scared. "I don't—remember that it was missing. I—don't use it every day. The professor's blood was on it? I don't understand. How could that be?"

Delgado got up, walked around behind her, and placed a hand on her shoulder while bending down close to her ear. "Because you stabbed him with it, Isabella. Then you hid it in your shredder basket. That's how it happened. Isn't that right?"

Isabella broke into tears. "No, that's not true. I didn't kill him. I wouldn't do that. I didn't like him, that's true, but I wouldn't kill him."

Shifting gears, Delgado asked, "Do you know what metoprolol is?"

"What?"

"Metoprolol," repeated Delgado.

"No," murmured Isabella, in a lowered voice, now almost a whisper.

"Can you explain, then, why a bottle was found in a chemist bag on your kitchen counter? And can you explain why that bottle had your professor's name on it?"

Isabella, looking confused again began to squirm in her chair and chew her lower lip. She appeared to be thinking.

Finally, Delgado demanded, "Well?"

Isabella snapped to attention, "Oh— that."

"Yes, that," Delgado agreed.

"Sometimes the professor would ask me to run errands for him. You know, like picking up groceries, stuff like that. A few weeks back he asked me to pick up some prescriptions for him from the chemist. That's what it was."

"But you didn't bring it to him, did you?"

"He said there was no rush. I was going to get it to him, but then when—"

"When you killed him?" offered Delgado.

"No. After—you know—after he was—"

"Murdered," finished Delgado.

"Yes. Then I just never got around to throwing them out."

"But you did take some out, didn't you, Isabella? You see," continued Delgado, "there should have been ninety pills in the bottle. We only found eighty. So where are the missing ten pills, Isabella?"

She sat there looking defeated and slumped down in her chair with tears running down her face. She had no answer.

"I'll tell you what happened to them," continued Delgado. "You took them and ground them up and put them in the professor's coffee cup in his office, an office to which you had constant access. Then, when he'd drunk enough to become lethargic and confused due to severely lowered blood pressure, you stabbed him in the chest with your letter opener. That's what happened, wasn't it, Isabella?"

Isabella appeared unable to move.

Inspector Delgado stood and declared, "Isabella Gomez, I'm arresting you for the murder of Professor Isandro de la Peña."

Delgado phoned Hunter and asked him to come to the station. When he took a chair in her office she cracked a rare smile.

"McCoy, you were right about Isabella Gomez. She was more than she seemed on the surface. Her alibi for the time of the professor's death didn't check out."

She told him about the search warrants, the murder weapon, the drug bottles with the professor's name, and the missing pills. They'd also checked the search engine history on her computer and found that three days before the professor's death, she'd looked up metoprolol on the Internet and presumably determined it could be useful to her in killing the professor.

"Here's the story as we pieced it together, with and without her help. Back in February of this year she came across the professor's report on the Mendez collection. Apparently the professor allowed his grad students free access to his office. Anyway, in the back of the report she claims that she'd found a loose note that the professor had written to himself, stating he'd just learned about a book called the *Christianismi Restitutio* that should have been, but wasn't, in the collection when he'd evaluated it. On this note he'd supposedly written 'I'll have to ask Mendez about it.'

"She also said the professor included in this note that he'd estimated the value of such a book at one million euros. We've never found this note. It wasn't in the report in his office when we got there. We think Isabella made it up. If it did exist, it would be a powerful motive for her to want the book badly enough to kill for it.

"She also told us she'd seen a note on the professor's desk calendar that Alfonso Mendez had asked him to provide a copy of the report for his daughter who'd just inherited the collection from her grandfather. We know this note exists. We've seen it.

"Fearing she would lose any chance of unearthing the book that we think she now wanted for herself, she began planning to kill the professor and frame Alicia for the murder. She was ultimately going to complete her degree under another professor while trying to find and keep the book for herself. We think she got the idea for how to do it when the professor asked her to stop at the chemist and pick up some medication for him.   Apparently he frequently asked his students to run errands for him. Once we'd arrested her and questioned her further, she admitted that she knew about Alicia's hypertension and her medication with the drug metoprolol.

"We think she saw her opportunity when she found that the medication she'd picked up for the professor was metoprolol.   We believe she made up the story about finding the note and giving Alicia the idea that he might have designs on the book.   Isabella thought this would make Alicia look guilty.

"When we asked Isabella how the professor had learned about the book in the first place, she initially said she had no idea he hadn't discussed this with her. Later, under intense questioning, she admitted that he'd told her he'd read about it in a ledger that Basilio kept in his library desk drawer."

Of course, thought Hunter. That explains the missing page in the ledger.

"Inspector, I believe you'll find evidence to back this up if you examine this ledger. You'll find that a page has been carefully removed. I believe this page described a meeting between Basilio Mendez and Director Lazodelavega of the Michael Servetus Institute. A meeting in which Basilio told the director about the book and that he intended to donate it to the institute. I've seen this ledger, and the removed page coincides with the very date that Basilio met with the director. You'll also find that this date overlaps with the time the professor was evaluating the collection. I think what happened was the professor took a break from his work on the collection, got into the library, read the ledger and learned about the existence of the book and its ultimate gifting to the Institute, and then removed the page so no one else would know about it. Then he planned to locate the book and take it for himself. Isabella must have gotten the professor to admit this when he was confused by the drug in his coffee before she stabbed him."

Delgado picked it up from there. "That would explain why the professor seemed to change his behavior after the cataloging. He was focused on getting the book. That's why his attitude toward Isabella Gomez, and almost everyone else, deteriorated considerably.

"Isabella also told us that she believed the professor had killed Basilio while trying to get him to reveal where the book was. We believe this too, and the evidence supports it. The professor was there the day Basilio fell off the ladder and he had a powerful motive. Pretty ironic that Isabella's motive for killing the professor was the same as his for killing Basilio: finding the book."

Delgado sat back, clasped her hands, and smiled.

Hunter thought about it all for a moment and then he had an idea. "Inspector?"

"Yeah?"

"Can you trace a text message to a cell phone?"

Delgado's brow creased in confusion. "I believe we can access such records. Why?"

"Remember I told you about the text message threat to Genevieve Swift, telling her to stop looking for the book?"

"Yes, I remember." Then it hit her. "Oh, I see where you're going with this. You think Isabella may have sent it."

"Exactly," agreed Hunter. Since Isabella and Alicia were friends, Maybe Alicia innocently told her about us. Isabella would see our looking for the book as unnecessary competition and decided to scare us off."

"I'll check it out."

"Thanks, Inspector."

"So, McCoy, I believe we have the professor's killer, and I think we know what happened to Basilio Mendez too."

"Good work, Inspector," acknowledged Hunter, with a slight bow of his head.

"Now, you just need to figure out who killed Alfonso Mendez."

Chapter 34

Hunter left Police Headquarters and slowly drove back to the hotel. Somehow, the day seemed a little brighter. He thought about that and what it meant. His mind kept returning to the fact that his real obligation was to Shay Blackwell. After all, Shay had hired him to find an old book that meant something to his late father. But somehow, he'd gotten caught up instead in all this police work, an attempted murder connected to the collider, and at least three murders related in some way to his search for the book.

But getting Alicia off the hook as a suspect in the professor's murder was somehow important to him. He wasn't sure why. He'd never believed she was guilty. But then he wondered why he felt that way? Was it because he actually believed in her innocence, or did he just need her to help him find the book? No, he had to admit it was more than that. Her murdering the professor made no sense. No evidence supported it and his gut told him she didn't do it. For that matter, Genevieve believed she was innocent, and he'd come to realize she had good instincts too.

As he drove, he thought of how complicated it had all become. As he thought about everything that'd happened since they'd started searching for the *Christianismi Restitutio*, he wondered if all of it was somehow related to this book or the message Servetus had supposedly written in it the night before his death?   After all, everyone murdered, Alfonso Mendez, Director Lazodelavega, and Professor de la Peña had some connection to this book.

Even the attempt on Rafael Mendez's life was at least peripherally linked since he was part of the family that supposedly had the book. Was it just a coincidence that Rafael was also a physicist assigned to the collider, and thereby a target for the collider killer?   But Rafael knew nothing about the book, and why would the collider killer, who presumably had his own agenda, care about an old book anyway? None of it made any sense. He just couldn't see any connection.

And then there was the threating note to Genevieve to quit the search. Why her? Why not him? Of course It now seemed likely that Isabella had texted the threat to Genevieve.   He'd know soon enough when Delgado checked it out.

Hunter continued to be stumped by the unanswered questions. If it turns out that Isabella sent the threat, she apparently wasn't the only one trying to stop them. After all, someone had tried to kill him at La Bodega. Was it Baltz? But then, who killed Baltz? Obviously who ever did that was trying to keep them alive. Why? And who was it? If he assumed, and it seemed reasonable, that both shooters were hired guns, whom were they working for? Was it possible that someone wanted him to find the book and was prepared to kill in order to do it, and someone else didn't want it found who had the same level of deadly intent?

Next his thoughts turned to Genevieve. Who tried to run her off the road on her drive back to Geneva?   It seemed likely that it was Rafael's potential shooter, the one he'd winged in the shoulder outside Rafael's apartment. If he were at the airport he'd have been sure I didn't get on the plane with Rafael. Maybe he somehow knew the car he'd been driving and assumed they were both in it when he tried to run it off the road. And, in spite of all this, they were no closer to finding the *Christianismi Restitutio.*

After he picked up Genevieve at the hotel, they stopped at Alicia's apartment to tell her the news. She was shocked to hear that Isabella had been arrested for murder but gratified to know that she was no longer a suspect.

Hunter told Alicia there were still a few loose ends they were trying to figure out. Maybe she could help.

"Of course," she said

"This could be important, so try to remember. Did you happen to mention to anyone that Genevieve and I were looking for the *Christianismi Restitutio* within twenty-four hours after we first met you in the hotel for dinner?"

"Within twenty-four hours? Let me think. What did I do now? Let's see. Oh, I remember, I had lunch with Isabella the next day at the university. And—I think I did tell her it. Yes. I did. Why? Is that important?"

"Later that day, Genevieve got a text message warning her off the search. We think it came from Isabella. Inspector Delgado will know soon. But at least we now know she would have known about us by then."

Alicia sat back in her chair and signed. "Oh, I can't believe it's over. I just want to go—"

"Soak in the tub," completed Genevieve, finishing her thought for her.

"Exactly. Wow. How'd you know? That's exactly what I want to do."

Genevieve grinned, "I thought you might want to do that, so I brought you this little present." She gave her a gift box of bath gel.

She hugged Genevieve and laughed. "It's just what I need. Thank you."

Hunter wasn't sure why, but he felt very paternalistic. Alicia surprised them both by suggesting that if they didn't have other plans she would like to see them in the evening to celebrate.

"You got it," agreed Genevieve. "We'll pick you up back here about eight and it will be our treat and our surprise."

"Great. See you then," replied Alicia.

In the car on the way back to their hotel, Hunter looked at Genevieve questioningly. "Our surprise?"

Genevieve smiled. "I saw advertising in our lobby for a festival tonight in a park not far from our hotel and her apartment. There is supposed to be food, music, dancing, and a flamenco show, all out in the open air. I think it's just what she needs, me too for that matter."

Back at the hotel Hunter made reservations for "dinner under the stars" at La Paloma's on the Green. Then Genevieve phoned Alicia and they worked out what to wear. Hunter smiled contentedly, happy to see them enjoying themselves so much. Later they drove back to Alicia's apartment, parked the Mercedes, and met her at her door.

"I feel so much better," she told them, and she looked it too. Dressed in a colorful peasant dress and sporting a big smile, she looked carefree and even younger than her twenty-five years.

"You look great," remarked Genevieve, taking her hands and dancing with her around the small living room. Both women laughed and hugged. Genevieve was wearing a peasant skirt and blouse and a bright flower in her hair held in place with a large fashionable clip.

"Hey, what about me?" quipped Hunter. Can I join the fun too?"

They all laughed and could tell the evening was just what they needed.

Hunter said, "The city park with the festival is only two short blocks away. I suggest we leave the car where it is and—"

"Just walk over," finished Genevieve.

"Just walk over," Hunter rolled his eyes and shook his head. They strolled to the park, Hunter in the middle with a pretty woman on each arm. The park was quite large with plenty of old oak trees giving it a refreshingly woodland feel. La Paloma's, a restaurant on the grass bordering the park, featured outdoor tables dressed in crisp white linen cloths. Each had an umbrella. The restaurant had both inside and outside seating. The forecast was for a beautiful star-filled night, so Hunter had made reservations for an outside table. Since they weren't going to eat right away, they decided to walk through the park and take in the sights. They encountered booths with every kind of Spanish art. The women were most interested in the jewelry. They also saw large oil paintings of the Spanish countryside, Madrid itself, and of course flamenco dancers.

One very large booth featured oils by an artist whose specialty was exact copies of original works by the great Spanish artists El Greco, Diego Velázquez, and Francisco Goya. The artist had painted these while seated before the actual masterpieces in the Prado museum.

Hunter commented to Genevieve, "You know, I think we saw this guy actually doing one of these paintings that day we took the tour. I remember thinking at the time that he was very good, since I could see both the original and his emerging copy."

"Oh look!" exclaimed Alicia with excitement. "Over there."

They turned and saw a large circle of people clapping their hands to a group of musicians who were part of the circle itself. People were dancing in the center of the circle. They weren't performers but just people in the crowd, mostly women and girls having fun, twirling their brightly colored skirts.

"Come on, Alicia, lets dance," coaxed Genevieve. So the two women joined the pulsing, laughing crowd of dancers while Hunter watched from the sidelines.

Overjoyed to see them having so much fun, he thought that even though they hadn't yet found the book, and though the threat from unknown sources was still out there, he'd successfully foiled the attempt to kill Rafael, while aiding in the arrest of the professor's killer and proving Alicia's innocence.

After a while Alicia came back to Hunter and asked where Genevieve was. Confused, he worriedly asked, "What? She was with you."

"We got separated for a little bit and then I couldn't find her."

Hunter was instantly on alert. This wasn't good. They looked everywhere in and around the group but couldn't see her. His anxiety growing rapidly, Hunter dialed her cell phone. He had seen her put it in her purse. She didn't answer. He knew she had it turned on and she usually kept the ring tone on high.

Damn, where is she?

The dancing had stopped and the crowd dispersed, moving toward the chairs set up for the stage show of flamenco dancers. Still she hadn't come back. Hunter didn't need his instincts to tell him something was wrong. He knew it.

Kestrel suspected that Hunter and the woman were more than just colleagues in search of that damned book. He'd been following them all day. He was tired of trailing them, waiting for the book to be found, if ever. He had to speed this up. That crazy Laurendeau had told him to make it happen. *How do you do that?* He wondered. *I don't even know how much they know. Are they anywhere near finding it, or are we all just wasting our time?* The idea had been in the back of his mind to force their hand, and he decided to do it when he saw the woman go into the women's toilet alone.

As Genevieve emerged and began to stroll toward the booths set up to sell crafts and local items, he moved in behind her, and with his gun covered by a jacket, grabbed her arm and pushed the gun into her back, whispering in her ear. "Don't make a sound or I'll kill you here."

She didn't move at first. Her cell phone rang. "Leave it." He used his gun as a prod. "Go where I tell you. Now."

The woman looked over her shoulder and directly at Kestrel. He thought he saw a spark of recognition in her eyes and started to push her toward the edge of the lawn at the back of the toilet building, to the car park.

Chapter 35

A CITY PARK IN MADRID

Frantic to find Genevieve, Hunter and Alicia searched the park for another two hours. She wasn't anywhere to be found. They even went back to the hotel room thinking she might have gone there for some reason. She hadn't. Alicia wanted to stay with Hunter and help him continue looking but he insisted on taking her home knowing he'd be better able to deal with this alone, unencumbered by having to look out for her.

After dropping off Alicia with a promise he'd call her as soon as he knew something, he returned to the park for another look around. Near the women's toilet on the grassy area leading to the parking lot behind he saw something on the ground that looked familiar. He picked it up. It was the flower that Genevieve had been wearing in her hair earlier. Attached to it was the broad flat clip Hunter had seen her put in her hair earlier.

His unspoken fear exploded to the surface. She'd been taken. She'd either dropped the flower accidently as she struggled with her attacker or she'd dropped it deliberately to alert Hunter. If she had been taken, it clearly wasn't Julian Baltz, the dead sniper in Salamanca. Who was it then?

His cell rang. It was Genevieve's number. He answered but said nothing.

"I have her, McCoy.

Hunter heard a man's voice, French accent, cold and hard.

"You harm her in any way, you're a dead man."

"You just might get her back, McCoy if you give me what I want."

"And what would that be?"

"First, let's have a little talk."

"I'm listening."

"I don't like having my schedule interfered with, and you've done that."

"What are you talking about?"

"The Mendez kid should be dead by now."

There it was. This guy's the LHC killer. What the hell does he want with Genevieve?

"Not only did you stop the hit, you hit me with a lucky shot."

"Believe me, luck had nothing to do with it," hissed Hunter.

"Let's be honest. We're both professionals. You couldn't hope for a clean shot with a handgun from that distance, and only one of six found me and even then you managed only a flesh wound. Still, I'll give you that."

"What do you want?"

"No one has ever slowed me down before, McCoy. I don't like it. I don't like you. Maybe all I want is a little revenge."

"Maybe? You don't know?"

"You know what? I might have a little fun with her first. I'll call you later."

"Wait . . . "

Kestrel hung up.

Genevieve was terrified. When he'd taken her from the park, to his van, he'd taped her mouth and tied her wrists together and her ankles as well. Then he'd pressed a cloth with what must have been chloroform over her nose and mouth and she'd passed out. When she awoke later, still taped and tied she had no idea how long she had been out. She determined she was in the trunk of a car and they were still driving. This went on for what must have been several more hours. She assumed they must be on a highway somewhere. Finally, she figured out by the change in traffic sounds and the periodic slowing of the car, that they were probably entering a city. After another half hour or so, they came to a stop.

The trunk opened and she saw it was nighttime. How long had she been in the trunk? He pulled her out of the car and she dropped on her behind and banged her head on the trunk lip. He put a hood over her head. He untied her ankles and made sure she could feel the hard steel of his gun pressed into the small of her back.

"Do not attempt to run." Grabbing her arm he pushed her forward.

"Up three steps."

Unable to see, she found the steps and did as she was told.

He opened a door and marched her forward across a room and then they stopped. Still unsteady from the cramped quarters of the car trunk and not being able to see, he told her they were going to go down a flight of stairs. He guided her down the stairs and then marched her to a heavy oak door to a room in the corner of the basement. He turned on a light from a switch outside the room, opened the door, and pushed her inside.

He removed the hood, and the bright light immediately blinded Genevieve. Rubbing her eyes she looked around and saw the room slowly come into focus. The room was the size of a small bedroom. It had a cot, a sink and a toilet. No windows. She saw her captor clearly for the first time. He was a man of medium height. About five foot ten inches but he looked very athletic and fit. He was dark,

French, she'd assumed from his accent. He didn't smile. Again, he looked familiar but she couldn't remember how.

"Now listen to me. If you expect to see your boyfriend again, you'll do exactly as I say. If you don't, you will never leave this room alive. I'm going to untie your wrists and remove the tape on your mouth. You will not cry out or attempt to escape. Do you understand?"

Terrified, Genevieve had no choice but to nod her head in agreement.

After freeing her remaining restraints, and the tape on her mouth, she rubbed her wrists and face and breathed deeply.

"Sit down," he told her, indicating the cot.

She did as she was told.

"Now look at me and listen very carefully to what I'm telling you."

Genevieve looked into his eyes and saw evil. If eyes really mirror the soul, this man's soul was that of a psychopath. She shivered in fear.

"I kill people for a living, both men and women, even a few children. I've been doing it for a long time and I'm very good at what I do. I tell you this so that you won't underestimate me. Having said that, I don't plan to kill you. You're valuable to me in another way. But I will kill you, in an instant, without hesitation, if you don't do exactly as I say. Do you understand?"

Genevieve surprised herself and heard her own weak, terrified voice say, "No. I don't understand. What do you want with me? What have I done to you?"

He stared at her with those black, soulless eyes and she felt her inside churn. Then he left, closing and locking the door from the outside.

Genevieve sat on the cot and look around her. The room was a square about 15 feet on a side. The walls were plaster and the plaster ceiling was normal height. She guessed about seven to eight feet. Aside from the cot, the sink and the toilet, there were no other furnishings in the room. She tried the door. As she expected, it was locked in some way from the outside.

Where was she? She knew she'd been in the car trunk for hours and that was after she'd regained consciousness. God. How was Hunter ever going to find her? She knew he'd be looking. He'd drop everything else and find her. She knew it. He'd get her out of this, somehow.

Then she remembered her cell phone. She still had her purse. She dove into it only to find it was gone. The killer must have taken it. Could Hunter track it? She'd read somewhere that the police could locate you by your cell phone. Something to do with GPS, she thought. If the man had it and it was still turned on, Hunter's people could surely find it.

With her options limited, she looked around again. Was there anything she could do to get out of here on her own? She listened. Carefully. Was there any sound? Any sound at all that she could identify? She listened. Nothing. Wait. There was a hum, something, very faint. Yes. Something was humming, maybe a refrigerator. That could be it. Was she in a house? Was this the basement of someone's house, but where? She might not even be in Madrid anymore. Where was she? Where was Hunter? What was he doing? She put her face in her hands and wept.

Hunter's cell phone rang. He saw it was a call from Genevieve's phone.

Hunter spoke first. "You're a dead man walking, but not for much longer. I want to talk with her now."

"Tell you what, McCoy, cut the bravado, give me what I want and you get her back."

Hunter thought, *here it comes.* "What do you want?"

"Why the book, of course."

"The book?" It didn't even register with Hunter at first.

"You know, that book you're looking for, the *Christianismi Restitutio*."

The book? What the hell does the book have to do with this guy? How could killing physicists have anything to do with the book? It makes no sense. What the hell was going on?

"And McCoy," continued the kidnapper, "I'll keep her until you find it and bring it to me. So I suggest you forget about looking for her and get on with finding it. She's out of the country anyway. You see, the only way to get her back is to abandon her for the time being while you find the book."

"I want to talk to her now."

"I'll be in touch," the kidnapper said, and hung up.

Chapter 36

MADRID

Hunter was torn. He couldn't just abandon her. But then the book was the only barter he had. Should he just quit trying to find Genevieve and focus on finding it? Getting the book and exchanging it for her might be the best way to get her back. But the thought of leaving her in the killer's hands and not trying to find her while he searched for it, was too unimaginable to contemplate.

He called Delgado and told her what had happened. "She's been kidnapped, Inspector. I just got a call."

"Has he made a demand?"

"Yes, but I don't understand it. He wants me to find the book we've been searching for, the *Christianismi Restitutio*. He says he'll exchange her for it. But here's the crazy part. He admitted that he was the one who'd tried to kill Rafael Mendez and that I'd wounded him when I stopped the kill.

"Inspector, do you see? He's your LHC killer. What I don't get is what do the murders of the physicists at the collider have to do with the book? There's no way they could be connected."

Delgado paused before answering. "I don't see it either, McCoy. But, a kidnapping and the collider murders are serious business. Get down here to headquarters, and bring your cell phone."

"Inspector?"

"Yes?"

"One other thing. He told me to not bother looking for her. He said she's out of the country."

Four hours later, neither Delgado nor Hunter was happy.   Delgado had reported the LHC connection to Interpol and then was promptly informed forty minutes later that she was no longer in command of the kidnapping on her turf. Because of the LHC connection, a full Interpol task force led by Interpol Agent William Zubriggen would be at her office within three hours.

Hunter knew Zubriggen.   He'd worked with him before. He was a no-nonsense professional. Finding the collider killer would be a priority with him and getting Genevieve back would be part of that effort. But Hunter had misgivings about Zubriggen. He wasn't convinced the man's focus on rescuing Genevieve would be as important as catching the collider killer. He told this to Delgado who had never met the man.

He gave Delgado the flower and hair clip he'd found in the park saying they might contain evidence of the killer's identification, possibly fingerprints or DNA.   When Zubriggen arrived, he'd been mad as hell when he learned that Delgado had already had the evidence scanned and processed by her own department's forensics people instead of turning it over to him. He told her he was now in charge and asked if she was capable of understanding that? Delgado seethed and reluctantly nodded her head. Hunter could see she had never been talked to in so rude and unprofessional a manner.

Zubriggen had never met Delgado but recognized Hunter right away.

"McCoy. So it is you? When I got the report on the assassin's sniper rifle and the request to compare it to the slug that killed the young physicist in Geneva, I saw the name Hunter McCoy, and I thought, could it be?   And guess what? It was."

Then, scowling, Zubriggen demanded, "So what the hell does all of this have to do with you?"

Hunter spent the next hour telling him everything.   In the end, he had to agree reluctantly with both Delgado and Zubriggen, the best way for him to contribute was to focus his efforts on finding the book. Zubriggen told them that the ballistic check on Julian Baltz' sniper rifle didn't match the bullet that killed the young physicist in Geneva or the slug taken from the wall at La Bodega. Hunter already knew that Baltz wasn't the collider killer. So who grabbed Genevieve, and who took the shot at him at the restaurant?

Hunter got his cell phone back after an hour in the skillful hands of Interpol's tech people. They'd tricked it out so that if he received a call from the killer, he was to push the pound key and that would immediately alert the Interpol tech team to track the caller. They were careful to caution him that the tracking could only start when he pushed the key. Because of the importance of catching the collider killer, the tracking team would be standing by twenty-four/seven.

Back in his hotel room, still frustrated by his inability to give one hundred percent of his time to finding Genevieve, Hunter reluctantly returned to his laptop. He knew he had to give his undivided attention to finding the book. Still it was hard and went against every instinct he had.

He was immediately drawn to the page with the Latin quote that he and Genevieve had seen earlier. He read it aloud in what must have been awful Latin, although he couldn't understand it.

He turned on Genevieve's computer and saw that she had typed a translation.

*"In the inhalation and exhalation there is
an energy and a lively divine spirit, since
He, through his spirit, supports the breath
of life, giving courage to the people who
are in the earth and spirit to those who
walk on it.*

Hunter thought the passage sounded a little like what they claimed to be looking for with their supposed research project about why Servetus dropped his pulmonary physiology discovery into the middle of a theological work. *Is it a quote from the Christianismi Restitutio?*

With the words inhalation and exhalation, Hunter figured it was probably in the section that addressed pulmonary physiology. He typed the phrase into the FIND feature, and hit go.

A minute later he had his answer. It was right there in the pulmonary section, first paragraph.

So if this is an actual quote from the missing book, perhaps Basilio did have it after all, Hunter mused. He wondered if there was any significance to the entry date, July 15, 1950. Then he looked to the bottom of the page. He hadn't seen this earlier.

Vegeu el llibre major de la clau

He examined the phrase. Even to his untrained eye, it didn't look like Spanish. Then it hit him. *I bet it's Catalan. Genevieve told me that was the language they spoke in Aragon. And the Servetus Institute is located right in the middle of old Aragon.*

He quickly found a Catalan to English translator on the Internet. He typed in *Vegeu el llibre major de la clau.* The translation came up instantly.

"See the ledger for the key"

Hunter clicked through the computer images of the ledger's pages, but nothing stood out as being unusual. He needed some idea where to look. He continued scanning for a few minutes and then saw that the ledger was dated too. *Now what was the date of the diary entry where I found the quote?*

He scrolled through the diary pages on her computer. There it was. July 15, 1950.

Unlike the diary, there were no printed dates on the consecutive pages in the ledger. Instead, Basilio apparently added the dated entries, as he needed them. Sometimes there were several different dates on a single page, each with its own entry.

Then he found the same date in the ledger, July 15, 1950. The entry read:

Sepultus est clavis haeresis
05915170425203872080208 3

Hunter examined it quietly for a moment. He thought it looked like Latin. Going back to the Internet, this time for a Latin to English translator, he had his answer.

Buried here is the key to heresy.

He considered the phrase and wondered if it meant the book was buried somewhere. More likely it referred to a key. Maybe the numbers are the key to where it's buried, or the key is buried in the numbers. Then it jumped out at him.

It's the date. July 15, 1950.

07151950

But it was backwards.

05915170 became 07151950.   July 15,
1950.

If I remove those numbers from the larger set I get:

4252038720802083.

Maybe this needs to be reversed too.

3802080278302524.

He could see it was too long for a social security
number or a combination and it didn't look like a phone
number. Maybe it was a number to a Swiss bank account.
   *Wait let me try something. I'm looking for a location.
The book has to be somewhere.   What if the numbers
represent map coordinates? There would have to be two of
them. So, if I divide the remaining numbers in half I get:*

   38020802 and 78302524

   *Coordinates are in degrees, minutes, and seconds, so
it could be 38 degrees, 02 minutes, 08.02 seconds.*
   He examined what was left.   He had 78 degrees, 30
minutes, 25.24 seconds. *This could be it*, he thought.   The
numbers fit the pattern needed for map coordinates: degrees
in whole numbers, minutes in whole numbers, and seconds
with a decimal.   And coordinates wouldn't change or be
lost after sixty years.   If he assumed the first set was
latitude and the second set longitude, he just needed to
know if the latitude was north or south and the longitude
east or west.
   Hunter looked for a website that would let him put in
map coordinates to locate a spot on the planet.
   Within minutes he found such a program.

He tried north latitude and east longitude and the map moved to a location in the desert of western China.

I don't think that's it.

Next he plugged in north latitude and west longitude and the globe spun again and zoomed in.

I don't believe this, thought Hunter, astonished. *What's going on here?*

The coordinates were for a site in Charlottesville, Virginia.

Chapter 37

GENEVA

Genevieve was beginning to lose track of time. She couldn't tell if it was day or night and was becoming increasingly disoriented. The man had only been back twice, each time to bring her food. So far he hadn't harmed her. But there was something about him that made her skin crawl. It was his eyes. They showed no human empathy at all. She sensed he viewed her as less than nothing, a thing, no more important than a stick of furniture.

No one she'd ever met had eyes like that. There was no soul behind them. Every person she'd ever met showed something with their eyes; love, happiness, concern, emotions of all kinds. Not this man. The evil she saw in his eyes reflected death. He was dead inside and he terrified her because of it.

The first time he'd brought her food she'd asked him what he wanted, why he'd taken her. He told her she'd go free when McCoy brought him the book, then left immediately without further explanation. Genevieve didn't understand. Our book? Does he mean the Servetus book? Was he the one who'd warned her off the search? Wasn't that Isabella? But then why would he do that? If he wanted the book why not let us find it and then try to take it? And why would a man who kills for a living want the *Christianismi Restitutio* anyway?

Thinking about the book turned her thoughts to Hunter. She knew he'd be looking for her. He wouldn't abandon her. But then if the only way for him to get her back was to find the book, maybe that's what he was doing. That had to be it. The man must have contacted Hunter and told him to find the book and that would be her ransom.

She sat on the cot, depressed, knowing they hadn't even been close to finding it. Worse, maybe it didn't even exist. *Oh, Hunter, where are you? Get me out of here.*

Again she tried to figure out where she was or if there was some possible way to escape. The door was solid and there was nothing in the room she could use to even try to pry it open. There was a heating vent in the wall above her bed but it was way too small for her to crawl through even if it led somewhere other than the furnace. She was imprisoned as surely as if she were in a real jail.

She'd noticed that if she stood on the bed and put her ear to the vent she could hear the humming a little louder. She made a cone with her hand against her ear and pressed it against the wall. She moved around the entire room this way. On the wall between the door and the sink she was definitely able to hear talking. Was the man back? She listened. It was definitely a man talking. What was he saying?

She recognized the voice. It was the kidnapper. She could tell. He must be talking on the phone because he'd talk and then there would be a pause and he'd talk again. It wasn't clear enough for her to make out any words. Then it stopped.

A few minutes later the door opened and he brought in food again, burgers from a local fast food place.

Genevieve stood and surprised herself by demanding. "Where am I? At least tell me where I am. What difference would it make to you?"

Kestrel paused on his way out the door. He looked at her with those soulless dead eyes. "All you need to know is that anytime you're with me you're very close to hell."

Enraged, she ran at him and struck him with her fist. He backhanded her so hard she bounced off the wall with her head and fell unconscious to the floor.

Some time later, she had no idea how long; the room began to come back into focus as she regained consciousness. She had to get out of here. There had to be a way. She looked around the room again as she'd done hundreds of times before. Under the sink was a metal plate, round, about 6 inches in diameter, next to the water pipes that went to the sink above. She'd seen it before but as it was too small to crawl through, even if it went somewhere, she'd left it alone. Looking at it now again, she wondered what it was for? She crawled under the sink and put her ear to it. She heard talking again, but surprisingly, it was much clearer. Cupping her hand into an amplifier she put her ear to the plate again.

"Laurendeau, I won't say it again, holding her will speed up the process. I've seen them together. He'll double his efforts to find the book. If it's out there, he'll get it. If not, they both die."

Genevieve made a promise to herself then and there. She wouldn't die here. Not at the hands of this monster. With a glimmer of hope and a lot of determination, she used her nail file and began to remove the circular plate.

Chapter 38

Just as Hunter was about to call Delgado to see if there were any leads to Genevieve or the kidnaper, his phone rang.

"Have you found the book yet?"

Hunter put his finger over the pound key and hesitated, then made a decision.

"I know where it is. It's in the United States, in Charlottesville, Virginia. But I'm not going to go there or find it until I see that she's all right."

"Impossible."

"I need to see for myself that she's all right. Only then will you get the book."

"Stay where you are," the kidnapper commanded and hung up.

Hunter hadn't pressed the pound key. His gut told him not to. Not yet.

An hour later the phone rang.

"Drive to the parking lot on the corner of Sommer and Main. Be there in exactly fifteen minutes, park in slot 362. Step out of you car and wait." He hung up again.

Hunter was there in eleven minutes, got out of the car and waited.

He heard a phone ring. *Where was it?* Then he saw it sitting on the floor at the back of the slot against the concrete wall. He picked it up and pressed 'answer.'

"Listen carefully, I'm only going to say this once. Tomorrow at exactly noon she will be sitting in the Midtown Restaurant. She will be at a table, inside, visible through a glass window. You can see her from the opposite side of the street where you will take an outside table at the Café Sonne. I'll be able to see you at all times and she will be continually in my crosshairs. Do not approach her in any way. Do not attempt to cross the street. Do not attempt to signal her in any way. You will come alone. If you violate any of these instructions, she will die immediately. Don't test me, McCoy. She means nothing to me and I'll kill her on the spot. After exactly two minutes, she will get up and leave. You will remain seated for one additional hour. You won't like the results if you attempt to follow her. By the way, the restaurants are in Versoix, a suburb of Geneva, Switzerland. You'd better get moving." He hung up.

Geneva? Geneva again.

He caught the red eye to Geneva. He decided to call Delgado when he landed. He wanted to know if they had learned anything about the kidnapper's identity. He knew he wouldn't tell her about the kidnappers call or what he was going to do in Geneva out of fear for Genevieve's safety.

He had four hours till noon after he landed. He called Delgado from the airport.

"Have you learned anything about the identity of the kidnapper from the flower or the hair clip?"

McCoy, I'm going to tell you again. Your 'friend' Zubriggen is in charge of this case and your job, your only job, is to locate that book."

Hunter was really getting annoyed with her. Then he got an idea. "Fine, Inspector. Can you at least tell me if they've identified him?"

"Yes we—I mean they— have. We know who we're looking for. Now leave it to us and do your job." With that, she hung up.

Hunter called Slocum at DIA.

"Slocum, can you find a number for me at Interpol headquarters in Lyon? An Eduard Gautier. I need it fast."

Still sounding peeved at his roll in this, Slocum answered. "Will wonders never cease? It's about time you brought Interpol into this. It's really a police matter you know."

"Slocum, cut the bullshit. The Director has assigned you to cooperate with me. Can you do it or do I have to ask him for someone who can?"

"Hold on."

Hunter waited and could actually hear Slocum's fingers flying over the computer keyboard. Within a minute he had it.

"Eduard Gautier, head of Information Technology, Interpol. That your man?"

"That's the one."

He gave the number to Hunter who cut off Slocum and called it immediately.

"Hunter. It's good to hear from you again. The Director told me you'd be calling—my director—not yours. Of course, my guy first got a call from Deacon asking for our cooperation. He told me you'd been temporarily reactivated. What can I do for you, old buddy?"

Eduard and Hunter had worked together on several high profile cases and the information transfer went equally in both directions, from DIA to Interpol and from Interpol to DIA. They'd always worked well together and never withheld important information from each other. Hunter hoped that would still be the case.

"Eduard, I need some information on the LHC killer case. I supplied some evidence to Interpol that had fingerprints or DNA information on it, information that could identify the killer. I need to know if they've matched it to a name."

"That's a hot case here, Hunter, Agent William Zubriggen is leading that investigation. You'll need to go through him to get that information."

"Eduard, I could do that. But, and you'll have to trust me on this, I need that information without going through him."

Hunter waited while Gautier contemplated this. Finally, "Hunter you know that's against regulations. The case officer in charge is the one to clear all pertinent information related to it. What you're asking is highly irregular."

"I understand."

Another long pause, followed by a huge sigh, "You're going to owe me one for this, buddy."

Hunter waited. After a few minutes Gautier was back on the line. "His name is Alan Moreau, but he uses the *nom de plume*, Kestrel. He's French from Marseille, five-foot-ten, brown eyes and hair, extremely fit and a stone-cold killer. He takes contracts all over the world. He's an efficient, ruthless, psychopath. And here's where it gets really interesting. He's dead."

"What?"

"He was reported killed on a yacht explosion in the Mediterranean a year ago. No body was found."

Hunter thought this over. "It seems there was a good reason they didn't find his body. Trust me, he's very much alive."

Hunter took a cab to the Café Sonne in the Geneva suburb of Versoix and arrived at almost 11:30 AM where he took a table and ordered coffee. He looked across the street at the Midtown Restaurant and could easily see the glass window Kestrel spoke of. He didn't know why but it helped to put a name to the bastard. Kestrel; what kind of name was that. Then he remembered; it was the name of a medium sized bird of prey, a raptor that survived by killing. It seemed an appropriate choice.

At exactly noon he saw her sit down, alone, at the table by the window. His relief was palpable. He allowed himself a moment of thanks and then he studied her. She was wearing the same blouse and peasant dress she'd been wearing when they'd gone to the park. She looked nervous, or he imagined she did. He wasn't sure. As he looked he could see that something was off. She never looked directly across the street, as if she'd been told not to. Still, he knew it was Genevieve. There was no doubt of that. She didn't appear to have any bruises and except for the very deliberate slow movements, looked okay. Hunter didn't doubt for a minute that if he didn't obey the instructions, and leave her there, Kestrel would kill her instantly, just as he'd said he would.

Then Hunter saw a waitress appear and talk to Genevieve. Genevieve looked nervously over the waitress's shoulder to the back of the room. Shaking her head, no, she said something to the waitress who then left her alone. A few seconds later, exactly two minutes after she appeared, Genevieve got up and walked back out of sight.

Hunter was a tangle of emotions. She was right there. He could grab the bastard and free her, now. He couldn't let her go back with him. She depended on him. Was he going to fail again? It took all of his will power to remain seated for another hour. But he did it, just as he'd been instructed. He knew he couldn't risk going after Genevieve since he knew the psychopath would put a bullet in her brain and not raise his heartbeat in the process. Hunter made a silent promise to himself then, that when he did find this Kestrel, he'd make sure his heartbeats stopped permanently.

After the hour he quickly got up and ran across the street. There was now a 'closed' sign on the window of the restaurant where she'd sat at the window and Hunter had to knock and show his Interpol ID. A man opened the door and allowed Hunter to enter. The place was empty except for the terrified man who identified himself as the owner, and the waitress he'd seen in the window. As hunter approached they both seemed to shrink back trying to disappear.

"Tell me what happened here."

The owner replied, "A man came in with a girl and told the few customers that were in the place to get out now. This was a police matter, he'd claimed. We were not to call the police or let other customers in."

"Hunter eyed the waitress who looked equally terrified, and then said, "What did you do?"

"I did as he asked. Everybody left." Then, as an afterthought, he said, "There were only two couples."

"Then what?"

"Then he told the girl to sit by the window but not to look out. He stayed back here," indicating the counter, "with a gun pointed at her."

Hunter looked at the frightened waitress. "You approached her and spoke with her. What did she say?"

She bit her lip and looked around nervously. "You're an American, right?"

Puzzled, Hunter nodded, "yes"

"Are you also her friend?"

Hunter sensed something. "Yes, yes, I am her very good friend. What is it? What do you know?"

"The woman at the window said 'Please remember this. It's very important. Tell my American friend to find Laurendeau.'"

"Laurendeau" What's Laurendeau?"

"I don't know. That's all she said. I can tell you she was scared. Then the man with the gun took her away. He told us not to move for an hour. We didn't. Not until you came in."

Hunter called Slocum. "Slocum, I need you to do a search for me. I've got a name for you. I don't know if it's a person, a place or something else. The name is 'Laurendeau' and it's probably in Geneva or at least in Switzerland, maybe not though. If you find something with a link to a man named Alan Moreau aka Kestrel, a hired killer from Marseille, that would be the link."

Then Hunter got an idea. Since Kestrel was, no doubt, the LHC killer, maybe Laurendeau is related to the collider.

"Here's another thread to look for. See if any of your searches relate in any way to the Large Hadron Collider."

Slocum, his earlier reluctance to cooperate apparently gone, said he'd get right on it.

Chapter 39

Hunter called Shay Blackwell to tell him he'd be flying back to Virginia immediately to resume the search there, but before he could get it out, Shay excitedly blurted out, "Hunter, I have some great news. I've found out the book does exist and it's somewhere here in the States, probably right here in Virginia. We just don't know where. I need you to get back here, now, to start looking for it."

"Shay, I believe that I know exactly where to look."

Still reluctant to leave Geneva, Hunter boarded a transatlantic flight to Atlanta and then on to Charlottesville. He went directly from the airport to the Blackwell home in the country. When he arrived, Shay Blackwell, his wife, and his daughter greeted him, and they all retired to the sun deck.

Hunter hadn't told him about Genevieve, but knew he had to now. When he'd finished telling them everything right up to the role of Interpol in trying to find Genevieve and the collider killer, they all sat stunned.

Finally Karen, Shay's wife spoke. "How awful. Oh, Hunter. This must be terrible for you."

Shay agreed, and followed it up with, "Of course you know if you do need the book to free her, it's yours."

"Thank you, Shay, I was sure you'd say that, but I hope it won't come to that."

"So," continued Shay, "Are you going to do as they say and put all your efforts into the search?"

"It's the only choice I have."

Margaret brought them all refreshments and Shay continued. "In that case, let me tell you what we've learned."

He went on to tell them that yesterday he'd received a sealed package from Hugo Alvarez who had been Basilio Mendez' personal attorney, friend, and confidant for many years. The package contained documents that told a story, much of which Hunter already knew.

The fourth copy found its way to the Calderon family in Spain. Then, in 1942, during the war, Señora Honoria Calderon entrusted it to Basilio Mendez for safekeeping. Later, in 1947, Basilio Mendez sent Shay's father the letter asking him to come to Spain to view it. It seems he intended to have George Blackwell take possession of the book and bring it back with him to America for safekeeping. After mailing this letter, Basilio had been surprised to find that the very same week, George had been sent back to Madrid by the United States Government to tend to some final embassy details. While there he visited Mendez and got the history along with the book, which he took back to the U.S. with him. When Shay's father returned and found the letter, he never opened it, since he already knew what it said.

Hunter knew this already. He had a moment of melancholy remembering how he and Genevieve had figured it out together. Now he had to find the damned thing and get her back. He learned that Basilio thought the book should not be kept in private hands, by his family, but should be made public at some point. However, he didn't trust the postwar Franco authoritarian dictatorship enough to give it to them. He'd had considerably greater faith in the postwar American government in the late 1940s than he did in his own. He'd arranged for George to hold the book for safekeeping until a time in the future when it might be safely returned to Spain. Then it would go to a suitable institution for access by scholars and the general public.

Some time later, George Blackwell informed Basilio Mendez that the book was secure and would be returned to Spain at any time that Basilio chose. Basilio replied that he didn't want to know exactly where the book was being kept, just that it was being properly cared for. Not content to have Basilio completely in the dark as to its location, George Blackwell sent him a code that, if he chose to do so, could be unlocked to tell him where it was.

The code he sent Basilio was:

> *In the inhalation and exhalation there is an energy and a lively divine spirit, since He, through his spirit supports the breath of life, giving courage to the people who are in the earth and spirit to those who walk on it.*

> *Sepultus est clavis haeresis*
> 05915170425203872080283

Shay continued the story. "Now Margaret, my daughter here, speaks Spanish and translated the first phrase. We don't know what it means. She said the second phrase looks Spanish but is somewhat different. She doesn't know what is says. And of course, we don't know what the numbers mean.

"So Hunter, your new task is to find out what these phrases mean and decode the numbers."

Hunter smiled.

"All right, what's so funny?" asked a puzzled Shay Blackwell.

Hunter with a smug look on his face replied. "Now I have a story to tell you," and explained how he'd cracked the code.

After they had digested all this, Shay said, "Well now that we have these coordinates you've worked out, let's get to it. The *Restitutio* must be located where they converge. It's the only explanation."

"I agree," said Hunter. "But we have a little problem. On the flight over I used the laptop to do some calculations. It seems that if the coordinates are correct, the best degree of accuracy we can expect is four hundred feet north or south of the actual location and about two hundred feet east or west. So it could be anywhere within eighty thousand square feet, or about two acres."

"Well where is this two-acre chunk of land?" asked Blackwell.

"Right on the University of Virginia campus—more precisely, in the area of the Darden School of Business Administration."

Shay grinned and straightened up. "That's got to be it. My father got his MBA in business at the University. He must have stored it there somewhere."

"I'll get right on it," said Hunter.

The business school was a red brick colonial-style structure with a beautiful white colonnaded entrance portico at the top of a two-sided stairway leading upward from the grass-covered grounds. Hunter knew from his own affiliation with the medical school that the Darden Graduate School of Business Administration was one of the top-ranked business schools in the country.

He got there early so he could have a look around before his meeting with the dean. Hunter figured that the business school itself occupied considerably more than two acres of ground, more like thirty acres. He walked around the business campus and reflected on the beauty of the brick buildings. Hunter learned that the business school library was called the Camp Library. On a lark, he had used the computerized library search engine to look up the *Christianismi Restitutio.* Not surprisingly, it wasn't among the library's holdings.

When he got to the dean's office, the dean, a very affable fellow, met him at the door.

"Hello, Dr. McCoy. I don't believe we've met. I'm Jim Driscol. Please come in. I must say I don't get many academic visits from the med school faculty. I'm delighted with the change."

"I know what you mean," said Hunter. "It seems the only way faculty from diverse colleges get together is when they serve on university-wide committees."

"You got that right. Well, since this isn't a university committee, to what do I owe the honor?"

Hunter didn't really know how he was going to proceed. He certainly didn't want to tell the dean that he was searching for a missing sixteenth century manuscript somewhere on his campus. He didn't think Dean Driscoll, for all his friendliness, would take kindly to tearing apart his domain to search for it.

"I'm doing a favor for Shay Blackwell," explained Hunter. "You probably know him because he's on the University board of trustees."

"Yes, of course. Mr. Blackwell has been a good friend to the college over the years."

"You may also know that his father, George Blackwell graduated from the MBA program here."

"I didn't know that, no," commented the dean. "He must have been in the first class or close to it. The Darden School of Business was inaugurated in 1954. Here, let me take a look."

The dean went to his shelves and took down a book whose spine read "Class of 1951" written in gold. "I have a copy of all the old yearbooks. We had a graduate degree in business even before the Darden School was built in 1954." He thumbed through the book and said, "Ah ha. Here it is. Sure enough, a picture of young George Blackwell."

Hunter took the book when the dean offered it and asked if he could have some time to examine it. If he could have it for a day, he'd return it to the dean promptly.

"Sure, no problem, anything for Mr. Blackwell. Now what was the favor you were going to do for him?"

"I think you've already done it."

Back at his loft, Hunter leafed through the yearbook. He noticed that George Blackwell's classmates had elected him class president. There were typical pages of professors teaching, group discussions, ground breaking ceremonies for new buildings, and then he saw it. It wasn't much, just a single picture with a caption below it.

It showed George Blackwell placing what looked like a metallic box into a hole in a concrete circle about four feet in diameter. There were two other students standing around. The caption read:

> MBA students place sealed time capsule on grounds of the new business school to be opened at some time in the future. From left to right are class president George Blackwell, Francis Evans, and William Snelling.

My God that's got to be it. He put the book in the time capsule. But what kind of time capsule doesn't have an opening date? 'Some time in the future' is not very specific. Where did they put it?

He looked through the rest of the yearbook, but found no other reference to it.

Wait a minute. I do remember that The Darden Business School buried another time capsule just a few years ago, shortly after I started with the medical school. That one won't be opened until 2057. But I don't remember any mention of an earlier one.

He checked the school's web sites, and the only reference he could find to a time capsule was the Darden Capsule, the one that wouldn't be opened until 2057.

Maybe the dean would know, Hunter thought.

Chapter 40

It had been three days since the killer had called. Hunter guessed he was giving him time to find the book. Hunter hated not actively trying to get Genevieve back himself. He could barely concentrate on the task at hand when he thought of the terror and fear she must be feeling. Still he knew that Zubriggen and his team were lasered on finding the man and, by extension, Genevieve too. He had to do everything he could to insure she wasn't hurt in the process.

He always carried the cell phone with him and saw to it that it was on and fully charged at all times with the ringer set to 'loud.' Again, he resigned himself to finding the book.

He returned the yearbook to Dean Driscoll and asked him about a possible earlier time capsule. "I've never heard of an earlier time capsule. The one we placed in 2007 is the only official one I know of."

"Maybe that's the answer. Maybe it wasn't official, but was just the work of George Blackwell and a few students. But then, I wonder how it got into the yearbook?"

"That wouldn't have been so hard," commented the dean. "It's not as though yearbooks were policed in those days. I'm sure the editors were just looking for interesting pictures to fill up space."

Hunter took another look at the photo with the time capsule. "Look here. Blackwell has one hand on the time capsule, but check out the other hand."

The Dean looked and saw what he as referring to. Blackwell had his index finger curled over his right thumb and his other three fingers were deliberately spread out, as if to indicate the number three.

Hunter stared at the picture. "He is trying to tell us something. It must mean three something. Three what? Wait! There are three of them in the picture. Maybe he is saying that the three of them know where it is. Or George is telling us that, if death takes any of them, the other one or two would know where it is."

"I don't know. It seems like a long shot."

"Or maybe he is saying there are three items in the capsule?" Hunter suggested.

"Or the hole is three feet deep," offered the Dean.

"In any case," Hunter said with a shrug, "it's all I have right now. I'll check with the Registrar's Office, or the Alumni Office, more likely, and see if they know the whereabouts of the other two in the photo. Unfortunately, we know that George Blackwell's already dead."

"Francis Evans and William Snelling?" repeated the alumni director. "What year did you say?"

Hunter told him it was 1950. "The university hadn't built the Darden School yet. The men would probably have been business majors, but I'm not sure."

"If they graduated, I'll find them. Records going back that far predate our computers, but at least the names of the graduates have been computerized from that era." He tapped at his keyboard. "Here we are. Evans, Francis Lee, graduated in spring 1951, business administration. Last known address, 6245 Pinehurst Lane, Fredericksburg, VA. There is no record of death. So he is likely to be on our active alumni list."

"What about Snelling?"

"Yep—Snelling, William Brendan, also graduated in spring 1951, in business administration. He didn't go far from home. After graduating he took a job in the University Development Office and stayed there until he retired in 1994. He is still in town. His address is 1106 Minor Rd. Charlottesville, VA. No record of death."

Hunter thanked the alumni director, and left.

He found the house and a man in his eighties, presumably Snelling, answered the knock to his front door. He was medium height with thinning white hair and slight build. He wore a golf shirt over gray slacks.

"William Snelling?" asked Hunter.

"Yes, I'm Bill Snelling. What can I do for you? I don't want to buy anything or join your church."

"Mr. Snelling, I'm not selling anything or asking you to join any religious group. I'm Hunter McCoy. I'm a professor at the med school here at the University. I wonder if you could help me with a mystery."

"Well, that sounds exciting. I can't imagine how I could help you, but won't you come in?" He stood aside.

"Would you care for some coffee? I just made a fresh pot. I'm alone these days, since my wife died two years ago, but my coffee is still first rate."

Hunter didn't want to waste time with niceties. All he could think about was getting the book and finding Genevieve. While Snelling went off to fetch it, Hunter looked around. The furnishings were old and somewhat dated, but the house was neat. Much like the man himself. He returned with the coffee and they sat down.

"Now then, what can I do to help you?"

"I've been asked to do a favor for Shay Blackwell," Hunter explained.

"I know Blackwell, but not well. He's on the board of trustees for the university. I did know his father George. We were in the same class together in the early fifties."

"Yes, I know. That's really why I'm here. I came across a picture of you, along with George Blackwell and a student named Francis Evans, in an old yearbook. You were burying a time capsule. Do you remember that?"

"Wow, that old thing. I haven't thought about that in years. Sure, I remember it. It was George's idea. He was class president, you know. We didn't really have any university sanction to do it. He said it would be a neat thing to do, as the university was getting ready to start a fundraising campaign to create a top-tier business college. Since we would all graduate before that happened, it would be a way to commemorate life in the business program before the era of the new school."

Leaning forward, Hunter asked, "So what did you put in it?"

"Nothing really important, a copy of the school newspaper, a copy of the class offerings, some 45 rpm records, junk like that. Like I said, it wasn't very impressive. Evans and I thought the whole thing was a little strange but George could be very persuasive. He'd used his own money to buy it. Moisture and temperature resistant containers were not cheap, even then. It had to withstand water, heat, cold, and the stress of being underground for many years.

There *was* something weird about the time capsule, though," mused Snelling. "I never could figure out why the thing didn't have an opening date. All George would say was, "I'll know when to open it."

"Was there anything specific George wanted to put in the capsule?"

"Well, that was strange too. Not only did he personally buy the capsule, he put a package in that was very well sealed. Now what was it he said? Heck, it's been so many years. Let me think. It was something like—oh, I don't remember. It was something about a country—Spain, I think. That's it, Spain."

With a sense of growing excitement, Hunter asked, "Mr. Snelling, can you tell me where the capsule was buried? Do you remember?"

"Yes, I can tell you, but you won't like it. Remember, we had no university permission to bury it. We selected a spot north of the campus in a wooded area that we thought would always stay that way. We were wrong. The university expanded and chose that very spot to build the new Darden School of Business. The Business Administration building now sits atop the site. I'm afraid the area was excavated when the foundation was laid."

Chapter 41

To say Hunter was profoundly disappointed wouldn't even come close. The book was the only real hope he had to get Genevieve back. How could it have been destroyed just like that? Unintentionally, but still destroyed.

He drove silently for some time. Finally, determined to not give up so easily, he decided to drive to Fredericksburg and see the other man in the picture, Francis Evans. He checked the map. It looked like a two-hour drive.

He reached Fredericksburg about three PM. He found 6245 Pinehurst Lane with no trouble. It was a modest house on a street of similar older homes. The maple trees lining the street formed a shady canopy that made the whole area feel comfortably warm.

The woman who answered the door was probably in her late seventies. She was slim and neatly dressed in navy slacks and a pink and white striped blouse. Classically beautiful, she clearly took good care of herself.

Hunter introduced himself. "I'm sorry to bother you. Are you Ms. Evans?'

"Yes, I'm Clara Evans."

"Mrs. Evans, I'm Dr. Hunter McCoy from the Medical School at the University of Virginia, I'd like to talk with your husband, Francis Evans, if I could."

Her hand went to her mouth and he could see that she was fighting back tears.

"I'm sorry, Mrs. Evans, is something wrong?"

"I'll be all right. Just give me a minute. Where are my manners? Won't you please come in?"

She told him that she had just buried her husband two weeks before and was still not used to people asking about him.

"I'm sorry for your loss," said Hunter, thinking he should probably leave, but knowing he had to question her.

"Please stay and have some coffee with me. It's actually comforting to talk about Lee."

"Lee?" inquired Hunter.

"Yes, he never went by Francis. He always used his second name, Lee."

He sat on a stiff sofa while she got coffee. The house was much like the one that Ed Snelling lived alone in, in Charlottesville. It was older with what looked like some valuable antique furniture. She returned with a tray of coffee mugs, cream and sugar, and delicious looking oatmeal raisin cookies.

Just as he had with Ed Snelling, Hunter explained that he was doing a favor for Shay Blackwell, the son of a college friend of her husband's. He explained about the picture in the yearbook and the time capsule. He further explained that the capsule had been inadvertently destroyed in the building of the Darden Business School in 1954. He was just going to ask her husband if he could tell them anything about it.

Hunter continued. "I should also tell you that most of the materials that went into the time capsule were typical bits of memorabilia. However, George Blackwell apparently also used the time capsule as a sort of safety deposit box for a rare and valuable book that he had been given by a Spanish compatriot from WWII, when he served as vice consul to the American embassy in Madrid."

Hunter left little out of the story that had been his life during the past several weeks. Maybe he needed the catharsis, since he appeared to be at the end of the line in his search, or maybe it was because Clara Evans seemed to be enjoying his company. He didn't know.

When he'd finished, Clara Evans stared out the window for a long time. After this period of reflection, she spoke. "Dr. McCoy. I think you should let me put something a little stronger in your coffee than cream and sugar. You're going to need it when you hear what I have to tell you."

Hunter felt his heart quicken. "My husband Lee had lasting memories of that time capsule," Clara Evans continued. "He knew especially that it meant a lot to George Blackwell. George was a little older than Lee and Ed. I suppose it was because of George's time away during the war years. Anyway, Lee told me his part in the time capsule burial shortly after we were first married in 1957. Initially he thought the whole thing was a bit of a lark.

"George bought the time capsule with his own money and organized the burial. He found the plot of land, and then the three of them made the concrete mold that would serve as the frame around the capsule. It wasn't an official university project, so only George, Ed, and Lee filled it.

"George told Lee, and he may have told Ed as well, I don't know, that what he was putting in was an old, rare, and important book that he had been entrusted with by a friend he made during the war years when he was with the American Embassy in Spain. Exactly as you just told me, it was very important that the book be kept safe for many years until the right time for it to surface arrived. Their time capsule was the perfect place for it.

"Then disaster struck, at least as far as the time capsule was concerned. The university got funding for the new Darden School of Business to be located on the north campus, exactly where they'd placed the time capsule a few years earlier. Lee was already working for a company in Lynchburg, Virginia at the time, and he kept up with the construction plans as they unfolded in 1954. George Blackwell had died by this time.

When the crews were ready to dig on the site, Lee was there ahead of time. He told the heavy equipment operator who was commissioned to level the land what they had done. The man, as it turned out, was very cooperative. He dug it up with his machine, breaking the concrete and freeing the time capsule. I guess he figured it was okay since the young man, my husband Lee, had told him about it before he dug. Lee took the time capsule away with him."

"My God," exclaimed an ecstatic Hunter, "it's still intact? What did he do with it?"

"Dr. McCoy, you look like a very healthy young man. If you'll follow me, I have something heavy for you to lift."

Hunter followed her into a room that functioned as an office. There on the floor in the corner sat a square stainless steel box with a lid and a lift handle.

Patting it, Clara said, "My husband never opened it. He said that he would respect the wishes of George Blackwell. All he ever said to me was that somehow, he didn't know how, when it was the right time to open it, he'd know. That's all he said, he'd know."

"But now, Dr. McCoy, after the story you've told me I believe the 'right time' that Lee had always talked about, has come. The best thing to do is to give the time capsule to George Blackwell's son, Shay Blackwell. You can take it with you and give it to him."

As he was preparing to leave with the capsule, Sara Evans hugged him and said that his coming today was just what she needed.

As he drove back to Charlottesville, Hunter was already planning strategy to get Genevieve back.

Chapter 42

Hunter drove straight to the ranch. He had to talk to Shay immediately. On the ride back from Fredericksburg he'd been devising a plan. He needed to get the capsule to Shay and they had to open it to verify the presence of the book. Then he had to get Shay on board with his plan.

He reached the ranch just after the family had finished dinner. Leaving the capsule locked in the trunk, Karen brought him to Shay's study where the two men looked at each other without speaking.

"I've got it, Shay, the time-capsule. It's in the trunk of the car outside."

"What? You have it? But how?"

"Wait. First let me bring it in and I'll tell you."

Hunter carried the heavy capsule in and set it on the desk that Shay had already covered with a large towel. The men stared at it. Finally Shay said. "You open it Hunter. It's been your search."

Hunter screwed the cap off. It was surprisingly easy after all these years. He carefully removed the contents. The largest item was a package wrapped in paper and sealed with tape. The little bit of additional material in the capsule included an old school newspaper dated June 21, 1950, a copy of class offerings, some photos of campus activities and two 45-rpm records. One featured Nat King

Cole singing *Mona Lisa* and the other had Patti Page singing *Tennessee Waltz*.

Then he turned his attention to the package. He carefully opened it and there it was, the *Christianismi Restitutio*. They both stared, saying nothing. Hunter could hear his own breathing, in and out, in and out. By God, he'd found it.

One of now only four known to still exist. Hunter was speechless. How could he describe it? All these years, sealed in a capsule, all he and Genevieve had been through to find it, and here it was. Hunter could tell it was old. It had a musty smell that had to be all its own, as the other items in the capsule didn't smell that way.

He hesitated to touch it, even though it looked sturdy. It had an ornately decorated leather cover, about 5 by 7 inches in size and approximately two inches thick. Carefully lifting this cover, which he assumed had been added by someone over the centuries to protect the rare manuscript within, he saw the original Servetus cover. It was identical to the copy he'd seen in the Paris rare book room with Genevieve. There was a Latin inscription that he could see included the words Christianismi Restitutio. Stamped near the bottom were the Roman numerals MDLII, 1553, the year of its publication. It looked intact and didn't appear to have suffered any damage from its long sleep in the capsule. Shay noticed there was something under the book. He carefully removed it and saw that it was an envelope. Written, in script on the outside, were the words, OPEN THIS NOW.

Hunter nodded to Shay as if to say. *It's yours, go ahead.* Shay opened it and read it silently to himself and then read it aloud to Hunter.

This copy of the *Christianismi Restitutio* by Michael Servetus is the property of my good friend Señor Basilio Diego Mendez of

Madrid, Spain. He entrusted it to my care in 1947 until such future time as it could be safely returned to Spain and made available to the public and to scholars. It is his intention to leave instructions with his attorney, as to the proper disposition of the book.

George Blackwell
July 15, 1950

Shay sat silently for a moment before speaking. He told Hunter that the materials Hugo Alvarez sent him included a plea to call him in the event the book was found.

Before he did so, Hunter told Shay what he needed concerning the book.

After hearing Hunter out and agreeing to his plan, Shay continued. "The attorney indicated that he had additional information for me regarding Basilio's wishes. I think we could call him now, get that information and still proceed with your plan. What do you think?"

"It can't hurt as long as I still have total discretion with the book."

Shay placed the call and put the attorney on speakerphone.

"Señor Alvarez," began Shay. "I am here with Hunter McCoy. He's located the fourth copy of the *Christianismi Restitutio* and we have it with us now. I'm calling because you asked to be informed in the event we found it."

"You found it? That's wonderful."

"Do you have Skype capabilities on a computer?" asked Shay.

"Yes, of course," replied Alvarez.

After a few minutes delay, while they made the connections, the three of them were face-to-face.

"Ah, there we are," said Alvarez, now able to see both Shay and Hunter. "Basilio Mendez would have been both happy and proud that the book had been recovered."

"Proud?" asked Shay.

"I'll explain that shortly. First let me give you Basilio Mendez' instructions for the *Christianismi Restitutio* as best I can. As you know from the materials I sent you, Basilio asked your father, George, to keep the book safe in the United States and to hide it and to not tell him where it was. It would insure he couldn't be pressured to give it up. He felt that he owed this to the memory of Señora Calderon. To that end he entreated me to be his agent. Over the years and right up to his death, this year, he and I collaborated on plans for the return of the book, and also what would happen if either of us were no longer around."

Señor Alvarez went on to describe how Basilio had met with Cristobal Lazodelavega, the Director of the Michael Servetus Institute and told him that he intended to donate the book to the Institute when it became available. He, of course, didn't tell Dr. Lazodelavega the book's whereabouts, because even he didn't know where it was.

"And I must say, Professor McCoy," Alvarez added smiling at Hunter, "you did a remarkable bit of detective work to find it. We are all in your debt. However, with the unfortunate death of Dr. Lazodelavega, a second caveat of Basilio's intentions comes into play.

"Mr. Blackwell, Basilio instructed me to tell you that in the event of the death or incapacitation of Dr. Lazodelavega, you are to have total discretion in the disposition of the book and in its ultimate final resting place. He had complete faith that you would do the right thing.

"And so, Mr. Blackwell, Alvarez said with a smile, I believe the appropriate American saying is 'The ball is now in your court.'"

Shay thought for a minute and then said, "Señor Alvarez, I've been wondering, why didn't Basilio try to break the code and find the book and return it to Spain after my father died? Wasn't Basilio concerned about its continued safety?"

Alvarez responded, "You must understand that the Franco Regime was still running the country and continued to do so into the 1970s, when the monarchy was re-established. Remember, Basilio so distrusted the regime that he decided to leave the book where it was at the time. He was confident that George had stored it in a secure and safe place."

Hunter had a question. "Why did Basilio work through Shay Blackwell when he finally decided to find the book, rather than confide in his own son, Alfonso?"

Hugo Alvarez gazed at Hunter for a long time before answering. "I believe you've met Alfonso, Professor McCoy." The silence that followed this statement, spoke volumes.

"Basilio and I talked many hours about this. After George died, he decided that when the time was right he would send his son to retrieve the book. He didn't know exactly when this would be, but he always thought Alfonso would be the one to do it. It gave him a certain sense of comfort to imagine that the Mendez family would hold fast to the trust that Señora Calderon had put in his hands, and that his only son, Alfonso, would be the one to complete the trust.

"By the time Franco was gone in 1973, young Alfonso, now in his early twenties, showed absolutely no interest in history, had no political point of view, was selfish, and thought his father was silly for spending so much time with books and history. Believe me, Basilio tried, several times, to interest his son in intellectual matters, but to no avail. In the end, he finally gave up on him."

Hunter thought about this. "So even though George Blackwell knew that Basilio didn't want to know where the book was, he sent him all the clues necessary to locate the time capsule."

"That's right," agreed Alvarez. "Mr. Blackwell, it seems your father felt that Basilio at least ought to have the means to find the book in case something happened to him. How prescient he was. Your father and mother were killed in that tragic boating accident and left you to be raised by your Aunt and Uncle, who were wonderful people but of very modest means.

"Basilio decided early on that he'd hedge his bet and invest in the education of both boys, his own son Alfonso and you, Shay. May I call you Shay?"

"Yes of course."

"And please call me Hugo. Anyway, Basilio hoped that in time, at least one of you would develop the character to find and return the book when the time was right. He anonymously helped your stepparents financially bring you up and send you to college. Further, by the time you'd graduated and become a successful and principled businessman, Basilio was becoming aware of the shortcomings of his own son, Alfonso. So, he continued to look out for you, Shay, helping you acquire financing early in your career to help ensure your success. But Shay, you should know that he only helped once or twice at the beginning of your career. Your success is totally your own and Basilio was very proud of you.

"He figured that if he could get you interested in finding the book when the time came, you would do the right thing and complete the task your father set out to do for him so many years earlier. You would be given the clues that would lead to the book and you would then return it safely to Spain. He took quite a chance on his ability to predict the future there, but that's what he did."

They were all quiet for a moment while Shay and Hunter pondered all of this. Finally Hunter spoke. "I just have one more question."

"What's that?" asked Hugo Alvarez.

"How did you manage to plant the unopened letter from Basilio Mendez to George Blackwell in Shay's files so that he could 'discover' it?"

Shay's head snapped around, and he looked at Hunter in surprise. Hunter pointed at the screen, indicating he should pay attention to the attorney. Shay returned his attention to the Skype feed.

Showing admiration as much as surprise, Alvarez said, "ah, so you've even figured that out, Hunter. *That* took a little planning. The letter is authentic. Basilio did write it. But he never mailed it, because George showed up at his house in Madrid before he put it in the post. The letter actually lay among Basilio's papers all these years. It had been folded and placed in the properly addressed envelope but never sealed. I wasn't his attorney in those early years. I began handling Basilio's affairs years later after his first attorney died. But, of course, as his executor, I went through all of his papers following his death— murder as we now know—and found it. It seemed the perfect way to get Shay interested and onto the trail of the book.

"I'm not without means, and, in spite of being an honest attorney, I have learned a few devious tricks over the years. I sealed the letter and was able to get it postmarked, as it would have been in 1947. Then I only had to get it in front of you, Shay, so you could 'discover' it. I'm ashamed to say that I hired a man who entered your house and placed the letter among the papers, but prominently, so it would be found quickly.

"And I have to say, with some considerable pride, the plan worked beautifully. Shay, you took the bait, as it were, and hired Hunter. And Hunter, your resourcefulness led to the cracking of the code, the discovery of the time capsule, and the recovery of the *Christianismi Restitutio,* just as Basilio hoped and George Blackwell planned. Shay, the disposition of the book is now in your hands, just as Basilio had always wanted."

Shay cocked his head and raised one eyebrow, "You know, Hugo? I wouldn't want you for an enemy."

Chapter 43

Hunter was on the evening flight to Geneva. He was relieved to be back on the hunt for Genevieve. He thought about all that had transpired since she'd been taken. Why hadn't that bastard, Kestrel called? Shouldn't he be checking on his progress in finding the book? And Genevieve must be terrified. He knew he should have insisted she go back to Paris. It just wasn't safe for her. Wasn't that the truth, he thought? None of this was her fault. It was his. He never should have left her out of his sight in the park. Well, he'd get her now, now that he had the book, patting the small satchel he carried with him and never let out of his sight. *Come on Kestrel, call.*

Slocum had finally gotten back to him regarding the search for the lead that Genevieve had left with the waitress in the café, 'Laurendeau.' "I know you don't want to hear how many Laurendeau's I had to go through to get this information, but—"

"You're right, Slocum, I don't. What've you got?"

"Okay, bottom line. Maybe this is what you want. A physicist, Arnaud Laurendeau, was on the Grand Council of the LHC until he was fired. I did some digging and it seems he kept trying to slow down the collider projects because he felt they were going too fast, no pun intended, and might actually create a catastrophe, maybe even blow up the world. The chairman finally had enough of him and canned him. He's kept a low profile since.

I did a lot of digging, and after he was fired he purchased two properties. One is his apparent residence, an expensive condo in Geneva overlooking the Rhone River. The other is an old house in the city center. Apparently no one lives there but he did have some interior work done."

"That's great, Slocum. Do you have those addresses?"

Slocum gave them to Hunter.

Hunter knew he had to contact Zubriggen and tell the Interpol agent everything. He knew he was also going to be in trouble. The kidnapper had called and he hadn't pressed *pound* to activate the search. He'd seen Genevieve in Geneva and hadn't told them. He knew the name of the kidnapper and presumable the LHC killer, and now he had a new name, Arnaud Laurendeau, who was presumably linked to all of it in some way. He decided it was time to bring the authorities in. But, by God, he was going to be a part of it. His priority was Genevieve.

He landed at Geneva International Airport the next morning and called Delgado first thing. He told her he had information relative to the kidnapping and needed to talk with Zubriggen. Could she make the connection?

"Hunter, has the kidnapper called? What have you found out?"

"He called. I didn't press the pound key to activate the search."

There was a long pause on Delgado's end.

Finally, a very slow and deliberate recitation of what he'd just said. "You—didn't—press—the pound key—to—activate—the—search!"

"Look," Hunter explained, I know Zubriggen, he's a smart tough cop, but he'll stop at nothing to get the LHC killer, and Genevieve's safety will only get a passing thought. I had to learn some things first, before I brought him in."

"And what have you learned besides how to get yourself jailed for interfering with an international police investigation by withholding evidence?"

Hunter told her about seeing Genevieve in Geneva, and about her clue regarding Arnaud Laurendeau. He didn't mention that he had learned the killer's name was Kestrel. He wasn't going to get Gautier in trouble for leaking that information to him.

"Look Inspector, I'm in Geneva now. I believe I know where she's being held. If Zubriggen can get here quickly, I'll wait and go in with him and whatever team he assembles. If not, I'm going alone."

"Now listen, McCoy, don't do anything until I get back to you."

"Make it fast, Inspector."

After closing the call, Hunter used his laptop and a mapping program to locate the old house Laurendeau bought and wasn't apparently using. He waited for the call from Delgado.

Forty-five minutes later, she called.

"He's on his way, Zubriggen and a team of six commandos on a private plane. They should arrive at the private jet terminal at Geneva International in a little under two hours. Zubriggen wants you there, waiting. And McCoy? He's pissed."

"I'll be ready for him. Thanks, Inspector."

"McCoy?"

"Yes?"

"For what its worth, I hope he lets you go in with them. I don't trust him either. And you're right. All he talked about was getting the LHC killer. The only time he referred to the hostage was when I brought it up. You get her out of there."

Hunter made one more phone call, this time he talked to Deacon directly. Then he waited for Zubriggen.

"Goddammit, McCoy, Who the hell do you think you are. I should jail you right now for withholding evidence. I'm in charge of this operation and I'll decide how it goes down, not you. I don't care how many top people you know this is my operation. Do you understand?"

"Zubriggen, let's cut the pissing contest. You know my boss talked to your boss and we're in this together. I accept that you're in charge. But don't forget for a minute that I'm on this team and I'm going in with you. Now I'll tell you where the house is and we can go over your plan."

Zubriggen's team had never seen their boss talked to that way before, much less his having to accept it. More than one couldn't hold back his amusement. That is until Zubriggen fixed them with an icy stare.

Two hours later they were in position around the house in the city center. One team member was assigned the front and right side of the two-story house and another the back and left side. The house had a front door leading up to a wide porch, a side door and a back door. Three would go in through the front, two through the back and one through the side. Hunter and Zubriggen were two of the three assigned to the front.

"Police. Open the door now," Zubriggen called and waited. The doors were locked. As previously arranged, they kicked in all three doors at once. With weapons drawn and rounds chambered, Hunter and the others entered. As the teams moved through the house Hunter could hear them calling "Clear" as each room was entered and found to be empty. Hunter was the first to stop at the basement door. It was closed. He opened it and carefully advanced down the stairs with Zubriggen and two others behind him. At the bottom of the stairs the team quickly determined no one was in sight. "Clear," Zubriggen called upstairs to the others.

The basement housed an old furnace with large air-duct pipes overhead. The only feature of the space was a corner room with a large oak door. Hunter ran to the door and called out, "Genevieve, are you in there?"

No answer.

Zubriggen had seen to it that his boys were well equipped. Hunter couldn't believe it. One of them even carried a crowbar. The man quickly set to work prying the door open. When it finally yielded to his efforts, Hunter was first in the room.

It was empty.

They saw the cot, sink and toilet. Food wrappers and a paper cup that still had a little coffee in the bottom confirmed that the room had been recently used.

"She was here," Hunter commented.

"Well she's not here now," Zubriggen said. His inflection implied that she might have been, had Hunter not gone out on his own and kept them in the dark.

Hunter ignored him and began searching the room looking for anything Genevieve might have left that could help them in any way. There was nothing in the toilet tank, in or under the cot or anywhere else he could immediately think to look. Then, he saw the small panel in the wall under the sink. It was held in place by two screws. Using his knife, he unscrewed them and pulled the panel free. In the space, wrapped around a piece of conduit, was a torn strip of colored cloth. He unwrapped it and pulled it out.

"She was here for sure. This is torn from the skirt she was wearing the day she was kidnapped. She put it here so we know we were on the right track."

Good girl.

By now all of the men, except those stationed outside were in the room after verifying the house was empty.

"All right, men, lets pull this room apart to see if there are any other clues," commanded Zubriggen.

Hunter returned to the panel where he'd found the cloth from Genevieve's skirt. He reached in and felt around to see if anything else was there. At first he found nothing then while reaching up he found what felt like a crinkled paper bag. He pulled it out. It was a bag from Burger King. He opened it and said to the others, "There's something written inside, here."

He carefully tore the bag open. Genevieve had written in lipstick,

COLLIDER GAS TUES
STOP THEM
GS

"GS, Genevieve Swift. She wrote this, Inspector, and hid it so Kestrel wouldn't find it. She knew we'd be coming and if she wasn't here, we'd find it."

"Smart girl. Gutsy too," admitted Zubriggen. "All right men tear this house apart and see if you can find anything else. McCoy, you come with me."

Outside, Zubriggen turned to Hunter. "Now let me get this straight, outside of the one time Kestrel called and you *didn't* inform us, you've received no other calls, and have had no other contact with him?"

"That's right, and I don't get it. I now have the book in my possession. If it's so important he has to kidnap Genevieve to get it, why hasn't he called back?"

"Exactly what I've been wondering. Maybe he doesn't really want the book at all, but kidnapping the girl was just a ruse to flush you out so he could kill you. I understand you interfered with his hit on the Mendez boy."

"I did."

"Today's Sunday, McCoy. He's got something planned for the collider on Tuesday and apparently it involves gas. We've got to stop it."

There's one other thing we have to do, Inspector."

"What's that?"

"We've got to find Genevieve."

Chapter 44

Laurendeau was addressing his group in a hastily called meeting in a small room he'd rented under an assumed name at the Airport Hilton. "I believe we need to change our tactics. The elimination of the new physicists assigned to the LHC programs isn't working. Not a single experiment has been cancelled. The protocols are proceeding as if nothing has happened. Our goal to stop experimentation until adequate safety issues are properly addressed is failing. I believe we now have no other choice but to focus our efforts more precisely on shutting down all collider experiments."

The group nervously shifted their gazes from Laurendeau to each other. Thorbjorn Asplund, the Norwegian physicist, raised his hand. "Arnaud, you're the only one of us whose actually worked at the facility. I'm not saying we shouldn't do what you ask, but how do you plan to stop the experiments if we agree to go ahead?"

Martin Hoffman nodded in agreement. "I understand their security is top notch and state-of-the-art."

Laurendeau clasped his hands and smiled. "I believe I know how, gentlemen, if you'll just leave it to me."

"But what do we do with Kestrel?" asked Kurt Walker. "Are we done with the eliminations? And what about the girl? She's still the incentive for McCoy to find the book."

"I've also come to a conclusion about the book," said Laurendeau. "Regardless of what message it might or might not contain, it just isn't necessary. We don't need it. We know what must be done. McCoy can find it and keep it. We're done with it."

Otto Fleischer sat stone-faced, saying nothing.

"But what about the girl, Arnaud? Do we just let her go?" asked Kurt Walker.

"I'm afraid not. She's already seen Kestrel. I'll have him deal with her."

No one seemed to object to this.

Laurendeau, surprised that his ideas were apparently being accepted so easily, decided to formalize it. "If we're all in agreement, I'll proceed and we're adjourned."

Otto Fleischer stood and put up his hand. "Not so fast, Arnaud."

Those who'd begun to rise sat back down and looked at Fleischer questioningly.

"What is it, Otto?" asked Laurendeau.

Fleischer stood, scowling. "If we're abandoning the search for the book. I want McCoy stopped as well. I'm sure this doesn't mean anything to the rest of you, but if McCoy is allowed to continue searching for the book, and somehow manages to find it, I don't like what it could mean for my religion."

"Religion? What are you talking about, Otto?" asked Laurendeau.

"I know you were all focused on the possibility that the Servetus message may have supported our arguments to reign in the LHC. That was fine. I was in agreement. But you seem to have forgotten that there was another part of the message. There was a reference to it containing information that could lead to the discovery of an ancient scroll that, if found, could severely threaten Christianity, as we know it today.

"In spite of what we've been doing here, I consider myself to be a deeply Christian man. I take this potential threat to my religion very seriously. I believe that God would be justified in sending me to eternal damnation if I didn't do all I could to prevent it's discovery.

"Gentlemen, I do not want to spend eternity in hell. I believe the eliminations we've sanctioned up until now have been necessary and indeed would be approved by God himself. But this, allowing the discovery of this piece of heresy to threaten my religion, would be unforgivable.

"I've happily paid for everything we've done up to now, and will continue through this next phase. In return, I want Kestrel to eliminate both the woman *and* McCoy, and I want the book if he has it. It has to be destroyed."

The others sat quietly for a moment. They'd never heard Fleischer give a speech before. In fact he'd rarely spoken at all at their meetings. This side of him presented an entirely new look to the man. Was he really that worried about going to hell? Most of them didn't even believe there was such a place.

Finally, Laurendeau stood. "All right, Otto, we'll follow your wishes. It's probably for the best anyway. If we leave him out there he'd only try to find what happened to the girl, and that might even lead somehow back to us."

When the others had left, Laurendeau called Kestrel and told him what he wanted him to do.

Chapter 45

The Swiss Federal Department of Justice and Police issued an arrest warrant for Arnaud Laurendeau. Zubriggen felt he now had enough evidence to bring him in on charges of murder and conspiracy. He and Hunter found no one home when they arrived at Laurendeau's apartment. With the authority of the warrant, they entered and began a thorough search. Genevieve wasn't there.

In Laurendeau's study, Hunter found all the usual things, a desk with a laptop on it, a two-drawer file cabinet on the floor next to it. A search of the drawers in the desk, revealed nothing of interest, but did show that Laurendeau was incredibly neat. Even the center drawer, which usually served to collect junk in Hunter's case, was clean with a notepad, an appointment book, and a divided tray in the front each with its own separate content of two sizes of paper clips, pencil lead, and two sizes of larger black clips. The same neatness carried over to the file cabinet. Every file was properly labeled. Zubriggen started through the files while Hunter examined the appointment book.

After a minute or so looking through the appointment book, Hunter turned to Zubriggen. "This is odd, Inspector, There isn't a single appointment indicated in this book. Why have an appointment book and not use it?"

"Maybe he keeps them on the computer. Check the computer's calendar."

Hunter did and was surprised to find that no password was required. "Same thing. Absolutely nothing here," he announced, after examining it for the current month as well as six months before and after.

"These files look pretty routine to me too," Zubriggen groused, "household records, bills, etc. Still, I'll have the forensics people come in here and go over this place with a fine-tooth-comb. If there's anything here, they'll find it."

On the way back to police headquarters, they talked about what to do next.

"Unless Kestrel is a fool and told her, she must have overheard a conversation of some kind in order to have gotten the name Laurendeau and the info about the gas at the collider on Tuesday." Zubriggen went on, "My guess is that she overheard one side of a phone conversation Kestrel had with Laurendeau."

Hunter agreed. "And she was clever enough to have gotten the name Laurendeau to me at the restaurant, and then left the note about the gas at the collider on Tuesday in the wall in her cell."

You are one gutsy woman. You kept your head and did the best you could even though you must be terrified. I'll find you, Genevieve, and I'll take Kestrel down in the process.

With no other leads since Kestrel hadn't called, they decided to focus their efforts on the collider. Maybe the link to Laurendeau or Kestrel, and even Genevieve was there. Zubriggen said he'd call on the LHC Security office and Hunter could check with central administration.

Under pressure from Deacon to Zubriggen's boss, Hunter had been empowered to aid in the investigation. Hunter decided to start with Laurendeau's previous employment with the Grand Council of the LHC.

On his way to the LHC head office building, where he'd scheduled an appointment with Giuseppe Ambrosi, the Chairman of the Grand Council, his cell phone rang. He didn't recognize the calling number.

"This is McCoy"

"Do you have the book?"

Hunter pushed the pound key immediately.

"Yes, I've got it. Now tell me—"

Kestrel hung up.

Hunter pulled over narrowly missing a car in the inside lane. He called Zubriggen's cell.

"He just called. I pressed pound immediately. Tell me your men were able to locate him."

Zubriggen said, "Hold on, I'll check and call you right back."

Hunter slumped in his car seat. His fists were clenching, he ground his teeth and slammed a fist into an innocent open palm. *I'll get you, Genevieve! If he harms you in any way he'll never know another quiet day. I'll—*

His phone rang. It was Zubriggen.

"They didn't get it. Not enough time."

Hunter paused before commenting. "It's got to be the collider. She wasn't in the house or Laurendeau's condo, and her note referred to collider gas on Tuesday, tomorrow. It's got to be the collider. She's got to be there somewhere."

Zubriggen agreed. He said they needed to focus all their efforts on finding out what was going to happen tomorrow. They had to stop it. If she were part of it, they'd find her.

"Inspector, you do what you have to, I'm going to find her."

He knew we'd be tracing the call, trying to locate him. That's why he hung up immediately after I told him I had the book. So he'll be calling back with instructions for an exchange, the book for Genevieve. He'll keep any calls he makes short and there will probably be several of them.

In the mean time, while he was waiting for the call, he decided to interview the Chairman of the Grand Council, Dr. Giuseppe Ambrosi. "What can you tell me about Arnaud Laurendeau?" asked Hunter, after he'd shown his Interpol credentials and had been invited into the office of the chairman. Ambrosi, an affable Italian of medium height wearing a plaid sport jacket, black tie and shoes that needed polishing.

"Arnaud Laurendeau? What about him? He doesn't work here anymore."

"I understand that. I also understand that you had him fired."

He'd asked Hunter to have a seat and then walked around behind his desk, piled high with journals, and had a seat himself.

"The man was an idiot. Oh, I don't mean he wasn't intelligent. He was. He was a world-renowned physicist with major publications. That's why we hired him. He was initially assigned to the ATLAS project and then we elevated him to the Grand Council. That's when he went around the bend, so to speak. He championed every crackpot theory about catastrophic consequences of proceeding with the collider experiments. He was worried about black holes, the Higgs, and even time-travelers from the future. It was like the man had lost all scientific perspective. When the best minds in the business investigated his claims and found them baseless, he only became more insistent. Finally, I'd had enough and had him removed."

"Have you heard from him since?" Hunter inquired.

"No, I haven't"

Then Ambrosi leaned forward, clasped his hands under his chin and put his elbows on the table. "Would you mind telling me what this is about?"

"It's about murder, kidnapping, and a possible eminent threat to the collider itself."

Chapter 46

"What?" Ambrosi jumped up. "A threat to the collider? What are you talking about?"

"Sit down and I'll tell you," Hunter said.

He explained that they had strong evidence that Laurendeau was responsible for hiring a killer that had been responsible for the murders of the young physicists assigned to the LHC. They'd found the killer's fingerprints in a house that Laurendeau owned downtown. Further, Laurendeau had been responsible for kidnapping a woman who was helping Hunter find a lost historical book.

"The idea seems to have been that I would find it faster with the incentive of freeing this woman, the kidnapped victim who was working with me, Genevieve Swift. It worked. I've found the book. But he hasn't called back to set up an exchange. We did find where he'd been holding her. It was in the basement of the house Laurendeau had bought in the city. She left clues that she had been there and that Laurendeau was behind it. She also left a note that said "collider gas on Tuesday. That's tomorrow. We've searched his apartment. He's gone and she wasn't there. We have no idea why he wanted the book."

"My God," said Ambrosi, stunned by the news, "the man must be insane."

"Very likely," agreed Hunter. "But we've got to find him, fast. Not only for the woman's sake, but to prevent him from carrying out an attack on the collider."

Ambrosi stood up again, clearly agitated. "Yes, of course. What can I do to help?"

"You said he worked in the ATLAS project. What's that?"

Ambrosi explained it to him.

"Dr. Ambrosi, if Laurendeau is planning to do something catastrophic with gas tomorrow, could you venture a guess as to what it might be?"

"I don't know. I guess it could be anything. Maybe the sick bastard's thinking of flooding the tunnel with some lethal gas. I suppose the ventilation system would be a good way to do that. You'll have to have security check everything out."

"We'll be doing that. My partner is meeting with your security chief now." Hunter couldn't believe he'd just called Zubriggen his partner.

Hunter thought for a minute and continued, "Is there any other gas, maybe something used in the physical experiments, that might be altered and could then possibly shut down the collider?"

"Yes, I'm afraid there are several possibilities. Hydrogen is the primary source of the protons that we accelerate in the tubes. I suppose that could be influenced if he managed to get to the source. Then there is the coolant gas for the huge cryomagnets. I don't know. It could be anything?"

Hunter needed something more concrete than 'it could be anything.' "Would Laurendeau know how the entire system works, I mean everything at the LHC?"

"Nobody knows everything about this place," replied Ambrosi. "The LHC is the most complicated scientific facility ever built anywhere. The particle beams are accelerated and kept on track by over 9300 magnets that are super cooled to -270 degrees by over 80 tons of liquid helium, and that's after they've been precooled by over ten tons of liquid nitrogen. The mechanics and maintenance of that distribution system alone requires the combined knowledge of hundreds of technicians. That's to say nothing of many other nonscientific people who maintain the ventilation, electrical, mechanical, plumbing, and communication systems. There's also a huge computer network called "the grid" that lets tens of thousands of scientists around the world instantaneously analyze the data recorded by the big experiments that we conduct here. Individual scientists pretty much learn only what goes on in their specialized regions of the facility."

"So would it be safe to say that Laurendeau would know the ATLAS area pretty well."

"Oh yes," said Ambrosi. "As part of the orientation for new scientists, they're familiarized with all the features of their area. This would include a tour and a detailed explanation of the specifics of the large and very sophisticated detectors that are the main scientific instruments in each area. In addition they'd learn about all the other things I told you earlier, the cooling, mechanical, electrical, and nonscientific systems. After that, it was felt they could focus on the science and not worry about the huge machines that dwarfed them in size. The first time someone actually walks into the ATLAS area, for example, and sees the huge detectors, it can be quite intimidating, I can tell you."

"Dr. Ambrosi, are you familiar with the ATLAS area?" Hunter asked.

"Yes, I am. As a matter of fact, when I first came to the LHC I was also assigned there. It's changed a little since then, but I still know my way around. Why?"

"It seems likely that if Laurendeau is planning something, it would probably be there, where he knows his way around."

Just then Hunter's phone rang
"McCoy, here."
"I'll call you with instructions. It will take a while."
The call ended again. It was Kestrel.
Once again a call to Zubriggen found that his team didn't have enough time. Hunter would have to keep him on the phone longer.

Hunter left Ambrosi after admonishing him to consider what potential damage Laurendeau could do. He'd told him to imagine he was a saboteur. What would he do to stop the collider?
While Hunter waited for a call from Kestrel he used the time to establish a way to contact the Interpol tracking team directly rather than having to go through Zubriggen. When they'd told him he needed to keep Kestrel on the line longer in order to trace him, he'd told them there had been no time to prolong the conversation as Kestrel ended it immediately after his short statements. They gave him some suggestions on how he could do it. After pressing 'answer' on his phone, he should delay before responding. Also, when he did respond, instead of saying 'McCoy" he should start talking instead. He should tell Kestrel he wanted assurance that Genevieve is all right—anything to keep him on the line longer.

After what seemed like an eternity, the call finally came in three hours later. Almost as if he'd anticipated Hunter's delaying tactic Kestrel began immediately "Listen carefully. Take the LII highway south to Arquette, ask how to get to the south shore of Lake Alpern and get out of your car and stand where the river Loo enters the lake. Be there in exactly two hours and come alone. Bring the book. Start counting now." Kestrel ended the call.

Hunter hadn't pressed the pound key. He didn't call Zubriggen. After what he'd seen at the house, he was more convinced than ever that the Interpol man's primary objective was Kestrel and not Genevieve's safe return. He knew her best chance was with him alone.

An hour later he entered the small Swiss town of Arquette, got directions to the site on the south shore of lake Alpern from a chemist on the main street. He had the book in its small satchel on the passenger seat beside him. He also carried his gun in a holster under his left arm.

He didn't believe for a minute that Kestrel would really let her go in exchange for the book. He drove another twenty minutes down a quiet road through a heavily wooded area and saw signs indicating Lake Alpern ahead. He could see a fast moving river occasionally coming close to the road and then disappearing back into the woods. It was running in the direction of the lake. Hunter assumed it was the River Loo. Eventually he saw the small sign the chemist had told him to watch for. It indicated the mouth of the river was off to the right down a single lane dirt road. Hunter drove for another quarter mile until the road ended in a small clearing at the shore of the lake. He pulled up and parked the car. No one else was around. In fact, he hadn't even seen another car for the past half hour. He got out and looked around. He couldn't see the river because of the nearby trees, but he could hear it off to the right where he also saw a small path. He took the satchel and started walking toward the sound of running water. After a few minutes he was there. He stood and looked around. The lake looked to be about two or three city blocks across at this point. There was a small point off to the right and he could see that the lake continued around it. Off to his left he could see all the way down to what he assumed was the far end of the lake about a mile away.

Everything was covered with trees, mostly pines. He saw no houses or any boats out on the lake. Kestrel had picked well, he decided.

"Put the bag down and your hands in the air."

Startled, Hunter turned toward the voice. *Where had he come from?* Standing six feet from him, with a gun rock steady in his hand aimed at Hunters heart, was a slim man of medium height with dark skin, hair and eyes, Kestrel. The eyes told him all he needed to know. This man wouldn't hesitate to shoot to kill. He had to be very careful here.

"Very slowly, toss that bag over by that rock," Kestrel directed," pointing to a large bolder near a pine tree at the start of what looked like another trail through the woods. "After you throw the bag to the rock, slowly remove your jacket, shirt, shoes, and pants. Do it now."

Kestrel's gun never wavered from pointing at Hunter's chest. After Hunter had complied, including his holstered gun, Kestrel told him to sit on the ground and not move. When he had done so, Kestrel examined his clothes. Taking Hunter's gun and a knife he'd been carrying, Kestrel pocketed them both and told him to get dressed.

Relieved to get his clothes back on even though his weapons were gone, Hunter growled, "Where is she?"

"Start walking down that path," indicating the one he'd seen by the rock, "and you'll see her."

Hunter did, and after another fifty yards the path ended in a small opening looking out onto a part of the lake previously unseen. There she was, sitting in a rowboat, about one hundred yards offshore, Genevieve. Relief flooded through him. She appeared to be all right.

"All right, Kestrel, let's do the exchange. The book is in the satchel."

An evil smile creased Kestrel's face and he just stared at Hunter. Finally, he spoke. "You don't get it, do you,

McCoy? I don't want your book anymore. I never wanted it. It was for that crazy group of scientists who hired me. Even they don't want it anymore. So, you see, you don't have anything to bargain with."

Hunter was confused. *What the hell was he talking about?*

"Oh, but you should know, your girlfriend out there in the boat?" he said while smirking, "You'll get her back in a few minutes, but some assembly may be required. You see she is sitting on an explosive charge rigged remotely to this 'dead-man-switch' that I've just activated—now."

Horrified, Hunter saw that man press his thumb on a small device in his non-gun hand. *A dead man switch! If he lets his thumb up, it will detonate the charge and kill Genevieve.*

Smiling, Kestrel snickered, "You've interfered with my work quite enough, and now that my contract to dispose of the physicists has been withdrawn by the crazies, you and your friend in the boat are just loose ends to clean up. But, I must say, I'm going to enjoy it. All that's left is for me to lift my thumb."

Chapter 47

Zubriggen was meeting with the head of security at the LHC. The man, Henri Couillard was a professional. Ex military, ex police, he managed a staff of one hundred and twenty highly trained security guards. To the man's credit, while he thought their security was unmatched, he took Zubriggen's news about an attempt on the facility with the seriousness it deserved. He explained to Zubriggen that their security also included a highly skilled technical staff of people devoted to thwarting cyber attacks on the LHC's computer systems. Computers were used for almost everything at the LHC. They controlled the thousands of large superconducting cryomagnets that accelerated and focused the proton beams around the beam pipes. They regulated the liquid helium that cooled the magnets to near 270 degrees below zero. They recorded the passage of subatomic particles produced by the collisions through the enormous detectors that filled the huge caverns at the collision sites around the collider loop. And, they linked the collected data to the tens of thousands of scientists around the world who then analyzed it

Zubriggen paced the office. "I don't think we're talking about a cyber attack here. Is there any way a single man, this Laurendeau, could physically shut down or damage the collider itself?"

Couillard, a powerfully built man with a shaved head and a permanent scowl, said, "It would be impossible. Even if he could somehow get past the guards at the gate and gain access to the control rooms that operate everything at the LHC, there are multiple layers of security in place to insure that no one but cleared personnel can gain access. None of these systems have ever been made public and none have ever been breached."

"Yes," said Zubriggen, "but what about Laurendeau. He used to work here. Presumably he'd know about the security. Didn't he have access once?"

"No. Everything around here is 'access-limited' and access is limited to areas where you work. Laurendeau did enter the ALTAS detector when he was assigned there, but even then he was only down there twice. Both times it was for orientation."

"I don't understand. Wouldn't he have to have access if he worked there?"

"No. Typically, the only people who ever go into the tunnel and detectors are technicians who maintain the equipment. The scientists do all their work from above. In fact, when the beams are running, no one is allowed in the tunnel at all."

"How do the technicians get down there?" Zubriggen asked.

Couillard told him. "There are eight elevators in the entire complex that go down. They're all two-stop elevators, one on the surface and one in the tunnel, spaced out around the seventeen-mile loop. Again, we have a multiple phase security check in place to ensure that no unauthorized personnel get down there."

Frustrated, Zubriggen tried to imagine how Laurendeau could attack the collider. He'd obtained a picture of Laurendeau from personnel and Couillard was circulating it to all of his people with the instruction to detain him immediately if sighted.

Hunter was out of options. The man was going to do it. He could see it in his eyes. He had to stop him, but how? If he rushed him, he'd let go of the switch. He had to keep him talking while he figured out a way.

"Look, Kestrel, don't do it. You said your contract is over. I'm not a threat to you anymore. Let her go. I'll leave you alone." He knew it was lame but he had no other ideas. He had to get him talking again. "Why did Laurendeau want the book in the first place?"

"Laurendeau? So you know about him, do you?" Kestrel was clearly surprised.

Maybe this was an opening, thought Hunter. "What could an old book possibly have to do with the collider?"

"I suppose it won't hurt to tell you, one professional to another," he remarked sarcastically. "He and his little group of crazy scientists thought the collider projects were too dangerous to proceed. They figured, by killing newly hired physicists, the authorities would shut the place down. But then Laurendeau found out that the book you were looking for had some kind of prophetic message that would justify their cause. He had to have it. So, they had me follow you so I could take it when you'd found it."

Prophetic message? What's he talking about?

Hunter continued to eye Kestrels left fist.

Was his thumb beginning to relax on the switch?

Since Kestrel's back was still to the lake and the boat, Hunter could see over Kestrel's shoulder that Genevieve was standing, or trying to. She was apparently tied, somehow, to the boat. He could see she was trying to get free. *Good for you, Genevieve. Keep at it.*

Hunter switched his eyes back to Kestrel. "But you couldn't wait, could you. You thought that by kidnapping Genevieve, you'd speed up my efforts, was that it?"

"Something like that, and," glancing momentarily at the satchel, "and since you now have the book, its seems I was right."

"So what's changed? Why not take it and let us go?"

"It seems my employers had a change of heart."

"I don't understand."

"He decided he no longer needed justification for what he was doing so he said he was going to take direct action on the surface of the collider itself. So, I'm out of a job, and you two are loose ends."

The two men were only six feet apart. Hunter had been getting closer as they talked.

Kestrel noticed. "Stop right there, McCoy. I'm not some jerk you can sneak up on and surprise. Back up to that tree over there."

Damn. If I do that I'll be about twelve feet from him.

Hunter looked back at the boat. Genevieve was still struggling with the rope, or whatever was holding her to the boat.

It looks like she's making progress. Don't look at her. I've got to keep him focused on me.

Kestrel held up his left hand and looked at the dead-man-switch. "Now, it's time to end this."

"Wait," cried Hunter, "I—I need to know something else."

I've got to keep him talking and looking at me and not the boat?

"Why Baltz? Why did you kill him?"

"'Who?" Kestrel's look of confusion told Hunter he didn't know the man's name.

"Julian Baltz, the man you shot on the rooftop in Salamanca. Why did you kill him?"

Kestrel laughed. "Was that his name? Baltz?"

For the first time, Hunter saw kestrel's gun waver away from his chest as he used it to gesture at the absurdity of the man's incompetence. "What a fool. Some sniper. There he was, out in the open on the rooftop. No cover at all. An amateur could have taken him out."

Hunter looked out at the boat. Genevieve was gone. At least he couldn't see her. Had she gone overboard or was she just lying flat in the boat? He couldn't tell.

"I would have let the fool do it, but I had just gotten new instructions from Laurendeau to keep you alive until you'd found that book."

Hunter looked around for a weapon, for anything he could use if he could get close enough. He was at the base of an old tree. All he could see were sticks. Most were dried and looked brittle, not good enough. He needed something stronger.

Hunter turned to Kestrel. "But up at the Institute, you hadn't yet got the order to keep me alive, so you took that shot at the restaurant La Bodega."

"Yes. Pity that. By the way, how did you know to duck at the last minute?"

"Your laser scope, I saw the reflection of the red spot on my forehead in Genevieve's reading glasses."

Kestrel nodded. "Damn, I hadn't thought of that."

I've got to find a weapon, soon.

Then he saw it, but it was out of reach. Kestrel was almost standing on it. It looked metallic. He could see it now, a broken piece of antenna, probably from an old radio someone had out here once.

"All right, McCoy, enough talk. It's time to get out of here."

Just as Kestrel looked down at his thumb on the switch, Hunter shouted, "Look, she's gone!"

As Kestrel turned his head Hunter could see his thumb coming off the switch. Then it all unfolded in slow motion. As Kestrel's head slowly turned to look out to the boat, his gun hand wavered ever so slightly off Hunter's chest. Hunter rocketed forward and clamped his hand over

Kestrels left hand covering his thumb in an iron grip. Kestrel fired but missed. Hunter grabbed Kestrel's left hand while keeping his grip on the dead man switch. They both went down and bounced in slow motion, Hunter's larger right hand squeezing Kestrel's left, forcing his thumb down. The scene continued in the slow motion of Hunter's mind and he slammed Kestrel's gun hand repeatedly on the ground. Hunter was clearly the stronger of the two men and finally, the gun bounced free, slowly spinning away.

Desperate to prevent the activation of the switch, Hunter covered Kestrel's left hand with both of his and tried to pry the switch away. Kestrel smashed his right fist into Hunters head with enough force to stun him. With a mighty jerk, Kestrel, tried to use the diversion to get free.

Hunter recovered and the two men rolled slowly on the ground. Hunter had to stop him but couldn't risk letting go of Kestrel's left hand. While trying to dodge the blows Hunter saw the antenna, about three feet behind them. He tried to shove Kestrel toward it while squeezing his hand and using his elbow to try and ward off the blows. If he could get close enough he could temporarily let go with one hand, grab the antenna and poke kestrel in the eye.

A little bit more, I'm almost there.

Just as Hunter was about to let go with one hand and grab it, Kestrel's foot kicked out and inadvertently sent the antenna spinning slowing another foot away.

Damn!

Hunter's superior strength allowed him to try again. He continued shoving Kestrel along the ground toward the antenna, still holding Kestrel's thumb down on the dead-man-switch.

Now, back within reach, he was ready to try for it. Squeezing Kestrel's hand with all the strength of his right hand, he let go with his left and grabbed the antenna.

As Kestrel's head slowly turned toward Hunter's face in slow motion, Hunter took aim and thrust the antenna directly into Kestrel's right nostril and pushed with all his might. Kestrel screamed and began to convulse.

Hunter had to hold on to the switch while the convulsing man's hand flew open. The explosion was enormous.

No! Oh, Genevieve. No. Not now, not after all this.

He rushed to the shore. The boat was gone and pieces of it were falling from the sky like rain. Nothing remained.

Oh my God!

Hunter, his arms hanging in defeat at his sides, hung his head and closed his eyes. He'd failed. Genevieve was dead.

Chapter 48

"Hunter, over here. I'm over here."

What? Genevieve? It's Genevieve's voice. How can that be?

"Hunter, help me, I'm in the water, over here."

Hunter shook off his confusion, and looked out at the boat, it was completely gone with wood pieces floating all over the small bay. Then he saw her. She was about twenty yards away tangled in brush near the shore. He ran to her and pulled her up and into his arms.

"Hunter, Hunter, is it really you?"

They clung to each other, neither able to speak.

She's alive.

She was still tangled in the brush and he could now see why. Both wrists were tied with a heavy rope that was also attached to what appeared to be an iron oar holder. She must have pulled it free from the boat and gone overboard before the explosion. He realized then that the water must have been shallow enough for her to be able to walk dragging the rope and oar holder with her. He freed her from the brush and pulled her from the water.

Back at the landing, Kestrel was still. The convulsions had stopped. Blood poured out of his nose where the antenna was lodged. The man was dead. Hunter knew he'd penetrated his brain through the roof of the nasal pharynx.

He retrieved his gun and used the knife to free Genevieve's hands. He retrieved the satchel with the book. Back at the car Hunter took a blanket from the trunk and wrapped Genevieve in it. He fired up the car's engine and turned the heater on high. In a few minutes, she was beginning to warm up from the dunking she'd had in the cold inland lake. When Hunter could see she was going to be all right, they headed back to Geneva.

Hunter stopped at a fast food place and, leaving the motor running to keep Genevieve warm, ordered her something to eat. The bastard hadn't even fed her in the past two days. She was famished and the food improved her outlook considerably. He was amazed at how quickly she'd bounced back from her captivity. Even though she was somewhat horrified at how Hunter had killed Kestrel, she was so happy to see him that she sat as close as you could in a bucket seat, clasping onto his arm during the entire drive. Vowing he wouldn't leave her again, they planned to drive to the LHC. Hunter thought he knew what Laurendeau had in mind and how he was going to sabotage the collider.

After making a quick stop in a clothing store to buy her a change of clothes and some shoes that didn't fit well, Genevieve changed in the car and they continued on their way. When they reached the CERN Building at the LHC they were shown in to the director's office immediately. Zubriggen had told security at the front gate about Hunter and Genevieve and said they were to be admitted at once if they showed up.

In spite of that, to say Zubriggen was surprised to see them was an enormous understatement. When the Director, the Security Chief, and the Interpol man heard about the rescue, the first two congratulated Hunter. Zubriggen, as if the rescue of Genevieve was unimportant, merely said,

"Did he tell you what Laurendeau was planning for the collider?"

Wanting to ignore him, but unable to because of the gravity of the situation, Hunter told them what he believed to be the plan. "Before I killed him, Kestrel said Laurendeau was going to take direct action on the collider itself, something about the surface.

"The surface? What the hell does that mean," demanded Zubriggen. "What's going on, on the surface?"

The Director thought for a moment and then said, "There is nothing special going on, at any of our surface sites other than normal routine maintenance activities, but there is something going on today at the main administration building. We have a special ceremony scheduled today at 3:00 PM to mark the opening of the new computer link to the American Tevatron Particle Accelerator near Chicago. Both the LHC and the Tevatron are in the hunt for the Higgs boson, and the agreement will allow scientists at both facilities to examine each other's data."

"Is that a big deal?" Hunter asked the Director. "Is that a reason for Laurendeau to attempt something spectacular to disrupt it?"

"Not really," the Director admitted, "We're fashioning agreements like this around the world all the time."

Hunter could see that the Director was mulling something over in his mind. He waited and then saw the Directors face light up as if he'd remembered something else.

"There is something," he said, "Something about the ceremony this afternoon."

Hunter and the others waited for the man to tell them what he'd recalled.

"Charles Dobson, the Tevatron's director, and a particle physicist, will be at that ceremony."

"What's special about Dobson," asked Hunter, thinking this was going nowhere.

"Dr. McCoy, remember how I told you I'd finally fired Laurendeau because of his crackpot ideas. How he insisted, despite all evidence to the contrary and the opinion of the world's best minds, that we risk creating giant black holes that could destroy the universe?"

Hunter gave the man his full attention. "I remember."

"Well," continued the Director, "Charles Dobson also had a run-in with Laurendeau. It happened at a conference we held right here at the LHC just two weeks before I fired him. Laurendeau had the stage and was delivering his drivel again. During the question session following his talk, Dobson took him apart pretty well as I recall. You could see the embarrassment and hate in Laurendeau's eyes on that podium. If looks could kill, Dobson wouldn't be here today."

"So if Laurendeau wanted to really make a statement with whatever he has in mind, he might time it to coincide with the ceremony," Zubriggen offered.

"And if that's true, said the Security Chief, we've only got a little over two hours to figure out what it is and stop him."

Hunter returned to Kestrel's statement that Laurendeau was going to take direct action on the collider and reminded them that he'd mentioned the surface. "What's on the surface that's vulnerable?" Hunter asked the Security Chief.

"Mostly buildings filled with supplies near the access points. And, of course, the helium tanks."

"Helium's a gas," Hunter pointed out. "The helium in those tanks would be in the gaseous state, wouldn't it?"

"That's right," the Director confirmed. "It doesn't take on the liquid state until it is super cooled by the refrigerators."

"How many tanks are there, Director?'

"Well, it's a little complicated. The helium is stored in low-pressure carbon steel tanks at ambient temperature. These tanks are located at eight points on the surface evenly distributed around the 17-mile ring. There are two size containers. The smaller are 3 meters in diameter by 12 meters in length and each stores 75 cubic meters of gas. These smaller tanks are located in sectors 2,4,6, and 8. They're stored vertically in the shadow of buildings on the site. The larger tanks, which had to be built specifically for the collider, are 3.5 meters by 28 meters, and hold 250 cubic meters each. These tanks are stored horizontally at all eight sectors around the ring. Four of these large tanks at each sector are always kept empty in the event that the helium in the system has to be purged or quenched in order to allow the system to heat up."

"You mean the super cooled helium needs a place to go?" Hunter asked.

"Exactly. All the other tanks, both small and large are filled with gaseous helium. In fact the amount of helium we use is enormous. It's almost hard to believe. We use an amount of helium equal to the world's entire annual production. These tanks hold over 100 tons of helium."

"So blowing those tanks and releasing the helium would shut you down, is that right?"

The director and the security chief looked at each other uncomfortably. Finally, the director answered. "It would be a disaster. You see, not only would we lose helium needed to cool the cryomagnets, but also, if he manages to damage the valves that control helium movement and allowed the super cooled helium to begin escaping, the proton beams could no longer be focused and would begin to drift. The punch of those beams is equivalent to a 400-ton locomotive traveling 60 miles per hour. The damage to the large detectors, like ALICE and ATLAS would be catastrophic."

Hunter picked up on the director's terror. "If he's planning an attack on the helium storage facilities, I imagine those tanks would be easier to get at than the detectors below ground."

Couillard, the security chief, sat bolt upright. "You're right, McCoy. If he could breach the security at these surface locations, he could plant explosives. Mind you, getting near those tanks still wouldn't be easy, but it wouldn't be as hard as getting below to the tunnel. He could do more damage by destroying the helium facilities than he could if he were able to actually get below to the tunnel."

Couillard immediately got on the phone and called his people and told them to immediately check the helium storage tanks in their sectors and to report anything suspicious to him right away.

"If he's done anything to the tanks, we'll know soon enough, Director."

While they waited, Hunter suggested that the ceremony with Dobson present would be the perfect time for Laurendeau to act.

Couillard got the first call within ten minutes. It was from Jacobson, the security man at point six. "Sir, the tank cluster has been compromised. We've found what looks like a bomb and a timer system. We'll need a bomb squad."

Within minutes five of the other seven sectors reported similar devices.

Couillard looked at Zubriggen. "We don't have a bomb squad on the site. I'll contact the Geneva Metropolitan Police."

"What the hell do you mean, you don't have a bomb squad? What kind of security is this?"

Ignoring him, Couillard made the call and was assured the team was on its way. After completing the call, Couillard looked directly at Inspector Zubriggen, and in a voice dripping with disdain said, "We have a standing agreement with the bomb-disposal unit at Metro to handle just such a contingency. We have done our job, Inspector."

"Humpff. Well—They'd better get here fast."

Couillard had told the Metro people that all of the devices were similar, based on the reports from each sector. Hunter figured that if the squad slowly disarmed one, the others would go more quickly.

Couillard put out an alert to all of his people to examine everything in their areas to look for similar devices. Then he turned to all those present, "We have less than two hours to stop him."

Chapter 49

Time was running out. While they waited for the bomb squad to inactivate the devices in the little time they had, Couillard, Zubriggen and Hunter set out to find Laurendeau. If their assumptions were correct, a phone call from him at the right moment would simultaneously activate all of the explosives that would shut down the collider for the foreseeable future. Laurendeau would see it as the perfect solution.

Hunter watched as Zubriggen called his men to see if Laurendeau had shown up at the apartment. They told him nothing had changed. Also, no one had been to the old house where Genevieve had been kept. As Zubriggen and Couillard went about coordinating with their men, Hunter and Genevieve slipped off to be by themselves. They found a table in the cafeteria off the main hallway.

"Genevieve, are you okay?" Hunter asked as they sat down and he took both of her hands in his. "It's been so hectic I haven't even asked."

Genevieve looked straight into his eyes and murmured so others sitting nearby wouldn't hear, "I'm glad that man is dead. I'm glad you killed him. I probably shouldn't feel that way, but Hunter, he was evil. He enjoyed killing and inflicting pain. He told me he tortured and killed Alfonso and that poor man, the director of the Institute. He smiled

when he said it. I felt sick for hours afterward. But I knew
you'd find me, and I wasn't going to let him defeat me.
When I saw you on the shore, I knew you'd get me away
from him. I just knew it."

Hunter could see the relief in her eyes. "There is so
much to tell you, and I need to hear your story too, but we
have to leave it for a while. Right now we have to stop
Laurendeau from sabotaging the collider. Your clue about
the name 'Laurendeau' that you left with the waitress at the
restaurant was the key to everything. This place may be the
super collider, but you're the super hero, or I guess I should
say heroine." Hunter squeezed her hands again. "And
leaving the food bag where you'd written 'Gas in the
collider Tues?' in the wall under the sink was incredible."

He quickly told her about Laurendeau's role in
everything.

Getting up, Hunter said, "You're staying with me,
Genevieve, but we have to find and stop Laurendeau. We
have to figure out where he is."

Genevieve retrieved her hands from Hunter's and as
she got up from the table she paused and thoughtfully
commented, "I don't know if it means anything, but I just
now remembered something, a part of a phone conversation
I overheard. Not a conversation, really, just a few words.
Kestrel said, 'From Calvin's chair?' He said it just that
way, like a question."

Hunter's brow furled. "From Calvin's chair?"

"Yes. Like whoever was on the other end of the
conversation said, 'from Calvin's chair,' and then Kestrel,
not sure he heard it correctly, repeated it as a question,
'from Calvin's chair?'"

"Genevieve, lets get to a computer, fast. I have an
idea." They raced back to the control room where the
director and the others had set up their command posts,
Zubriggen for Interpol, Couillard for LHC Security, and the
director for everything else.

When they got there they learned that the bomb squad had reached the first of the explosives and had determined that it was a very sophisticated weapon that was designed to be detonated by cell phone, and, the entire device itself had been booby-trapped to prevent its dismantling. They were moving cautiously.

They only had fifty-two minutes until the ceremony.

Knowing time was running out, Hunter told the director he needed access to a computer linked to the Internet, now. He took them to his office and set them up at his desk. Genevieve pulled up a chair beside him and they started searching.

"My guess is," said Hunter, "Laurendeau is going to activate the bombs from a site that has some meaning or significance. Maybe he no longer needs the Book and the Servetus quote to justify his acts, but he might feel like he was honoring Servetus by detonating the explosives from the very site where his chief tormentor had his greatest moments. So let's see if we can find out where Calvin's chair is. Maybe it's still there."

They used Google and typed in 'Calvin's chair in Geneva.'

"Look at that first one," shouted Genevieve, "the Cathedral of Saint Peter in Geneva."

They opened the site and learned that it was the very place that John Calvin gave his fiery sermons during the mid-16th century. It appeared to be an imposing Romanesque-Gothic church. It was located in the center of the city. It had become a Protestant church in 1563 and Calvin preached there from 1536 to 1564. It quickly evolved into a leading center of Protestantism. But what caught Hunter's eye was that it had a very tall tower. One that Hunter imagined would give an unimpeded view of the valley to the northwest that housed the surface structures and helium tanks for the eight sectors of the Large Hadron Collider.

"Genevieve, he could be up there, make his cell phone call and watch all of the explosions from a single vantage point. Plus, he gets the added satisfaction of doing it from John Calvin's home church, essentially from Calvin's chair. The very man who almost single handedly had Michael Servetus arrested, tried, and murdered. It's perfect. It's like he'd be getting revenge for Servetus who he somehow imagines actually supported him with his supposed message in the book."

"Plus," added Genevieve, "What better place to do it from than a church if you're convinced God is on your side?"

"It fits," Hunter agreed. "Let's go."

When they got to the car, Hunter checked to see that he was fully armed. He wasn't leaving Genevieve out of his sight. She was coming with him. They raced from the collider across town toward the city center, speeding almost everywhere. On the way, he called Zubriggen and told him where they were going. They followed the GPS unit's directions that gave an estimated driving time of twenty-three minutes. If they were right in thinking he'd be there, they couldn't afford to lose any time. Hunter figured if he were stopped, he'd flash his Interpol credentials and keep going.

They were racing through the city streets passing cars and getting irritated looks from drivers and pedestrians everywhere, so far no interference from police. The traffic got heavier as they approached the city center. Hunter estimated they were still several blocks away when up ahead, what was either a fender-bender or a stalled car, had brought traffic to a complete stop. He checked his wristwatch, 1:48 PM, twelve minutes until the ceremony. They had to get there fast.

Seeing no way around the tie up in the traffic, Hunter pulled the car over and parked illegally half on the curb and opened his door. "Come on, we have to go on foot."

Genevieve got out quickly and he lead her, running, in what he assumed was the direction of the church. Finally, at a corner, looking up, they were able to see the steeple of what had to be the Church of Saint Peter. They raced toward it and rounding a final corner saw the neoclassical facade of the cathedral that he'd recognized from the picture on the Internet site.

Crossing the courtyard, racing past people milling about, they ran up the stairs toward the main front doors. They were open, as if inviting the citizenry to come in. Suddenly they were in the enormous cathedral with its high arched columns of stone and curved ceiling. Like most Gothic cathedrals, one immediately got a sense of great empty space. Rows of empty wooden pews covered the floor space. A central fixture near the front was the elevated pulpit from which Calvin must have preached. Light filtered through the stained glass in the chancel.

"Hunter, over there." Genevieve pointed toward the left at the far end of the nave. There, against a colonnaded stone pillar, was an ornately carved wooden chair. Next to it on a black metal stand was a green sign that read 'Calvin chair.' They'd found it. It was empty with a small rope connecting the wooden arms to prevent people from sitting.

All right, Laurendeau, where are you?

Desperate, Hunter looked around and saw that immediately next to the chair was a recess that appeared to lead to a stairway. On the wall to the recess, was a metal plaque that simply said 'North Tower.'

Hunter took Genevieve's arm and led her up the stairs. "Stay with me but let me go first. If he's anywhere near here, I think he'll be up in the tower."

They climbed hundreds of steps up the narrow winding stairway toward the tower. Hunter checked the time, 1:56, four minutes left.

As they neared the top, Hunter looked at Genevieve and puts his finger to his lips, as if to say no noise. She nodded. He removed his Berretta and silently chambered a round. With Genevieve behind him he poked his head up through the opening, which turned out to be the floor of the tower room. It was a square room about twenty feet on a side with three vertical slit openings on each of the four sides looking out at the surrounding countryside. In a chair, looking out toward the northwest sat a solitary man. Laurendeau.

Hunter stepped into the room and the man turned quickly. In his hand was a cell phone, his finger poised over a key, presumably the send key.

The two men stared at each other for a moment, neither saying anything. Hunter's gun was drawn but pointed downward, not directly at the man.

"I have to do it, you know," Laurendeau said with a sadness that surprised Hunter. "There's really no other way. The threat to God's creation is too great to be ignored."

Hunter saw a small boyish figure, clearly the man in the photo that Couillard had circulated to his security people. He appeared to be calm and relaxed as he looked at Hunter and his gun. "You can't stop it, you know. Even if you were to stop me, I have another man who will detonate the charges if for some reason my call fails. I've already dialed the number. All I have to do is press 'Call.'"

This was not good news. There was someone else with a phone? Who did he have out there to call if he failed? If he was counting on Kestrel, he was out of luck. But what if it were someone else? How could he stop that? Hunter had to stall him until he could get to that phone. As he walked laterally away from the stairway opening to the room he was careful not to approach any closer to Laurendeau.

"Why are you doing this?" Hunter asked, trying not to sound threatening.

"Why? I think you know why, or you wouldn't be here. Those fools just wouldn't listen to reason. We tried everything, logic, arguments, even the testimony of scientists. They were just too blind to what they couldn't understand. In the end, I knew the only way to stop them was to take more direct action. That's why my group of five committed ourselves to stopping them."

Group of five? He has a group? What if one of them is the second caller, and not Kestrel? The danger would still be out there even if I could stop him here.

He decided to take a chance. He remembered that Lazodelavega had said a science fiction writer, an American named Kurt Walker had asked about a fourth copy of the *Christianismi Restitutio* and told him it contained a message from Servetus that made important predictions for the future. And he lived in Geneva. He could be a member of the group.

"I hope your not counting on Kurt Walker to bail you out. It's too late for him."

Obviously startled, Laurendeau stood up and looked around, as if trying to find Walker. "How do you know about Walker?"

Hunter continued bluffing. "Oh, we know all about your little group. We have them all."

Really upset now, Laurendeau began to pace but held his cell phone up and pointed it at Hunter as if it were a weapon. "Asplund, Hoffman, and Fleischer? You have them? Good God, it's all coming apart." He sat back down dejected but with the phone still pointed at Hunter.

Hunter memorized the names, Asplund, Hoffman, and Fleischer. "So your group thought arranging the murder of young physicists was the answer." He said it as a statement not a question.

"We didn't like it but knew they'd be part of the unsafe experiments. Eliminating them was justified as part of the greater good, if it got the council to take us seriously." Just then, Genevieve stepped up and into the room and Laurendeau saw her for the first time.

"And what about me? Was eliminating me part of the greater good?"

It wasn't until that moment that Laurendeau finally got it and put the whole picture together. He squinted his eyes and looked at her, and then swung his gaze back to Hunter who was about six feet away from her, as if seeing him for the first time. "You. You're McCoy. You're Hunter McCoy, the man hired to find the *Christianismi Restitutio.* And you. You're his partner. Yes. The Swift woman."

Genevieve stepped toward him. "Yes. You had me kidnapped by that psychopath, who would have killed me had I not escaped."

Escaped, thought Hunter? Then he got it. He knew what she was doing. He decided to take another chance. "You should know that we've arrested Asplund, Hoffman, Fleischer and Kurt Walker. If you're counting on one of them to activate the bombs on the helium tanks, they won't be much help, I'm afraid."

Now Laurendeau was really upset. He began to hyperventilate. Laurendeau wasn't aware of it but Hunter had seen enough in his medical training to recognize it when he saw it. "Christ, you even know about the helium tanks?"

"Yes, and we even know about today's ceremony with your old nemesis, Dobson." Suddenly, Hunter knew he'd made a mistake. Laurendeau looked at his phone, suddenly remembering it was there and remembering the importance of the 2:00 PM time. It was now several minutes past 2:00.

Seeing he was getting ready to press 'Call,' Hunter tried one last stall. He could see that Genevieve had slowly moved farther to the right away from the stairway opening. The three of them were now at equal distances from each other in a triangle.

"So Laurendeau, who's your backup caller, since we have everybody in custody?"

Now regaining his confidence and with a little attitude in his body language and voice answered, "While, I don't believe I'll need him after all, but just so you know, you don't have *him* in custody."

Like they'd rehearsed it, Genevieve made her move. She ran to the slit windows to Laurendeau's left and his head and eyes followed her. That was all Hunter needed. Genevieve's run and Laurendeau's head swivel all shifted to slow motion. He tackled Laurendeau and knocked the phone out of his hand in a single move. As they tumbled to the floor, Laurendeau's other hand came out of his pocket and fired a small, previously unseen, handgun at Hunter, just as Hunter shot him. Laurendeau missed but Hunter didn't. Laurendeau jerked back and lay on his back staring at the ceiling,

Then in a weak voice, but with a sardonic smile, Laurendeau whispered so both Hunter and Genevieve could hear, "You lose, McCoy, my hired gun is still out there with instructions to call in and activate the bombs at 2:15 PM if they hadn't already gone off. What time is it McCoy?"

Hunter checked his watch. "It's 2:18." Then Hunter turned to Genevieve and said, "Take a look out the window to the northwest. Tell us if you see any smoke?"

"No nothing," Genevieve answered. "I wonder what could have gone wrong?" "Oh, now I remember. Hunter killed your psychopath, Kestrel, during my 'Escape.' Was he your mystery caller?"

Laurendeau never heard her. He was already dead.

Chapter 50

"Good to see you again, my boy." Deacon surprised Hunter by showing up at the Grand Council chairman's office. Security Chief, Couillard, Zubriggen, and Erwin Gisel, the Bomb Squad Captain, were already present when Hunter and Genevieve arrived a few minutes earlier. Zubriggen was talking. "We've got the others in custody, all but Walker. He's currently on a United Airlines flight from Geneva to New York. The FBI will arrest him, as soon as he lands.

"We hit the jackpot when we caught up with and interrogated Otto Fleischer. We found phone links between Fleischer and Julian Baltz, the sniper from Salamanca. When we confronted him, he admitted he'd hired Baltz to stop you and Genevieve from finding the book. Apparently he was worried that you'd find some secret message that would screw up the faith of millions. Imagine, a guy whose faith tells him to commit murders."

Zubriggen then looked at Genevieve for the first time. "Fleischer claims he didn't send you the threatening text message and didn't have anything to do with running you off the road. We think Kestrel was responsible for that after McCoy eluded him at the Zaragoza airport. He followed you from Zaragoza and thought you were both in the car. We're pretty sure Kestrel shot Baltz in Salamanca to stop him from killing you after Laurendeau decided he needed that book you were looking for."

Hunter confirmed this when he told them that Kestrel admitted he'd shot Baltz.

Chairman Ambrosi turned to Hunter. "I don't know how to thank you, Dr. McCoy," and bowing to Genevieve, "and you too, young lady. You two, almost by yourselves, saved the collider."

Hunter could see Zubriggen stiffen at this, but the Security chief, Couillard, enjoyed it immensely. "You're correct Mr. Chairman, and to think Hunter is only temporarily assigned to Interpol at that. I'd say they could definitely use more people like him in full time command positions," as he looked directly at Zubriggen.

"Thanks, but no thanks, gentlemen," Hunter said as he looked at Deacon, diffusing the tension. I'm sure any spare time I have will be taken up by Colonel Wogen, here."

Deacon smiled. "I'll do my best to keep your time obligation to the Department of Defense at a minimum, Hunter."

"What is the status of the explosives on the tanks?" inquired Hunter, turning to Couillard.

"Captain Gisel tells us that his men are almost finished deactivating them. And when they're done, we'll be significantly beefing up our security at those surface tank sites."

That night, before flying back to Washington, Deacon took Hunter and Genevieve to dinner on the DIA's tab. He told them he'd happened to be in France on Intelligence business when he'd gotten news of the final showdown at the LHC and had immediately flown to Geneva.

Following dinner, they were having cognacs; "So, Hunter" asked Deacon, "Did this Servetus guy really write something about sabotage to the LHC way back during the Inquisition?"

"I don't know, Deacon, I haven't had a chance to look at it. Somehow I've been too busy."

On the flight from Geneva to Paris, Genevieve snuggled as close to Hunter as the airline seats would permit. It was as if she wanted to physically stay attached to him. He had no objection at all. She wanted to know how he'd found the book. So, he told her the whole story about breaking the code leading to Charlottesville, and the discovery of the time capsule. About half way though the flight she turned to him.

"Do you really have the book?"

"Right here," he said, patting the satchel on his lap.

"And you haven't looked at it?" Genevieve asked in disbelief, showing signs of coming out of the fog of the last several days.

"Just when Shay and I unwrapped it. I've been a little busy what with rescuing damsels in distress and saving the collider."

Genevieve laughed and hugged his arm again. "And, just so you know, both the collider and the damsel are very, very glad you did."

Hunter appraised her readiness to return to the mission. "Do you think you're ready to look at it?" he asked, patting the satchel again. "I mean this book has caused you a lot of pain."

Beginning to show enthusiasm for the first time since the rescue, she nodded.

Hunter opened the briefcase on his lap and extracted the book, now wrapped loosely in linen cloth. As he handed it to her he said, "You might want to start—"

"With the last several pages." Interrupting him for the first time since it all ended.

They both laughed so much that passengers in the adjacent first class seats looked curiously at them wondering what was so funny.

"Okay, now I know you're getting back to the old Genevieve."

Turning serious for a moment, she kissed him on the cheek and said, "I'll never be the old Genevieve again for a lot of reasons."

They stayed close for a moment, before she said. "Okay, let me see it."

Even though she was used to seeing and handling rare texts, Genevieve appeared surprised by the relatively small size of the *Christianismi Restitutio*, not much bigger than a paperback novel. "When I think of everything we've been through to find this, I would have thought it would be larger somehow. It looks so small."

Holding the linen cloth between her fingers, she carefully turned to the back of the book until she found the handwritten message in the last six pages of the *Restitutio*. She looked at Hunter. "Have you translated this?"

"Nope."

She smiled at him, knowing that Hunter would consider rescuing her more important than deciphering the book. The knowledge made her feel special and wanted.

"Truthfully, I really haven't looked at it," he said.

"It's in Greek," she said. "That's curious. Why would he write in Greek?"

"Can you translate it?"

"Of course, silly. All right, here goes."

I write this now, on the eve of my execution.

I have been condemned for stating beliefs that are so obvious to me that I would have thought them to be equally obvious to any contemplative reasoning person. But I was wrong in thinking thus. Fear, not reason, has prevailed and my arguments have been twisted and turned against me by those who have much to lose personally by acknowledging the truth of my statements.

Just as it is clear from scripture that God was Jesus' father, and that Jesus did not exist before he was born on earth, it is equally clear that Jesus was separate from God and subordinate to God. Any attempt to make Jesus, the Father, and the Holy Spirit equal and in some way one, not three Gods, is purely a political fabrication and the work of philosophical compromise. I'll have none of it.

So even now while I prepare to burn for this and other 'heresies' I'll explain another truth that would it be known to the court would no doubt be added to my list of 'heresies'.

Just as God the Father created Jesus and sent him to earth as a man, a millennium and a half before, he has continued to send other messiahs over the ages right up to today and surely into the future. Jesus and his fellow messiahs, both male and female, were sent to earth by God to further the glory of his creation and to protect it from harm.

Some, surely with the blessing of God, will labor in the field of natural philosophy and medicine and like the freshening of the blood in the lungs as I've described, may even find ways to produce the 'breath of life' itself, where none existed before.

But there will be dangers. When God looks at his creation and sees that mankind has produced forces that collide head on to

*threaten it, his sons and daughters can, and
must, prevent these forces from prevailing.*

*I come to these conclusions, not
through introspection or philosophy, but
rather through reading a most remarkable
ancient scroll dating from the time of Christ.
This ancient scroll is preserved and
suspended in the heavens above at the
unholy trinity.*

*I'll be put to death tomorrow. But
someday in the future, a messenger from
God may arrive, perhaps even here in
Geneva, not to correct this injustice to me
but to prevent some unholy force from
accelerating a threat to God's very creation.*

*By the grace of God, I pray that these
words will survive and give credibility to my
insignificant life.*

*Jesus, son of the eternal God, have
mercy on me.*

Michael Servetus

Genevieve spent the rest of the flight thinking about
what she'd read. Hunter, exhausted, had fallen
immediately asleep.

"Ladies and gentlemen we are beginning our final
approach into CDG International Airport. Please put your
seatbacks in the upright position and close you tray tables
in preparation for landing"

Genevieve rewrapped the book in its linen and put it
back in Hunter's satchel.

Hunter and Genevieve walked up the single flight of
stairs to her second floor flat in a five-story brick walkup

on a shady quiet street in Paris. They were both anxious to leave Geneva and its horror behind.

He wasn't surprised to find her place was bright and neat. It suited her personality. The living room was quite large and had lots of windows since it occupied a corner of the building. The room was brightened by the sunlight and the light pastel color scheme she'd used throughout. While most of the furniture was standard stuff, he recognized a few antiques. She used a nineteenth century French copper flour bin as a vase for a collection of dried flowers and grasses. On the wall next to her writing desk he saw a wonderful nineteenth century Louis Philippe Mirror.

"Your place is beautiful, Genevieve."

"Let me show you the rest and then we can get down to business." She took his hand and showed him her small kitchen, with its small wrought iron-railed deck overlooking a tiled courtyard centered with a wonderful sycamore shade tree. When she led him to her bedroom, they paused and looked knowingly at each other. He took her in his arms again and for a long time they kissed while slowly removing each other's clothes. Finally, they made love with an aching abandon that knew no danger, no uncertainty, and no end.

Later, showered and dressed, Hunter went out and returned with a take-out lunch purchased from a corner deli that they ate in her small kitchen. Hungry from their erotic workout, they devoured the lunch. As Genevieve cleaned up, Hunter examined more of the antiques throughout her apartment. When she was finished, she told him they'd use the kitchen table as their workspace.

Genevieve got her laptop, placed it on the table, and they each took a chair. After she'd read the Servetus message on the plane, she'd written out a translation and typed it onto her computer while Hunter slept.

"I wondered, when I first saw it, why Servetus chose to write his last message in Greek. He could read Latin, Greek and Hebrew in addition to French, German, and his native Catalan. So why select Greek?"

Hunter looked amused. "I know you're just dying to tell me."

"Okay, consider this." She looked at the translation on her computer. "He starts out by reiterating his opposition to the concept of the trinity; nothing new there. A large part of the book is about that. He sums it up by saying:"

> *Any attempt to make Jesus, the Father, and the Holy Spirit equal and in some way one, not three Gods, is purely a political fabrication and the work of philosophical compromise. I'll have none of it.*

Genevieve continued. "Next he gets really heretical, by suggesting that Jesus isn't the only messiah. There are many of them, both men and women. Here's what he says:"

> *Just as God the Father created Jesus and sent him to earth as a man, a millennium and a half before, he has continued to send other messiahs over the ages right up to today and surely into the future. Jesus and his fellow messiahs, both male and female, were sent to earth by God to further the glory of his creation and to protect it from harm.*

"But what he wrote next is probably the most interesting," as she pointed to Hunter's copy of her translation.

> *I come to these conclusions, not through introspection or philosophy, but rather through reading a most remarkable ancient scroll dating from the time of Christ. This ancient scroll is preserved and suspended in the heavens above at the unholy trinity.*

"I think he's telling us where this scroll is, and I believe I know. It's suspended in the heavens above at the unholy trinity." Having said this, Genevieve sat back crossed her arms and looked smugly at Hunter.

Hunter looked at her, ran his hands through his hair, and let out a big sigh. "That's it? All we have to do is die and go to heaven to get this thing?"

Still looking smug, Genevieve continued, "You're half right, we do have to go to heaven suspended above, but we don't have to die first."

Hunter got up and paced around the table. "Well that's a relief. So you've figured out another way to get to heaven."

Genevieve enjoyed his confusion. "Right, we use a telephone."

Hunter now completely confused, yet knowing there had to be more to the story, resumed his seat. "Okay, Sherlock, let's have it. No more games."

"All right. Here it is. Look at what he says.

> *This ancient scroll is preserved and suspended in the heavens above at the unholy trinity.*

"Start with 'suspended in the heavens above.' I'll admit I had an unfair advantage over everyone's earlier attempts to decipher this phrase. I typed in into Google to see what might come up. And guess what?   The phrase 'suspended rocks,' 'suspended in the air,' or 'in the heavens above,' are traditional descriptions given for the Metéora, six Medieval Greek orthodox monasteries, built on natural sandstone rock pillars, at the northwestern edge of the Plain of Thessaly in central Greece. The nearby town is Kalambaka.   And get this. One of the six monasteries is called The Holy Trinity." Genevieve, with a smile on her face, again sat back smugly and waited.

Hunter thought about this for a minute.   "And you think because of his negative view of the concept of the trinity he was enjoying a little dark humor by calling this monastery in Greece the 'Unholy Trinity'?"

"Exactly.   But I was skeptical too, Hunter until I looked a little deeper. I wasn't able to find any evidence that Servetus ever traveled to Greece, much less Metéora, but he could have, and I think he did."

Still skeptical, Hunter waited for her to explain.

Genevieve pointed at the text. "Look what he says."

I come to these conclusions, not through introspection or philosophy, but rather through reading a most remarkable ancient scroll dating from the time of Christ.

"He says he *read* the scroll. I don't think he was told about it, or had a copy read to him, I think he actually read it. And to do that, he had to be there. I'm guessing for a fifteen hundred year old scroll to be in good enough shape for Servetus to have actually read it in the fifteen hundreds, it had to have been discovered shortly before he saw it. And, if it somehow managed to survive for the four hundred years since he'd read it, I think it's still there, at the monastery.

Hunter considered this. She could be right. Then he had an idea. "Why don't we call the Servetus Institute and ask if they know whether Servetus ever traveled to Greece. Maybe there's some record of his having traveled to Metéora."

"Good idea," agreed Genevieve.

Hunter made the call, not sure who he'd talk with at the Institute, now that the director was dead. He was surprised to find that the new director of the Institute was Vincenzo Lazodelavega, the late director's only son, who, it turned out was also a medieval scholar. Hunter introduced himself and was surprised to hear that Vincenzo knew about him and that his late father had spoken well of him.

"Vincenzo, I have a Servetus question for you. Is there any record that he ever traveled to Greece?"

"Greece? Not that I recall. But that doesn't mean he didn't. During his twelve-year residence in Vienne, practicing medicine as Michel de Villeneuve he was quietly working on his theological treatises and we know little of his travel during that time. It's entirely possible. Why do you ask?"

Hunter decided to tell him the truth. "Genevieve has translated the message Servetus left in the fourth copy and believes that she has also cracked the obscure language that Basilio referred to. We think it leads to an ancient scroll hidden somewhere in Metéora, Greece."

"I see. All right, I'll scour the records and see if I can dig up anything on his travels."

Hunter's cell phone rang twenty minutes later. It was an incoming call from Vincenzo. He put it on speakerphone so Genevieve could hear. "Hello Vincenzo. What've you got?"

"Good news, Hunter. We checked our records and believe we have convincing evidence that Michael Servetus did visited Holy Trinity Monastery at Metéora, Greece in the summer of 1547, six years before his execution. So, if the scroll is there, it's very likely he could have read it."

Hunter and Genevieve silently gave each other a high five.

Chapter 51

Genevieve continued with a little more Internet searching before they called the monastery. They learned that most of the ancient documents stored in the Metéora monasteries were transferred to the Monastery of Saint Stefanos for safekeeping after World War II. So if the scroll had been at Holy Trinity Monastery at one time, it would likely be at St. Stefanos now. They also learned that St. Stefanos was now a convent, with almost all of its nuns holding advanced degrees including doctorates in everything from history to science.

Genevieve called St. Stefanos and was connected to Sister Ophelia, the Abbess. After introducing herself as a Renaissance scholar from the National Library in Paris, she explained about the Servetus note and the scroll.

The Abbess told her that much of the work done at the monasteries in the old days was to copy ancient manuscripts onto parchment. Some of the monks were truly artists. Their skill in calligraphy and drawing were unmatched and their work helped preserve a considerable written history. Unfortunately, much of their work was stolen or destroyed during World War II.

"I'm sure that something as old as a first century scroll would have disintegrated by now," she told them. "It wouldn't even have survived until Servetus' time in the fifteen hundreds. I don't see how Servetus, if he had been there could have read such a scroll."

"Here's an idea, Sister Ophelia," Genevieve offered. "Let's think about the Dead Sea Scrolls. When they were discovered in 1947, we learned they'd been removed from a cave where they'd been buried for almost two millennia. The conditions in the cave preserved them for two thousand years.   They've been preserved ever since and are in relatively good shape. Suppose the scroll Servetus saw had been buried, you know, like the Dead Sea scrolls were, but wasn't found until the fifteen hundreds.   If that scroll somehow made its way to Holy Trinity Monastery, it may have been intact enough for Servetus to read just a few years later. And, if one of the monks from that time copied it to a parchment, you might still have that, even if the original scroll was eventually destroyed because of failure to preserve it."

Sister Ophelia acknowledged the possibility. Then she said, "Now it's coming back to me. Michael Servetus. His great heresy was denying the holy trinity. Yes, now I do remember. Yet you think such a document would be in a monastery dedicated to the Holy Trinity?

Recognizing the irony, Genevieve said, "Yes, Sister, I do, but I get your point."

Hunter, who had been listening on speakerphone, feared that maybe they weren't any closer after all.

Sister Ophelia told Genevieve she would carefully examine their records and call her back if they had any documentation relative to the scroll. She called back within the hour.

"We do have a parchment dated to around 1545 that might be what you're talking about. It had been done by a monk at Holy Trinity, and was based on all that remained of a papyrus scroll that had mysteriously arrived at the

monastery of the Holy Trinity several years before 1545 by
a visitor from Oxyrhynchus, Egypt."

"What does it say?" asked Genevieve.

Sister Ophelia sighed, audibly enough for them to hear
over the phone. "Which do you want first, the good news
or the bad news?"

"Oh no," groaned Genevieve.

Sister Ophelia continued. "The good news is we have
something. Now here's the bad news. It seems the original
papyrus from Oxyrhynchus, Egypt was in such bad shape it
was almost unreadable by the time the monk got it. So he
gave us his best interpretation of what *might* have been on
the scroll based on talking with the Egyptian man who
brought it to the monastery in the fifteen hundreds. And
even there he copied only a part of this already second-
hand story onto the parchment that we've carbon-dated to
approximately 1545."

"You've carbon dated it?" asked Genevieve in surprise.

"We're very technologically up to date here, Ms. Swift,
even if our monastery is very old."

Genevieve recovered. "And what did the monk
interpret?"

"Do you have a fax machine?" Sister Ophelia asked.

Genevieve did. She used it often in her work with the
library.

What arrived was a photocopy of the Monk's
parchment in Greek, followed by an English translation,
obviously done by the monastery. She read the translation.

> *Elsafty, an Egyptian, brought here a jar
> that contained fragments of a scroll that his
> ancestors had unearthed in Oxyrhynchus in
> northern Egypt south of Cairo many years
> before. Elsafty was not a Christian but he*

told me a story. Age had destroyed most of the scroll but his ancestors were able to read part of it before that too began to fade. It is completely unreadable now. They told him it spoke of the sayings of the prophet, Jesus. Many were similar to those in the Christian bible. Others were not. I will include only one.

And Jesus said to the crowd gathered, "some call me messiah, and truly I have come to help you now. The father's love and mine know no bounds for his creation. But know that you are not alone. The father will send others after me as long as the world is in need. Trust in the father and trust in your love for one another.

Hunter and Genevieve sat quietly for several minutes, each thinking their own thoughts. After all that had been reported about the profound significance of the ancient scroll, it really came down to the few words they'd just read.

"You know what this reminds me of?" Hunter finally said, breaking the silence. "You know that game where you have several people sitting in a circle and one person tells a secret to the person to his left? That person repeats the secret to the person on *his* left, and so on around the circle. Finally, the last person to receive the secret repeats it out loud."

"Right," Genevieve said. "I know the game."

Hunter continued. "And when the person who started the secret hears it and repeats out loud what he'd *actually* said—"

"Everyone sees that it's changed so much it hardly bears any resemblance to the original," Genevieve finished, starting to get the point he was making.

"Exactly," agreed Hunter. "I think we can apply that here. Right from the beginning, the ancient scroll from Oxyrhynchus has been misinterpreted and improperly embellished. And it only got worse as it made its way through history. We'll never know what it actually said."

"Just look at what we *think* we know about the message of the scroll," Hunter said. "This Egyptian guy, this Elsafty, who brought the disintegrated scroll to the monk, never read it himself. It was already unreadable. The parchment says his ancestors *'told him it spoke of the sayings of the prophet, Jesus.'* "Therefore, we have to assume the most authentic version we now have, is whatever Elsafty, the man who brought it from northern Egypt told the monk at Holy Trinity monastery. And, even then, we don't know what he *actually* told him. What we have is the monk's *interpretation* of what he told him. And on top of that, the monk only chose to record *a small part* of what Elsafty told him. So already we know that the original wording of the scroll has undoubtedly been both lost and altered.

"I think we have to assume that Servetus could only have read the monk's parchment, unless of course he'd been able to interview the monk himself or even Elsafty. But since we know that Servetus was here in 1547 and the monk's parchment dates to around that time it's a sure bet that Servetus never read the original scroll, but had to rely on the monk's interpretation instead."

Genevieve agreed. "And now that we have the *Christianismi Restitutio* with Servetus's actual handwritten message, we know what Servetus got from reading the monk's already thrice-removed interpretation. Here, let me read it for you:"

> *"But there will be dangers. When God looks at his creation and sees that mankind has produced forces that collide head on to*

threaten it, his sons can, and must, prevent these forces from prevailing."
"I'll be put to death tomorrow. But someday in the future, a messenger from God may arrive, perhaps even here in Geneva, not to correct this injustice to me but to prevent some unholy force from accelerating a threat to God's very creation."

"Wow. We can already see Servetus taking enormous liberty in his interpretation of the monk's version," Hunter added. "The monk said nothing about '*Geneva'*, or '*preventing a force from creating a threat.*'"

Genevieve agreed. "Laurendeau didn't know how right he was when he told Kestrel to forget about the book, that the message probably wouldn't help justify his case for murder and sabotage anyway.

"And here's something else," he added. " I got a call earlier from Zubriggen telling me about his interrogation of Otto Fleischer after they'd arrested him. He told Zubriggen that Kurt Walker, the American science fiction writer, had found a website that referred to an 18th century scholar, a guy named Renaldo Quintaro.

"It seems, this guy claimed to have actually seen our fourth copy of the *Christianismi Restitutio,* and the message Servetus wrote." Hunter patted the book as he said this. "The website gave Quintaro's interpretation of what Servetus wrote. Even there, we don't know exactly what it said since it's been pulled down and they can't trace it. Fleischer told Zubriggen what Walker *claimed* it said; that it referred to a future world wide catastrophic event that would be prevented by a time traveler from the future coming to Geneva specifically to stop the Large Hadron Collider."

Genevieve looked at Hunter with an incredulous smile. "So let me see if I have this correct. Walker saw a website, that no longer exists, and interpreted what he saw to Laurendeau, even though what he saw was an interpretation of an interpretation of an interpretation. He tells Laurendeau that four hundred years ago, a scientist predicted that a time traveler from the future would come to Geneva specifically to sabotage the Large Hadron Collider in order to protect the future from its catastrophic discoveries.'"

Genevieve, really getting into it now, added, "Again, we see the story changing. The words *collide* and *accelerating* from the Servetus note are taking totally out of context, with Walker implying they refer to the Large Hadron Collider."

Hunter smiled, nodding his head with incredulity spreading across his face.

Genevieve, continued, "That interpretation is really a stretch. What Walker told Laurendeau bore no resemblance even to the Servetus message, not to mention the monk's interpretation of whatever was in the disintegrated scroll."

Hunter agreed. "When scholars get their hands on this book, they'll easily discover there was nothing in the monk's parchment to back up Laurendeau's claims to protect the collider. And they were going to use this nonsense to justify murder and sabotage."

Genevieve shook her head in amazement at the absurdity of it all. "And last but not least, there's the other thing, the supposed threat to Christianity that so worried Fleischer. It turns out it was nothing. There was no serious threat to Christianity, none at all. Remember what the parchment said.

*'The father will send others after me as
long as the world is in need. Trust in the
father and trust in your love for one another.'*

"Right," Genevieve agreed. "Even if the monk's interpretation is true, these 'others' he referred to were not being equated to Jesus. It turns out that Servetus was every bit as guilty as Laurendeau of reading into the message just what he wanted to see. Here, look at what Servetus wrote:

*Just as God the Father created Jesus
and sent him to earth as a man, a
millennium and a half before, he has
continued to send other messiahs over the
ages right up to today and surely into the
future. Jesus and his fellow messiahs, both
male and female, are sent to earth by God to
further the glory of his creation and to
protect it from harm.*

"Notice that Servetus inserted the word 'messiah' and the phrase 'Jesus and his fellow messiahs.' He seems to be putting them on equal footing with Jesus. None of this was in the monk's parchment. And, of course, he also added both male and female messiahs."

They both sat quietly for a few moments contemplating all of this. Finally Hunter spoke. "I think Laurendeau would have liked the Servetus message in the back of the Christianismi Restitutio, had he lived to read it. I think he would have believed himself to be one of those messiahs, sent back from the future to protect God's creation. The madman would have seen it as justification for the murders and the sabotage, at least to himself. Remember what he said in the north tower? 'The threat to

God's creation is too great to be ignored.' He'd never even seen the Servetus message and he said that."

"Servetus could at least be forgiven," added Genevieve, "He'd never actually hurt anyone and was going to be executed the next day. On the other hand, Laurendeau and his gang, including Otto Fleischer, deliberately murdered several innocent people."

This prompted another moment of silence. Then Hunter got up and paced for a minute. "Think about Otto Fleischer and his irrational fear. He told Zubriggen that he believed he'd suffer eternal damnation if he failed to prevent the discovery of the book. He was terrified of Satan and Hell. He even used old-testament bible stories to justify his attempted murders. How could he think God would approve murdering innocent people in order to prevent the discovery of some supposed heresy? I mean, I'm no philosopher, but isn't that why we have free will, so we can evaluate ideas for ourselves?"

Genevieve considered this for a moment. "I'm reminded of a quote from Saint Teresa of Avila, the sixteenth century Spanish nun, mystic, and writer."

"And what's that?" asked Hunter.

She thought for a moment trying to get it right.

"I'm quite sure I'm more afraid of people who are terrified by the devil—"

"Than I am of the devil himself," said Hunter, finishing the quote for her.

"Exactly right," laughed Genevieve in surprise.

They both agreed she had it right.

Epilogue

Ed McCoy was waiting near the luggage belt at Sawyer International Airport in Marquette. Hunter spotted him first. "Hi Dad. How're doing?"

Giving Hunter a hug and patting his back, he said, "Okay, son, now that you're back"

"Why, what's happened?

"Nothing"

"Nothing?"

"Well, Toivo and I have been fishing a lot. The trout are running real good this year on the Yellow Dog. In fact, when we get home tonight I'm going to fix you one of the best brook trout dinners you've ever had," Ed said with a big smile on his face.

"Great," Hunter remarked. "I'm looking forward to that."

They took highway 553 into Marquette, and then the Big Bay Road out to Anue on the big lake.

Hunter traveled light and only had one suitcase since he kept a good supply of clothes at the cabin. As they pulled into the driveway, Hunter felt a sense of relaxation he hadn't felt since he'd left several weeks before. It was good to be home.

He and Genevieve were both looking forward to seeing each other again at the International Physiology Meetings later in the fall in Paris. As difficult as it was to part, she had to get back to work, and he had to check in at home, with his dad. He'd stayed on with her in Paris for another week. They promised to keep in touch until then.

Shay Blackwell told her that after the book was returned to him and he'd gifted it to the University, she'd be the first scholar allowed to examine it in full, at her convenience. Shay also told her that he'd talked with Vincenzo Lazodelavega, and they'd agreed that the book would rotate between the University's new rare book room and the Michael Servetus Institute, giving scholars on both sides of the Atlantic equal opportunity to study it. Shay felt that this would be in the spirit of what Basilio had wanted all along.

As they walked into the cabin Hunter could immediately see that something was different, more light was coming in than he'd remembered. Then he saw it. A large part of one wall was gone and had been replaced by three huge glass sliders. And beyond that, on the side facing the lake was the complete foundation for the sunroom they'd been planning to add.

"Dad. It's great. How did you manage to do this?"

"I'm not without talent you know," he said beaming. "After I got the plans done, I got the county to approve the building permit and then thought, what the heck, I'll just get started. Toivo has a backhoe and we dug out trenches for the footings. It didn't take long at all. Then I did the cement block work myself. It wasn't too bad. After that was done Toivo and I would take just an hour or so each day to put up the two by ten floor joists. Then we covered them with the plywood under floor you see now."

Hunter stared at the work. It was beautifully done. Sitting on the plywood were their two Adirondacks chairs.

"After dinner," said Ed, "we're going to sit out there and have a drink and you're going to tell me everything you've been up to.

Later, about 9:30, Hunter and Ed retired to their Adirondacks chairs on the new deck. Hunter made drinks for them both, a large perfect Manhattan on the rocks with a twist for him, and Jack Daniels for his dad. There was just enough of a breeze off the big lake to blow the mosquitoes away. It was warm enough with their jeans and sweaters for the two men to enjoy their drinks and each other's company well beyond midnight.

Hunter told Ed everything. Well, almost everything.

Author's note to readers

This story is a work of fiction, and all characters and events are products of my own imagination with the exception of Michael Servetus. Michael Servetus, a physician, was burned at the stake as a heretic in 1553, largely due to the influence of John Calvin. It's also true that three copies of his *Christianismi Restitutio* (The Restoration of Christianity) have survived to this day and are kept, one each, in the National Library of France, the Austrian National Library, and the library of the University of Edinburgh. The fourth copy of the *Restitutio* with its execution-eve message that represents the focus of the search in this book is entirely fictitious.

The reference to Galen and his influence on a millennium of medicine is essentially true. He was the first to develop a general theory of function for the mammalian body in which everything had a purpose. His views remained largely unchallenged until the 17th century.

As an emeritus professor of physiology, I got the idea for this book after learning that Servetus had curiously inserted his scientific findings on pulmonary circulation into his theological book the *Christianismi Restitutio,* the very book that resulted in his condemnation and execution. Even more curious is the fact that the section on pulmonary circulation encompasses only six pages in what are otherwise some 700 pages of theology and letters.

The Michael Servetus Institute does exist in Villanueva de Sijena. The Institute is a public non-profit educational and research institution located in Villanueva de Sijena, a town of 500 inhabitants in the Aragon region in northeast Spain. It was founded in 1976 with the objective of studying the life and works of Michael Servetus and spreading his intellectual and scientific legacy. I hope those associated with the Institute will forgive the liberty I've taken in describing it.

The Darden School of Business does exist on the University of Virginia campus in Charlottesville. It was founded in 1954. It is named after Colgate Whitehead Darden Junior, a former Democratic congressman, governor of Virginia, and president of the University of Virginia. The story of the time capsule with the book in my story is totally fictitious.

The Large Hadron Collider does exist outside of Geneva some 300 feet beneath the Swiss/French border in an oval some 17-miles long. It is the world's largest High-energy particle accelerator and was built by the European Organization of Nuclear Research (CERN). It did suffer several construction accidents and delays during the attempts to get it up and running.

It's true that segments of the public, encouraged by detractors of the LHC, had expressed fears that the experiments might create black holes and endanger the earth. There have even been fears, raised by some scientists that the many delays in getting the system operational could be due to interference from time travelers coming from the future. Those who subscribe to this theory suggest that some unspecified discoveries made by the collider teams were so detrimental to the future that time travelers were sent back from the future to prevent their discovery. The overwhelming majority of physicists believe such fears are nonsense. I'm delighted to note that at this writing, the Higgs boson has recently been detected by the LHC and the world is still here.

The Monasteries of Metéora in central Greece are real and spectacular. Holy Trinity and Saint Stefanos monasteries are functioning today and the sisters at St. Stefanos are indeed unusually highly educated. After looting and destruction during World War II, the majority of valuable documents were collected and stored at St. Stefanos. The entire story of the ancient scroll and the monk who copied it is fictitious.

Don Stratton

DON STRATTON

Don Stratton is Ellis and Nelle Levitt Distinguished Professor Emeritus of Physiology at Drake University. His textbook, *Neurophysiology*, was published by McGraw Hill. *Unholy fire* is his first novel. Don is originally from the Upper Peninsula of Michigan, and currently lives in Venice, Florida, with his wife, Pauline and their dog, Gracie.